AF243972

KD EASLEY

A RANDI BLACK MYSTERY

MURDER at TIMBER BRIDGE

BOOK ONE

NukeWorks
Publishing

NukeWorks Publishing
Fulton, Mo 65251 USA

ISBN 978-0-9825294-9-2

Cover design by A&J Creative Services

Cover illustration by James Bratten

Edited by Alice Peck

Visit KD at www.kdwrites.com

Printed in U.S.A.

For Justin and Clint

*In memory of Willie, who gladly shared his personality
with Wilson and his short life with us.*

Acknowledgements

If I personally thanked everyone that had a hand in bringing Randi and her cohorts to life on the page, there wouldn't be room left for the actual story, but there are a few people that I have to make mention of. First, to the ladies at Al Scheppers who finished reading every chapter with the question, "what happens next?" and kept me tied to the keyboard until we all found out. To the members of AHunt who have all managed to achieve writing success, thank you for your friendship, your support and for listening to me rant when things turned dark and the words wouldn't come. To my kids who put up with Hamburger Helper and noodlestuff as I tried to carve minutes of writing time out of crowded days. To the Guppies who still offer support, advice and friendship and never look at me funny when I say, "that would be cool place to find a body." For Sister's in Crime for making me feel like a professional, and the Oklahoma Hat Ladies, who let me be an honorary Oklahoman whenever I went to their writer's conference. To Alice Peck, Chief of the Echo Police, for making me look good and to Susan McBride because she took the time to befriend me when I still didn't know enough to ask the right questions. And finally, to my Mom, who supported me in my writing, critiqued me impartially, celebrated my rejections and disappointments with parties, and never let me become lazy in my writing.

MURDER at TIMBER BRIDGE

Chapter 1

Shots whizzed overhead. I crouched behind a century-old oak tree and tried to locate the gunmen. The underbrush rustled as the body of my son crashed to the ground beside me. I yelped and shoulder-blocked my ancient barricade as I leapt in surprise.

"Dammit, Devin."

"Sorry, Mom. You're on your own."

"Shit!"

I sank to my knees beside my son and rubbed my newly bruised shoulder. Shots peppered the area around us.

"You'd better get out of here," Devin said, as the leaves to our left rattled under another barrage.

I nodded, but didn't speak as he shoved his gun into my hands and motioned me away. He flashed a weak okay sign as I stuck his weapon under my arm and slid to the bottom of the ravine. I blocked him out and crouched behind a thicket as I listened for movement, but the woods were silent as birds, bugs, and humans waited for the next fusillade. Sweat dripped into my eyes. I blinked them clear and covertly searched for the safest route out of harm's way.

My position started to feel exposed, so I dashed for a big maple that offered more cover. Shots rattled around me. I hit the dirt and closed my eyes, making myself invisible because I couldn't see. It worked—the shooting stopped. My breath escaped in a silent rush of relief.

I hunched in the leaf clutter waiting for the thud of shots around me. Nothing broke the stillness but the raucous call of a crow in the distance. I relaxed enough to move; inched around the clearing on knees and elbows, keeping my profile low. The muscles in my arms began to shake with fatigue. My abs burned. My vision blurred as sweat ran down my face. In the movies, they make this look easy.

I stopped to wipe my face and stretched against the stitch in my side. I promised to get up and run every morning if I could just get through this day. The muscles in my arms stopped burning and my breathing slowed. I let my mind wander. A shot whistled overhead, abruptly snapping me to the present. Shit! These guys were trying to kill me. Still on my stomach, I laid down the spare gun and peered around the tree I cowered behind. The underbrush crashed near my feet. My heart jumped into my throat. I rolled onto my back and took aim. As I tightened my finger on the trigger, a boot connected with the barrel. The gun jerked from my grasp and rattled off into the underbrush.

"Easy, Randi. I'm on your side."

"Jesus, AJ! I almost shot you," I hissed.

"You wouldn't shoot me, darlin'." He winked as he eased down beside me.

"Think you made enough noise?" I asked. "Now they know exactly where I am."

"I'm pretty sure they already did," he said.

By the crinkle around his eyes, I could tell he was smiling. At least one of us was having a good time.

"Do we make our stand here, or try to sneak around somewhere else?" he asked softly.

I mopped my face with the tail of my shirt. "I've had it. I say we make our stand here."

"You gotta get in better shape, darlin'."

I mentally stuck my tongue out at him and eased up for a look. AJ rose beside me and took a shot to the head. I ducked.

"Shit, shit, shit!"

I lifted Devin's weapon, checked the ammo and eased to the right on my stomach. A cold barrel pressed into the small of my back. I froze.

"Gotcha, little sister."

"Dammit!"

I smacked the ground in frustration. Chad laughed. Leaving Devin's gun where it lay, I pushed to my feet. Every muscle in my body protested. Almost forty years old and still trying to prove I'm as tough as my brothers, a retired Army Colonel and an ex Navy SEAL. They are so far out of my league, we might as well be playing on different planets. I gotta be nuts. The only thing I've ever been able to match them in is marksmanship.

My older brother Steve, the retired colonel, radioed "Game Over." Dark shapes detached themselves from trees and bushes and converged on him. I searched the underbrush for the gun AJ'd kicked out of my hands. Devin and Travis, my twins, raced from the trees covered in paint. Devin and Travis always manage to get covered in paint. I think they take target practice at each other after they go out of the game. What can I say? They're fifteen; they don't know any better.

Travis dumped his gear and flopped at my feet. His sandy blond hair, matted with sweat and orange paint, blended with the leaf litter like camouflage. I nudged him in the ribs with the toe of my boot and nodded toward his brother. He rolled up onto his elbow, green eyes sparkling, as he watched Devin sneak through the trees. Chad never knew Devin was there until he squashed a red paintball on Chad's head. It looked like blood running through Chad's black hair. He hooked a foot behind Devin's legs and the two of them toppled to the ground with a thud. Travis chucked acorns at them as they wrestled, every shot right on target. Chad and Devin emerged from the underbrush, covered with leaves and dirt, appearing more like twins than Devin and Travis ever have. Travis grabbed a pinecone and yelled, "Go long". Chad and Devin took off at a run as my quarterback hopeful fired the pinecone missile. I shook my head at their antics and untucked my shirt. Sweat trickled from between my breasts and soaked the waistband of my pants.

AJ peeled off his paint-covered mask and traded high fives with Chad and Devin as they trotted back toward the group. His black hair stuck up in spikes. He used his tee shirt to wipe his face, then peeled the shirt over his head. His dark eyes turned my way and caught me admiring his abs. A grin tugged the corners of his mouth as he winked. I turned away and felt the blood rush to my face. Leaves rustled as he moved away. I took the opportunity to admire the view—even in baggy field utilities, it was spectacular. Maybe nicer than the front.

My sister-in-law, Sara Beth, says when AJ strolls down the street in tight jeans, women walk into parking meters. He does tend to have that effect. Mentally I fondled those abs and buns as I reached down to snag my paintball gun from the ground. When I straightened, Chad was standing in front of me, smirking. My face flamed, as if Chad could read my thoughts.

"What ya blushing for, Sis?"

"I'm not blushing, I'm just hot." I fanned my face for emphasis.

"Yeah, hot for AJ."

"Give me a break. He's just like another brother."

"I don't think you ever looked at me or Steve that way."

My face was burning. I wondered if I was old enough to be having a hot flash.

"Leave me alone, Chad."

He laughed. I unhooked the spare ammo pods from around my waist and hung the belt over my arm as Chad left to join the guys. AJ does still have an effect on me, but we had some history that I didn't intend to repeat. I wished my body would get in line with my brain on that. I jogged/hobbled to catch Chad. The paintballs in my ammo pods rattled as they banged together. It sounded like I was shaking a cat food box. Chad heard me clattering behind him and slowed so I could catch up. I slowed my half-hearted trot to a walk, so he paused. He shook his head at the wait and started off again as I drew even and fell into step.

"How come you never capture anybody else, Chadly?"

"You're the only girl."

"What does that have to do with anything?"

"It's not polite to shoot women."

He winked and chucked me under the chin like I was a little kid.

"Hey Chadly, something I need to tell you."

He stopped walking to listen.

"I noticed you're getting a little grey in your beard there. Might be time for a little Grecian Formula."

He laughed and shook his head.

"Oh, Ran, that was so lame. Is that the best you can do?"

His teeth flashed white against his perfect little Van Dyke when he grinned.

"Face it, Sis, I always know what you're gonna do next."

I smirked. That knowledge went both ways. I knew as soon as he got home he'd be standing in front of the mirror checking his beard for grey.

We stepped out of the woods into the clearing where Steve and AJ were waiting and it struck me how much taller AJ is than my big brother. Steve's posture is so erect that you don't realize he's not a tall man, but he's a good four inches less than AJ's six-two. I ducked my head before Chad caught me staring again and slid down to sit at the foot of a big oak tree. I moaned in pleasure as I relaxed the muscles in my back.

"I'm wiped out."

"You ought to go to the gym with me," Chad said.

I snorted. A trip to the gym with Chad would be like sending a high school kid out to pitch game one of the World Series. I'm not in his class. He's the ex Navy SEAL.

"On your feet, Randi," Steve yelled. "We're burning daylight."

"What? We have a time limit on getting to the parking lot?"

Chad and the boys snickered. Steve turned and started out of the woods, ignoring me. He was just pissed because our team lost. I stuck my tongue out at his retreating form.

"Move your ass, Randi," he snapped over his shoulder.

"Move your ass, Randi," I mumbled as I crawled to my feet. "Maybe you should have stayed in the army, Colonel."

As you've probably gathered, Steve and I don't operate on the same wavelength.

Devin and Travis bounced ahead of us toward the parking lot. I stopped to watch my almost grown babies for a minute. Devin, lean as a distance runner, his dark hair falling below his collar. Travis, tawny hair almost military short, broad at the shoulder, a good three inches under his brother's six foot. Totally opposite in looks, but seemingly connected by radar as they zigged and zagged through the trees and over brush. They were ready to play another round. I wished I had half their energy.

Chad, just a few steps in front of me, snapped branches at me as we ducked through the trees. Sometimes, I wish he were still in the Navy. I glanced toward the parking lot and sighed. It seemed further away than when we started. I stared at my feet and stumbled through the underbrush on rubber legs. My boots felt like they weighed forty pounds apiece. Chad shot a quick glance over his shoulder and made a rude comment. I flipped him off without looking up. He just snickered. *Asshole.*

Head down, eyes half closed, I trudged through the woods. A sticker bush encircled my pants leg. I jerked free, tripped and banged into an ash tree. I swore and rubbed my elbow.

"I hate trees, I hate sticker bushes, and I hate these stupid combat boots," I snapped as I tripped again. Mostly what I hated was feeling inadequate. I actually like playing paintball. It's all the booyah army stuff that puts me in a bad mood.

Just once I'd like to come to the range dressed in comfortable clothes. But when you play war games with a bunch of ex soldiers, you have to dress the part. I'd have camouflage underwear if it were up to them. If Alden, Missouri is ever threatened by terrorists, my brothers could mobilize an attack force to rival a small nation. The only civilian in a family of warriors, I just fumble along in their wake. They include me in their games from habit. I join in because, hey, anything they can do I can do. I know, I know. It's stupid. I don't think you ever outgrow your childhood.

Chad snapped another branch at me. I ducked, took a step, and my forty-pound boot caught on a wild grapevine.

"Shit," I yelled as I started to fall.

I could hear Chad laughing as I tumbled forward. My gun went flying as I hit the ground. Paintballs spilled from the hopper and rolled around, bright pink against the green and brown leaves. I pushed onto my hands, spit out a mouthful of dirt, and found myself face to face with a head. A growl rumbled deep in my throat. I rose, arms flailing, and teleported backwards, landing on my butt in a multiflora rose bush. My knees were shaking and my heart hammered in my chest.

"Ahhhh, shit. Oh, Jesus!"

I fought my way clear of the thorny bush and tried to stand on shaky legs. My stomach heaved. I hugged a tree for support and deposited my breakfast at my feet. Chad stopped laughing and ran toward me.

"Jesus, Randi. What is it?"

I sank to my knees and flapped a hand weakly toward my discovery. He turned to where I pointed and morphed into cop mode. Chad's a vice cop. He's a UC, an undercover guy, and spends most of his work time hanging out with druggies and prostitutes. I guess a dead woman in the forest wasn't that far off his area of expertise. He stepped forward and moved the underbrush aside with the barrel of his gun. His ponytail flopped across his back as he shook his head and fumbled his game radio from the pocket of his utilities. He keyed it twice. Steve stopped and looked back over his shoulder. Chad motioned them back and Steve and AJ turned around. I closed my eyes and lay my forehead against the rough bark of a tree.

My stomach twisted and I gagged again. Eyes pinched closed, I pressed against the tree trunk until it hurt, trying to refocus my brain so my stomach would settle. A hand cupped my elbow. I jumped and let out a squeak. I hadn't heard AJ. He lifted me to my feet, guided me to a fallen log, and pressed my head down between my knees.

"Deep breaths, babe."

I sucked in air and tried to gain control of my stomach.

"You okay?" he asked.

I nodded. I couldn't speak. I was afraid I'd lose it again.

I took a deep shuddering breath and sat up. AJ was already moving away, pulling his tee shirt on. I guess cops can't go around half dressed. AJ's a detective with the Alden PD, so is my brother Steve. I guess, like Boy Scouts, they're always prepared. AJ slid a notebook from his pocket and started to write. I wondered idly if he had his cuffs and sidearm stashed in there somewhere too.

Steve headed the boys off before they caught sight of the head and sent them to the truck with orders to call their granddad and get a ride home. They grumbled, but moved toward the parking lot. They know better than to argue with the Colonel.

"Is that head attached to a body?" I asked.

"Don't know yet, darlin'," AJ answered.

A shudder rippled along my spine. I wrapped my arms around my knees and rested my chin on them. Chad stood off to my left with his cell phone to his ear. The diamond stud in his earlobe glinted in the light that filtered through the trees. I could already hear sirens growing closer. I sat on my log and watched as Alden's Finest went to work.

I was invisible—an outsider observing the pros. A crime scene team roped off the area and took photos, then started clearing leaves from the head. My stomach was still in a knot and my hands would have trembled if I hadn't had them clasped around my knees. I wanted to look away, but couldn't. I sighed in relief, as a pink silk sleeve was uncovered. I hadn't tripped over a head. It was a body. I don't know why that was better, but somehow it was. Finding a body was bad, but finding a head—that was just gross. I tore my gaze away from the crime scene and stared off into the woods trying to think about something else. Grocery list. That was good. Eggs, milk, bread, pink silk shirt. Dammit.

I glanced back at the body. The pink sleeve tugged at my memory. The blank face was turned toward me and I forced myself to take a good look. I knew this girl, or had at least seen her recently. Maybe at work. I stared at nothing. Focused inward as I tried to put a name to the once pretty face. Booted feet and camo-clad legs stepped into my line of sight blocking my view just as a name was percolating up through my brain. As my focus moved from the body to the legs, the name vanished. My concentration broken, the reality of what I was staring at hit, and a shudder racked my frame once more. I closed my eyes and wished myself at home in a nice hot shower.

Lost in my daydream shower, I started as my log shifted. Chad settled next to me and slipped a bottle of water in my hand.

"You okay, Ranna?" He asked.

"Yeah."

I took a drink and shivered. The warm September day was starting to cool. Chad peeled off his field jacket and laid it across my shoulders.

"She looks familiar, do you know who she is?" I asked.

"Got a pretty good idea."

That admission wasn't followed by a name, but I was pretty sure I'd remember it myself when I had a minute to think without the distraction of a dead body at my feet. I slipped my arms into the sleeves of Chad's jacket and hugged it close. Right now I just wanted to go home. As usual, Chad seemed to read my mind.

"The crime scene boys and the coroner will be here for a while. Why don't you let me drive you home?"

Sweet as that sounds, he wasn't asking to be nice. He wanted me out of the way. I didn't care. I was cold, tired, sore, and wasn't all that eager to watch them load the body bag. I let Chad pull me to my feet without an argument. His bearing was stiff and, even in his paint-spattered clothes, I saw a glimmer of the naval officer that lurked under his disheveled exterior. The clean-cut guy that returned from the service was unrecognizable until you saw him at a crime scene. When he's not working undercover, the spit and polish sneaks out from beneath the long hair and punk clothes.

AJ stepped away from the cops ringing the crime scene. "You working tonight?" he asked.

I nodded.

"I'll stop by later."

I waved an okay and followed Chad to the parking lot. Emergency vehicles, lights flashing, were scattered across the gravel lot. As we stopped at the truck, Harold Baker, the owner of The War Zone, jogged toward us, his beer belly proudly leading the way. He huffed to a stop in front of Chad's Ranger pickup, jerked off his Ruger cap to wipe away the sweat and jammed it firmly back in place.

"What's all the ruckus?"

"Randi stumbled onto a body out on the paintball range," Chad answered.

Harold's face went pale.

"Damn teenagers are always running around out there after hours. My God. This is awful. Randi, are you alright? Can I get you a drink? Do you want to come in and sit for a while?"

I shook my head and gave him a half smile.

"One of the detectives will be by to talk to you later," Chad said.

"I'll be here. My God, I can't believe this. There's a bunch of kids getting ready to play a round. I'd better catch 'em before they stumble into the middle of the crime scene." He turned and hurried toward the door of the shop.

I hoped the murder investigation wouldn't keep Harold shut down very long. He'd owned Sure Shot—the shooting range, and the paintball field—The War Zone, for almost two years. A great old guy, he reads Soldier of Fortune magazine, drinks Budweiser beer and hates terrorists and drugs. I was pretty sure he was an old soldier, but I'd never heard him talk about it. He'd be the right age for Vietnam, though. Three evenings a week, at Sure Shot, he taught women how to shoot and take care of a weapon. Sometimes I got to help him. Harold Baker was one of my favorite people.

I sank onto the truck seat with a sigh, lifted my curly brown hair off my neck, and tucked it through the back of my camouflage ball cap. Twigs and leaves fell onto the seat. I tried to comb the rest out with my fingers without much luck. While Chad stood outside talking to another officer, I pondered cutting my hair short before our next paintball weekend. Nah, probably not. I'd hate for Chad's hair to be longer than mine.

Chad and I are twins. When we were kids, we looked a lot alike. Now he's six feet tall to my five-eight, and he has muscles where I've got boobs, so the resemblance is harder to see. It's still there in the dimples we share when we smile, the dark brown hair, the deep brown of our eyes. But Chad's eyes have a menacing glint that wasn't there before he went into the Navy. Mine usually just look tired.

Chad finished his conversation and slid behind the wheel. We drove toward town without talking. Chad was tense. His knuckles were white as he gripped the steering wheel and his biceps bulged against the fabric of his tee shirt.

I stretched my neck and swallowed a groan as my muscles protested. I absently picked twigs and leaves from my ponytail as we drove and wished I didn't have to go to work. I tend bar part-time for my ex-husband, Morgan Black, and I was due there in a little over an hour.

I started tending bar for Morgan about five weeks ago. I left the ad department of The Alden Sentinel because the sports editor grabbed my ass one too many times. After I clocked him with my computer keyboard and gave him a black eye, I decided a career change was in order. Morgan offered me a job. Since jobs aren't that plentiful around Alden, I took it. My Mom's still in shock. My brothers think it's funny.

Morgan and I didn't have the calmest divorce on record. I caught him banging Wendy Miller in the backseat of my car one night in the parking lot behind the bar. We'd been married a little over five years. They hadn't been all that smooth, but I never dreamed he was cheating on me. Apparently, I was the only one in Alden that didn't know about Morgan's extra curricular activities. We've been divorced more than ten years now, and I seem to be mellowing where Morgan is concerned. He's a good father and a good businessman, just a lousy husband.

Lids at half-mast, I sagged against the headrest and ran through a list of people that might cover for me at the bar. It was no use. I was just going to have to go in. I leaned forward and opened my eyes as Chad swerved onto the shoulder. The man walking alongside the road stopped, glanced at the truck and sketched a salute. Chad hooked a finger at him in a 'come here' motion. He eased out of his backpack and ambled toward the open window.

"Mouse," Chad said.

"Commander. Ma'am."

He nodded toward me. I cocked my head to see him better. He was probably close to sixty. Lean in an underfed kind of way. His eyes were a startling blue and lines like cracks radiated away from the corners. His beard was grey with a hint of red, but his hair was a dull brown and pulled into a ponytail.

I glanced away as a siren wailed and came closer. The sheriff slowed and gave us a once over. A nod from Chad and he continued on to Timber Bridge.

"What's goin' on?" Mouse asked, shrugging at the departing sheriff's car.

"Little trouble over at Timber Bridge." Chad answered. "What are you doin' out here this afternoon?"

"Just walkin'."

Mouse ducked his head and glanced quickly around as he answered.

"Uh huh. You around here last night?" Chad asked.

"No, suh."

"If you saw anything unusual around here last night, I need to know about it."

"Wudn't out here last night, suh."

You might want to head on into town, Mouse."

"Yes, suh."

He snapped off another salute, nodded to me, and turned away. I'd seen Mouse around for years, but I'd never really paid attention to him. He was just part of the scenery. I looked him over as he moved off toward town. His combat boots, worn at the heel from years of use, shone with polish. His jungle fatigues, threadbare at the knees and seat, were clean. For some reason that surprised me. I just assumed he'd be dirty. He shouldered his pack, stuck his hands into the pockets of his field jacket and shuffled off. Chad watched him for a minute, lost in thought. I sat quietly glancing between Mouse and Chad.

"You think Mouse had something to do with the murder?"

Chad didn't answer. He shifted into first and eased onto the road. I didn't ask again. I knew from experience Chad wasn't going to talk tonight. I'd catch him tomorrow and get all the details. A moment later, we passed Mouse still trudging home.

"He in Vietnam?" I asked.

"Uh huh."

"How do you know him?"

"He deals a little weed."

"He one of your contacts?"

Chad was staring through the windshield, fingers tight on the wheel, body rigid in the seat beside me. He didn't answer my question. Probably didn't hear it. I gave up and stayed quiet until we stopped in front of my red brick house. I coaxed my body from the truck and turned toward the sidewalk.

"You ought to take off work, Ranna. It's been a rough day."

"I can't. Morgan's out of town. We can't get by without two bartenders on Saturday night. Unless you want to go in for me."

"Not a chance. If I'm not back at Timber Bridge soon, Steve's gonna go postal on me."

Chad started to pull away. I called his name and he stopped.

"You don't actually think Mouse had anything to do with this, do you?"

He didn't answer, just waved, and drove off to The War Zone. As I trudged up my short walk past the dying stalks in my flowerbed, I saw two shake shingles amongst the flowers. I picked them up and noticed two more at the bottom of the hill next to the road. Lovely, the roof's coming off, just what I needed. I tossed the shingles onto the porch and sank down on the steps. The leaves rustled as Mrs. Litton's cat, Bill, popped out of the flower stalks and sat down next to me. Bill lives next door, but he visits a lot. We companionably admired the flowers scattered across what used to be my tiny front yard. The patch of grass that dropped downhill into the ditch and was a real pain in the butt to mow, so I turned it into Bill's personal jungle. Solved my problem, and made the neighbor cat happy, a two-for-one deal.

"Mouse wouldn't hurt anyone, Bill," I said.

I wondered briefly why I was so sure of that. I didn't even know the guy. I was too tired to ponder it for long. Bill rolled his head under my hand and grabbed my fingers with his teeth. I scratched behind his ears and gave him a final rub before I staggered to my feet and went inside. Wilson, my Jack Russell Terrier, raced down the hall from the kitchen as I pushed into the living room. He bounced around my legs in greeting as I tried to pull the door closed behind me.

"Hey, Wilson. You want to go outside, buddy?"

He raced ahead to the kitchen, then stared at me in puzzlement as I stopped at my bedroom to toss in my paintball gear. I piled my stuff just inside the doorway and gazed longingly at the bed. The urge to crawl in and sleep till morning was almost overwhelming. Wilson yelped to get my attention. I sighed and went through the kitchen to let him outside. He charged, barking at the squirrels. Bill shot across the yard, blindsided the dog, and leapt to the top of the fence. Wilson whirled in confusion, searching for his invisible attacker. Laughing, I slid the door closed and went into the bathroom. Paint-spattered clothes covered the floor. Looked like Dad stopped off here with the boys before he took them to the farm. I scooped up their cammies and trudged upstairs. Their bedrooms are at the front of the house. Devin's is a disaster area. You need a tetanus shot to go in. Travis's room is perfectly neat. The only similarities in décor were the rock band posters, but even here their tastes varied—Nickelback for Travis, he tends to try and blend in with the crowd. Metallica for Dev, I think he just likes the look. I don't know that I've ever heard him play any Metallica. Maybe he listens to them on his iPod. They both share an affinity for busty blonde swimsuit models and Taylor Swift. Were I to snoop a little, I'd probably find a collection of Chad's old Playboy magazines stashed away. If I were guessing, Travis would have them filed in a Science Digest binder on his bookshelf. Devin's would be under his mattress. I've decided not to try and find them.

My office overlooks the backyard. The boys have moved into my space and now retired video game systems, sports equipment, guitars and small animal cages fill every nook and cranny. I dumped their paint-spattered clothes next to the rest of their gear and peeked at the cages. No inmates right now. I think the boys are biding their time. I had a full-blown conniption fit when I found a snake in there last month.

I started dropping my camo on my way to the shower as the phone rang. I grabbed it and sagged onto a chair at the kitchen table.

"Hello."

I leaned over to unlace my boots and got a good look at the kitchen floor. Geez, I really needed to mop.

"Miranda, it's Mom."

I knew that. No one but my mom and my second-grade teacher have ever called me Miranda. My second-grade teacher never phones.

"The boys are here with me. They can spend the night if you want. That way you can go straight home after work."

"Thanks, Mom."

"I wish you would get a better job. That bar is a terrible place to spend time."

"The Jolly Roger is the safest place in town, Mom. It's always full of cops."

"It's not proper for a mother of teenagers to work in a bar."

I rolled my eyes and stifled a groan.

"It's a good job, Mom. I make good money and I have my days free."

We have this conversation every time we talk.

"It's not proper, you're a single woman."

What that has to do with anything, I've not yet determined. Maybe one of these days I'll ask her to explain, or maybe I won't. She went on about the bar and I zoned out while I finished unlacing my boots. I tuned back in just as she finished.

"...Devin wants to talk to you. You just be careful at that place."

"I will, Mom."

Devin came on the line.

"Dude! Mom, I heard you found a head at The War Zone."

"It wasn't a head, it was a body."

I gave a shudder as I thought of being face to face with that body.

"Oh," he said losing some enthusiasm. "That's not nearly as cool as finding a head."

I rolled my eyes again and sighed. "Don't make trouble for Gran and Granddad tonight."

"We won't. Gotta go, Mom. Me and Granddad are working on the Mustang."

"Granddad and I," I said as the phone clicked in my ear.

I cradled the receiver, dragged myself into the bathroom and stood in the shower letting the water pound on my shoulders. I was sore and bruised and my butt was still stinging from the multiflora rose scratches. My brothers never fall into rose bushes. They never trip on grapevines either.

I slumped against the wall of the shower in a stupor until it suddenly turned cold. I squealed, flailed around getting the soap rinsed from my hair and thrashed my way past the shower curtain. I toweled off the goose bumps and shivered into jeans and a long sleeved tee shirt. While I dressed, I also did some inventive swearing at the stupid water heater. When I finished (dressing and swearing), I wasn't cold anymore.

Combing the tangles from my hair, I ran some gel through it with my fingers and did the dark bar makeup routine. The magazines say if you feel rotten, take extra time with your face. According to them, it'll make you feel better. Since I hardly ever wear makeup, any time at all was extra. I gave my lashes a last swipe of mascara and tried a smile at the mirror. It came off more like a grimace. The extra mascara hadn't done the trick, I still felt like hell. I let Wilson in, told him I'd be late and slipped into my boots. I grabbed my keys and ran out the front door, tripped over the damn cat and stumbled down the stairs.

"Jesus, Bill. Go sleep on your own porch."

Bill flipped his tail at me and stalked toward home. I crossed my fingers as I jabbed the key in the ignition of my truck. If it started on the first shot, I might make it to work on time.

Chapter 2

eedless to say, I didn't get to work on time.

"You're late, sweetcakes."

"Piss off, Lex," I said, as I stepped behind the bar.

He snickered as I dodged around him and into the office. I threw my jacket on the chair and emptied my purse onto the desk. Lex poked his head in while I dug through the mess searching for my gun.

"Got everything you need, precious? Nail file, lipstick, tampons."

"A gun." I snapped.

He ducked out laughing. My Kel Tec P32 peeked from under a Happy Harry's grocery store receipt. I shoveled the rest of the junk back into my bag and palmed the tiny automatic. My P32 was about the size of a shirt pocket and slightly less intimidating than a water pistol. I liked it because it was small. I carried it because Morgan preferred his bartenders armed. We cashed paychecks at the Roger for the shift workers at the brick plant. On Friday and Saturday nights, there was a lot of money on the premises. He wanted to make sure we didn't lose any of it.

The holster for the .32 snapped onto my belt behind my right hip. Purse lint caked the gun sights. I took a quick swipe with a bar towel to remove it, checked that my little peashooter was loaded and snicked it home. It weighed less than my cell phone and the tail of my tee shirt covered it completely.

Lex made another rude comment as I took my place behind the bar. I considered using the .32 on him, but decided that was maybe a bad idea. It would probably just make him mad. Morgan keeps a .45 under the bar. That was a little more appealing, but I could hardly lift the damn thing. I'd probably shoot myself in the foot if I tried to use it. Lex was probably safe. I don't think I could actually shoot anyone with anything more deadly than paint anyway. I was definitely too tired to try it tonight.

My reverie was broken when someone rapped an empty bottle on a tabletop. The universal 'give me another' signal. Cigarette smoke swirled around the nicotine stained ceiling, trapping the light before it reached the floor. Squinting through the smoke-induced gloom, I tried to locate Kira Reynolds, our cocktail waitress. She was lost somewhere in the shadows. I sighed, grabbed a fresh Bud from the cooler, slogged from behind the bar and traded it for an empty and two bucks. Kira mouthed a thank you as she rushed past with her tray. The jukebox started thumping as I made my way blindly to the bar and I lost the use of my hearing as well. I felt like Helen Keller.

By the time I stumbled back, Kira was standing at the bar with a Birkenstock perched on the rail while she waited on an order from the kitchen. She may be the only person in town that owns Birkenstocks. She looks like a blonde gypsy fortuneteller and you never know what she's going to be wearing when she shows up for work. Tonight it was an ankle length navy blue skirt and a long gauzy white shirt tied at the waist with a psychedelic scarf. Her hair was hidden beneath some sort of multicolored turban and a quartz point dangled from a silver chain around her neck. Every time she moved, the tiny bells sewn onto the hem of her skirt jingled like a wind chime. Her colorful garb usually made her easy to spot in a room full of feed caps and denim. She went tinkling away with her order as one of the dart players rode the banister down from the mezzanine and tumbled to the floor. He staggered to his feet and the bar patrons awarded him a round of applause. He tottered to the bar grinning, got a fresh pitcher and made his way upstairs at an unsteady but slower pace.

The mezzanine, where the dartboards hang, runs down one wall and over the bandstand. Not for the first time I wondered at the soundness of the reasoning that had drunks with sharp objects overlooking the dance floor. In their defense, I don't think anyone's ever been punctured, but the tables underneath the dartboards have bull's-eyes painted on them for a reason.

I mixed drinks and tried to stay out of Lex's pawing range. Lex is Arlen Lexington; he's been tending bar at the Jolly Roger since he moved down from St. Louis. I guess he's a good bartender. When he smiles, his teeth gleam beneath his mustache and his eyes sparkle. He looks like a bandit, an extremely well-built bandit. The local girls love him and leave him huge tips. I think he's pond scum. That could be because he gets a lot bigger tips than I do. It also might be because Lex cops a feel any time he thinks he can get away with it. He's worse than the sports editor. I'm not about to let some guy run me away from another job. I work in cowboy boots and retaliate with the occasional instep mash.

"Oops, sorry," sheepish grin.

What can he say after he just grabbed my ass? Good thing for him we don't have a computer. I'm deadly with a keyboard. When AJ or my brothers are in residence, Lex backs off. I wished one of them would show up now. I was too tired to put up with his shit tonight. Lex must have read something in my face because the last time I glared at him he strolled to his end of the bar and stayed there.

The front door opened and I glanced over. A tall skinny guy in a cowboy hat strolled in. He moved with the loose-jointed gate of a dancer. First looks were deceiving, he wasn't skinny just lean and muscular. A pair of sunglasses mirrored the room as he looked around. His gaze flitted over Lex before he ambled to my end of the bar. The crowd parted in front of him like magic and he took a vacated stool in front of me.

"What'll it be, Tex?" I asked.

He hooked a finger in the corner of his shades and eased them down so he could peer over the top. The eyes staring from the shadows of his hat were such a light blue they were almost without color. The temperature in the bar seemed to drop twenty degrees. I suppressed a shiver.

"Beer," he said.

I dropped a coaster on the bar in front of him and sat a draft down. He shoved the shades back into place, lifted his draft and spun toward the room. I let out my breath in a rush. This guy was frightening. I caught Lex's eye and nodded toward the cowboy. He motioned me over.

"You need me to get rid of him?" Lex asked.

"Nah, just keep an eye out."

"You got it, angel."

I went to the sink to wash up some glasses. When Tex spun around for another beer, I jumped and dropped a beer mug. It clattered into the sink without breaking. I dried my hands, pulled another draw for the cowboy, and placed it on the coaster. Our fingers touched as he reached for the glass. I jerked and a smile flashed across his face before he turned away. Ick. I took a drink of water and sat the bottle on the counter behind the bar. Kira slapped her tray down in front of me and rattled off an order. I mixed her drinks and watched as she leaned toward Tex.

"Hey, cowboy," she said. "Where's your horse?"

He didn't even look at her, just drained his beer, thunked the empty on the bar and stood.

"You know, you have a seriously dark aura," Kira said.

He stared at her silently for a minute, then turned and touched the brim of his hat as he glided toward the door. Kira caught my eye and I curled my lip.

"He can't help it, Randi. He's a very troubled soul," she said.

Chad came in as the cowboy and his troubled soul walked out. They brushed passed each other without a look. Chad took the stool vacated by the stranger and ordered a burger. I drew him a Bud Light and slid it across the bar.

"How's it going, Chadly?"

"I've had better days."

"You know that guy that was leaving as you came in?"

"Didn't see him."

He drained his beer and I poured a second.

"Find out who the girl at Timber Bridge was?" I asked.

"I know her."

I did too, that was the problem. The vision of her at the bar was clear, unfortunately, it didn't come with a name, but I was sure it was from last night.

"Well, what's her name?"

"I can't say anything, Ranna, her family hasn't been notified yet."

"Come on, Chad. It's not like I'm gonna call the newspaper."

"Randi, don't. Not tonight. It's been a long day."

I at least had the good grace to look contrite.

Chad turned his attention to his cheeseburger, and I left him alone to eat in peace. He said he'd talk to me tomorrow and left as soon as he finished. AJ came in next. Things were starting to slow down so I ordered a couple of burgers and came out from behind the bar. My muscles were screaming for a break. I almost whimpered in relief as I crawled onto the barstool. AJ wasn't much more talkative than Chad so we chewed in companionable silence for a while. When Lex left at eleven, I limped behind the bar. AJ sat with his back against the wall nursing a Coors Light and scanning the crowd. I guess that gets to be a habit when you're a cop. I straightened bar bottles, restocked the cooler and finally the clock made it to closing time. I hollered last call, sent a few six packs out the door and wished everyone would go home.

"AJ, you want another one?"

He shook his head.

"Okay if I stick around while you close tonight?" he asked.

I shrugged and kept washing glasses.

"How come Lex leaves at eleven?" AJ asked.

"I don't know. Got to get his beauty sleep I guess. Why?"

"I don't like you being here by yourself. It's not a good place for a woman."

"Have you been talking to my mom?" I asked.

"What?"

"Never mind."

I ushered out the last drunk and locked the door. As I dragged my tired body back across the room, I spun around and lifted my tee shirt uncovering my gun.

"I can take care of myself."

His only response was an eye roll.

"I managed okay while you guys were gone," I mumbled.

AJ watched TV and ignored me. I wiped off the tables, swept the floor and finished straightening up. AJ switched off the TV and slumped against the bar as I shut off the main lights. I drew a Bud Light and sat down to count the cash drawer. AJ sat on full alert; eyes sweeping the dark room, ears tuned to dog whistle range while I counted. He was kind of giving me the creeps. I didn't finish my beer, just dumped it, zipped the deposit in a bank bag and went to lock it in the office. When I came back with my purse, AJ was standing by the door.

"Let's go," he said.

I let us out and glanced over my shoulder. The only illumination in the place was behind the bar. The rest of the room was completely black. I felt a chill as I locked up. AJ pulled me away as I checked to make sure all was secure. I'd left my truck parked in a pool of light next to the road. AJ hustled me across the lot. The rest of the weed-choked gravel drive was in shadow. The Roger squatted in the dark. The only sign of life, a neon Miller Lite sign glowing in the window. I walked across this lot every night without giving it a thought. Tonight, it felt creepy. AJ's next question did nothing to quell the feeling.

"You still wearing your gun?" AJ asked.

"Yeah, why?"

He didn't answer.

"AJ...Why?"

"Not now," he said shaking his head. "Make sure you keep it handy when you're home by yourself."

"Right, AJ. Nobody even locks their doors around here, but I need to carry my gun. What's going on?"

He jerked open the truck and shoved me in.

"AJ, dammit. Tell me what's going on."

He closed the door on me without answering. I turned the key in the ignition. It didn't even click.

"Come on," I muttered.

I tried it again. Nothing. I stomped the throttle and twisted the key. Nothing, it was completely dead. I smacked the steering wheel in frustration.

"Don't do this to me tonight," I pleaded.

AJ stood outside, sweeping the parking lot, hand resting on the butt of his gun. I noticed he had his holster unsnapped. A shiver rippled up my spine. I was getting the heebie jeebies. I stomped the accelerator and twisted the key simultaneously. I might as well not have bothered. AJ opened the door and pulled me off the seat. I stumbled into him when my feet hit the gravel and he slid his arm around me.

"Leave it, we'll get it tomorrow."

I already had the creeps so I went with him to his truck without comment. He relaxed a little when the engine started and we crunched across the drive. We wove slowly through the dark streets of downtown. Even the stoplights were off. AJ scanned the empty streets like he expected a gang war to break out at any minute.

"AJ, you're scaring me silly. What's going on?"

"Nothin'."

"Right."

We turned off Main, passed the Quick Mart and crossed over to Evergreen. I was planning to run into the store for lunchmeat and cheese on the way home. I turned to tell AJ and lost my nerve. He didn't act like he planned on making any detours. I flipped on the radio, received a dirty look, switched it off and we rode in silence the rest of the way. AJ turned onto Nichols, slowed, and pulled into my driveway. He scanned the neighborhood, apparently saw nothing threatening and relaxed a little more. As I pushed open my door, he snatched his keys from the ignition and slid out from under the wheel.

"You don't have to escort me to the house."

He smiled and followed me without comment. Bill uncurled from in front of the door and stretched before strolling out of the way.

"Goodnight, Bill."

"Who's Bill?" AJ asked.

"Mrs. Litton's cat."

"Why doesn't he sleep on his own porch?"

"I don't know. He likes mine better, I guess."

AJ rubbed Bill behind the ears while I fumbled my key in the lock. When I opened the door, Wilson barked, shot between my feet and went after the cat. Bill smacked him on the nose. Wilson yelped and ran back into the house.

"Your dog just got his ass kicked by Mrs. Litton's cat, darlin'."

"Shhh. Not so loud," I said. "You'll hurt his feelings."

AJ snickered and pushed into the living room flipping on the light. I let the dog out into the backyard and eased into a kitchen chair to pull off my boots. I could hear AJ upstairs opening doors and flipping on light switches. I rubbed my aching feet and tried to think of some clever torture for Lex. If it weren't for him, I could work in tennis shoes. AJ thumped down the stairs, got a Pepsi from the fridge, and dropped into the seat across from me. I slumped back and propped my feet on the trashcan.

"What was that all about?" I asked.

"Just making sure nobody was here."

AJ picked up one of my aching feet and started massaging it. I groaned and he smiled. I jerked my foot out of his hands and scooted up in my seat.

"Did you..." I swallowed and started again. "You didn't really think someone was in my house, did you?"

"Not really."

"This have something to do with the girl at Timber Bridge?"

"Maybe."

"Why were you so uptight at the bar?"

"She was a barfly. Didn't seem like a good idea for you to be there alone."

"Oh."

I leaned my head over the back of my chair and closed my eyes. A picture of her still nameless face painted itself on my eyelids and it was driving me nuts. I knew this girl and I could not come up with her name. I opened my eyes and looked at AJ.

"I've never seen a dead body before," I whispered.

AJ took my hand and gave it a little squeeze.

"Who was she?" I asked.

"Lisa Woods."

The name unleashed more pictures, Lisa laughing and flirting at the bar Friday night. Sharing drinks with a couple of other women—all of them with shiny hair, glossy lips, talons for fingernails, a pitcher of margaritas on the table in front of them. I remembered them because they made me think the bar had been invaded by a pack of real estate saleswomen. Just a little more polished and mature than our normal girls night out group. I remembered watching as they shot down the guys that tried to interest them in a game of darts, or pool. Lex had kept their margarita pitcher full and I figured he'd be looking at a twenty-dollar tip come closing time.

"Randi?" AJ said.

I blinked away the pictures and came back to the kitchen.

"You okay?" He squeezed my hand.

I nodded. "Yeah. I knew she looked familiar, I just couldn't think of her name. How did Chad know Lisa? I'm not sure she was even in high school when we graduated."

"She's been known to turn the odd trick."

"She was a hooker?" That pretty well shot down my real estate saleswoman analogy. I thought I was a better judge of character than that.

"Not really a pro, more like gifted amateur."

"I still can't believe she was murdered. People don't get murdered in Alden."

"People get murdered everywhere, Randi."

"What happened to her?"

AJ paused to gather his thoughts before he spoke.

"I'll tell you, if you really want me to, because I want you to know exactly what happened to that woman, Randi. I need you to be on your guard, especially working the hours you do, but the information stops here. Most of this won't make the papers. If it did we'd have a panic on our hands and we'd spend all our time soothing fears instead of investigating the murder."

"Okay."

"Are you sure?"

"I guess."

I didn't even know what he was going to say and I was creeped out.

"This stays between us, darlin'. Don't mention it to anyone. Not even your Granny Bert or Sara Beth, okay?"

I nodded.

"She was naked except for her shirt. The killer had sliced off the buttons and it was hanging open. At some point, the bastard cuffed her hands behind her. We found a pair of plasti-cuffs lying near the body, they'd been cut off, but there were ligature marks on her wrists where they'd dug into her skin before he removed them."

AJ stopped talking and looked up.

"You sure you want to hear this, darlin'?"

I nodded. Although by that time, I was pretty sure I didn't want to know the rest.

"She had knife cuts on the inside of her thighs and on her breasts. We didn't find the knife." He paused a minute then went on in a softer voice. "It appears she may have been raped. The autopsy will tell us for sure. There were marks on her neck...the sick sonovabitch raped and strangled her." His voice rose at the end. He took a deep breath, then continued again softly. "I can't wait to catch this bastard. Come on, babe. I don't want to talk about this any more tonight."

AJ gently pulled me to my feet and led me into the living room. We sat down on the couch and he turned on the TV. I wasn't paying much attention. He might be able to shut it out. I was still thinking of the pasty white face of the girl I had seen at The War Zone. What a horrible way to die.

"Relax, darlin'," AJ said.

His hand brushed the hair from my neck and started kneading the muscles there. I lowered my chin to my chest and blew out a tired breath. I didn't feel noticeably more relaxed, but I was trying.

"I don't want you to walk around looking over your shoulder, Ran. Just be careful when you're alone at night. We'll catch this guy."

He turned me away from him and started working out the knots in my shoulders. I was definitely not relaxed now. I tried to keep the tremble from my voice when I spoke again.

"You don't have any idea who the killer might be?"

"Not yet. We'll know more after the autopsy."

His thumbs moved down my backbone working the muscles loose. My skin tingled everywhere he touched. I sighed and let my shoulders relax. He lifted my hair and pressed a kiss against my neck. I jerked away and pulled my shirt down before he slipped his hands underneath. He laughed softly. I leaned against the cushions, and laid my head back. I definitely wasn't thinking about dead bodies anymore. Okay, so AJ's not exactly like another brother.

"We don't want to do this, AJ."

His fingers trailed through my hair and brushed my cheek. My skin felt hot under his touch. I tried to ignore it.

"Well, actually," he said. "I think we do."

"That's not what I mean and you know it."

"Why are you afraid of me, Randi?"

I ducked away from his hand and scooted closer to the end of the couch.

"I'm not afraid of you."

"Uh-huh."

"I just don't want to deal with this right now."

"Why, you dating somebody else?"

"You know I'm not."

"Then what's the problem?"

"I just don't want to do this right now. How do I know you won't leave? I won't go through that again. Last time you left, I married Morgan."

AJ shook his head and relaxed against the cushion beside me.

"Don't lay that on me, darlin'. It's not my fault you married that asshole."

Well, it was and it wasn't, but I wasn't going to go into that with AJ. Not tonight, not ever.

"You just left, AJ. I was devastated." My voice cracked. Shit.

He reached over and brushed the hair away from my face. I willed my eyes not to tear up.

"Gimme a break, Randi. I was a twenty-year-old kid. You scared the hell out of me."

"So you ran away for twenty years."

"Jesus, it's not like I left with another woman. I was an Army Ranger."

"Well, while you were off playing GI Joe, I was left here with Morgan the ass." And a broken heart, I added silently. And a pregnancy I had no idea how to deal with.

AJ sighed and shifted beside me.

"This isn't going well, is it?"

I shook my head.

"I better get outta here, darlin'. It's almost three and I've gotta get the race car ready to go in the morning. You working tomorrow night?"

"No."

"Come to the races with me?"

My heart did a little stutter step. God help me, I still wanted him. It was like I was caught in a time warp, sitting with him on the couch on a Saturday night, him asking me if I was going to the races. AJ drives a sprint car, twelve hundred pounds of motorized testosterone. They rumble the ground, fill the air with rooster tails of dirt and assault your ears with their pounding roar. An orgasm on wheels. If I had any sense, I'd say no.

"I don't know," I answered. "I might." God, I was hopeless.

"Can I take Devin even if you don't go?"

I laughed. He was bribing me so my son could crew for him. I snapped out of my time warp and followed as AJ stood from the couch and moved to the door. He pressed a kiss to my lips and my knees went weak. It was safe to say I was probably going to go to the races tomorrow.

"I'll bring your truck over in the morning, darlin'," he said. "Now lock up and don't open unless you know who's on the other side."

"Yes, sir."

I snapped off a smartass salute before I closed and locked up behind him. My lips still tingled from his kiss. I banged my head against the door and closed my eyes. He made me feel like an inexperienced kid. Maybe I should date more. Hell, maybe I should just date. I sighed and shut off the lights as I wove through the darkened house.

"Come on, Wilson. It's bedtime."

Wilson charged onto the bed and dove under the covers. Wilson really likes to sleep. I peeled out of my clothes, slipped a tee shirt over my head, and put my .32 on the bedside table. Wilson was snoring before I made it all the way into bed. I turned off the lamp and lay in the darkness. Visions of Lisa Woods' white face kept playing like a movie in my head. I wouldn't have minded having AJ here now. I turned over and fluffed my pillow. Wilson sighed, repositioned himself, and started snoring again. I lay awake and watched the moon shadows crawl across the walls. When the sky outside my windows began to lighten, I finally fell asleep.

Chapter 3

The smell of coffee and the rustle of newspaper woke me. I lay still and tried to decide who was in my house. I decided it must be Chad. Steve would have knocked and the boys don't make coffee.

The sun was shining through the window, but my body was telling me it was still too early to get up. I rolled over and tried to go back to sleep. Wilson hopped onto the bed and started licking my face. It was no use. I went from horizontal to vertical and groaned. Every muscle in my body hurt.

"Bout time you got out of bed," Chad called from the kitchen. "I thought you'd died."

"What are you doing here?" I snapped.

"That's not very nice. I came to take you to breakfast."

"Oh, hang on." I pushed away from the bed and hobbled down the hall to the bathroom.

"What time is it?" I asked.

"Almost ten-thirty."

"Where's my truck?"

"Still dead. We hauled it to Dad's."

"Great."

"Mrs. Litton's cat is on your roof."

I poked my head from the bathroom door.

"The roof?"

"Yeah."

"How did he get up there?"

"I don't know."

I went into the bedroom, my hobble slowly easing to a walk. My Mizzou sweatshirt peeked from the pile of clothes in the hamper. I tugged it out and sniffed it. Clean enough for a weekend. I slipped it over my head and dug in my dresser until I found my last pair of jeans. I didn't need to go to breakfast. I needed to stay home and do laundry. I sucked in my stomach to get the jeans zipped and remembered why I kept them buried in the bottom drawer of my dresser.

My hiking boots were next to the door under my paintball gear. I dug them out from underneath and stepped into them before I shuffled back to the bathroom. I brushed my hair into a ponytail and stared at the face in the mirror. Dark bags huddled under my eyes and red lines marked the whites. Nothing short of stage makeup was going to help today, so I didn't bother. I clomped into the kitchen dragging my bootlaces and pulled a Pepsi from the fridge.

"Morning, sunshine."

"Hrmph. Why are you so chipper this morning? You didn't get as much sleep as I did."

"It's not the length of the sleep, it's the quality."

"You got a new girlfriend or something?"

"You know, there are things besides sex that will put a smile on your face in the morning, Sis."

"Name one."

He hesitated and I laughed as I dropped into the chair across from him. He rattled the newspaper into submission while I bent to lace my boots. When I was finished, he handed me the paper folded over so the murder article was the first thing I saw. I drained half my soda and started to read.

"How can you drink that shit first thing in the morning?" Chad asked.

"Better than coffee."

I finished the article and shoved the paper across the table.

"Not much in there." I finished my Pepsi and tossed the empty into the trashcan. "That all they have or just all they're sharing?"

"They don't have much yet. Forensics is still doing their thing."

"That the case-file?" I asked nodding toward a manila folder tucked into his waistband.

"Uh-huh."

"Gonna let me see it?"

"Not supposed to do that. You know the rules."

"What are you doing with it? You don't do homicide."

"Professional courtesy," he said with a grin.

"The Colonel know you have it?"

All I got for an answer was a smile.

"Get your jacket and I'll take you to Mabel's," Chad said. "Maybe the file will accidentally fall open in the truck on the way to town."

I stuck a baseball cap on over my ponytail and followed Chad. I looked at the house from the driveway. Sure enough, there was Bill, sitting on the roof surveying the world.

"Should I tell her where he is?"

"Who?"

"Mrs. Litton. Should I tell her Bill's on the roof?"

"Nah, he'll come down when he gets hungry."

Mrs. Litton, ice blue curls gleaming in the sun, was weeding the flowerbed in her front yard. I find it hard to believe a weed would have the audacity to sprout in her garden. In her role as official neighborhood snoop, she stood and watched to see exactly who I was getting into the car with. I waved and slid into the truck. Chad handed me the file and backed from the drive.

"You tell Steve or AJ I let you see this and I'll deny I even know you."

"I won't tell."

I read the preliminary report, riffled through the crime scene photos, and shoved it all into the file.

"Her family know yet?" I asked.

"Steve did that last night. I'm glad I didn't have to. I hate notifying next of kin."

"Any idea who they're looking for?"

"Nothin' yet. We'll find him though."

"Yeah, that's what AJ said. Right after he drove me home from work and searched my house for intruders."

"Get used to it, sis. At least until we find out where she was when she met up with the asshole or why he killed her. You're just going to have to deal with a bodyguard any time you're out after dark."

"You don't have to do that. I learned how to take care of myself while you guys were off protecting the world."

"Well, we're home now. You can relax."

I shook my head and smiled. Chad has always been overprotective. There weren't many guys brave enough to ask for dates when we were in high school. We rode the two miles into downtown, then circled around the square until we found a parking space at the courthouse. Mouse, dressed the same as yesterday, was standing on the corner. I waved as we drove by. He crossed the street as we got out of the truck and hurried away in the opposite direction.

"What's going on with Mouse?" I asked.

Chad was standing beside the truck watching him move off down the street.

"Guess he doesn't want to talk to me."

"Why's that?

"Let's eat I'm hungry," he said sidestepping the question.

He started across the street to the café. I sighed and fell in beside him. Mabel's Café hasn't changed since it opened in 1957. Black and white tile floors, red and white plastic tablecloths, red plastic covered chairs, and a counter with twelve stools running down the kitchen side of the room. Tiny Kellogg's cereal boxes frame the pass-through window to the kitchen. The shelf over the front door holds a collection of bowling trophies. Mr. Muley, an ancient mule deer head, stands guard over the hallway that leads to the bathrooms. If you're searching for classy dining, Mabel's is not your place. If you want biscuits and gravy and gossip, you're in luck. The main attraction is an octogenarian waitress by the name of Bertie Mae Jennings. She's my grandma.

Granny Bert's been waiting tables at Mabel's forever. She has bright red hair, compliments of Miss Clairol, and bright red lipstick from the Avon lady. Her fingernails are like talons and match her lips. She can carry eight plates at a time without losing a single french-fry. When she dies, Mabel will probably have to close down.

Mabel sat at the front table smoking and drinking coffee. The shellac on her bleach blond beehive glittered in the morning sunlight. She winked as I went by and waved her cigarette in my direction, showering ashes across the tabletop. Most of the morning coffee crowd was gone and families were packed in for breakfast. There wasn't an empty booth or table so we parked on stools at the counter. The die-hard coffee drinkers were huddled at the far end having a shouted conversation with Leroy and Alvin in the kitchen. Granny leaned over and planted a big red lipstick kiss on Chad's forehead.

"It's rude to eat in a hat," she said to me as she snatched it off.

She took one look at my hair and shoved it back onto my head. Chad laughed quietly beside me. I elbowed him in the ribs. He retaliated by squeezing my leg just above the knee, the most ticklish spot on the human body. I squealed and twisted away. My cap fluttered to the floor.

"For God sake you two. Act your age."

I laughed and reached down to retrieve my hat from where it had fallen. Chad turned and planted his elbows on the counter.

"Your brother was just here with that good looking boyfriend of yours," Granny said.

I straightened from the floor and shoved the hat over my hair.

"He's not my boyfriend, Granny."

"Humph."

"Hey Bertie, how 'bout some coffee down here," yelled Fred Baxter.

Fred's retired from the brick plant. He's deaf as a post and spends ninety percent of his time at Mabel's. I think he's sweet on Granny Bert.

"Don't get your shorts in a twist, Fred or you'll be wearing this coffee instead a drinkin' it."

I smiled. I think Granny's sweet on Fred, too. She hollered an order through the window and scooted down the counter with the coffee pot. A few minutes later, she plunked plates in front of us. We didn't get to order. It doesn't work that way at Mabel's. Granny takes a look at you, decides what you need to eat that day, then bribes you into eating it by promising you sweet rolls. I must have looked bad. My plate had the works, B and G's, hash browns, eggs, and what looked like a half pound of bacon.

"You're lookin' a little peeky this morning, hon. You need something else, I'll bring you a sweet roll," she said.

I dug in. Chad had a manly breakfast of steak and eggs. No biscuits and gravy, no promise of sweet rolls. Guess Granny didn't think he was as needy as me. I cleaned my plate and listened to my arteries harden while Chad finished. The breakfast crowd was clearing out by the time we finished eating.

Granny sat down next to us with a cup of coffee. "So what's going on with that girl you found yesterday?" she asked.

"What have you heard?" Chad asked.

"Just that Randi fell over the body of a girl out at The War Zone."

"How do you do that? It just made this morning's paper, Randi's name wasn't in the article and I know Steve didn't tell you anything."

She didn't answer. Granny Bert's grapevine was legendary. She knows everything about everyone and she always knows it first.

"So, what's the deal?" She asked again.

"Nothin' much to tell yet, Granny," Chad answered.

"Humph. Not safe for a young girl on the streets any more. You have your gun Randi?"

"Yeah, Granny. Do you?"

"I don't have nothin' to worry about. Nobody's gonna mess with an old lady like me."

"It's in your purse, isn't it?"

Granny winked. Chad sighed and shook his head. The thought of Granny Bert with a gun concerns him. I think it's cool. I hopped off my stool and gave her a hug goodbye.

"You bring those boys down for breakfast some morning next week. They're gonna be grown before I see them again."

"Okay, Granny, I will."

My boys think going to Mabel's for breakfast is punishment. They aren't old enough to appreciate Granny Bert yet. I was almost thirty before I could chill enough to enjoy her. My uptight brother Steve can only stand her in small doses, even after all these years. He must have been awfully hungry to come in this morning. Either that, or AJ twisted his arm. AJ enjoys my Granny. Chad and I crossed the street to the truck and made our way back to the house.

"Oh, Ranna, I almost forgot. I was supposed to tell you Dad and Devin are going to work on your truck."

"Great, it'll be months before I get it back again. Maybe years."

Chad laughed.

"Don't laugh. You have a vehicle."

"They won't keep it for months," he said.

"They've been working on that Mustang for years."

"You have a point there."

"Oh, thanks, I feel much better now."

Chad snickered again.

"The boys want to go to the races at California tonight. You want to go?" he asked, changing the subject.

I hesitated. "I don't know."

"Why the hesitation?" he asked. "You've only been a couple of times this year."

"I don't much like watching AJ race."

"Still got a soft spot for AJ, don't ya?"

"No."

"Liar."

"Shut up."

Chad was grinning as we stopped in front of the house.

"Thanks for breakfast," I said, as I climbed from the truck.

"Randi, wait."

"What now?"

"Check around with the guys at work. See if you can get any idea where Lisa's been the last few days. Be nice to get a handle on where she was and who she was with before she died."

"Why me?"

"You're a bartender. People talk to you."

"I'll ask around. I'm almost sure she was at the Roger Friday night, but I'm not sure who she was with." Well, I did know, sort of. I just couldn't put names to faces.

"See what you can find out. I'll be back for you at three," Chad called as he accelerated away.

"I never said I was going," I muttered.

Mrs. Litton caught me before I made it inside. I took a quick look at the roof. No cat. Bill is a mostly welcome visitor. I could do without his owner.

"Who was that handsome young man that gave you a ride home last night? Was it that new police officer?"

Geez, don't you ever sleep?

"Yeah, AJ Weleski. My truck broke down and he gave me a ride home."

"Well, that was nice of him."

"Yeah, he's very nice. I really need to get inside. I'll talk to you later."

She waved and I escaped. As soon as Mrs. Litton goes to the beauty shop, everyone in town will be talking about how AJ and I are getting together again. "God, save me," I groaned. Wilson gave me a worried dog look, so I patted him on the head and filled his food and water dishes. He sniffed at them, then whined at the door, so I let him out. He made the grand tour, watering all the fence posts. The next-door neighbor's stupid black lab was asleep against the fence so Wilson watered him too. He returned looking pleased with himself. I shook my head and let him in. After a shower, I flopped down on the couch. Wilson, always ready for a nap, curled behind my knees and sighed.

My dreams were full of knife-wielding madmen and dead women in pink silk. When someone pounded on the front door, Wilson and I levitated off the couch and stood stupidly in the middle of the living room trying to determine the cause of the noise. Adrenaline had my heart racing and visions of the killer flashed through my head as the door opened. I jerked out my .32 and pointed it at the opening as my son Travis ambled in. He yelped and hit the floor. I squealed and collapsed onto the couch. Wilson, thinking it was playtime, jumped on Travis's head and started biting his ears.

"Jesus, Mom. What the hell is wrong with you?" Travis asked from the floor.

Good question. I sat in shock staring at the gun in my hand. Chad eased through the door behind Travis and stepped over him into the living room.

He stared at Travis on the floor and me with the gun.

"Damn, Randi."

"Just shut up, Chad. I was asleep."

I slipped the gun into my holster and stood.

"You always sleep with your gun?" he asked trying not to smile.

I ignored him. Travis pushed the dog away and stood up. I glared at Chad, walked into the bathroom and slumped against the counter. When I was certain I wasn't going to be sick, I splashed my face with cold water and went out. Travis was standing in the living room and I pulled him into a bear hug.

"I'm sorry sweetie. Jesus, I almost shot you."

"Chill, Mom. It's no big deal."

He ducked away from my hug and shuffled out the still open front door. Oops. How incredibly uncool. First I try to shoot him, then I mortally embarrass him. I have to remember, no hugging teenagers in front of witnesses. I sighed and walked across the porch behind Chad and followed him to the truck. Travis slouched down in the seat, not nearly as cool about that little incident as he wanted me to think. I stuck my still shaking hands into my pockets and took a deep breath. Chad draped an arm over my shoulder.

"Relax, Ranna, nobody was hurt."

"They could have been, though," I whispered. "I could have killed him."

I squeezed my eyes closed and a tear tracked down my cheek. Chad brushed the tear away, pulled me into a hug, and held me until I was in control.

"You have a cigarette, Chad?" I asked as I slipped out of his arms.

"I thought you quit."

"I did."

"Oh."

He fished a pack of Marlboros from his pocket, shook one out and handed me his lighter. I tried to light the cigarette, but my hands were shaking too much. Chad took the lighter and lit it for me. I took a drag and blew smoke toward the treetops.

"I don't think I want to go to the races tonight. I've had all the excitement I can stand for one weekend," I said.

Chad handed me the cigarettes and his lighter as he slid into the truck beside Travis.

"Tomorrow you throw what's left of those away," he said.

"I will."

"You sure you're okay? Why don't you go to Mom and Dad's?"

"Nah, I'll be fine. I'll just stay home with Wilson. We'll watch movies and eat ice cream or something," I said. "I'll see you guys when you get home."

Travis gave me a half salute as they drove away.

I turned to go into the house. Mrs. Litton poked her head out of her front door.

"Randi, I thought you quit smoking."

"I did."

"Oh."

She glanced at the cigarette burning in my hand and the pack I was holding in the other, a confused look crossed her face before she ducked inside.

I groaned. By tomorrow, someone will have told Mom I've started smoking again. Wonderful. I walked into the house, sank onto a kitchen chair and smoked another cigarette. I knew Lisa had been at the bar Friday night. I needed to figure out who she was with or who else from the bar might know the other girls' names. I didn't have a clue. Friday night had been madness. I decided to call Kira to see if she remembered. Though to be honest, she'd be more likely to know what men were there. She didn't pay much attention to the women; they didn't tip her as well.

Kira's phone rang nine times. I was getting ready to hang up when she answered breathless.

"Kira?"

"Oh my God. Randi, is that you?" she squealed. "Did you really fall right on top of a dead body? I heard it was Lisa Woods."

"No, not right on top of it, and yes, it was Lisa."

"I would have wet my pants."

"I was too surprised."

I heard a male voice in the background. Kira said just a minute and through the muffled phone, I heard her say "Would you quit?" and giggle. Well, now I know why it took so long for her to answer.

"Did you know her?" I asked when she came on the phone again.

"Who?"

I swallowed a groan. "Lisa Woods. Did you know her?"

"Oh," she giggled. "I knew who she was. I saw her around the bar some. She hung around a lot when Lex was working. Why?"

"I was trying to remember the names of the girls she was with Friday night."

"Gosh, Randi, I don't have any idea. Is it important?"

"Probably not. You ever see that cowboy in there before?"

"That guy's a creep. He's been in a couple of times. I think he was there Friday night."

"He was?"

"Yeah, he didn't sit at the bar, you might not have noticed."

"He's kind of scary. I wish I could just forget all this for a while."

"It's probably bad feng shui. All that bad energy can really mess things up. I could come over and help you with it if you want. I mean later, not right now." She giggled.

I slapped a hand to my forehead. "Thanks Kira, I think I'm just going to have to deal with the energy that I have right now."

"Well, take a hot bath with some scented oil. Oh, and light some candles. Aromatherapy really helps. I don't guess you have any crystals, do you? Well, never mind, do the hot bath and candles. That's what I do when I want to relax. I'll bring you a stone the next time I work. It'll make you feel a lot better."

"Thanks." Ugh. "I need to get off here, Kira." I could feel my IQ shrinking. "Let me know if you remember anything about Lisa."

"If I do I'll call ya."

"Yeah that's fine. You might ask around, see if anybody else remembers anything about Lisa or her friends."

"Okay. If I hear anything, can I report it to your brother?" she whispered.

"He's married."

"Not that one, the other one. Chad. He's hot."

"Sure. I guess if you run into him before you see me you can." I stared cross-eyed at the phone. "I really gotta get off here, Kira. I'll talk to you tomorrow at work."

"Okay, I'll see ya, Randi."

God, just what Chad needs, a woman with all her brains in her boobs. I called two other people with the same lack of result, then gave up and flopped on the couch with Wilson. I surfed through the channels and found a movie. It must have been a good one. I fell asleep before the opening credits were over. When I woke, the TV was off, Wilson and I were covered with a blanket and someone was sitting in the chair next to the couch. My heart went into overdrive. I bit my lip and tried to determine who was there.

"Relax, Randi, it's me," he whispered.

I let out a breath I didn't know I held and tried to slow down my heart rate. It was AJ.

"What are you doing here?"

"I came to see you. When you didn't answer my knock, I opened the door and found you and Wilson sacked out on the couch. He sure is some watchdog."

"He's my friend, not my protector."

"Good thing."

"Did you pick my lock?"

"Yeah."

"They teach that at cop school?"

"No, I picked that up on my own."

I sat up and ran my fingers through my tangled hair.

"You look good all tousled like that," AJ said.

"I bet you always say that to a woman after you break into her house."

"Yeah, it's a great line. I use it all the time."

"Do any good at the races?" I asked.

"Second."

I stood, went to the kitchen and blinked in the light of the fridge. When I could see, I grabbed a couple of beers. AJ took one and I slumped onto the couch. Wilson, buried in the covers, was snoring. I scooted him over and AJ sat next to me.

"I hear you almost shot Travis this afternoon."

"I don't want to talk about that."

"Okay, what do you want to talk about?"

"I don't know, baseball, world trade, the weather."

AJ laid his hand on the back of my neck and lightly ran his fingers under my hair.

I shivered.

"Baseball sounds good," he said.

He pulled me against his chest and wrapped his arms around me, kissed the top of my head and rested his chin there.

"Have I made it to first base yet?"

"No."

I could feel him laughing in the dark.

"AJ, do you know when Lisa was killed?"

"They're pretty sure it happened Friday night, why?"

"She was at the bar Friday night with a couple of other girls."

I felt him tense as he shifted into cop mode.

"You remember who they were?"

"Not really. They're a lot younger than me. You know how it is, I recognized their faces from school, but they weren't part of our crowd."

"That's not a lot of help, darlin'," he said as he relaxed.

"Sorry. Where are the boys?"

"Went home with Chad. Nobody here but us."

I felt him smile in the dark. He kissed the top of my head again and brushed his fingers across my breast. I stiffened and felt him laugh again.

"Relax. I'll be good. You're safe with me tonight. Just go to sleep."

I turned in his arms, laid my head on his chest and closed my eyes. He scooted down, rested his head on the puffy armrest, and pulled me close.

"AJ, do you know Mouse?"

"Yeah."

"What's his deal?"

"Came back from Nam screwed up. Been in some trouble."

AJ squirmed beside me and slipped the blanket over us. He kissed me softly on the cheek and closed his eyes.

"AJ," I whispered.

His breathing was slow and even. If he wasn't asleep, he was faking it well. I sighed. I'd ask him more about Mouse in the morning.

I woke still wrapped in AJ's arms. Wilson was standing next to the couch sending me a telepathic "I need to go out NOW" message and dancing around. I agreed a pit stop sounded like a good idea and started to sit up. AJ tightened his arms around me.

"If you squeeze me, I'll pee."

He laughed and let me go. "I need to get ready for work anyway. Unless you have a better idea?"

I hesitated; several things sprang to mind.

"Nah, I guess you'd better get to work."

"You were undecided for a minute there," he said.

"No, I wasn't."

"Yes, you were."

I let Wilson outside and headed for the bathroom, brushed my teeth, untangled my hair and strolled into the kitchen. AJ put his coffee cup down as I came in.

"Looks like you found the coffee pot."

"Yeah. Can I use your shower?"

"I guess."

"Want to join me?"

My breath caught. I swallowed and squeaked, "No."

"Liar."

I stuck my tongue out at him. AJ was laughing as he closed the bathroom door. I let Wilson in. He buried himself in a blanket and went back to sleep. I took my mind off the naked man in my shower by making an omelet. By the time AJ finished, I was putting plates on the table. I glanced at him and started to ask about Mouse. His muscles rippled as he walked into the kitchen clad in nothing but jeans and socks. My stomach tied itself in a knot. I forgot what I was going to ask. I took a deep breath and forced my eyes from his abs. A slow smile spread across his face.

"Stop laughing at me," I said.

"I'm not laughing, darlin'."

"Your eyes are."

"That for me?" he asked, nodding toward the omelet.

"Yeah, help yourself."

"Shower would have been more fun than cooking eggs," he said as he sat down.

"Aren't you late for work or something?" I asked.

"I've got time for breakfast."

The look on his face said he had time for more than that. I ignored the thrill that rolled through my insides and sat down.

"You need to get used to me, Randi. I'm not going away this time."

"I thought that before."

AJ finished eating and stepped away from the table. I watched as he pulled his tee shirt over his head and snapped his holster on his belt. Leaning across the table, he brushed my lips with his, slipped on his shoes and sauntered to the door.

"I'm not twenty any more, darlin'. I went to the Army and grew up. You've got to learn to trust me."

The door closed behind him and I stared blindly down at my omelet. I picked up my fork and put it down without taking a bite. I finally called Wilson and sat the plate down in front of him. He was ecstatic. At least one of us was happy.

Chapter 4

After AJ left, I mopped and straightened the kitchen. While I waited for the floor to dry, I pulled myself onto the counter and poked around in the cabinets for something to eat. There weren't many choices, a bag of egg noodles and a can of Campbell's Cream of Mushroom soup. It was definitely time for a trip to the grocery store.

I lifted the bag of noodles and found an open cookie package. Ahhh, that's better. I tore into it and found a lone chocolate-covered graham cracker. The chocolate had started to go white around the edges and the cracker was almost petrified. I ate it anyway.

When the floor was dry, I hopped down and let Wilson in. He flounced in wagging his tail, joyously trailing muddy paw prints across my newly cleaned kitchen floor as he trotted to his favorite napping spot in the recliner. I scooped him up before he got there, muttering as I went down the hall.

"Thanks, Wilson. It hasn't rained in ages. Where'd you find the mud?"

He answered by washing my face with his tongue. I wiped his feet with a tea towel and let him go. He checked to make sure his food dish hadn't disappeared, then continued to the living room for his nap. I mopped the floor again. And sponged the mud from the carpet. Now there were telltale clean spots marching down the hall. I should have put in hardwood floors. I decided I'd had all the housework I could handle for one day. I needed to go to the farm.

Chad wanted information and I could get it from a place he'd never think of. Chad had been gone for close to twenty years. He was still getting reconnected to the small town pipeline. Because I'd never left, I still had mine. I knew who to call for straw bales, where I could get the best Halloween pumpkin, and who could fix my plumbing quick and cheap in an emergency. I also knew the person that could tell me who Lisa's friends were, my dad. Dad was the high school principal in Alden for twenty-two years. He knows every family in the county and remembers almost every kid that ever walked his halls. I was sure he would remember Lisa Woods.

I dragged on my freshest pair of jeans, a flannel shirt, and stuffed my feet into my hiking boots. I stopped in the kitchen to make sure Wilson had food and water, then scooped my keys off the counter, locked the door and stopped short at the sight of my empty driveway. Shit! No car. I pondered my options and finally called Chad to see if I could borrow his truck. I left my number on his pager and waited on the porch steps for his call. My butt was starting to go numb before my cell phone chirped.

"What's up, Ran?"

"Uh, I'm kind of stranded. Don't guess I could borrow your truck for the day, could I?"

"Nope, don't guess you could."

"Please, Chad."

"Forget it, Ran."

Chad's Ford Ranger pickup is his baby. Shiny black with chrome everything and that's just for starters. The V8 squashed under the hood makes it as meaty as it is beautiful. He's spent the last two years customizing it and I wasn't going to have an easy time talking him out of it for an hour, much less the rest of the day.

"Come on, Chadly, please?"

"You remember what happened the last time you used my car?"

"That wasn't my fault. That lady ran a red light."

"Doesn't matter. When it comes to vehicles, you're disaster central."

That's actually only true when it comes to Chad's vehicles. It started when we were kids. The only time I ever asked to borrow his bicycle, it disappeared from in front of Mabel's Café. Then, there was the incident with his Camaro, but that really wasn't my fault. I was minding my own business when this crazy woman flew through a red light and smashed right into the driver's door. For the last ten years, I've heard about that damn car. Lucky for me Chad was out of the country when it happened or he might have killed me. It was old news by the time he made it back home, but he still won't let me forget it.

"Come on, Chad. I'm stuck here."

A big sigh came over the phone.

"I know I'm going to regret this."

I pumped my fist in the air with a silent yes.

"Thanks, Chadly."

"I'm telling you right now. If it gets even one little scratch I'm gonna take it outta your hide."

"Relax, nothin's going to happen to your truck. I promise."

I lifted my eyes to the sky and made a quick plea to the god of cars.

"Don't promise what you can't deliver."

"Ooh, gotta go, I'm getting another call. Talk to you later."

I shut off my phone and stuck it in my purse. While I waited for wheels, I sat on the front porch steps and smoked Chad's last cigarette. I could see Mrs. Litton peeking through her front window. She was still trying to decide whether or not I'd really quit smoking. I turned and waved. She ducked behind the curtains. I laughed. My other next-door neighbors are perfect. They pull into the drive, the garage door rises, the car disappears and you don't see them again until the next time the car leaves. I'm sure they go outside to feed the dog or mow the grass, but I've never seen them do it. I keep wishing I'll get another set of neighbors like that, but I think Mrs. Litton is here to stay. She's lived in that house for thirty years.

When Chad parked at my curb a half hour later, I ran down the steps and hopped in the truck. Bill blinked down at us from the porch roof. I hadn't even known he was there.

"Catch any criminals today?" I asked as he nosed the truck downtown toward the police station.

"Yep, pretty much have the crime problems in Alden taken care of. The Jennings gang will have to move on soon."

"Speaking of gangs, did the boys get to school this morning?"

"Yeah, I dropped them off. We were going to run by the house for their backpacks, but they said there was some kind of assembly today and they probably wouldn't need anything."

I wondered if that was true.

"You sure they didn't just say that because they didn't have their homework done?"

Chad laughed. "I did wonder about that actually. Oh, they did say Morgan was picking them up after football."

Chad pulled into the Quick Stop parking lot and stopped.

"I gotta run in here for a second, you need anything?"

"Nah, I'm good."

He got back in the car with a pack of smokes and a Mountain Dew and we took off.

"Any leads on your murder case?" I asked.

"It's not my case, Randi. I'm Vice. I'm just helping Steve and AJ with some legwork."

"Vice can't be that time consuming in this town."

"You'd be surprised. There are a lot of drugs in this area."

"Think the murder is drug related?"

"Doesn't feel like it. Not getting any vibes from my contacts."

"Do they have any leads?"

"I don't really know. I'm having lunch with AJ and Steve. I'll probably hear what they have then."

"And share it with me later?"

"Why don't you just join the force? Then you wouldn't have to wheedle the info out of me and put my career in jeopardy."

"I've never jeopardized your career. And I don't want to be a cop. I don't like the uniforms. They are terribly unflattering to women."

"I'll pass that along to the chief. Let him know he's losing a lot of female recruits 'cause the uniforms are ugly."

"Well, they are."

Chad shook his head. We parked on Main, in front of the police station. It's square concrete and glass ugliness squats in the middle of the block. In a town full of turn of the century architecture and cobblestone streets, it's an eyesore. Local graffiti artists try to beautify it periodically, but mostly, it's just an ugly hulking brown blob half way down Main Street. Chad wasn't thinking about architecture as he slowly eased out from behind the wheel. He was thinking he was seeing his baby for the last time. I slid across the seat before he could change his mind.

"I swear I'm not going to hurt your truck, Chad."

"Yeah, I know."

"You need me to pick you up after your shift?"

"Nah, I'll catch a ride with somebody."

I turned the ignition and Chad leaned in the window, started to speak, stopped, took a deep breath and straightened without speaking.

"I got it, Chad. Not one scratch, I promise."

He turned and went into the station with a backward wave of his hand. I resisted the little devil on my shoulder that was urging me to goose the throttle and leave black marks the length of the street. The way my luck was running, I'd mow down some innocent old lady. I smirked at my silliness and pointed Chad's black missile toward the farm and Dad.

The farm is a little over six miles from the city limits. It used to be about ten, but Alden has kind of grown out toward it. I could smell fresh-cut grass as I parked in front. The house was sparkling with a new coat of paint since the last time I was there. Dad was keeping busy in his retirement.

A big yellow tomcat hopped onto the rail of the wrap-around porch as I scuffed across the drive. He was the latest in a long line of yellow Toms that had shared that porch with us. We moved here after Grandpap died. Steve was just a baby then. Chad and I were born here. The farm's been in Mom's family for three generations.

I wandered around until I found Dad in the machine shed. The mower was sitting out front, still warm from use and Dad was buried elbow deep in the engine of my Ford. Parts covered the workbench behind him. I sighed. It didn't appear my truck was going to be running any time soon.

"Hey, Dad."

He spun out from under the hood.

"Well, hi. Didn't hear you drive in. Sounds like you had an exciting weekend."

I cringed and wondered if he heard I almost shot Travis, or if he was just talking about finding the body.

"Is it terminal?" I asked, nodding at the truck.

"Nah, Devin and I will have it running good as new before long."

"Soon, I hope. I'm kind of lost without a vehicle."

"Oh, shouldn't take more than a week or so. That what brought you home, just checking on the truck?" he asked as he wiped his hands on a grease rag.

"Well, that's one thing. I wanted to pick your brain too."

"Your mom probably has lunch ready. Why don't we go in and you can start picking my brain over food."

My stomach grumbled and I remembered that Wilson had gotten my breakfast and all I'd had to eat today was a stale chocolate-covered graham cracker.

"Sounds good to me."

I trailed him from the shed to the house and we clomped across the porch together. The porch sags probably six inches from the center to the edge of the house where the foundation has settled. That'll probably be Dad's next project. We pushed into the kitchen. Dad hung his Tractor Supply cap on the rack by the door and ran his fingers through his silver gray hair. I had a sudden glimpse of what Chad was going to look like in another twenty years, tall, slender, distinguished. Dad brushed a kiss on Mom's cheek. She smiled at him and her eyes crinkled at the corners. The smell of cooking sausage and melted cheese filled the kitchen. My mouth started watering. Mom's mac and cheese is legendary. She won't even give me the recipe. Says I wouldn't ever come to visit if I could make it myself. She could have a point.

I stood in the entry, watching Mom cook while Dad washed his hands at the sink. She was wearing a bright yellow apron over her blue dress. Her makeup was flawless and not a strand of her curly ash-blond hair was out of place. As usual, I felt like a slob compared to her. She smiled at Dad and he nodded in my direction.

"Look what I found wandering around outside, Alice."

Mom raked me in a head-to-toe glance and her emerald eyes dulled with disappointment. It was a look I was intimately familiar with.

"Hi, sweetie," she said, then turned back to the stove.

"Hi, Mom."

I straightened my shirt and wiped the toes of my boots on the back of my pant legs. I tried to remember whether or not I'd combed my hair before I left the house. Mom has that effect on me. I've never seen her without her hair and face perfect. Even in the middle of the night, she always looks put together. I've been known to run to the grocery store in my sweats and I'm not above shoving a hat over my hair if I'm in a hurry to get out of the house. Mom just shakes her head and wonders where she went wrong. She slid the sausages from the skillet onto a plate and turned toward the table.

"I hope you're not going job hunting dressed like that."

"Nope, I have a job." I paused. "What's wrong with the way I'm dressed?"

"For heaven's sake, Miranda. You look like a truck driver. You'll never catch a man dressed like that."

"Maybe I don't want to catch a man."

Mom's look said my last statement was too stupid to justify a response so she went on to her second favorite topic. My job.

"I'm telling you, that bar is no place for a nice woman to work. You get all kinds of riff-raff in there."

"It's a cop hangout, Mom. We only get the nice riff-raff."

Dad, already biting his lip, snickered. Mom glared at us both, sniffed and tossed her head. A ladylike gesture of disdain I'd never mastered. When I try it, someone usually hands me a tissue.

"I can't believe you went to work for that...that...man."

I grinned at Dad and sat down at the kitchen table. Mom never did like Morgan. While she put lunch on the table, I let my gaze wander over the kitchen. It hadn't changed in my lifetime. Probably not in Mom's either. The fridge was short, rounded on the corners and yellowed with age. The linoleum on the floor was black and white with worn spots in front of the sink and stove. White eyelet curtains fluttered at the windows and Fiesta Ware canisters held sugar and flour. I could feel myself shrinking. In this kitchen, I was forever ten years old. Mom filled our plates and joined us at the table. We boosted our cholesterol in silence. When we finished, Dad asked what I needed to know.

"You knew Lisa Woods, didn't you?"

"The young lady that was murdered? That was just terrible," he said shaking his head. "She graduated ten or twelve years ago. Class of ninety-four I think."

"I don't know how you remember stuff like that."

"It's a gift," he said.

"You remember who she used to hang around with?"

"That's easy. They were all cheerleaders. Ellen Martin, Amy Elder, and Tina Bishop."

I dug a Quick Stop receipt from the bottom of my purse, grabbed a pen from the Lake of the Ozarks mug on Mom's desk, and wrote down the names. Tina Bishop was married to Ellen's brother Tom, so she would be Tina Martin now. I thought she worked at my bank. I'd have to check. Tom graduated with me. I didn't know Ellen except to recognize her face and didn't remember Amy Elder at all.

"Is Amy married?"

"You have to remember her," Mom said. "She married Lyle Caster. They're divorced now. I play bridge with her ex mother-in-law, Martha. I can tell you Martha didn't think much of her. Why do you want to know who that poor girl's friends were?"

"She was at the bar Friday night, but I couldn't remember the names of the girls she was with. I just thought Dad could refresh my memory."

"Why don't you keep your nose out of it and let your brothers handle it? You're not a police officer."

"Just thought I could help."

"You think you can get information the police can't?"

Uh, well, I just did. I had the good sense not to say that out loud as she continued.

"Miranda, I don't know what's going to happen to you, running around in the woods like a teenager. If you'd been behaving like a normal grown woman you'd never have stumbled over a dead body to begin with."

"Someone would have found her eventually. It could have been a little kid."

"Just because you tripped over her doesn't mean the police need your help to find the killer."

I closed my eyes, counted to ten and took a deep breath. "Nah, you're right Mom, they don't need my help." Even though Chad asked for it.

I pushed back my chair and carried my plate to the sink.

"I'd better get going, thanks for lunch."

"Just going to eat and run again. You never just come over for a visit."

I wonder why. "Sorry. Can't stay today, lots to do."

"I'll walk you out. I need to get back to work on that old Ford of yours," Dad said.

I fumed in silence as we crunched across the gravel driveway.

"Your mother loves you, Randi."

I blinked away the tears that filled my eyes.

"I guess I'll never be what she wants."

Dad stopped and slid his arm across my shoulders.

"You're perfect just the way you are, punkin."

"Thanks, Dad."

We continued arm in arm to the truck.

"I see Chad loaned you the Ranger."

"I'm not going to hurt it."

He laughed.

"I hope not. I'd better get yours running again before there's a murder in the family."

"I'm not going to hurt Chad's truck."

Dad just grinned and waved as he sauntered to the machine shed.

"That lady ran a red light," I muttered under my breath as I angled under the wheel.

Chapter 5

I turned into First Bank and parked the truck at the far side of the lot where it would be safe. I cashed a check with the teller and asked if Tina Martin still worked there. The teller directed me down the hall. It was a corner office with a window overlooking a small flowerbed and the parking lot. Through the window, I could see Chad's truck sitting in solitary splendor at the edge of the lot. I knocked on the doorframe and stuck my head in.

"Tina?"

"Yes," she said glancing up from her desk.

"Can I talk to you for a couple of minutes?"

"Sure. Have a seat."

I sat down in her client chair and tried to decide how to begin. Being my normal organized self, I hadn't planned anything past going to the bank and finding out if Tina still worked there. I tried to ease into it.

"Uh...I'm Randi Black."

"I know who you are. You're Chad Jenning's twin sister."

"You know Chad?"

"God, I've had a crush on him since grade school. Speaking of crushes, someone told me at lunch today that you and AJ were dating again."

I shook my head. Mrs. Litton worked fast.

"You aren't?"

"Not really."

"Oh, well you know how rumors are around this town. So, what can I do for you today? You need a loan or something?"

"I wanted to talk to you about Lisa Woods."

"God wasn't that horrible. Poor Lisa."

She swallowed and took a deep breath before she continued.

"I just saw her Friday night."

Her eyes filled. She blinked and fanned her face while she dug in the desk drawer for a Kleenex. She dabbed at her eyes without smudging her mascara. Her nose didn't even turned red. I stared through the window while she flipped open her compact and repaired the invisible damage. Chad's truck was still safely alone at the edge of the lot. When her compact snapped shut, I turned toward the desk. All sign of tears had vanished. Amazing, like a magic trick—or maybe some secret female rite of passage that I'd somehow missed out on. I was so absorbed by her flawless makeup that it took me a minute to tune in when she started talking.

"...who would do something like that to Lisa...Did you really find her body?"

"Unfortunately, yes. I did."

"What was it you wanted to know?"

"Do you know who she was dating?"

Tina shook her head, a sad smile on her face. "It would be tough to narrow it down."

"No one steady?"

"No way. She was the original good-time girl. That's why she didn't stay married very long."

"I didn't know she'd ever been married."

"Divorced, they only stayed together a few months. Lisa wasn't really into monogamy."

"Did she still see her ex?"

Tina dropped her gaze from mine and stared at her hands folded on top of the desk.

"I'm married to her ex."

"Oh, I thought you guys were married right out of high school."

"It was almost a year after. He and Lisa tied the knot the day after graduation."

"Ah."

I mentally scratched that possibility off my list and tried to get my thoughts in line.

"You said you saw her Friday night. That was at the Jolly Roger, right?"

"Yeah, we were all there. Kind of a girls' party night. We all left for home around midnight, except for Lisa. She told us she had a date later."

"And she was meeting him at the Roger?"

"She never really said. I assumed she was. When we left, she was sitting at the bar talking to that good looking bartender."

When she mentioned Lex, I paused for a mental eye roll. "You're sure she didn't say who she was meeting?"

"Not to me, but Lisa and I weren't very close. We didn't have much in common anymore. If she mentioned it to anyone, it would have been Ellen. They were like sisters."

"I guess I'd better talk to Ellen."

"She works at the Nail Palace. She's a nail technician there."

"A nail technician?" I had a vision of bins full of nails and technicians in white lab coats measuring and sorting them.

"Yeah, she does manicures and stuff."

"Oh," I laughed. "That kind of nail technician."

I glanced at my hands and curled my fingers so my nails didn't show. I really should get out with the girls more. I stood and hooked my purse strap over my shoulder. "Thanks for your help, Tina. I'd better go and let you get back to work."

"Are you working for the police department now?"

"Nah, I thought I saw Lisa at the Roger Friday night. I just wanted to confirm it before I told Steve or AJ."

"Ellen probably has more information than me. Sorry I couldn't be more help."

"Hey, that's okay. I know she was waiting for someone, maybe that's the lead they need to catch up with her killer."

"You really think so?"

"I guess not, but it would be nice. The thought of a killer walking around Alden is kind of creepy."

As I strolled out of the office, Tina grabbed her cell phone and started punching numbers. Dammit, she was probably calling Ellen to tell her I was on my way over. I should have asked her not to do that. Geesh, I suck at being a detective. I opened the door of the Ranger and tossed in my purse. As I scooted behind the wheel, something I'd seen as I walked across the parking lot registered. I stepped back out and closed the door. There was a dent centered about six inches below the window, and a scratch running the entire length of the bed.

"Oh for Christ's sake," I snapped.

How could this possibly have happened? I was watching the truck almost the whole time I was in the bank. I groaned. Chad was going to kill me.

"Dammit! Shit!" I yelled and stomped my foot.

I glanced away from the truck. A young woman was glaring at me as she herded her two small children across the parking lot. I glared back. I might have even snarled. Her eyes went wide and she pushed the kids ahead staring over her shoulder. I resisted the urge to make a face and stick out my tongue. I collapsed onto the seat and banged my head against the steering wheel. I debated calling Chad for less than half a second. I was not telling him this on the phone. I'd wait until tonight after he'd had a couple of beers. Okay, I admit it, deep down I'm a coward.

I checked my watch. It was almost time to go to work. If I hurried, I could stop by the Nail Palace on the way to the Jolly Roger. Before I pulled out, I decided to call and make sure Ellen was there. I dialed the number and waited while it rang six times. Maybe they were already gone for the day. As I was about to punch off the call, someone answered.

"This is Randi Black. I wonder if I could speak with Ellen Martin?"

"Sure," the receptionist chirped. "Hang on. I'll get her."

The phone thunked down on the desk and I listened to scraps of conversation while I waited. "Missy Waterton is pregnant and I hear the father..." then the speakers moved out of range.

"Hey, come back! What about Missy Waterton? You can't just leave me hanging like this!" I yelled at the phone.

I waited in frustration while other tidbits of information drifted through the phone. I tried not to listen. I really did, but it was just too much fun. Wendy Miller was getting a divorce. I was smirking about that when I heard my name mentioned.

"That Jennings girl, you know the one that works at the bar..."

"...divorced you know..."

"...shacking up with a cop..."

"Hey, I'm not shacking up with anybody," I yelled.

"Excuse me?"

"Uh...sorry. I wasn't talking to you." The receptionist had picked up the phone.

"Ma'am. Uh...I...Um...Ellen can't...Um...Ellen's already left for the day. Would you like to leave a message?"

"She's not there?"

"Um...yeah, she had a...doctor's appointment and had to leave early."

"You're kidding me."

"No ma'am."

I stabbed the off button on my phone, and puffed out my breath in frustration. "Doctor's appointment my ass," I mumbled and tossed the phone on the seat as I pulled out of the lot.

I was still muttering under my breath as I drove toward work. If Chad was going to kill me tonight, I was going to have one last Jolly Roger cheeseburger, the condemned sister's last meal. I drove carefully. Stopped at all the lights, signaled all my turns, and wished with all my heart I hadn't borrowed Chad's truck this morning. I made it to the Roger without any more disasters, but that didn't improve my disposition much.

When I burst into the bar, Morgan was flipping through a sales flier. He glanced over the top of it as I tossed my purse behind the bar and sagged onto a stool.

"What's the matter with you?" Morgan asked.

"Somebody hit Chad's truck in the bank parking lot, Ellen Martin is avoiding me, I didn't get the whole scoop on Missy Waterton's baby, and somebody's spreading around the rumor that AJ and I are living together."

Morgan drummed his fingers on the bar and stared at me for a long minute. Trying to decide which piece of information to respond to first, I guess.

"Uh, well...Ellen Martin's a ditz," he finally said. "I don't know why you even want to talk to her. As for Missy Waterton, she's not pregnant, that I know of. God, I hope she's not pregnant."

His face paled and I wondered how long he and Missy had been dating.

"Jesus, Morgan. Missy Waterton? She's like, what, twelve years younger than you?"

"She's a sweet girl, Randi."

"Remember you said that when she's eight months pregnant and hates your guts."

Morgan cocked his head at me and smirked. "Did I hear you say somebody hit Chad's truck?" he asked.

I sighed. "Yes."

"Chad is going to kill you."

I thumped my head down on the bar. "Just shut up and pour me a beer. I'm having the start of a really rotten day."

He twisted the top off a Sam Adams Light and scooted the bottle across the bar. I took a long drink.

"I didn't know you and AJ were dating again."

"I don't want to discuss it. Order me a cheeseburger while you're over there."

Morgan smirked and called in my order. He came back to the bar and started scanning the flier again.

"What ya reading?" I asked.

"Stuff from Kauffman Security, they're trying to sell me a security system for the bar. They put in a couple of those little wireless cameras last week as a free trial. They came by and removed them a little while ago. I was just reading about how the system works. You can hook them to a computer or they can record directly to a DVD. Sounds pretty cool. They recorded onto a DVD while they were installed. They're supposed to mail a copy to me so I can compare the quality to a video-based system. Video is usually black and white, these are in color. Might be kind of slick."

"Why do you need security cameras?"

"Insurance mostly, supposed to make my premiums go down. And, if I ever get shorted at the bar, I can tell which bartender is making off with the loot."

I rolled my eyes at that.

"Speaking of bartenders, how are you and Lex getting along?" Morgan asked as he pushed another bottle across the bar.

"He's a first-class jerk."

Morgan laughed. "You can handle him."

"Thanks a lot. You picking the boys up after football practice?"

"Yeah. They can spend the night with me. I'll take them to school tomorrow."

"That works. Hey, Morgan, you ever see a guy in a cowboy hat in here? Skinny guy, six foot tall or so, wears sunglasses all the time."

"Not that I remember, why?"

"Kira said she's seen him in here a couple of times before. I just saw him Saturday night for the first time. He's kind of creepy. Just wondered if he'd ever been here in the day time."

"I don't remember him."

I polished off my burger and went behind the bar to rinse the plate. Morgan tossed the flyer on the counter next to the beer cooler and wiped his hands on a damp bar towel.

"Mind if I cut and run?" he asked. "It should be pretty quiet tonight. Mondays aren't all that busy. The dart tournament should be done by ten. If it's dead after the tournament go ahead and close up."

"Might as well, I'm already here."

"Thanks."

He snatched his jacket from the office and pulled it on as he scooted toward the door. He acted like he was afraid I'd change my mind.

"You stopping in later tonight?" I asked.

"I'll bring the boys in for dinner."

"Okay, see ya."

I washed the few dirty glasses, then dragged a stool behind the bar so I could sit and watch television. An hour or so later, the after work crowd trickled in. The Roger stayed hopping till a little before seven when the dart players invaded. They were easy. They just sent a runner down for a pitcher when they ran dry. The rest of the bar was quiet.

Morgan came in with the boys around eight and they ate their weight in cheeseburgers. Elisabeth Appleton, Alden's classiest call girl, came in around nine. I guess Mondays are slow in her business too. Her nanny, Ann Marie, was with her. I'm not sure, but I think she's a working girl also. Chad would know. If he didn't kill me later, I'd ask him.

I like Liz. She's close to my age. She moved here almost ten years ago from Kansas City after some asshole started killing off members of her profession. She's a beautiful woman, very elegant. If you saw her walking down the street, you wouldn't guess what she does for a living. She has an eight-year-old daughter named Becca, who's going to be as pretty as her mom in a few years. The nanny, Ann Marie, has that Meg Ryan girl-next-door look about her. She's from Kansas City also. She joined Liz a couple of years ago to take care of Becca. She said she liked the quiet and safety of a small town better than the city.

Ann Marie left the Roger to pick up Becca from a scout meeting. I visited with Liz until Chad came in around ten. While Chad watched the bar, I cleared the tables in the dart room. I could hear the soft rumble of voices as Liz and Chad talked. She was giving him some information on a couple of new girls in town that were working at the Jungle. I guess if you're a hooker, it can't hurt to be friendly with a vice-cop. Keeps down the competition.

No one else was in the bar. I wiped down the tables, swept the floor, and bagged the trash. While Chad and Liz chatted, I took the plastic bags to the dumpster. I chucked in the first sack and a dark furry shape shot toward me with a hiss. I squealed and stumbled back. It was just a cat. Jesus, scared me to death. Soft laughter wafted across the parking lot. I turned. Tex strode toward the entrance, teeth flashing in the dark as he smiled.

"We're closed," I said.

My heart was thundering in my chest and I took a sliding step toward the door. He stopped, hooked down his shades and glared from the shadows of his hat.

"Slow night," I said. "Sorry."

I took another step back. Tex spun on his heel and ambled to his truck. I leapt through the back door, slammed it and rammed the bolt home. I stood in the dark hallway waiting for my pulse rate to slow. That guy really gave me the creeps. Those pale eyes almost glowed in the dark like a cat's.

When I finally scuffed into the bar, Liz was leaning close to Chad, talking softly, one hand on his arm. It looked like he was getting ready to kiss her. I cleared my throat and they leapt apart. Liz said something I didn't catch, waggled her fingers in goodbye and left.

"That cowboy was out in the back lot just now, Chad. You should walk Liz to her car."

He hopped off the barstool and followed Liz out. I swept the floor of the hallway and the back-bar before he reappeared. There was a suspicious smile on his face, but I didn't tease him. Now was not the time to get him miffed.

I locked the doors behind him and while he finished his beer I started counting my tips.

"Was he still there?" I asked.

"Who?"

"The cowboy. Jesus, you've heard me talking about him."

"There wasn't anybody in the parking lot, Ran."

Chad definitely had his mind on something else. Or, someone else, unless I missed my guess. I fiddled around doing nothing jobs that didn't really need doing while I tried to get up the nerve to tell him about the truck. I pulled the register drawer and started counting the deposit. Chad watched the Cardinals game on TV. I miscounted the money and started over again. Finally I just shoved it all in the bank bag.

"Uh, Chad. I need to tell you something."

"What's that?"

"Uh, somebody kind of dinged your truck today while I was at the bank."

"Oh yeah?"

"Yeah. Just thought I ought to tell you."

"Yeah, thanks...Wait. What?" he turned away from the TV and gave me his full attention. Uh oh, it finally sunk in.

"Please tell me I did not hear what I think you just said."

"I said, someone kind of dinged your truck today while I was in the bank."

"Tell me this is a joke."

"Okay. It's a joke."

"It's not though, is it?"

I shook my head. "Please don't kill me. I found some good information for you, and I wasn't even in the truck when it happened. That counts for something, doesn't it?" I said in a rush.

Chad sighed. "How bad is it?"

"It's not that bad. I'll show it to you when we leave."

Chad glanced at me from the corner of his eye and grinned.

"I'm really sorry."

"Don't worry about it," he said.

"I thought you were going to kill me. I've been in a panic all day. Dammit, why are you just smirking at me?"

"I bet AJ something would happen the first day you drove the truck. I won."

"How much?"

"Fifty bucks," he said.

"I should get half of that."

"Not a chance, kid. You ready to get out of here?"

"Yeah, let me put the deposit in the safe."

I ducked into the office to lock up the deposit. He might say he wasn't mad, but I wasn't going to relax until he actually saw the truck.

Chad walked around slowly and surveyed the damage. He finally decided it wasn't a killing offense. The knot in my stomach went away for the first time since I left the bank parking lot. I huffed a big sigh of relief and sank onto the seat. Chad eased behind the wheel and drove me home. He escorted me to the door and Wilson met us when we went in. I shooed him out back for a run and sat at the kitchen table.

"Tell me what they found out today," I said.

"You first."

Cops always do that. I sighed.

"Okay," I started. "Missy Waterton is pregnant."

Chad stared at me to see if I was joking. He finally decided I wasn't. "What exactly does that have to do with anything?"

"Nothing, it's just something I found out today."

"Did you, maybe, learn anything about Lisa Woods?"

"I'm getting to that."

"Tonight?"

"You're so impatient."

"Randi."

"Okay, okay. Lisa was at the Jolly Roger Friday night with Ellen Martin, Amy Caster, and Tina Bishop, I mean Tina Martin. Anyway, Ellen, Amy and Tina left around midnight. Lisa told them she was meeting someone later and sat down at the bar to talk to Lex."

"Okay, I can talk to Lex. Do you know who she was waiting for?"

"Tina didn't know. Ellen Martin might, but I didn't get a chance to talk to her today. I'll try to catch her tomorrow, if you want.

"Wouldn't hurt anything. Someone in the department will have to verify anything you tell me, but it'd be nice to know if Ellen knows anything. Then we can prioritize the interviews. They won't be all that important unless she's got some really good info."

"You know, Kira thinks that cowboy was at the bar Friday night too."

Chad rolled his eyes at the mention of Kira's name.

"What cowboy is that?"

I thunked my head on the table in frustration. "The one that left as you came in the other night."

"I didn't see him."

"The one that was in the parking lot tonight."

He shrugged.

"Ask Lex about him, the guy gives me the creeps."

"Why?"

"His eyes are almost white. He's creepy."

"Hmm. Creepy eyes. That puts him right on the top of my suspect list."

"You can be such an ass, Chad."

He laughed. I walked around his chair to get a Sam Adams from the fridge and sat across from him.

"So you gonna tell me what you guys learned today?" I asked.

"The forensics report came back. She was raped, then strangled. She received a blunt force trauma injury to the head shortly before she died, so she was probably unconscious when he killed her. She struggled at some point. She wasn't unconscious the whole time. She had bruises on her arms and face, and shallow cuts on her legs. They think she died where you found her. It didn't appear that the body had been moved post mortem. ME thinks the killer scraped under the nails after she was dead and wiped the body down with some kind of soap or cleanser."

"You got DNA from the rape kit, right?"

"Nada."

"No semen, no hairs?"

"Not a thing."

"She was raped. And there's no DNA?"

"You got it."

"The rapist wore a condom?" I asked in disbelief. "And shaves his...eew."

"We assume he wore a condom. We didn't find one at the scene. That he might have shaved hadn't occurred to me."

Chad squirmed in his seat at the thought.

"It was a clean crime scene, that's for sure. It looked like the CSI guys had already been there."

"This reeks of serial murder. Nobody else sets a crime scene that carefully. He was probably sitting in the woods watching and laughing at us."

"I don't think so, Randi. If some psycho was slicing up chicks and leaving them lying around in the woods we'd have heard something before now. Contrary to popular fiction, serial killers aren't that plentiful. Besides, anybody who watches CSI or Court TV knows how evidence is collected. Hell there are books about it, probably web sites on the Internet. The guy's done his homework, but he's not a crime scene investigator. There's something he forgot, something he missed, or something he didn't think of. We'll find it."

"Maybe."

"Count on it, Ran. We'll have this guy in a week, two weeks tops."

Chad stood and stretched, then fished his keys out of his pocket.

"I gotta go, Ranna. It's almost midnight. I'll give you a ride in the morning after I go to the gym, then you can use the truck."

"You're going to let me use it again?"

"Sure. You're my sister."

"Yeah, but that truck's your baby."

"I'm getting kind of tired of it anyway. I may start on a new project before long."

"Liar."

Chad sketched a wave over his shoulder as he headed out.

Chapter 6

After Chad left, I let Wilson out for his last run of the night. As I came through the kitchen, someone knocked on the front door. I stopped in my tracks and checked the clock. It was after midnight, close to twelve-thirty. My heart thumped in my chest. Who would be coming over here this late? I eased my .32 out of the holster and crept into the living room. The knock came again, more impatient this time. I shoved the curtain aside and tried to see the porch. The angle was wrong. I couldn't see anything but the corner post. For the first time, I wished I had a spy hole in my door.

"Who is it?" I asked.

"It's AJ. Let me in."

My breath whooshed out in relief as I unlocked the deadbolt. As AJ came in, I snapped the .32 in my holster.

"You're being careful, that's good."

"What are you doing here?"

"Brought you a car. Thought you could use some wheels 'til your truck's on the road again."

I opened the door and stared at the car parked in my drive. AJ's red '69 Mustang sparkled under the streetlights.

"You brought me the Mustang?"

"You can't have my truck. It's got my police radio and all my cop stuff in it."

"AJ, I can't drive that car."

"Sure you can."

I shook my head and walked to the kitchen. AJ trailed me down the hallway. I leaned against the kitchen counter.

"You've had that car since high school. I'm not going to drive it."

AJ stepped in close and trapped me with his hands on either side.

"You drove it in high school," he said edging closer. "Why not now?"

I could feel his breath move the hair by my ear. His body pressed against mine and I tingled all the way to my toes. I swallowed and tried to remember what we were discussing.

"I just don't want to," I stammered.

His lips brushed my temple and my knees went weak. I held onto the counter so I didn't slither to the floor at his feet.

"Take the car, darlin'. Chad's going to wind up with a nervous breakdown if you drive his truck another day. And I'm liable to end up broke."

"That was a lame bet."

"Just playin' the averages, darlin'. Didn't figure it could happen again."

"What if something happens to your car?"

"I'll fix it."

He brushed the hair away from my forehead and tucked it behind my ear. I ducked under his arm and scrambled away so the kitchen table was between us. He grinned, tossed the keys on the table, and took my place against the counter.

"Drive it or leave it parked. It's up to you. Either way you're gonna have to give me a ride home. Unless you want me to stay here."

I snatched the keys from the table. "I'll take you home."

AJ laughed. "Let's go then."

I let Wilson in, pulled on my leather jacket and followed AJ to the car. By the time I'd locked the house, he was sitting in the driver's seat.

"I thought I was supposed to be driving you home."

"You can drive back. Did you know you have a cat on your roof?"

"Yeah, that's Bill from next door."

"He the one that smacked around your dog the other night?"

"Yeah, that's him."

"How'd he get on your roof?"

"That's a good question. As far as I know, no one's ever seen him get up there. He just appears."

AJ shrugged and started the car. I relaxed and closed my eyes as we started through the neighborhood. AJ flipped on the stereo as we turned onto Evergreen. An Eagles tune came on and I smiled. I had a lot of pleasant memories associated with this car and that music. When we bounced off the pavement and onto a rutted track, I jerked out of my memory trip and stared through the window. AJ was driving toward the river.

"This isn't the way to your house."

"We're gonna make a stop first."

"We're going to the bluff, in the middle of the night?"

"Sure, gotta problem with that?"

"I am not fooling around with you in the backseat of your car when I have a perfectly good bed at home."

AJ turned my way and smirked. "We can go back if that's what you really want to do."

"No, that's not what I want."

"I didn't think so. Relax, Ran. I just want to talk for a while."

"We could have talked at my house."

"Neutral field. I thought maybe if we got away from stuff, we could talk like we used to. You know, when we were friends."

"That was a long time ago, AJ."

He didn't answer, just parked on the bluff facing over the river. The spot we've always parked. If you sat on the hood of the car, it felt like you were hanging out in space, because you couldn't see the river. We used to come up here when we were kids and try to throw rocks to the other side. As teenagers, we came to drink beer and fool around. I lost my virginity here in the backseat of his Mustang, the summer after my senior year. AJ had just finished his sophomore year in college. I started making mental wedding plans. Three weeks later, he left for basic training. I smiled to myself and shook my head. When I glanced at AJ, he was smiling.

"I'm sorry," he said.

I turned away and stared through the windshield. The tree branches moved across the sky in the breeze.

"Think we could start over?" he asked softly.

"I guess we could try."

AJ reached back between the seats and lifted out a six-pack. We left the comfort of the car for the view from the hood. Relaxed against the windshield, the six-pack nestled between us, the night creatures rustling in the darkness. AJ opened a Coors Light and passed it to me. Our fingers met and I felt the heat of his touch even after he moved away. The moon was just rising above the trees, and the stars twinkled in the clear night sky. The wind rattled through the leaves that hadn't yet fallen from the branches. I took a deep breath and sighed. It felt like a hundred other nights I'd spent on this spot by the river. AJ took my hand in his and pressed a kiss into the palm. I shivered, though the night wasn't cold. Shoulders touching, fingers laced together, we talked, and listened to the night. The moon made its way across the sky, and the night sounds tapered off until the only one left was the breeze sighing through the trees. My eyes started to grow heavy. AJ nudged me awake and we slid off the hood. When my feet touched the ground, AJ wrapped me in his arms. I laid my head against his shoulder and breathed in his scent. It felt right, it always had. It felt like the clock had turned back twenty years.

"I had to leave, Randi. I wasn't ready to be married."

"You could have at least told me you were going."

You didn't tell him you were pregnant, a little voice whispered. I ignored it.

His lips brushed mine as I lifted my head from his shoulder.

"I'm sorry, Ran. I handled it badly. I'm sorry I wasted all those years. I'd like to make up for that."

He stared at me until I dropped my eyes. I was sure this was a bad idea and I knew I didn't have the willpower to push him away. He kissed me softly and opened my door. I sank into the seat and we drove silently back toward town.

I don't know where AJ's thoughts were as we sliced through the darkness in the sparkling red Mustang. Safe to say they weren't anywhere close to mine. I was thinking about a scared and pregnant eighteen-year-old. Did I really want to get wrapped up in AJ's life again? If the feeling in the pit of my stomach was any indication, the answer to that was a resounding yes.

AJ parked in front of his parents' old farmhouse and swiveled from behind the wheel. I took his place and he pushed the door closed.

A soft kiss goodnight, a hushed goodbye, then he melted into the darkness. A light came on and silhouetted him on the porch as I drove away.

As I meandered home in the quiet early morning, I locked the scared eighteen-year-old back into the cubbyhole where she belonged. She had no business here now. If I wanted to let AJ into my life again, that was my business. If I chose not to tell him about...well, in this case, what he didn't know wasn't going to hurt anyone. I shook those thoughts from my head. I was too tired to deal with it right now.

The roads were empty and I turned the Mustang loose. No bad vehicle karma here. This car and I were old friends. I passed Mouse, trudging slowly toward town, backpack slung over his shoulder, brown paper bag clasped tightly in his hand, a slight stumble to his gait.

I turned the Mustang off Evergreen and glanced around. The only light in my neighborhood was in Mrs.

Litton's front window. I checked the roof as I walked across the front yard. Bill was nowhere in sight. I saw Mrs. Litton's curtain jiggle as I stepped onto my porch. I swear the woman never sleeps.

I stumbled down the hall to my bedroom without turning on the lights. I was suddenly too tired to function. I pitched my clothes toward the hamper and crawled into bed with Wilson. I thought I'd lie awake half the night, but I was asleep as soon as my head hit the pillow.

It was after noon when I woke. I don't know what time I made it home. I do know Wilson was standing at the foot of the bed with his legs crossed when I opened my eyes. He probably thought I had died. I let Wilson out for his morning constitutional, and ate a bowl of cereal for breakfast. I guess it was really lunch. When Wilson came in from yard patrol, I filled his bowl. While he crunched doggie goodies, I made my plan for the day. First, I was going to talk to Ellen. I stared critically at my hands. I could definitely use a manicure. I called the Nail Palace to see when I could get an appointment with Ellen. Oh lucky me, she had a cancellation at twelve forty-five, could I make that? I glanced at my watch. It was doable, so I said yes. I was afraid if I gave her my name, Ellen would suddenly find the need to be elsewhere, so I set the appointment up for Miranda Jennings. Hey, that used to be my name. I took a shower and dressed in jeans and a St. Louis Cardinals sweatshirt. The playoffs were starting tonight and the Black residence was baseball central. Unless Alden was the scene of a tremendous crime wave, come game time, cops and teenagers were going to overrun my living room and beyond. I needed to get food, beer and soda before I came home.

I told Wilson to guard the house and that we were having company tonight. He likes to be kept informed. My face lit into a smile as I climbed into the Mustang and fired the engine. It rumbled in a nice testosterone-laced way. I resisted the urge to rap the pipes before I backed out of the drive. I wondered if it was the car or the memories that went with it that made me so happy. Didn't really matter, I loved that car.

I wound out of the neighborhood and pointed the Mustang towards the bar. I passed Mouse on the way. Dressed the same as always, pack over his shoulder, trudging down the shoulder. No sign of hangover—must be a professional drinker. I waved. He nodded. I stopped in the parking lot of the Jolly Roger and slipped inside.

"Hi, Morgan," I said.

"Hey, Randi. What's up?"

"Are you working tonight?"

"Huh-uh. Lex comes in at four."

"Can you get the boys after football practice?"

I perched on a barstool and scooped up a handful of peanuts. Morgan swiped the bar in front of me with a towel.

"I guess. Why?"

"Baseball party tonight. Wanna come?" What the hell was I saying?

"You inviting me to a party at your house?" he asked.

I grabbed some more peanuts and crunched for a minute.

"Uh...I guess."

"Is this a date?"

"You wish."

"I might stop by for a little while."

"Good, can you grab the pizzas on your way over?"

"I knew there was a catch."

"I'm sorry. I have a ton of stuff to do. It'd be a big help if you would."

"Okay, I'll get the pizza and the boys."

"Thanks. You're a sweetheart."

I hopped off the barstool and scooped up another handful of peanuts.

"That's not what you used to call me," he said.

"I'm not married to you any more," I shot over my shoulder.

"Can I bring a date?"

Missy Waterton? I wondered.

"Only if she likes baseball. Does she?"

"I don't think so."

"Then leave her at home. I'm not spending the night explaining the infield fly rule to your latest girlfriend."

"That's probably better anyway. She might be a little uncomfortable going to a party at my ex-wife's house."

I checked my watch as I stepped outside. Time to get my nails done. The salon was within walking distance of the Roger, so I left the car in the lot. My steps got slower the closer I got to the Nail Palace. Every instinct I had was telling me to turn around. The building was small and white with big windows across the front and frilly curtains showing at the sides. Well-dressed women flipped through magazines as they waited for their appointments. I stared down at my boots, jeans, and sweatshirt. I was a bit underdressed. Didn't know you were supposed to dress up to get your nails done. I took a deep breath and strolled through the entrance like I did it every day, but I scanned the waiting room like I was entering enemy territory. I'd never had a manicure, didn't know what was involved. The receptionist hung up the phone and scribbled in her appointment book as I came in. She glanced up when I stopped at the desk.

"Hi, I'm Miranda Bl...uh Jennings, I have an appointment with Ellen at twelve forty-five."

"Sure, she's almost ready. Have a seat, and I'll let her know you're here."

I sat down to wait. A woman strolled out of the back and stopped at the desk to pay her bill. My jaw dropped when I heard the amount. I did a quick inventory of the contents of my wallet. Probably gonna have to use my credit card. I stared at her nails as she wrote the check. I don't know how she could hold the pen. Her nails were at least two inches long and looked like they'd been tie-dyed. My stomach went queasy. She turned and smiled at me as she was leaving.

"Nice nails," I stammered.

"Thanks, Ellen's the best."

Ick. I am not leaving here with tie-dyed, nails. They would look ridiculous at the paintball range. I swallowed the urge to run and picked a magazine out of the pile on the table next to my chair. I flipped through the pages ogling the latest in nail fashion and hairstyles. These women could not possibly have real jobs. I bet they never did the dishes or cleaned a toilet either. I glanced up as Ellen walked into the reception area. She scanned the appointment book, then glanced around the room. I went back to my magazine.

"Ms. Jennings, I'm ready for you now."

She paused. I sat, still thumbing through the pictures.

"Ms. Jennings," she said again.

I jumped. Shit, that's me. I stood and started forward. Ellen widened her eyes and took a step back. Jeez, I didn't think my nails looked that bad.

"Hi, that's me." I said.

"You're Randi Black."

"Uh-huh."

"It says Miranda Jennings in the book."

"Yeah, that's my maiden name."

"Oh," she said swallowing hard. "Well, follow me, I guess."

I trailed her past the hair dryers. She pointed to a chair at her workstation. I sat and she shoved my hands into a bowl of warm soapy water. While I soaked, she poked around in a drawer and laid out clippers, files and other implements I couldn't identify.

"I'd like to ask you a couple of questions while you work. Is that okay?"

"I guess," she answered. She snatched one of my hands from the bowl and picked up the clippers, her focus totally on my fingers.

"Tina Martin said that you and Lisa Woods were really close. Do you know who she was meeting at the bar Friday night?"

"No, she didn't say anything to me."

Her hand tightened on mine when she said that and I knew she was lying. But, why?

"It would be really helpful to the police if you could tell me what you know."

Way to go, Randi. Make it sound like you're working for the cops. Ellen stopped filing and stared at me. She looked scared.

"I'm afraid to say."

She finished with my right hand, and started on the left.

"Please, Ellen. It's really important."

She shook her head. "I can't."

She was terrified. I could see it in her eyes, feel it in the tremble of her fingers.

"Ellen, you can trust me."

"You're too close to them."

Now I was at a loss. Too close to whom?

"I don't understand."

She wasn't even pretending to work on my nails now, just sitting there with my fingers in her hand.

"Ellen, help me out here. Who am I too close to?"

"The cops. You're related to two of them and sleeping with another one. Please. Please just go and leave me alone."

Ellen wasn't making any sense at all, or I was missing something really important here. Either way, I didn't have a clue what had her so scared or what AJ and my brothers had to do with it.

"I'm not sleeping with AJ," I said for lack of anything better.

"It doesn't matter."

I was going nowhere fast. My two days of playing Nancy Drew had just pointed out how inept I really was; just another case of me trying to live up to the skills of my brothers. I started to pull my hand away and leave Ellen in peace when I thought of something that might get her to talk.

"Ellen, what if I could give the police your information without telling them how I found out?"

I could see Ellen thinking it over, trying to decide if she could trust me.

"Could you really do that?"

"Sure."

That is until one of them threatened me for withholding evidence in a murder investigation.

Her silence stretched between us. I figured she wasn't going to say any more when she started buffing my nails. She put down the buffer and twisted open a bottle of clear nail polish.

"She didn't tell me a name," she said as she started coating my nails with polish. "She just said she had a date with a policeman."

I jerked my hand away.

"And you think it was AJ or one of my brothers?"

"No, maybe, I don't know. She had a date with a cop and now she's dead. What am I supposed to think?"

"Did she say anything else?" I asked.

"That's all she said. 'I have a date with a cop'."

Ellen took my hand back and finished applying polish.

"You don't have any idea who it might have been?" I asked.

Ellen shook her head, her eyes never leaving my fingers.

"You have pretty hands," she said. "They'd look great with long nails. I could do that for you sometime, if you wanted."

"Thanks. I'll think about it." Not. I just can't see myself lobbing a football with the boys or traipsing around with my paintball gun while wearing two-inch, tie-dyed nails. Maybe camouflage. I'd have to give that some thought.

Ellen finished. I dug my wallet out, sifted through the bills and pulled out a five. I held it out to her. She shook her head and turned to walk up front. I followed her to pay for the manicure.

"Don't worry about it, Randi. This one's on me," she said blinking back tears. "I just hope you can help find who did that to Lisa."

"I hope so too," I said.

I dropped the five on the desk and pushed outside. I was as exhausted as if I'd worked all day. Getting a manicure can't possibly be that tiring all the time. If it were, no one would ever do it.

I walked back to the Roger. My nails felt heavy and thick. I couldn't stop playing with them. Before I made it to the car, I'd already chipped the polish on one. That was a great investment, Ran. I mumbled as I unlocked the car. At least it was only five bucks.

My next stop was the grocery store to stock up for the party, then home to unload and let Wilson out for a run. While he was outside, I opened a bag of chips and sat down at the kitchen table. If what Ellen said was true, one of Alden's finest could be a real sicko. Just the thought gave me goose bumps. I grabbed the phone and called Chad's pager. While I waited for him to call back, I made a list of all the cops I knew. I scratched off Steve, Chad, and AJ. If it was one of them, I didn't want to know. I sorted through the rest and made marks by the ones who were coming over tonight. Then I made another check next to everyone I remembered being at the bar Friday night. Jody McIntire and George Williams were the only names with two check marks. So, I guess I'd try to talk to Jody and George while they were at the house. I wondered how that would go.

"So, you were at the Roger Friday night. Did you take Lisa Woods to The War Zone and rape and kill her?" I snorted at myself and walked over to let Wilson in when he barked.

A few minutes later, Chad strolled through the front door. I squealed when I saw him.

"You scared the shit out of me, Chad."

"You're supposed to keep your door locked, Ranna."

"You're supposed to knock. What are you doing here anyway?"

He draped his jacket over the chair back. "I stopped by because you paged me and I was hungry. Did you know that cat's on your roof again?"

"I saw him."

"Got any food?" Chad asked.

"For the cat?"

"No, ass. For me. I just said I was hungry."

"Oh," I said laughing. "I think there's sandwich stuff in there."

"That'll work. So, what'd ya need?"

Chad started hunting in the cabinets searching for edibles. I sat at the kitchen table and scooted my notes in front of me.

"I talked to Ellen Martin today."

"The girl that was with Lisa at the Jolly Roger Friday night?"

"One of them. I told her I wouldn't say who told me this so you have to keep it to yourself."

"You know I can't do that, Randi."

"Can't you keep it to yourself for a little while?"

"I'm not making any promises. So what did she tell you?"

"She didn't know the name of the guy Lisa was waiting for, but she did say something interesting."

"What's that?" Chad asked as he rooted around in the fridge for the mayo.

"She said Lisa had a date with a cop."

"What!" Chad straightened up and hit his head on the freezer door. "Ouch! Dammit." He rubbed his head. "No way a cop did that. At least not one from Alden."

He spread sliced turkey, cheese and lettuce on the counter.

"Think it over, Chad. You said the crime scene was clean."

"I also said anyone with half a brain and a television would be able to do that. Where's the bread?"

"It's on the counter and don't bite my head off. I'm just passing along information."

"Sorry, Ran. I don't believe a cop would do that."

He slathered mayo on his bread, slapped the sandwich together and slouched against the counter.

"You going to tell Steve and AJ?" I asked.

He chewed, swallowed and took a drink before he answered. "They won't buy it, Ranna."

That meant no. I stared through the sliding glass doors at the backyard. Chad finished his sandwich and wiped off the counter.

"You coming over to watch the game?" I asked.

"Yeah, you want me to get some more chips on the way over?"

"This isn't the only bag I bought. Besides, they aren't all gone yet."

"They will be by six," he laughed.

"Will not."

"Uh huh."

"Did you come by this morning on your way to work?"

"Yeah, saw AJ's car so I didn't stop. Didn't want to interrupt anything."

"AJ didn't spend the night here."

"Yeah, whatever."

"Did he tell you he did?" I asked.

"No, he wouldn't though. Officer and a gentleman and all that." Chad winked, snatched a handful of chips and started down the hall. "Got to get back to work, Ran. Lock this door after I leave."

I waved as it closed behind him.

"Great, Wilson. Now everybody thinks AJ and I are sleeping together."

Not that sleeping with AJ would really be so bad. It made me go all tingly just thinking about it. Wilson cocked his head at me and decided I wasn't talking about food. He trotted down the hall to the recliner for a nap. I decided to fix something to eat. I stopped in the middle of making a sandwich and slapped the counter.

"Dammit, I forgot to ask about Mouse."

Wilson ran in from the living room, got a whiff of lunchmeat and sat at my feet staring at the counter. I handed him a bite of turkey and finished making my sandwich.

Chapter 7

was still chewing when the telephone rang. It was Devin calling from school.

"Mom, I need my biology worksheet."

"Well hi, Devin. Nice to talk to you, too."

"Mom, I left my biology worksheet at home. I have to have it before class or I'm gonna get a detention."

"Plan ahead, bud. Stuff like that won't happen."

"Mom, if I get a detention I'll miss the next football game."

"Prior planning, Dev."

"Mom, please, I'm begging you, please, please, please bring my paper to school."

I could feel my resolve weakening. I knew I was going to end up going to the high school. Coach Waters would never forgive me if his star wide receiver missed Friday night's game. I gave it one more shot.

"I'm trying to get ready for the party tonight. I don't have time. You'll just have to do without."

"Mom, please. I'll do anything you ask."

"Clean your room."

Silence came over the phone. I grinned to myself. If it got his room clean, it might be worth the trip across town.

"Okay."

His answer was soft. Barely audible.

"I'm not sure I heard you, bud. Did you say you were going to clean your room?"

"Yes, Mom."

"Okay, where is the paper?"

"It's on the floor next to my bed, under the green pillow."

"Of course it is. What time is your class?"

"It starts at two-thirty."

I checked my watch. It was two-fifteen already.

"I'll try to get it there. A little advance notice would have been nice."

"Gee, Mom. If I'd thought to check this morning, I'd already have it."

"Don't get smart, I'm doing you a favor."

"Sorry, thanks, Mom."

I started to tell him he was welcome, but I was talking to the dial tone. I trotted upstairs and walked into Devin's bedroom. I couldn't see the floor. There wasn't even a path to the bed. Wilson trotted in behind me, and rooted under a duffle bag at the doorway. I followed his progress by watching the pile of stuff on the floor shift. He popped out next to the bed, hopped up and burrowed under the covers. I pushed my way through the mess and grabbed the green pillow from the floor. There wasn't a biology paper there. I stepped sideways and felt something squish under my foot. Eeyou. I lifted my foot to look. The remains of a handful of red paintballs drizzled off my shoe. I wiped the goo on the green pillow and said a few choice words. Wilson stuck his head out to see what was going on. I ignored him and he rooted underneath the pillow. Something crackled as he spun around in circles. I pushed him aside and lifted the pillow off the bed. The biology worksheet was there, crumpled from Wilson's feet and Devin's head. I smoothed out the creases, and pushed a path to the door. Wilson hopped off the bed, trotted through the mashed paintballs, and ran down the hall to the stairs leaving little red doggy prints as he went. I groaned and checked my watch. I didn't have time to clean them off before I left. I stumbled downstairs, shooed Wilson outside and ran to the car. Even with the Mustang,

I'd be lucky to make it to the high school before two-thirty. The trip would be fun, though.

I slid to a stop in the parking lot scattering, gravel across the drive. Then I raced to the front entrance of the high school, barreled through the door, then stuttered to a more sedate pace as I made my way to the office. I grinned as I glanced at my watch; two minutes to spare. Devin's homework safely delivered, I started toward the door, mentally reviewing my list of things I still needed to get done before the party. I still needed to make the nacho meat. I'd wanted to vacuum the carpet, but I'd have to forgo that and remove the little red doggy prints instead. I was almost outside when Maggie Peterson spotted me.

"Randiiiii," she warbled.

"Shit."

Maggie is president of the PTA and a royal pain in my butt. I looked left and right for an escape route but she was on me before I could find one. Dammit, I didn't need this today. I swallowed a groan and stopped moving as she plucked at my arm.

"Randi, I'm so glad to see you. I heard about you finding that body. It must be so hard for you with just the boys there and no husband."

"I..."

She went on before I could say anything. She has the mistaken idea that my divorce was the most devastating moment of my life and that I haven't quite recovered from it. I have a sneaking suspicion she might be one of Morgan's conquests.

"I just wanted to tell you, Randi, that any time you need a hand with those boys you just let me know. My Timmy would just love for the twins to come stay a day or so."

Her Timmy was the biggest pothead at Alden High and if my boys so much as strolled down the street with him, Chad would knock the hell out of them. I couldn't very well tell that to Maggie so I smiled and thanked her for being so thoughtful. She continued on without a break, segueing into her canned speech about how it was time to start making money for the senior all-night party. I sighed and checked the time. The afternoon was getting away from me and red paintball goo was slowly drying into my carpet.

"Can we do this another time? I really need to go, Maggie."

"Oh, I'm sorry, hon. I'm sure it's hard to get everything done when you don't have any help."

Right now, the only reason I was having trouble was because she wouldn't leave me alone. I finally managed to get away and push outside. Maggie was still talking as I ran for the car. A tall dark handsome figure was lounging against the rear bumper. He straightened as I skidded to a stop in the gravel.

"Hey, darlin'."

"AJ, you...uh, startled me."

"We need to talk."

"Uh, okay. How'd you know I was here?"

"I followed you. You ran two lights and broke all the speed limits on your way across town."

I thought over my reckless trip. I guess I could have slowed down a little. I did arrive two minutes early.

"You here to write me a ticket?" I asked.

"No, but I should."

"Would it help if I said I'm sorry?"

"Christ, Randi, that's my car. You know how much trouble you'll get me in if you get busted in it?"

"I said I'm sorry. It was kind of an emergency."

"Kind of an emergency?"

"Yeah, Devin forgot his biology homework."

"That was an emergency?"

"Well, okay. Maybe not an emergency, but if he didn't turn it in he would get a detention and then he couldn't play in the football game this week. And he promised to clean his room if I bailed him out this time."

AJ tried to keep from smiling.

"I can see where that could cause you to break all those traffic laws. Life or death situation like that."

I stared at the gravel and scuffed my toe in the rocks.

"It seemed important at the time."

"Uh huh."

"So, uh, was that all you needed to talk to me about?"

"No, that came up on the way. Thought we could chat for a little bit about a guy in a cowboy hat."

"What about him?"

"I talked to Kira. She mentioned seeing a guy in a cowboy hat at the bar Friday night. Chad said you'd mentioned a cowboy, so I'm following up."

Damn, I'd forgotten to ask Ellen and Tina about the cowboy. I dug in my purse for my car keys and stepped around AJ to unlock the Mustang. He followed me with his eyes but didn't move from his spot on the bumper.

"I don't know much."

"More than me apparently. I never heard of the guy before."

"I told Chad. He didn't think it was important."

"It's not Chad's case."

I sighed. "What do you want to know?"

"I want you to come down to the station and look through some pictures. While you're doing that I'm gonna ask you some questions. When you answer those, I'll probably have some more. That's how this stuff works."

I checked my watch.

"Do we really need to do this now?" I asked.

"Randi, there's a murderer in this town. A woman is dead. We don't know why or if he's going to do it again. It's pretty important we get this done right away."

I sighed. "Okay. I'll follow you to the station."

I pulled in behind AJ and parked in front of the station. Jody McIntire walked out the door with Chad as I stopped. They nodded to AJ and Chad burst out laughing at something Jody said as they crossed the lot to Chad's Ranger. I got out of the car as AJ opened the door and motioned me inside. I pushed the party details out of my mind and stepped into the station.

AJ put me in an interrogation room, dropped a huge book of mug shots on the table and left. I opened the book and started flipping through the pictures. AJ came back, handed me a Diet Coke and straddled the chair across the table. I looked at the Coke and then up at him.

"Pepsi machine's broke. Sorry."

I went back to scanning mug shots. AJ sat quietly while I paged through the book. After fifteen minutes, my eyes were watering and the photos started to run together. At thirty minutes, I was just turning pages, no longer looking at the pictures. I leaned back in my chair and rubbed my eyes.

"You need a bathroom break?" AJ asked.

I shook my head, stared up at the clock, and sighed.

"You in a hurry to get somewhere?" he asked.

"I'm having a party at my house tonight, as you well know. I was just thinking about everything I still need to get done."

"Sorry, darlin'. This first."

I huffed out my breath and turned another page in the book. AJ began to ask questions. Who was the cowboy? Did I know his name? How many times had I seen him? Who did he hang out with? As I answered, he made notes. When he started over again with the same questions, I slammed the cover of the book closed.

"I'm done, AJ. I've told you all of this before. Rewording your questions isn't going to make me think of anything new. I've seen the guy twice and he spoke one word, beer. Let me go home. I'm not going to recognize his picture unless he was wearing his cowboy hat and shades when they took it."

He cocked his head at me and narrowed his eyes. I looked again at the clock over the door. It was almost five. I sighed and rubbed the bridge of my nose. My head was starting to pound.

"Christ, Randi. Would it kill you to cooperate a little?"

I stared at him in surprise.

"I am cooperating. I'm the one that told you guys about the damn cowboy in the first place. What the hell do you want from me? Jesus, no wonder people hate cops."

"Damn, darlin'. That was a little harsh."

An amused sparkle had replaced the annoyed look on his face.

"I'm sorry, I...never mind. I'm getting a headache."

"Go home, babe. It was a long shot that you'd find him in there anyway. Do me a favor; give me a call the next time he turns up."

I told him I would and stood to go. He pulled me toward him and gave me a kiss.

"You don't really hate cops, do ya?"

I shook my head.

He gave me a squeeze and nudged me toward the door. "I'll see ya later for the game."

He scooped the mug shot book off the table as I turned to go. I gave a little finger waggle to the dispatcher as I stepped out of the building. I wasn't in the mood for a party anymore. I drove home dreading the evening to come. Wilson shot inside when I opened the back door and stood guard in the kitchen as I started the nacho meat cooking. I left him in charge and went upstairs to scrub away his little red footprints. I ran downstairs when I smelled smoke. The pan of hamburger was preparing to erupt into flames.

"Shit."

I jerked the pan off the burner and dumped the ruined beef into the trash. Piss on it. They'd just have to do without nachos tonight. I turned on the exhaust fan and opened the back door to get rid of the smoke. Wilson trotted out. I opened a beer and stood on the patio with him to get away from the smell.

At six, I turned on the Cardinals pre-game show. My TV is my one luxury. It's a 60-inch plasma screen. It took me three years to save up for it and I probably should have used the money to buy new furniture. The couch looks good, but the cushions are shot, and the recliner squeaks every time you move, but the TV is perfect. It hangs across one wall of the living room surrounded by all the accoutrements required by a modern television; DVD player, digital cable receiver, X-Box. The shelves are filled with testosterone movie favorites like Top Gun and

Terminator, and games called Morrowind, Burnout and Halo3. I don't know how to play any of them. My gaming skills petered out with Super Mario Brothers, and I can just barely play a movie since videotape went the way of the 8-track. I just recently figured out how to program the clock on the DVD player. That collection of electronics accounts for my entertainment budget for the next decade, but it ensures regular visits from my brothers. Even my Dad sneaks over to watch a little TV once in a while. Guys come to my house just to drool over my electronics. All serious baseball watching takes place in my living room.

At six-fifteen, the boys came charging in carrying pizza boxes and soda. Morgan followed them looking a little uncomfortable. The last time he was there was to pack the night he moved out. I handed him a Bud, turned the oven on low, and stuck the pizza boxes inside to keep warm. Devin relieved me of one of them as he headed for the living room. Travis raided the fridge for sodas.

"Are the nachos ready?" he asked.

I shook my head.

He frowned and followed Devin to the living room. I stuck more soda in the fridge to get cold.

The Cards were playing our archrivals the Cubs in the first round of the playoffs. The Cubs hadn't won a pennant in almost a hundred years so we were looking forward to this series. It's always fun to beat the Cubs and make fun of them. Morgan stood in the kitchen and stared around him.

"Did you know you've got..." he started.

"A cat on the roof? Yeah, I know."

"Oh. Is it yours?"

"No, he lives next door."

"How's he get up there?"

"Haven't figured that out yet."

Morgan sat down at the kitchen table and popped the top on his beer. Someone knocked on the front door. I heard it open, then voices, then feet thudding down the hall. Four strapping high school football players trailed into the kitchen behind Travis. They looked hungry. They always look hungry.

"We might need more pizza," I said to Morgan.

"Hey, Mrs. B," the first one said.

"Hi, Alan. You guys hungry?"

They laughed at my foolish question. I handed them two pizzas from the oven. Travis raised his eyebrows at me and I handed over one more.

"You weren't joking about more pizza were you?" said Morgan.

"Not really."

I searched around for the cordless, found it on top of the fridge and ordered pizza reinforcements. That done, I slumped into the chair across from Morgan and opened another beer.

"You've redone the kitchen," he said.

"Couple of years ago."

"It looks good."

"Thanks. Chad and I did most of it."

Morgan shifted in his chair. I got up and pulled chip bags out of the pantry, opened them and poured them into bowls. Devin padded into the kitchen and tiptoed up behind me. I handed him a bowl of chips without turning around and he went back into the living room—teenage food radar in action.

"Your brothers gonna lynch me when they find me here?" Morgan asked.

"Nah, they figure I can handle you. I don't know about AJ, though."

"That's comforting."

Steve came into the kitchen carrying a bag of pretzels and tossed them on the counter.

"Hey, Morgan. What's up?"

"Steve," said Morgan.

"Beer's in the fridge, Stevie," I said.

"Thanks, Ran. I could use one. Where's the nachos?"

"I didn't make nachos."

"You always make nachos."

"I just didn't feel like it today. Sorry. I'll make 'em next time."

Steve grabbed a Coors Light and disappeared down the hall. Not before he shot me a disappointed look over his shoulder. I was beginning to hate nachos. I glanced at Morgan.

"What's with the nachos?" Morgan asked.

"I just didn't make any. Jeez."

"Sorry."

I waved away his apology and changed the subject. "Steve's here and you're still alive."

"Steve's not really the one I'm worried about."

I smiled at his comment as I walked down the hallway. "Devin, you guys got your homework done?"

"Ah, Mom. It's a playoff game and we've got company."

"You'd better hurry up then, hadn't you? Take a shower and put your football stuff in the wash. It smells like a locker room in here."

The boys came grumbling out of the living room carrying their pizza and chips. Devin dumped their laundry in the washer. They hefted their backpacks and tromped upstairs, trailed by their friends. I heard the shower running and a few minutes later, thumping music pounded the ceiling over my head. The house started filling with cops. Morgan migrated with the kitchen chairs to the living room. Guys who weren't quick enough to snag chairs as they appeared, were leaning against the walls or lying on the floor. I was in the kitchen when Chad came in at the top of the third inning.

"What'd I miss?" he asked as he grabbed a Bud Light from the fridge.

"Not much. Cards are ahead by two. Have you seen AJ?"

"He'll be late. Where's the nachos?"

I acted like I didn't hear the question. The boys tumbled down the stairs and slapped their finished homework on the kitchen table. Chad left to watch the game. While I checked their homework, the kids filched several more bags of chips and scooted into the living room. I removed the remaining pizzas from the oven and stacked them on the table. The doorbell rang and a few minutes later Morgan walked down the hall with the pizza reinforcements and dumped them on the counter.

"You ready to pass these out?" he asked.

"Yeah."

"I'll do it."

"You're a guest, Morgan. You don't have to do that."

He grinned and picked up a couple of boxes off the stack and took them to the hungry hordes in the living room. He was in the kitchen for another batch when AJ strolled in.

"What are you doing here?" AJ asked, glaring at Morgan.

"I...uh."

"I invited him," I interrupted.

AJ continued to glare and Morgan backed out of the room.

"You're late. Rough day?"

"You could say that."

I handed him a Coors Light. He opened it, swallowed it, and tossed the can away.

"That should help. You want another one or should I just hook up an IV?"

He grinned and popped the top on his second.

"Why'd you invite Morgan?" he asked.

"I don't know. Seemed like the thing to do at the time." Truthfully, I didn't know. It just sort of slipped out. "You're not going to kill him are you?"

"Nah, the boys like him."

I snickered. AJ pulled me toward him and kissed me just as Morgan reappeared in the kitchen.

"Uh, sorry. Didn't mean to intrude."

He started backing down the hall. I laughed. AJ glared at me. I laughed harder. Morgan flattened against the wall as AJ brushed past. When AJ was gone, Morgan came in and leaned against the table.

"I didn't know you guys were dating again."

"I'm not sure we are."

"He doesn't like me much anymore."

"He never did like you much."

"I guess that's true...I'm going to get out of here, Randi. Thanks for the invite."

"It's only seven thirty."

Morgan stared at the floor for minute.

"Tell the truth, this is kind of uncomfortable. I'll just tell the boys I'm leaving."

"Sure, okay. Thanks for picking them up tonight."

"Any time, Randi, You know that."

He gave me a long searching look before he went to tell the boys goodbye. That caught me by surprise. Occasionally, I remembered why I married him. He's handsome and can be real sweet when it suits him. I saw him out, then made my way to the living room.

AJ wrestled Travis out of the recliner and sat. I settled on the floor in front of him. He laid his hand possessively at the base of my neck and brushed his thumb back and forth. I felt chained to the floor and found it difficult to concentrate on the game. When the chip bowl emptied, I jumped up to get more, glad for an excuse to escape. When I walked into the kitchen, George Williams was getting a Bud from the fridge.

"Hey, George. Did I see you at the bar Friday night?"

"Yeah, I was there with my wife. First time we'd been anywhere since the baby came."

"Oh, yeah I forgot you guys just had a baby. How's he doing?" Scratch George off my list of psycho cop suspects.

"He's great. Doesn't sleep much though."

"That will get better."

"I hope so."

George returned to the game. I opened the pantry to get another bag of chips. When I turned around, Jody McIntire was standing right behind me. Jody's maybe five seven and built like a tank. He goes to the gym every day and looks like he's on steroids. He just started working down here a few months ago and I don't really know him. Chad invited him to watch the game.

"Hey, sweet thing. How you doin'?"

"Fine, Jody. You need a beer or something?" I asked.

"Huh-uh, I wanted to talk to you."

I held the chip bag in front of me like a shield.

"Uh, okay."

Jody moved closer and I felt a shiver ripple up my spine. I was standing with my butt against the counter so I couldn't step back.

"You dating Weleski?" he asked.

"Not really, we're just friends. Why?"

"Cause I'd like to take you out sometime. You're pretty hot."

God save me, I must have forgotten my sleaze repellent.

"Uh, I don't date much. Not a lot of time. You know, working at the bar, the kids' games and stuff."

"I bet we could find time. I could meet you after you close the bar some night."

Gulp, not in this lifetime.

"Thanks, but I don't think so."

"What's wrong, Twinkie, you don't like cops?"

Twinkie? "It's not that. I'm just not looking for a relationship right now. If you'll excuse me, I'd like to watch the rest of the game."

I brushed past Jody and started down the hall. His next words brought me to a halt.

"I'll be watching you."

I swung around to stare at him. "What the hell does that mean?"

"It means what I said. I'll be watching you. Sooner or later you'll go on a date with me. I always get my girl."

This guy was a nutcase.

"Uh, I'm really not interested, Jody."

"I'll change your mind. I like a challenge."

My lip curled. I turned away and hurried into the other room. AJ moved his legs and I slumped against the recliner.

"You okay?" he asked leaning over my shoulder.

"Yeah, fine. Why?"

"You look like you just found a roach in your soup."

More like a spider.

"Nope. I'm fine." I lied.

My heart was beating a little fast. Something about Jody McIntire had all my alarm bells ringing. I tried to settle in and watch the rest of the game. Every time I glanced away from the television, Jody was staring at me. It was creepy. I don't remember much about the game. I think we won. I sent the football team home and the boys to bed when it was over. The rest of the guys started trickling out soon after. Chad and AJ stuck around to help clean up the mess.

"You tell AJ what I told you this afternoon?" I asked Chad while AJ was in the kitchen.

"You mean your psycho cop theory?"

"It's a good theory."

"No way. I know all these guys. None of them would do something like that."

"Maybe it's a sheriff's deputy or a highway patrolman."

"Sis, it's not a cop."

I decided to drop it for now and changed the subject.

"You know Jody very well, Chadly?"

"Yeah. We hang out. He's wanting to get in on an undercover sting we've got going. He's a good cop, but a little too intense to go UC."

Intense was kind of an understatement in my opinion.

"Why the question?" Chad asked.

"Um, no reason, really."

Chad knew me too well. He stopped what he was doing and stared at me.

"What's up, Ranna?"

I sighed. Sometimes having a twin is a pain in the ass. I didn't want to tell him about my encounter with Jody in the kitchen. They were friends. But I needed to say something. I wished I'd never brought it up.

"Nothing, really. He's new here, I don't really know him. I was just wondering."

"He's okay," Chad said. "A good guy. A good cop."

He stuffed the last pizza box into the trash bag and went outside to put it in the can. Chad was a good judge of people. Maybe I was over-reacting and Jody was an okay guy, but he made me really uncomfortable.

Chad left a few minutes later and AJ and I sat on the couch. Wilson, worn out from stealing pizza and chips, curled in a ball in the recliner for a snooze. I leaned against AJ and he draped his arm around me.

"What happened in the kitchen that made you look like you saw a ghost?

"Nothing."

"Don't lie to me, Randi."

"Jody McIntire asked me for a date."

"You get asked out so seldom it's a shock to your system?"

"It was just the way he asked. Do you know him?"

"I guess. He came down here from Clark City."

"Uncle Bill is police chief there."

"Yeah, he gave him a good reference. You're not going to dump me for Jody McIntire are you?"

"No way. I think he has a few screws loose. If I had to pick a cop to finger for your psycho murderer, he would be the one."

AJ tensed beside me.

"What makes you think the murderer's a cop?"

"I guess 'cause the crime scene was so clean."

I clapped my hand over my mouth as soon as the words left it. Chad was gonna kill me.

"Chad showed you our case file."

"No he didn't."

"Randi, he could get busted off the force for that. I will have a talk with him about this."

"Don't, AJ. He didn't show it to me. I kind of looked at it while he was sacked out on the couch the other night."

AJ knew I was lying. I smiled my little please don't be mad at me grin and tried to look innocent.

"It's not Jody, Randi."

"You have any other leads?"

"Not really. Nobody saw Lisa with anyone. Nobody saw or heard anything weird at The War Zone. We got a big bunch of nothin'."

"Then how do you know it wasn't a cop? How do you know it wasn't Jody?"

"Jesus, Randi. I just know, okay. Jody's a damn good cop."

I sighed. AJ gave my shoulder a squeeze, kissed the top of my head and stood.

"I need to get home, darlin'. Got an early day tomorrow."

I followed him to the porch, and we kissed goodnight. It was an awesome kiss. After that, I wasn't sure he was still leaving. I wasn't sure I still wanted him to. After a long moment of indecision, AJ finally walked down the stairs. I closed the door and turned around to find Jody standing at the end of the hall. I squealed and pulled my gun.

"What the hell are you still doing here?"

"I wanted to talk to you some more. I waited outside on the patio for everyone to go home. I didn't think AJ was ever going to leave. Thought you said you guys weren't dating."

"We're not," I said as I backed against the door.

"Sweetheart, that wasn't no goodnight peck between friends. I thought you were just going to drop down and go for it right on the porch."

"Jody, get out of my house," I hissed.

"You gonna shoot me if I don't?"

"I might." Probably not, but I wasn't going to say that.

"Bad idea, shootin' a cop. Pretty hard to explain. What with my weapon still in the holster."

"Jody, please leave."

"Okay. Relax, Twinkie," he said holding his hands out in front of him.

I kept the gun pointed his way and walked forward as he backed toward the kitchen.

"I like chicks that aren't afraid of guns. The tough ones are the most fun. You're going to be a real challenge."

"OUT!"

"I'm going, but here's a little piece of advice before I do, sweet thing. If you're going to point that gun, you'd better be ready to shoot."

As he said the last word, he lunged forward, peeled the gun from my hand and ejected the clip. It clattered to the floor. He placed the empty weapon gently in my hand.

"Good night, Twinkie."

I stood in stunned surprise and watched him step outside and disappear into the dark. I shook myself out of my stupor and set the lock. My knees were shaking as I sank onto a kitchen chair. My hands were trembling and my heart was beating so hard I thought I was going to pass out. Jesus, was I being stalked by a cop? When I could stand, I scooped up the clip and slapped it back into my gun. I flopped onto the couch and Wilson hopped up beside me. I ruffled his ears as he softened up the cushion and got ready to go to sleep.

"You aren't much of a watch dog, buddy."

He snorted at me and buried himself under the blanket. I lay on the couch, wide-awake, cradling my .32. Wilson snored, and snorted, while I waited for the sun to come up.

Chapter 8

When the boys came down for breakfast, I roused myself off the couch.

"You sleep in your clothes last night, Mom?" Travis asked.

"Fell asleep on the couch," I lied. Well, the couch part was true.

The boys shot matching eye rolls at me as they picked crunch berries out of a mixing bowl that now held an entire box of Cap'n Crunch.

"If you eat all the crunch berries, all you have left is Cap'n Crunch," I said.

"Yeah, but it makes pink milk, Mom," Travis said.

I couldn't really argue with that.

"Just make sure you put the cereal back in the box."

"Yeah, yeah." Devin waved a hand in my direction without taking his eyes off the task of crunch berry removal.

While they ate their crunch berries, I took a shower. It didn't do much to wake me up; my eyes were gritty and red.

After I dropped the boys at school, I went home and crashed. I slept fitfully, dropping into dreams, then jolting awake as I felt myself falling—my standard stress dream. At four, I dragged myself off the bed, totally un-rested, and took another shower to wake up. The shower didn't do the trick so I added caffeine. Not to the shower—I drank the caffeine—but I'd read about some caffeine soap in the paper the other day. Right now it didn't sound like a half bad idea. I dressed, blinked my eyes into focus and took off to the high school to get the boys from football practice. They tumbled into the car smelling of boy sweat, dirt, and grass and filled me in on their day as we drove home. I fed them hamburger mac and cheese, and sent them upstairs for homework and showers. While I was cleaning the kitchen, Chad arrived to watch the playoff game with the boys.

"You have bags under your eyes the size of blimps, Ranna."

"I didn't get much sleep last night."

"Doesn't look like you got any. You're never going to make it 'til midnight."

"I don't have any choice." I checked the time. "Shit, I'm late already. I've gotta run."

I yelled goodbye up the stairs to the kids and snatched my purse off the counter as I left. Lex was his normal charming self. I retaliated by working in my hiking boots for a change.

"Bitch," he said after a particularly good stomp. "Why don't you watch where you put your feet?"

"Why don't you watch where you put your hands?"

He grinned. "Call a truce?"

"I will if you will. I'm too tired to fight tonight."

"I'll be good."

"You'd better or Friday night I'm wearing heels."

Lex laughed. "Okay, you win. I don't have anything to combat that."

I was still smiling to myself over our truce when the cowboy strolled in. My eyes went wide as he parked on a stool in front of me. He gave me his icy over-the-shades stare and ordered his usual. My hands were trembling as I pulled his draw. As soon as I could get away, I ducked into the office to call AJ. He wasn't at the station, so I dialed his cell. I got an out-of-area message and it cut off before I could leave a voicemail. I hoped he'd see my number and call. Just to be sure, I dialed his pager, punched in my number, and added 911. If that didn't get me a callback, I was out of luck. I eased behind the bar, secretly hoping the cowboy had taken himself off somewhere, but my luck wasn't that good. He motioned for a refill as I stepped back into place.

I drew his beer and waited for AJ to get in touch. Dammit, why wasn't he calling? Better yet, why wouldn't the damn cowboy just leave? A half hour went by, then an hour and still no phone call. I was getting more wound up by the minute. Lex touched me on the shoulder and I dropped the glass I was drying. It hit the floor in an explosion of slivers.

"Sorry, angel. Didn't mean to startle you. You okay?"

"I'm just tired, sorry."

"Why don't you pack it in? I can close tonight."

I glanced at the cowboy. Should I stay? Nah, I was getting out of there. If AJ wanted to talk to the cowboy, he should have called back. I wasn't gonna stick around and baby-sit until he found the time to get in touch.

"That would be great, Lex. I'm exhausted."

Steve strolled in the door while I was getting my purse from the office. He was leaning against the bar when I walked out. The cowboy was at the other end. He tilted his glass at me. I pointed to Lex and turned to Steve. Lex poured the cowboy a beer and stayed at that end of the bar watching him.

"What are you doing here?" I asked Steve.

"Dropped by to see if Lex could do bodyguard duty. AJ and I are going to be tied up for a while."

"You can walk me to my car. I was just getting ready to leave."

I wanted to get Steve outside so I could tell him about the cowboy. I moved toward the door and looked over my shoulder hoping he was following only to see him still slouched at the bar.

"I thought you had to close tonight," Steve said.

"Lex is gonna close for me. I'm beat. What's AJ working on?"

"The Woods murder."

"You got a new lead?" I asked.

"We have a new body."

I stopped and glanced out of the corner of my eye at Tex slouched at the other end of the bar. He sat up a little straighter on his barstool. Without moving, he seemed to lean closer to us. He said something to Lex that I couldn't hear. Lex answered and Tex eased off his stool and pushed past us, leaving his full glass on the bar. I glanced at Lex and he turned his palms up in an I don't know gesture.

"What was that about?" I asked.

"He asked if Steve was a cop. I said yeah and he took off."

I looked at Steve.

"That's the cowboy AJ wants to talk to about the murder."

"Shit!"

Steve ran outside. A truck sprayed gravel as it peeled out of the parking lot. I could hear the rocks thunking against the side of the building. I walked out as Steve was coming in.

"Get a license number?" I asked.

"No, covered with mud."

"Sorry, I was trying to get you outside so I could tell you."

"Don't worry about it. I've got a description of the truck. I'll call it in, we'll find him."

He slipped his phone from his pocket, gave a description of the vehicle to dispatch, and told them to keep an eye out.

He snapped the phone closed and looked at me. "You ready to go?"

I nodded and followed him out to the Mustang. I asked if he knew who the new murder victim was.

"Don't know yet. McIntire found her. Took a noise call on a party at Timber Bridge. The body was in the creek. He collared a guy at the scene. We have him in custody."

"Somebody local?"

"Nah, some college kid. You need me to follow you home, Randi?"

"I'll be okay, Chad's at the house with the boys."

"Good, I really need to get back to the station."

"Steve, you think the guy you've got is the murderer?"

"Too soon to tell, my gut says no. I think the poor kid was just in the wrong place at the wrong time."

"Stevie...do you think it could be a cop?"

"What the hell makes you say that?"

"Nothing, never mind. I hope you catch him."

"Yeah, I'd like to get this thing solved. I haven't been home before two a.m. since you tripped over Lisa."

"You'll break it soon."

"I hope so, Ran."

I thanked Steve for the escort and drove toward the house. Chad's car was on the street, so I parked in the drive. The boys were in bed and Chad was watching TV. I opened a Coors Light and flopped on the couch next to him.

"You're home early."

"Lex offered to close the bar."

"You look beat."

"I didn't get any sleep last night."

"Yeah, you said that earlier. AJ stay too late?" he asked with a grin.

"No, AJ left right after you did. I closed the door behind him and turned to find Jody McIntire standing in my hallway. That guy's not right."

"What do you mean?"

"He's just weird. He asked me for a date, I told him no and now it's like he's on a mission. He gives me the creeps."

"He's a damn good cop."

"Well, he must be a peach of a guy if he's a good cop." I snapped.

"I didn't mean that, Randi, I was just stating a fact."

"I think he's crazy. He was also at the bar Friday night."

"So."

"So, I made a list of all the cops that were at the bar Friday night, and he was one of them. He hasn't done anything yet to make me think he couldn't be the killer."

"You're convinced the killer's a cop, aren't you?"

"Yes." A picture of Tex's ice blue eyes flashed through my mind. "Well, maybe."

"Did you tell AJ about Jody?" Chad asked.

"I told him he asked me out. I haven't talked to him today. Wouldn't do any good to tell him, he likes Jody, too."

"What's that supposed to mean?"

"Means the good ole boy network is in full force."

"That's unfair, Randi. We know him a lot better than you do. What, you've talked to him twice?"

"Whatever. I'm too tired to argue with you. That's not the first time I've been asked on a date. I know what's normal and what's not."

"You haven't dated since you got divorced."

"How would you know? You weren't even around."

"Okay, you haven't dated since I got back."

I slouched at the end of the couch and picked up the remote.

"I might have dated before, you wouldn't know."

"Yeah, you might have, but you didn't."

"Steve said they found another body at Timber Bridge," I said, changing the subject.

"Shit."

"They have a guy in custody. Guess who made the collar?"

"Who?"

"Jody McIntire. I think he did it and is trying to frame some poor college kid for it."

Chad just rolled his eyes.

Okay maybe that was a little farfetched.

"Steve say anything else?"

"Said he didn't think the guy they had in custody was the killer."

"That why you think McIntire did it?"

"Maybe. Or maybe it was my buddy Tex, from the bar. He didn't waste any time getting out of there tonight when he found out Steve was a cop."

"You need to make up your mind, Ran. Is it the cowboy with the creepy eyes or Jody the psycho cop?"

"Maybe they did it together."

"Now there's a thought. I'll run that by the guys."

"Go home, Chadly."

He struggled up off the couch and started for the door.

"Think I'll head down to the station first and see what I can find out. I'll talk to you tomorrow."

"Chad, please talk to Jody. He really scares me."

"If it will make you feel better, I'll ask him why he came into your house, okay?"

"Thanks, Chadly."

"Don't thank me for making an ass of myself with one of my co-workers. I'm a little old to be beating guys up, 'cause they looked at you wrong."

"You'll be my hero forever."

"Whatever. Goodnight, Ran."

Chad left and I crawled into bed. My .32 was on the bedside table next to the phone and Wilson the watchdog was asleep at my feet. Exhaustion kicked in and it didn't take me long to fall asleep. At six the next morning, the telephone startled me awake. I mumbled hello. Nothing answered but silence. I started to hang up when a familiar voice spoke.

"You sicced your brother on me. Not nice, Twinkie. Not nice at all."

"Leave me alone, Jody."

"You'll come around and all the family detectives in the world won't stop it."

"Why are you doing this?"

He ignored my question and left me breathless with his next statement.

"By the way, won't do you any good to sleep with your gun, Twinkie."

I jerked to a sitting position and stared through my bedroom window. There was laughter from the phone and then a click as Jody punched off.

Chapter 9

To say Jody had me freaked out would be an understatement. I was a basket case. My first instinct was to call Chad or AJ, but I was afraid they wouldn't believe me. Hell, I could hardly believe this was happening. Cops don't stalk.

I dressed, snapped my .32 into my ankle holster and retrieved my 9mm from the gun safe. An ankle holster? Two guns? I know, I know, but I have two brothers, three if you count AJ, and two sons, my life is ruled by testosterone. I think it rubs off, I often get the urge to buy needless electronic gadgets, hell I own a sixty-inch television. Just another case of me trying to fit in, it's the basic tenant of my life. Chad would make fun of me if he knew I was carrying two guns, but I didn't care. I slipped the holster on my belt, threw a jacket on over my tee shirt and took the boys to school. It was the beginning of a long day. I spent my time cleaning house and jumping at shadows.

I took a shower, washed my hair and spent some extra time with my makeup. The makeup thing was getting to be a habit, must be the manicure. I flipped through my closet, passed by the Henley's and flannel shirts, and stopped at a white blouse with puffy sleeves and long cuffs. I tucked it into my jeans, unbuttoned it as strategically as possible and bloused it out over my belt until I was satisfied that I was as sexy as I was going to get. I stopped in front of the full-length mirror before I left. Not bad for forty. Hell, not bad for twenty. I was ready for work.

I pulled the door closed behind me, started across the porch, and stepped on Bill's tail. He howled, I squealed, and he ran through my legs. I kicked him while I was trying to get my balance. He hissed and swatted at my pant leg as he shot off the porch. I stumbled off the top stair, lost my footing, and bounced down the stairs on my behind. The sleeve of my sexy white blouse caught on the stair rail and ripped as I fell. I swore. After I hit bottom, I glanced quickly around to see if any of my neighbors saw my graceful exit.

"Dammit, Bill. That was my favorite shirt," I snapped as I crawled up the stairs.

Mrs. Litton peered around her front door. I should have known she would see.

"Are you alright, dear?"

I nodded and she disappeared inside. Bill blinked at me from behind the leaves of a hosta in my flower garden. I sent a superheated glare his way. He didn't appear to be singed. I went inside to change shirts.

Wilson greeted me like I'd been gone for days. I stripped off the ruined white shirt and pushed my arms into a long-sleeved tee. My hair was a disaster and I felt closer to fifty than twenty as I stepped carefully across the porch.

As I walked into the bar, I shoved my sleeves to my elbows and tucked my tee shirt into my jeans. My cell phone flipped off my belt and skittered across the floor. I scooped it up and snapped it in place. Lex tapped at his watch face. I sent the superheated glare his way. He should have disintegrated into a smoldering pile of cinders. He just winked. I was gonna have to work on my technique. The look didn't seem to have much power anymore.

I was late, my trip down the porch steps had ensured that. It was a habit I was going to have to break, or I'd wind up unemployed again. I took my place behind the bar and Morgan motioned me toward the office with his head. It wasn't a friendly motion. Oh shit, I thought. He's going to fire me. I wasn't gonna get the chance to mend my ways.

I stepped inside and pulled the door closed. If I was going to be fired, I didn't want Lex listening to every word. I was working on what argument to use to wheedle my way into Morgan's good graces. When he spoke, it took me a minute to focus.

"What did you say?" I asked.

"I said, what's with the iron?"

I stared at him in confusion. My mind simply refused to switch gears.

"Your gun," he said. "I know I told you I wanted you to have it on you when you work, but it has to be concealed. The customers get a little squirrelly about firearms in the bar."

He turned toward the safe and spun the dial. I was slowly making my way out of my imagined conversation and into the one that was actually taking place.

"You're not firing me?" I asked.

He shot me a puzzled look, his hand still resting on the safe.

"What?"

"Never mind. What did you say?"

He huffed in exasperation.

"You can't wear your gun in the open like that, Randi."

"Oh. Right, I know that."

I reached down to unsnap the holster from my belt and Morgan grabbed my arm. A big scrape started at my wrist and disappeared beneath my shirtsleeve. Souvenir of my tangle with the porch rail. I hadn't even noticed it.

"What have you been doing, Ran?" Morgan asked.

"Nothing. I just had a little accident with the cat as I was leaving."

"The one on the roof?"

"No, the one on the porch."

"I didn't think you had a cat."

"I don't."

"Oh." Morgan paused and tried to sort through that, decided to just ignore it. "You can put your gun in the safe."

I dropped the nine in its holster inside the safe and flipped it closed. I flexed my foot and felt the comforting weight of the ankle holster there above my hiking boot. Morgan glanced at the bulge in my pant leg and smirked.

"You're wearing two guns?"

"Just spooked about the murders, I guess."

"I heard they found another body. That's all anyone's been talking about all day."

Jody had me so whacked out, I'd scarcely given the second murder a thought. Funny, since I thought Jody was the killer.

Morgan sat down at his desk as I stepped out of the office and joined Lex behind the bar. I needed a drink. I settled for a soda. It was still quiet, too early for the after-work crowd.

Lex sidled up beside me and brushed his fingers down my arm next to the scrape. I sucked in my breath at the unexpected touch.

"What happened to your arm?" he asked.

"I fell down the steps."

"What a klutz."

"I'm not. I stepped on Bill. He was asleep on my porch."

"You have a guy named Bill sleeping on your porch?"

"No dammit, Bill's a cat."

"Right."

I glared at his back as he walked down the bar to mix a drink. I scooped some ice into a bar towel and stuck it on my arm. Now that I knew it was there, it ached all the way to my shoulder. It was already turning purple. I was going to have a beauty of a bruise.

The Thursday night crowd started trickling in and someone played the jukebox. Lex and I started working together behind the bar, tossing bottles and glasses around like we'd been doing it for years. It was fun, and the time passed quickly. I almost forgot how sore I was from my tumble.

It was after two a.m. when we rolled the last drunk out the door. My bodyguard hadn't shown yet. I sat on a stool and Lex slid a beer down the bar. My feet were aching and I groaned as I unlaced my boots and eased my feet out. Tomorrow I was wearing tennis shoes.

Lex pressed himself up and sat on the bar beside me. I wondered briefly why he hadn't left at eleven like usual, but before I could ask he spoke.

"So, you have a cat named Bill?"

"No, my neighbor has a cat named Bill. He just likes to sleep on my porch."

"Not anymore," he said laughing.

"Ass."

Lex chuckled. I pelted him with an ice cube. He hopped off the bar and started washing glasses. I leaned over and shoved my feet back into the boots. Muscles screamed in protest. I should never have sat down. I stifled a moan as I stood. Lex looked at my boots and smiled.

"Shithead," I said.

He flipped soapsuds at me.

"I'm working in tennis shoes tomorrow."

Lex grinned and wiggled his fingers. "Oh, goody."

"You touch me, you better be wearing a cup."

He cringed.

I wiped off the tables and swept the downstairs, my bootlaces leaving trails in the dust piles. Then I hobbled up the stairs to straighten the dart room.

"You're gonna trip on those laces."

"I'm being careful."

I promptly stepped on a bootlace and thumped down on my hands and knees.

Lex laughed outloud. I didn't even bother with a glare. It hadn't worked all day. I didn't have any reason to think it would now. I gathered my dignity and continued to the mezzanine. Someone pounded on the door as I was coming down.

"OPEN UP, POLICE!"

Lex shot me a questioning look. I shrugged and unlocked the door. AJ strolled in.

"I love saying that."

I shook my head and went to put the broom away. When I came back, AJ was nursing a Coors Light and Lex was getting ready to leave.

"Everything's done except counting the money," he said as he hopped over the bar.

"You didn't get your tips."

"You keep them and we'll call it even," he said.

"Thanks."

"What's that all about?" AJ asked.

"Nothin'. Lex and I have just reached an understanding."

AJ raised an eyebrow in question. I didn't elaborate. I did the deposit, locked it in the safe, and grabbed my purse. AJ was slouched against the bar half asleep. I nudged his shoulder and he raised his head with a yawn.

"What'd you do to your arm?"

"I stepped on a cat and don't you say one word about it."

"Okay, you ready to go?"

"Uh huh."

"Chad had to go back to the station so the boys are with Morgan."

"He gonna take them to school?"

"Yeah. You can sleep in. Wish I could. I'm wiped out."

I hobbled toward the Mustang and noticed AJ's truck wasn't in the parking lot.

"Where's your ride?"

"In the shop. Some kind of computer problem or something."

"How'd you get here?"

"Caught a ride with a patrol officer."

"Just drop me off at home and take the car. I don't have anything I have to do tomorrow 'til work. I can get a ride from Morgan."

"Okay."

As we got into the car AJ said, "If you stepped on a cat, how'd you hurt your arm?"

"I don't want to talk about the cat. Okay?"

"Sorry. I was just wondering."

AJ glanced at me once and started to say something.

"Not another damn word about the cat." I warned.

He grinned but kept quiet for the rest of the drive. When we stepped onto the porch, AJ took my key and unlocked the door. I glanced around, but no cat eyes peered back at me. I stepped into the yard and checked the roof, but I didn't see Bill there either.

Wilson greeted us and trotted behind me into the kitchen. I let him out and rooted around in the fridge for a beer, I was out of Coors Light. I grabbed a Budweiser for AJ and a Bud Light for myself. When he came downstairs, I handed him the beer and we went into the living room. I sank to the floor by the couch and pulled off my boots. AJ stretched out behind me and turned on the TV. He rested his hand on the back of my neck and played with my hair. When I turned around to say something, he was asleep. I turned off the TV, covered him with a blanket, kissed him on the forehead, and turned off the light.

I dropped my clothes on the floor and slid my pocket gun into the drawer of my bedside table before I crawled into bed. Every ache and bruise clamored for attention as I pulled up the blanket. I rolled onto my side, closed my eyes, and remembered my 9mm was locked in the safe at work. With AJ sleeping in the next room, it didn't seem like something I needed to worry about. I relaxed and felt the tension of the last couple of days melt away. My last thought before I drifted off to sleep was, it would be nice if AJ were curled up next to me instead of on my couch. My eyes snapped open and I lay in the dark staring at nothing. When did getting back together with AJ start to seem like a good idea? It didn't just seem like a good idea, it seemed right. Like I'd found something that had been missing for a long time. I flopped over onto my back, took a deep breath and blew it out. Wilson wiggled around under the covers until he was comfortable again and licked my ankle. The tingle I got just thinking about AJ said it was the right thing to do. The little voice in the back of my head kept telling me I was just asking for another heartache. They hadn't reached a consensus by the time I'd fallen asleep. Apparently they came to one while I slept.

AJ woke me in the morning with a kiss. I opened my eyes as he brushed the hair away from my face and ran his fingers around my jaw and across my lips.

"Sorry I fell asleep. That wasn't exactly what I had in mind when I came in last night," he said as he sat on the edge of the bed.

I smiled as he bent down to kiss me. I felt it all the way to my toes. He tossed the covers back and ran his hand underneath my shirt. My skin tingled beneath his touch. He raised my shirt and kissed my breast and a car horn sounded out front.

"Shit, that's Chad. He's giving me a ride to work this morning."

"You told him you were spending the night here?"

"Well, yeah. I told him I might."

"Is there really something wrong with your truck or did you just make that up?"

He laughed. "It's really in the shop."

"How'd you know I was going to let you spend the night?"

"Just a hunch."

"Pretty confident weren't you?"

"Uh-huh." He pulled my tee shirt down and kissed me again. "To be continued," he whispered as he rose to leave.

His steps scuffed down the hall and the front door closed behind him with a quiet click. I groaned and smacked the bed. Wilson stared at me in alarm.

"Think I'll start the day with a cold shower, bud."

He stuck his nose on his paws and scrunched his face at me, trying to determine if I was talking about food. I retrieved my gun from the drawer and placed it on the bathroom counter while I took my shower. I was rinsing the soap from my hair when I heard a noise. I peeked around the curtain. Jody McIntire was standing in my bathroom, my gun swinging from his finger. I froze in stunned silence.

"Morning, Twinkie," he said.

"What the hell are you doing here?"

"Just stopped by to say good morning. AJ was here last night, thought I'd wait till he left."

"How thoughtful."

I was trying to be tough, but my voice trembled. His lips twisted into an ugly smile.

"Give me a few minutes, Twinkie. I'll make you forget all about that asshole."

My lip curled in disgust. "Not likely."

He shot forward and ripped the shower curtain down, leaving me standing bare assed in front of him. I was shivering from fear and cold. I tried to reach the towel. Before I could grab it, he snapped it out of reach. I huddled against the wall as he took a slow tour with his eyes.

"Not bad," he muttered. "Not bad at all."

Bile rose in my throat. I swallowed it down.

"How 'bout I take you on a little trip around the world. I can guarantee you'll enjoy it."

"Get out of here," I hissed.

My eyes filled with tears and I desperately blinked them back. For some reason it seemed terribly important that I didn't cry in front of him. I tried to glare.

Jody stepped closer and ran his hand down my ribcage. I flinched at his touch and slapped at him. He jerked away, the twisted grin gone from his face.

"You need to learn some manners."

This from a man who had broken into my house and now had me cornered in my shower. An unwanted giggle bubbled up—a product of my fear and his incongruous words.

"Why are you here, Jody?"

His eyes raked slowly up and down my body, leaving no doubt why he was there. Jody read the revulsion on my face and smiled in satisfaction.

I crouched and covered myself, the urge to giggle forgotten in a rush of panic.

"We'll do this another day. Give you time to look forward to it. See you around, Twinkie."

He palmed my gun and backed out of the room, and closed the door, leaving me drained and shivery. I grabbed a towel and clutched it around me as I perched on the edge of the tub. I listened for some sound outside the bathroom, but heard nothing but the drip of the shower. Still I couldn't open the door. My skin started to itch as the soap dried, and I sat waiting for the courage to leave the room. An hour passed. Wilson snuffled at the bathroom door, and whined softly. I shook myself out of my stupor and showered off the soap residue. Belting my robe, I scooted down the hall to my bedroom.

My .32 was lying on the bed. I threw on some clothes, grabbed the gun, and searched the house room by room until I was certain I was alone.

Wilson stood patiently at the back door when I came into the kitchen. I opened it for him and sat down at the table to think. A cop that could be a murderer was stalking me. Who was going to believe this? I dialed Chad's pager and waited. Ten minutes later, the phone rang. I let the machine get it in case it was Jody. When Chad's voice came on, I grabbed it.

"Chad, can you come over here?"

"What's wrong, Ranna?"

"I..." I paused and took a deep breath. "I really need to talk to you."

There was a pause on the other end. Finally he said, "It's going to be a few minutes. I'll get there as soon as I can."

"Thanks, Chad."

I dropped the cordless on the table and started to cry. I swore and wiped my eyes. I had to pull myself together. When Chad arrived forty-five minutes later, I was almost calm again.

"What's wrong?" he asked as soon as he saw me.

I stood, Chad wrapped his arms around me and the tears came again. AJ's kiss and promise from that morning seemed like a lifetime ago. Chad held me until I started to sniffle, then handed me a box of Kleenex and a glass of water. I blew my nose, and tried to get myself under control.

"Ran, tell me what happened?"

I tried to work out how to start. Chad sat across from me and waited.

I finally said, "Jody was in my house this morning while I was taking a shower."

"Jody McIntire?"

I nodded.

"Was in your house this morning?"

"He came in while I was taking my shower."

"Randi, why would he do that?"

"I don't know. He broke in. He scared the hell out of me. I think he killed Lisa Woods and now he's harassing me."

I told him the whole story, everything about Jody that was creeping me out. In his defense, he listened without interrupting. He still wasn't buying my story.

"Ranna, I find it hard to believe Jody would break into your house and harass you while you were taking a shower."

"Seriously, Chad. You still think I'm making this up?"

"No. Yes. Shit. I don't know. I think you're freaked out about these murders and it's got you jumping at shadows. Look, Ranna, this whole thing runs to pattern. Bobby Nolen, Gary Baker, Andy Carlisle."

"What about Andy Carlisle? What are you getting at Chad?"

"Steve and I have been bailing you out since we were in middle school. If you didn't like somebody, we made sure they left you alone."

"Andy Carlisle? You beat up Andy Carlisle. I loved him. He broke my heart freshman year. We went out one time and after that he wouldn't even talk to me in the halls. I never said anything bad about Andy Carlisle. Never. I can't believe you did that, and I can't believe you think all I want is for you to beat up some guy that I think has the cooties. I'm not a little girl anymore, Chad. Jody really scares me."

"Okay, okay. Relax. I'll talk to him again. "Will that make you happy?"

"I don't think talking is going to do anything this time."

Chad rubbed his temples and sighed.

"Look, I said I'd talk to him, and I will. That's it. I'm not going to make more of an ass of myself than that."

"What do I have to do to make you realize this is serious?"

"I believe you think this is serious." Chad rubbed his temples. "God, I don't have time for this. Listen to me. The killer is not a cop and it's not Jody McIntire. If Jody is guilty of anything it's having bad relationship skills. I'll tell him to back off." He ran his hands through his hair and shook his head. "I have twenty things waiting for me at the station. I gotta get back to work. I'll talk to Jody this afternoon. Jesus, you have no idea how awkward this is."

"Chad, wait," I said as he rose to leave.

"Look Ranna, I love you, and I appreciate your help finding Lisa's friends, but now it's time for you to step back and leave this investigation to the pros."

He walked out and closed the door behind him just short of a slam.

"God damn cat!" I heard him mumble as he stumbled off the porch.

I smiled. "Way to go, Bill."

I sat down at the table and tried to decide what to do now. Deep down, I knew Chad believed me, or he would if he was really listening. This murder case had everyone on edge and Chad's everyday vice stuff kept him pretty wound already. I wasn't going to be able to depend on Chad for help. AJ definitely wasn't going to listen. Or more to the point, I wasn't going to tell him. He had too much going on with this murder case to give much attention to something he didn't want to hear. I was going to have to take care of Jody myself. I climbed the stairs to Travis's room and breached the inner sanctum. I needed his computer. My laptop was dead and my budget didn't stretch to a replacement. Devin's laptop was probably buried under a mound of unwashed socks and empty Mt. Dew bottles. Travis was just going to have to deal with it.

I woke up the computer and Darth Vader's face appeared. I googled Jody by name, but all I could find was his blog. That was creepy reading, but it didn't tell me what I wanted to know. I thought for a minute and googled people search sites. Without more information, I wasn't going to find anything I needed to know about him there either. I thought for a minute, then decided to call in a favor.

I called Loretta Anderson at the police station. She owed me because I'd gotten her a date with Chad. They didn't really hit it off, but the debt was still outstanding. I got through to Loretta and told her it was time to pay up.

"What kind of a favor do you need, Randi?"

"Just some information."

"Like what?"

"You know that new cop, Jody McIntire?"

"Sure, he's kind of cute."

"He asked me on a date. I want to find out something about him before I say yes. Can you get your hands on his personnel file?"

"Jeez, you don't want much."

"You said you'd do anything."

A sigh came over the phone.

"Please, Lor?"

"What do you want from his file?"

"Could you accidentally get me a copy of it?"

"Randi! I could get fired for doing that."

"It's really important, Lor."

"I thought you were dating AJ."

"Sort of. I mean, not really, not officially anyway. At least I don't think so."

That senseless statement left Loretta momentarily speechless. Before she could ask me what it meant, I went on.

"Please, Lor. I need this information. It's more important than you could possibly know."

"This doesn't have anything to do with a date, does it?"

"I can't tell you what it's about, but I could really use your help."

Loretta sighed again. "Can you meet me for lunch at Mabel's?"

"Sure, what time?"

"I'll be there at one. Get a booth in the rear. I don't want anyone to see me give you these papers."

"Thanks, Lor. You're a sweetheart."

"An unemployed sweetheart if I get caught. You'd better tell me what's going on when this is over."

"I will. Thanks, Lor." I hoped I'd still be alive when this was all over.

Chapter 10

arrived at Mabel's by a quarter to one. Mabel was sitting in her usual spot at the front table drinking coffee and smoking a cigarette. Her beehive hairdo was listing a little to port. Either it had been a busy morning or Mabel had had a rough night. I grinned to myself as I walked past. Ann Marie was sitting at the counter, so I took a stool next to her and waved at Granny.

"Hey, Ann Marie," I said.

"Hi, Randi. How ya doin?"

Granny dropped a Pepsi off in front of me as she headed down the counter with the coffee pot. I took a drink and wondered idly if Ann Marie was acquainted with Jody. It was possible, being that she was a working girl. At least I thought she still was. It would be kind of embarrassing if I mentioned it and she wasn't.

While I was trying to figure out how to broach the subject of Jody, Granny swung back by.

"You doing okay, sweetie?" She asked Ann Marie as she paused on her way past. Ann Marie nodded. Granny looked at me.

"You here for lunch?"

I nodded. "Loretta's gonna meet me here in a few."

She nodded and continued down the counter to deposit the empty pot and start a fresh one. She paused at the window and rattled off an order to the cook.

I was screwing up my courage to ask Ann Marie about Jody, just as he walked past the front window of Mabel's. He glanced in and flashed me a smile.

Ann Marie shot him the bird with one perfectly manicured middle finger. He made a gun shape with his finger and pointed it at her as he continued on.

"Son of a bitch," Ann Marie whispered.

"You know him?" I asked.

She lifted her coffee spoon from her cup, tapped it against the rim and placed it carefully on the counter.

"Yeah, I guess you could say that." She finally said.

"Uh oh. I sense something less than respect for our new officer."

"He's not worthy of respect."

"He asked me out."

The words popped out without thought on my part. Ann Marie stiffened on the stool beside me.

"Stay away from him, Randi. He's bad news."

I looked a question at her and she continued.

"Look, he's nice looking, but he's trouble with a capital T."

"Why, what's he done? Have you had a run in with him?"

"I have, but that's nothing. It's what I've heard about him that's scary. He...he's." She stopped and picked up the coffee spoon she'd just laid down. "I'm not going to get into specifics. I can't afford for anything I say to get back to him. I've got enough skeletons of my own to deal with, but trust me on this, okay? You need to stay away from that guy. He's dangerous. He'd be bad enough without the gun and badge. With them, he's out of control."

"I, he...He broke into my house this morning."

"Randi, you don't want to get caught alone with him."

"I don't know what to do. I've talked to Chad, but Jody's everybody's best bud down at the station. I'm not sure Chad is really taking me seriously."

"File a restraining order. Go to the Chief if you don't think your brother can do anything about it."

"I can't do that, Ann Marie. Chad would never forgive me if I went over his head like that. What if...Would you tell Chad what you wouldn't tell me? He'd believe it coming from you."

Ann Marie snorted a laugh. "Randi, don't take this the wrong way, I'm sure your brother is a good man. Lord knows Liz thinks he walks on water, but I'm an ex hooker and a recovering addict. Chad can say all the nice things to me he wants, but when push comes to shove, what it boils down to is I'm a hooker and he's a cop."

"Chad's not like that, Ann Marie."

She patted my hand as she slipped off her stool and picked up her purse to go.

"I can't help you, Randi, except to tell you to steer clear of Jody McIntire."

She glanced down at her watch. "I need to go, I'm late. Be careful, girl." She left a dollar on the counter and walked out the door.

We were nearly the same age, Ann Marie and I, but there were years and years of living looking out of her eyes. I liked her and wished we could be friends. Girlfriends, real do-your-hair and share-your-deepest-secret girlfriends, were almost non-existent in my male-dominated life. I picked up my glass and moved to a booth in the rear to wait for Loretta—another almost girlfriend. I tapped my worse-for-wear manicure on the plastic tablecloth and wondered if I was lacking some gene that kept me from making deep female friends. My mother would probably say it had something to do with my job and the fact that I seldom took the time to do my hair and makeup.

Granny Bert slid into the booth across from me with a cup of coffee.

"Is there something wrong with me?" I asked.

"What?"

"Nothing, I'm just having a mother-daughter moment. I don't even have to be around Mom anymore. I can play both parts all by myself."

Granny patted my hand.

"Don't let Alice get you down. She wanted a passel full of girls and got a bucket full of boys and a tomboy instead. You can't live up to someone else's dream. All you can do is be yourself."

I smiled at Granny Bert and felt better than I had all day. Granny Bert's a wise, wise woman.

"Do you know Ann Marie very well?" I asked.

I was sure she would. Granny collects information about people like some folks collect glass figurines. It's her hobby.

"Ann Marie is a fine young woman. She's working her way through college. Only has one more year to go."

"I didn't know that."

"She's come a long way from that frail little thing that showed up down here a few years ago."

"What do you mean, Granny?"

"Ann Marie was married to a fella that smacked her around something awful. Liz tried to get her out of there when she first moved down to Alden, but Liz couldn't convince her to get away. She finally got her down here after the bastard nearly beat Ann Marie to death. She... well. I've said enough. Her story is hers to tell, but I'm real proud of her. She's finally getting her life straightened out."

"I thought Morgan was bad, but he never hit me."

"There's always somebody has it worse than you. At least you have family around."

I leaned across the table and gave Granny a kiss.

"I don't know what you've been doing with yourself lately, but you look like hell, Randi."

"Thanks, Granny," I said with a smile. "It's been a rough couple of days."

"Man trouble?" she asked.

"Not exactly."

"Anything I can do?"

I thought of Granny toe to toe with Jody and grinned. "I don't think so, but thanks. You ever see a guy in here wearing a cowboy hat and sunglasses?"

"Just Eddie Malcolm."

"This guy's not really a cowboy. At least I don't think so."

"Nobody in here with a cowboy hat but Eddie, why?"

"Guy comes in the bar sometimes. He's kind of creepy. I just wondered if you'd ever seen him."

"Sorry, hon. I'd remember if I did."

Loretta came in the front and I waved her back. Granny left, came back with a cup of coffee for Loretta, then went to the kitchen to get our food.

"Did you get it?" I asked.

"Yes, I got it. I was scared to death I was going to get caught. Jesus, you look like hell today."

"That seems to be the general consensus," I said.

She passed me the folder and I stuck it into my purse.

"So," she said. "Tell me what's going on."

"I can't right now, but I promise I'll tell you when I can."

Loretta sighed, "Okay. So, are you seeing AJ or what?"

"I don't know."

"You don't know?" she said enunciating each word precisely. She wasn't buying it.

I ignored her sarcasm and smiled as Granny slid plates down in front of us. Chicken fried steak and all the trimmings for me, chef salad for Loretta. Loretta started to eat. Just looking at the chicken fried steak made me feel better. God bless comfort food.

"Come on, Randi, are you and AJ a couple or what?"

"I told you I don't know."

"How could you not know? God, Randi, he's gorgeous, he's a nice guy. If AJ was interested in me, I sure wouldn't have to stop and think on it."

"He didn't run off and break your heart."

"Jeez, that was twenty years ago. Give the guy a break."

I sighed. "We'll see. Who are you dating now?"

"No one special."

"You only say that when it is someone special."

Loretta became real interested in her chef salad and ignored me. I let her eat in peace. She took one last bite and scooted out of the booth.

"Sorry I can't stay and chat. I gotta get back to the station.

"Hey, that's not fair. Who is it?"

"I'm not telling."

"Ooh, you must really like him a lot."

"I do."

"You might as well tell me, I could just ask Granny Bert."

"She doesn't know."

"Bet she does. She knows everything."

"She doesn't know this. I really do need to go, Randi. Maybe I'll see you at the bar later."

I waved as Loretta left and turned my attention back to lunch. I finished eating, promised Granny I'd bring the boys in for breakfast on Saturday, and drove to the house. Wilson patrolled the yard while I sat down at the table with Jody's file and tried to find a clue to what was going on.

I copied down his social security number, phone number, and address, stuck the file in my purse and invaded Travis's room once more. I pulled up Google and opened the people search sites again. There were a zillion of them. I clicked on ussearch.com, it looked the least like a scam, and plugged in everything I had on Jody. A few seconds and the site told me they had information as long as I had money. I plugged in my credit card number and waited. Instantly information started scrolling down the screen: former employers, school and military history, nothing that really told me much. He had a general discharge from the military. That was interesting, but my military contacts weren't going to help me this time. They were on the dark side. I went back over his former employers. Clark City police department leapt off the page at me. I smacked my forehead. I must be brain dead. Uncle Bill's the police chief there and I already knew Jody used to work for him. I hoped Loretta didn't find out that I didn't really need her information after all. I certainly wasn't going to tell her. I went into the kitchen, sat down with the phone and punched in the Clark City PD number. I hoped my cousin Deana answered.

"Clark City PD."

"Deana?"

"Who is this?"

"It's Randi."

"Randi, how are you?"

"I'm fine. You got a minute, I need some information."

"What kind?"

"I'm trying to find out something about a cop who used to work there. Jody McIntire."

"That bastard. What do you need information on him for?"

"He works down here now."

"God, I'm sorry. So what do you need?"

"He asked me for a date."

"Jesus, Randi. You do not want to go out with that guy."

Wilson barked at the door. I untangled myself from the phone cord and stretched to open it for him. He ran in and I shoved the door closed with my foot.

"Are you listening to me, Randi? Don't go."

"Why not?"

Dee spoke to someone on her end, then came back.

"Look, I can't talk right now, Dad's coming this way. Are you going to be at home tonight?"

"I have to work. Come down, we can talk at the bar. I really need to know what's going on with this guy."

"Okay, I'll be down, but it won't be till late."

"You can crash at my house, if you want."

"I'd better not, I'm supposed to work tomorrow. I'll come down for a while tonight, though."

I was a little spooked after listening to the ominous non-information from Ann Marie and then Deana. I wondered if there was any way to get them both to tell their stories to Chad. I'm sure Deana would talk to him, but Ann Marie, I doubted.

I wondered what information Deana had that she didn't want to share over the phone when the front door slammed. My heart jumped in my chest. Then I heard the boys clattering down the hall. Travis bounced into the room and grinned.

"Dad wants to know if you're working tonight."

I looked at the clock, shit, late again.

I hurried down the hall to change clothes. I pulled on a long-sleeved Henley, squeezed into a clean pair of jeans, and shoved my feet into tennis shoes. I threw a flannel shirt over the top to cover my holster and ran upstairs to ask the boys if their dad was taking them to the football game. He was, so I took off.

The road to the Jolly Roger was empty of traffic. I smiled. I might not be late after all. On the shoulder up ahead someone sat, knees up, arms draped across them, head down. I squinted and saw a backpack sitting on the ground next to him. It was Mouse and something was wrong. I angled off the pavement and stopped a few feet away. Mouse stiffened, but didn't raise his head. I stepped out of the car.

"Mouse. You okay?"

He looked up. Blood trickled from his nose. One eye was swollen shut. His normally spotless utilities were rumpled and grass stained, the spit-shined boots, spattered with mud. I grabbed a bottle of water off the seat and a handful of McDonald's napkins from the glove box and ran toward him.

"Who did this to you?" I asked.

He took the napkins from my hand and held them to his nose. I handed him the water. He poured it over his head, then took a drink.

"Mouse, what happened?"

He shook his head once, slowly, like it hurt.

"You need an ambulance or something? Should I call the cops?"

At the mention of cops, he jerked and pain etched creases through the mud and blood covering his face.

"No cops," he whispered.

"Did a cop do this to you?" I asked.

"Don't matta," he answered.

"Mouse, let me get you some help."

A car stopped across the road. I turned to look. Jody McIntire was staring at us. My blood went cold. I stifled the urge to race to my car and lock myself in. Mouse swallowed hard and glared back at him.

"Is that the guy that hurt you?" I asked.

"Twinkie, get the hell away from that guy," Jody yelled.

"He's been hurt, he needs help." I answered.

"You need any help, Rat?" Jody sneered.

Mouse gave the slow head shake again.

"Get the fuck outta here, then," Jody said.

Mouse eased slowly to his feet. I could see the pain on his face as he reached down for his pack. He hung it over his shoulder and started limping slowly down the road. I turned toward Jody.

"You just get in your little car and go home, Twinkie. That piece of shit don't need your help."

The window of Jody's car whispered closed and he whipped onto the road. I trotted over to catch Mouse.

"Mouse, let me give you a ride into town."

"You betta do as he says."

He clenched his teeth with pain as he hobbled along.

"You can't walk all the way home the shape you're in. Let me give you a ride."

He thought about it for a minute, then finally turned and followed me to AJ's car. He slumped in the passenger seat and I U-turned toward town. Mouse sat silently staring out the window.

"Mouse, you know who my brothers are?"

"Yes, ma'am."

"Let me tell them what happened to you."

"Don't matta. They cain't do nothin'."

"Dammit, Mouse. You can't let him get away with beating up an innocent citizen."

He turned away from the windshield and stared at me for a minute. I kept driving, waiting for him to answer.

"You can let me off here," he said.

"I can take you home, Mouse."

"Here's fine."

I sighed and pulled over.

"Let me get you some help, Mouse."

He stepped out of the car, grimacing with the effort, then he looked in at me.

"I don't need no help. I ain't much of a citizen and I definitely ain't innocent."

He slammed the door closed and slowly limped down the street. I smacked the steering wheel with my fist. Jody had no right to harass Mouse. The guy never hurt anybody. I drove away and turned toward the Roger. I was seriously late now. If I didn't watch myself, Morgan really was going to fire me.

Chapter 11

hurried into the bar expecting some smart remark from Lex for being late. Instead, I got concern.

"You okay?" he asked.

It stopped me in my tracks and my surprise must have shown.

"You just look a little pale."

"I'm okay, but thanks."

I stashed my purse in the safe and joined him behind the bar. This day had already been a week long. I hoped I was up to the Friday night madness. The rush starts around five and it was going pretty well by the time I got there. It wouldn't even start easing up until after ten. And Lex and I were on our own. Morgan had the boys tonight.

By eight, the tables were all full and the bar was stacked two deep with cops. Two brutal murders in less than a week had those guys looking for escape. I didn't think they were going to find it at the Roger. Thanks to an article in today's paper, it was all anyone was talking about. There seemed to be lots of theories, but nothing really new that I could pick out of the chatter.

Chad came in for a beer around nine and sat down in front of me.

"We need to talk."

"Can't right now, Chadly. Too busy. You want a beer?"

He glared across the bar at me. I took a step back. He spun away and included the bar in his dirty look. Deana arrived while he was still scanning the room. There was a crush at the bar, so she gave me a little finger wave as she grabbed a drink and went to the mezzanine to throw darts until the mob downstairs thinned out. I didn't get a chance to talk to either of them till after ten. When it finally slowed down, I leaned against the bar behind Chad.

"What's up, Chad?"

"I want to know what the fuck you thought you were doing letting Mouse in your car."

"What?"

"Don't you ever stop to think before you do anything?"

"Somebody beat the shit out of him, he could barely move. All I did was give him a ride to town. You want to yell at someone, talk to Jody. He's the one that beat the crap out of Mouse."

"I'll deal with Jody later. Right now, I'm talking to you. Stay away from Mouse."

"Chad, what the hell's wrong with you?"

Our voices were low; no one could hear what we were saying. That we were arguing was obvious by our body language. No one came close or interrupted.

"Randi, you don't know anything about that guy, just stay away from him."

"Mouse has been around almost as long as I can remember. He collects aluminum cans and spends the afternoons hanging out with Harold swapping war stories. I'm pretty sure he's no threat."

"God dammit, Randi. He did ten years in Leavenworth for rape and assault."

I stepped away from the bar and banged into the liquor shelves. The bottles clanked against each other. I stared at Chad and swallowed. "I didn't know that," I whispered.

"There're a lot of things you don't know, Randi. Stay away from my case, and stay away from Mouse."

"I didn't think it was your case."

"Everybody is working on the murders. We've got meter maids running down leads on this thing."

I stepped forward and leaned on the cooler. Chad was still glaring. I poured a beer, drank off almost half, and poured the rest down the sink.

"How long have you known about Mouse, Chad?"

"I don't know, long time."

"Why didn't you ever tell me?"

"Didn't think you'd ever be around him."

"Been nice to know that kind of thing."

"For Pete's sake, Randi. Why would you need to know that? When were you ever going to be around Mouse?"

"I don't know."

I spun away from Chad and made a tour through the tables picking up empties. I tossed them in the trash and eased back behind the bar. Chad had a beer in front of him. He took a sip and centered it on the coaster in front of him.

"I don't think Mouse did it, Chad."

"Yeah, I know. You think it's Jody."

"I was telling the truth this morning."

"He tells the story a little bit differently."

"Oh, so now you're going to believe that asshole over your own sister?"

"Dammit, Randi, give me a break. You've put me in a terrible position here. It's just your word against his. If you want to file a report against him, we can do that. But without any evidence, all we have is your statement against his and like it or not, Jody's a cop. When push comes to shove, they'll take his word before yours. It's not fair, but that's the way it works."

I sighed in frustration. He was right and I knew it. I was going to come off the loser if I tried to butt heads with Jody, he had a badge to back him up. I almost motioned Deana down to talk to Chad, but even if he believed whatever she had to say, there still wasn't any evidence to support my claim. Until I had something concrete to show the police, I was on my own.

I flicked a towel across the surface of the bar wiping an imaginary spill and left Chad to nurse his beer.

Forewarned is forearmed. I'd just have to deal with Jody without Chad's help.

I looked up from my contemplation of the bar rag and caught Chad watching me.

"What?"

"I believe you, Ran, but I've got nothing to go on here. You could file a restraining order if you want."

"Will it keep him away from me?"

"Not if he wants to get close to you. It does give me a leg to stand on if he keeps bothering you."

"What do you think I should do, Chadly?"

Chad sighed before he answered. "I don't know, Ran. I...I believe what you've told me, okay. But, I know Jody. I work with him. I don't think I'm a good one to give you advice here. I'm caught in the middle and I don't really know what you should do."

"Maybe we can talk about it later, after I think it over."

"Yeah, we could do that."

Kira stepped up to the bar with her tray and rattled off an order. Tonight she was dressed all in black with silver trim. She looked like an old black and white photo that the silver had started to leach out of. I filled her order and made change while she drooled over Chad. He didn't notice.

"She has the hots for you, Chadly. She told me."

He turned to stare at Kira, then back at me. The expression on his face was priceless. I laughed and refilled his glass. It felt good to laugh, a little of the tension that had clenched my gut since morning trickled away.

"Tell me about the new murder. The paper said you'd caught the killer, but that's not what scuttlebutt says and I haven't seen Steve or AJ here celebrating yet."

"The paper got it wrong, as usual."

"You guys did arrest somebody, though, right?"

"No. We questioned somebody."

"So you think the same person killed both women?"

"Yeah, the same sicko did the job. No evidence, no clues, no nothing. At least nothing we could use by the time we got to the scene. She'd been dead a while, probably a week or so before Lisa. There wasn't a lot of evidence left for us to work with."

Chad emptied his beer and handed me the glass. "I need to go, Ran. Let me know what you decide. I'll walk you through the process if that's what you want to do."

"I'll call ya."

I waved him out and went back to work. Things were slowing down. I was washing glasses while Lex kept up with the few diehards still at the bar. My feet were aching even in my tennis shoes, and I needed toothpicks to hold my eyes open. Lex put a cheeseburger and fries on the bar in front of me.

"Take a break, angel."

I smiled my thanks and sank gratefully onto a stool. "I'm almost too tired to eat."

"You'll feel better if you do," he said, stealing a fry.

"Probably."

I picked up the burger for a bite. I was so tired I had to tell myself to chew. Kira dropped her tray on the bar and leaned in, one foot propped on the rail. Deana took the stool next to me and Lex poured her a beer.

"Hey Randi, I got something for ya," Kira said. "I meant to give it to you earlier, but we got busy and I forgot."

She reached into her pocket, pulled out a small, black silk pouch with a silver drawstring and handed it across the bar. I opened the little bag and tipped the contents onto the bar. Four rocks rolled across the surface.

"Well, uh, thanks, Kira. I guess."

"These crystals are going to help you so much. I picked them out especially for you."

She poked at the four stones and picked up one.

"This one is clear quartz. It raises your energy level and keeps you tuned into your spiritual side." She dropped that one in the bag and picked up a purple one. "This one is Amethyst. It's good for easing stress and healing bruises or strains. The black one is Hematite. It absorbs bad energy, the other one is a tiger-eye. It's good for clearing confusion."

She dropped the last three stones into the bag with the clear quartz, pulled it closed, and handed it back to me.

"You'll need to cleanse those crystals before you use them. I can come over to your house sometime and show you how if you want."

Dee was biting her lip to keep from laughing. Lex scooted down the bar and busied himself filling the beer cooler. I tucked the silk bag into the pocket of my jeans and thanked Kira again for thinking of me. Dee snorted into her glass and I sent her a glare.

"Did you ever find those girls you were looking for?" Kira asked.

"Yeah, I talked to them."

"Sorry I couldn't help more, I just don't pay that much attention. If it's not somebody that's here all the time, I just don't notice."

"Yeah, I know, it's crazy here. Especially on Friday nights." Truth was, Kira's radar just wasn't tuned to females. The number of people in the bar at the time had little to do with it.

Kira floated off to coax tips from the remaining drunks, as Dee reached over and grabbed a French fry from my plate.

"That one for confusion ought to really be a help for ya, cuz," she said.

I punched her in the shoulder and put a protective arm around my plate as I finished my burger. I savored the last bite and reluctantly joined Lex behind the bar. Deana scooted over in front of the sink where I was working and got serious.

"So, tell me the story of Jody McIntire," I said.

"He was a good cop. The guys all liked him a lot. But he's screwed up, too many steroids or something. He has a real short temper. Tends to be a little rough on suspects; they come in with a lot of extra bruises. Not just guys either. He even smacks around the women."

"He didn't get in trouble for that?"

"He always had some story. The perp fell down some stairs or tripped. Something. It was always weak and he always got away with it."

She glanced around to see if anyone was listening and placed her glass carefully on the bar.

"Did he really ask you for a date, Randi?"

"Uh-huh."

I had stopped washing glasses and was just talking to Deana. Lex was watching us from the corner of his eye. Deana put her hand on my arm.

"Don't go out with him."

I jumped. Her intensity surprised me.

"I'm not going to, he scares me. He snuck into my house while I was taking a shower. It's like I'm being stalked."

Deana bit her lip. "He left Clark City because he ended up in some trouble over a woman."

"What kind of trouble?"

Deana took a breath and blew it out.

"He asked a female officer for a date. She wouldn't go, so he started stalking her. She and I were good friends. She told me some of the stuff he said."

"Like what?"

"Like, I really dig chicks with guns. Or, you can't resist me forever, Twinkie."

My face blanched.

Dee nodded. "I see he hasn't gotten any new lines. You need to tell someone, Randi. He's dangerous. He scared Marie so bad she quit the force and moved out of state. She said she would wake up and he'd be in her house, or she'd find notes on her pillow. It was creepy. She was terrified."

"I told Chad. But I don't have any proof. There's nothing I can say that Jody can't refute."

"That's the way it was in Clark City. Marie went to her superior and filed a harassment complaint. Jody blew it off. All the guys sided with him. She didn't have a chance. Nobody ever saw him do anything. There was never any evidence, just her word against his."

"I can't believe Uncle Bill would let that go on."

"It never made it that far. I offered to tell him, but Marie was afraid. The guys were all pissed off at her anyway because of the harassment thing. She said it wasn't worth it. She wasn't going to be able to be a cop around there anymore. It sucks, but she was probably right. The guys would have made her life a living hell."

"That's bullshit, Deana."

"I know. She didn't even tell me where she moved. I haven't talked to her since she left. Jody took some heat over the harassment charge. They didn't follow up on it, though. Marie left and Jody put in his notice. I guess that's when he came down here. Be careful, Randi. He's weird. He likes being a cop. It's all a big power trip to him."

"Where did he work before he came to Clark City?"

"He was in Kentucky somewhere. When I tried to get information from them, I got stonewalled. I think he did the same thing there, but I couldn't really squeeze much out of them. Didn't matter. By that time, he was getting ready to leave and Marie was already gone."

"Thanks, Deana."

"I don't know how much help it's been. He's still bothering you."

"At least I know what's going on. I was beginning to think I was nuts. Chad's convinced I just want him to beat up the latest guy that's pestering me, and everybody else thinks Jody is a great guy. Do you think I should file a restraining order against him?"

"I don't know, Ran. If you do, it's gonna piss him off. Might just make things worse. It gives you some protection because, if he continues to harass you, you can take legal action. He's smart though, and I think he'd still find a way to get to you. I'm not sure it's enough benefit to counteract how angry he would be. That piece of paper won't do you much good if you're dead."

"Do you think...Geez, Dee. Dead."

"I shouldn't have said that. I didn't mean to scare you worse, It's just that I've worked a lot of domestic cases where a restraining order just seemed to be the match that lit the fire. It's not much of a weapon. I think staying on your guard and telling your friends and family what's going on will do you more good and cause less backlash. You have to do what feels right, but I think in this case it might be the wrong tack to take."

"Thanks Dee. I think." I wasn't sure if talking to her had made me feel better or worse.

Deana glanced at the clock and drained her glass.

"I need to go, Ran. Come up some weekend. We'll go into St. Louis, catch a ballgame or something."

"I will. Sure you don't want to spend the night?"

"No, thanks though. Be careful, girl."

"Always. See ya."

Deana moved toward the door. When I turned back, Lex was watching her walk away. I grinned.

"Her Dad's a police chief. Both her brothers are cops."

He turned toward me and laughed.

"All the chicks in your family that well protected?"

"I guess so. There's only Deana and I."

"Enough to make a man give up on women."

Surely, that comment was just about Dee. Lex wasn't interested in me that way. Okay so he'd grabbed my butt a few times, but that was just him being a jerk. I took another quick glance at him. Nah, he was definitely talking about Dee. I started in on my sink full of dirty glasses again. The bar was almost empty and I was counting down the seconds until we could lock up. With just minutes to go before last call, Jody strolled in and took a seat at the bar. I stiffened as Deana's words tripped through my mind—won't do you much good if your dead. Shit. My heart rate shot up into stroke range. I took a deep breath and tried to retrieve the calm I'd spent all day cultivating.

"Hey, Twinkie. How 'bout a beer?"

I pulled a draw, threw down a coaster, and slammed down the glass. Beer sloshed over the rim and soaked the little cardboard disc. Jody drained half of it and smiled at me.

"Ahhh. That really hits the spot."

I moved away to take care of someone else. Every time I looked up, Jody was staring at me. It was like being on display.

I hollered last call and Jody tipped his glass at me. I pulled him another draft and walked over to Lex's end of the bar.

"Who's the fireplug that keeps staring at you?" Lex asked.

"Jody McIntire. He's a cop."

"You don't seem all that happy to see him."

"He's an asshole."

"Want me to kill him?" Lex asked.

"Hmm, tempting, but I guess not."

I hoped that was a joke. With Lex, you couldn't really be sure.

Kira escorted the last drunk outside. Jody still sat at the end of the bar. "We need to lock up, Jody, time to go." I said.

"I'll just wait for you. AJ and Steve are tied up, they sent me to play bodyguard tonight."

My stomach muscles contracted. There's no way I was leaving with this guy.

"That's real nice of you, Jody, but I'll be fine."

"Nope. No can do. AJ asked me to see that you arrived home safe and sound."

He smiled and a chill crawled up my spine.

"Thanks anyway, Jody. I'll be fine."

"I'm staying, Twinkie."

This time he wasn't smiling.

"The lady said she doesn't need your services," Lex said over my shoulder. "I suggest you leave."

"And if I don't. What you gonna do? Call the cops?" he sneered.

"I don't need to call the cops. I can take care of you myself."

Lex was standing so close I could feel his body tense. I stepped to one side and saw he was up on the balls of his feet ready to go over the bar if needed. He could get over in a heartbeat; I'd seen him do it to break up fights. Since he hired Lex, Morgan didn't even keep a bouncer. Jody and Lex locked stares. Jody broke first. Lex kept his gaze lasered in on him until he eased off the barstool and stalked out.

"I'll see you later, Twinkie," he called over his shoulder as he pushed through the door.

I rammed the deadbolt home behind him, and sank down onto a barstool. Lex handed me a beer.

"I think that boy's done a few too many steroids."

"Thanks for getting rid of him."

My voice was shaky. Hell, so were my hands. I watched as Lex finished cleaning up the back bar. He handed me the cash drawer and I started on the deposit. I had to restart three times, before I got the money counted. My mind was not in top form. I divided the tips and Lex shoved his half in the front pocket of his jeans. I locked the deposit in the safe and walked out into the bar.

"You preparing for war?" Lex asked, as I snapped my 9mm into its holster.

"I'm preparing for Jody."

"Not a good idea to shoot a cop."

"I'll try not to kill him." I said with a grin.

It probably came off more like a grimace, but I was trying. Lex trailed me outside and locked up behind us.

"Lex, would you mind following me home?"

"I could do that."

"Thanks."

I started the Mustang and sat in the lot until the headlights came on in Lex's truck. He trailed me through town and stopped at the curb when I pulled into my drive.

"You want me to come in with you?"

I shook my head.

"I'll stay till you're inside."

"Thanks."

I turned and started fitting the key into the lock. My hands trembled and the keys dropped to the porch with a clatter. Jody was getting into my house. Maybe it was time to install an alarm system. That seemed a little much for

Alden. People would think I was nuts. Even the cops in the family would think I was being overly cautious. Besides, I couldn't afford an alarm system. I still needed to get the roof fixed. Wilson barked on the other side of the door. I took a deep cleansing breath, Kira would have been so proud of me. Then I squatted down to pick up the keys and gave the lock another try. The key slid in and turned with a click. Lex hollered a question as I turned the knob.

"Hey, did you know there's a cat on your roof?"

I laughed. "Yeah, I know."

I waved goodnight and stepped inside as Lex drove away. Wilson ran through my legs and bounced up and down as I made my way to the kitchen. He went out for his run and I paced around the house turning on lights, searching under beds and inside closets. No unwanted visitors, just dust bunnies. I finished and turned all the lights off, let Wilson in, and sat down at the kitchen table. My 9mm rested on the table in front of me. My .32 was in the holster at the small of my back. I huddled in the dark, listening to my heartbeat. When the front door opened, my heart rate doubled. I stumbled to my feet, set myself in a shooter's stance, and snapped the action on the nine. The person at the door stopped at the sound.

"Randi?"

I blew out my breath in relief and sagged onto the chair.

"Come on in, AJ."

"Why are you sitting in the dark with your gun?"

"Why don't you ever knock?"

"Sorry, the lights were out, I thought you were asleep."

"Where'd you get the key?"

"Chad gave it to me when I told him I was stopping by. He said you'd probably be in bed, and I didn't want to get busted breaking into your house. I'll give it back to Chad tomorrow or give it to you."

"You might as well just keep it."

"So, darlin', you gonna tell me why you're sitting in the dark with your gun?"

"I...um. Have you talked to Chad today?"

"About what?"

"About me. Did he tell you anything?"

"Randi, what are you talking about?"

"There was a guy at the bar tonight that really gave me the creeps, so I had Lex follow me home. But I was still kind of freaked out, so I was just sitting here. Working up the nerve to go to bed I guess." Before AJ could ask for details, I walked over and hugged him.

"I'm really glad you're here."

I should have told him all of it, but I still hadn't figured out what I wanted to do about Jody. I didn't want AJ involved until I made a decision. I should have told him then and there, but at the time, my reasoning made perfect sense.

"What are you doing here, AJ? It's after three."

"I thought I might sneak in, finish what we started this morning."

"That was actually yesterday morning."

"Okay, I'm here to finish what we started yesterday morning."

"Could I get a rain check? I think I'm too tired to enjoy it."

"Are the boys home?"

"No, they're at Morgan's."

"Hmm. How about I spend the night and we finish up in the morning after you're all rested."

"That's the best offer I've had all day."

"But I don't have to sleep on the couch, right?"

I laughed. "You don't have to sleep on the couch."

AJ smiled and kissed me again. God, I must not be tired, I must be dead. It was a serious kiss, but I just wished he'd stop so I could go to bed.

Chapter 12

A slamming door snapped my eyes open what seemed like minutes later. I blinked at the clock on my bedside table, but couldn't decipher the glowing shapes. Noises from the kitchen invaded—the open and close of the refrigerator, the smack of a banging cabinet door. Eight a.m. my brain finally transmitted. The warm body next to mine moved and I was suddenly and completely alert. My lips curved into a smile as I rolled toward AJ.

"You've got raccoon eyes, babe," he said.

"And you need a shave."

His left hand slid beneath my tee shirt and traveled up until his thumb brushed my nipple.

"That's not all I need, darlin'."

He leaned toward me for a kiss as Devin stuck his head into the bedroom. We sprang apart like guilty teenagers.

"Mom, Uncle Steve's on his way. We're supposed to be at The War Zone at eleven. Hey, AJ."

"Morning, Dev."

Devin closed the door and disappeared.

"That was rather uncomfortable," AJ said as he got up.

"It could have been worse."

"Not likely. I think I'm doomed to an eternity without sex."

I laughed and scooted up to sit against the headboard as AJ stepped into his Levi's.

"Did I know about the game at the War Zone today?" I asked.

"I don't know about you, but I didn't. I had other plans for this morning."

"Rain check." I said with a smile.

He dropped a kiss on my forehead.

"Oh, you can count on that, darlin'."

He zipped his fly and left the bedroom to find out from the boys what was going on. I dressed in jeans and a tee shirt, combed my hair, removed my raccoon makeup, and joined them in the kitchen. As I walked in, they all started chattering at once. I held up a hand for quiet.

"First order of business, we go to Mabel's for breakfast. I promised Granny Bert."

"Ah, Mom!" the boys chimed in concert.

"Sorry guys, has to be done."

"But Mom, Uncle Steve is on his way here right now."

That was Devin. I glanced at the clock. It was only twenty after eight.

"I'm pretty sure we have time to eat. You said we weren't supposed to play until eleven."

"But we have to change clothes and get all our gear together..."

"Travis, enough. We're going to Mabel's."

"But what if Uncle Steve doesn't want to go?" Devin asked in a small hopeful voice.

"Then he can wait for us here."

Both boys geared up for more argument, so I shot them with the mom look and they retreated into silence before trudging from the kitchen and up the stairs to their rooms. I dropped into Devin's vacated chair and looked at AJ.

"Do you know what's going on yet?" I asked.

"Not really, guess we'll find out from Steve when he gets here."

I got up and grabbed a Pepsi from the fridge while AJ made coffee. As AJ was pouring a cup from the completed pot, Steve knocked and walked in. AJ grabbed a second mug and filled it for Steve before he sat down.

"Why aren't you guys ready to go?" Steve asked.

"Well, good morning to you too, Stevie. Did you forget to tell us we were playing paintball today?" I asked.

"I left a message on your cell phone last night."

"Oh, I didn't check my messages after work. The first I heard about it was when the boys came in this morning."

"Yeah, I called Morgan and asked him to drop them off if they didn't have any plans. He has a meeting with a real estate agent in Ashland this morning, so he said he'd bring them home on his way."

"Well, I'm glad the two of you saw fit to let me know the boys weren't spending the weekend with their dad. Did it ever occur to you I might have made plans?"

"But Morgan said he only picked up the boys last night for the football game because you were scheduled to work."

"That's not the point, Steve. You guys just went around making plans and nobody bothered to check with me."

"But Morgan said..."

"Steve, I don't give a porcupine fuck what Morgan said. You should have checked with me."

Behind me, AJ choked into his coffee cup as he tried to swallow his laughter.

"But I left you a message..."

"Dude, you're not gonna win this one," AJ said laughing out loud. "Just apologize and move on."

"But..." Steve looked at AJ, then at me, and blew out his breath. "I'm sorry, Randi."

"Thank you. Now, want to fill us in on our plan of the day?"

Steve sank into a kitchen chair and took a gulp from his coffee cup. AJ winked at me and tried to hide his smile. Steve cleared his throat and started to speak.

"Um, I ran into Harold yesterday afternoon at Happy Harry's. He said things were pretty slow at the Zone. Even though the crime scene had been released, there hadn't been anyone out to play. He asked if we wanted to come out for a game. I told him I could probably get some people together. I told him you might not want to play in the woods, so we would use the urban venue."

"That was sweet, Steve. Thank you." Ugh, I hate the urban course.

"Then you'll play, I mean, do you want to play... today?"

I didn't really want to play paintball, especially not an urban game. But, I figured AJ wasn't going to get out of it even if I said I wasn't going. That ruled out the chance of getting back to our morning plans, so I told Steve I would go. He smiled in relief, like it was vitally important that I be part of the game. I'm not; I'm the weakest player, but I guess every team needs some cannon fodder. If they were shooting at me, no one else was being fired on.

"Good," Steve said. "Great. I'll just holler at the boys and have them start getting their stuff together."

"Whoa there, Colonel. First we're going to Mabel's for breakfast. I already promised Granny Bert."

Steve's face fell and he looked just like the boys when I'd relayed the same message to them earlier. I had trouble trying not to laugh.

Just then, Chad came through the front door. AJ got up to pour another cup of coffee. The boys heard him come in and ran down from upstairs.

"Steve, why don't you call Sara Beth and have her meet us at Mabel's for breakfast?"

He sighed and walked outside with his phone to make the call. When he came back in, we left for Mabel's. Devin rode with Chad, Travis and Steve squeezed into the backseat of the Mustang. Steve told us on the ride to town that Sara and the kids were going to meet us, as well as the rest of the players. Before I could ask him who else was playing, Travis asked him a question about his new paintball gun.

Lex pulled up beside Chad as we parked outside the restaurant. Before we got inside, Sara Beth drove up with the kids. Steve waited for them by the door while the rest of us headed for the big double booth in the rear corner. We were sorting ourselves into seats when Jody walked in. I elbowed Chad before he could slide into the booth.

"What's he doing here?" I asked.

"He's playing with us today," Steve answered before Chad could say anything.

Chad squeezed my arm in warning before I could tear in to Steve.

"How the hell did he get invited to our game?" I growled at Chad.

"Steve asked him before he even talked to me. What was I supposed to say, Ran? Steve doesn't know what's been going on with Jody."

That brought me up short. He didn't say, "Steve doesn't know what you told me." Chad believed my story. Just knowing I wasn't the only one that thought Jody was a menace and a killer made me feel better.

"He's not the killer," he said reading my thoughts.

I looked away from Chad and found Jody smiling across the room at me. I gave him a PMS glare, but it didn't have any effect. I must need a refresher course.

Chad slipped away from my side as Sara Beth and I scooted onto the seat. I looked over and saw him give Becca's long black braid a tug as he leaned in to speak to Liz. Becca's giggles rang out across the restaurant. Chad came back wearing a small smile on his face, like he knew a joke that he wasn't sharing.

"Business?" I asked as he sat down.

"What? Oh, yeah, business."

His blush told me he was lying. Before I could pick at him about the blush, Granny Bert came over to visit. She left lipstick kisses on my boys and my brothers and scooted back to the kitchen to place our orders. Chad studiously avoided me by talking across the table to Lex.

Granny Bert came out of the kitchen a little while later with plates balanced the length of both arms, passed them around and went back for coffee. While we dug into breakfast, Steve outlined our battle plan.

"We're playing an urban game today," he said.

I knew that; Steve had told me at the house. And I knew he did it for me, but I really hate urban games. I wondered if it was too late to talk AJ into skipping the game and going back home to bed. Probably, but it was a nice fantasy. I smiled to myself and dug into my breakfast.

Everyone was talking. It seemed like ten different conversations were going on. Jody was at his most charming and had Steve and AJ laughing almost too much to eat. I noticed Chad's smile and laughter seemed a little forced. I hoped he was watching Jody with a different mind set, even if he didn't think he was a killer.

The conversation settled down a little as everyone got serious about their food. Steve used the lull to start sharing game details. Steve gives a lot of details. The guys were rapt with interest. My kids were enthralled. I stifled a yawn. I kept my focus on my plate so Steve wouldn't notice my inattention. Another reason was that Jody was sitting right across the table staring at me. Even when he'd been busy entertaining everyone else, his gaze spent a good deal of time on me. I could almost feel his eyes boring into the top of my head. When I forgot and looked up, the slimy bastard winked.

"What's with him?" Sara Beth whispered to me. "Steve really likes him, but he kind of gives me the creeps."

"Me too. I don't like him at all."

"If AJ catches him staring at you like that there's going to be bloodshed."

"Nah, AJ likes him. All the guys do."

"Well I don't like him. I hope Steve doesn't think he's gonna invite him over to my house."

I smiled as Sara turned back to her plate, and wondered if Jody gave off invisible creep waves that only women could pick up. Before I could ask her, Nathan slipped away from Steve and crawled under the table. A minute later, his blond curls popped up next to Jody.

"Get outta here, kid," Jody snarled.

Sara dropped her fork and glared at Jody, her hand twitched like she wanted to slap him.

Nathan cocked his head at Jody. "You're not very nice," he said.

"No, he's not," Sara said.

Jody ducked his head at Sara and smiled. "Sorry, I'm not used to children."

"So I noticed."

He gave Nathan an awkward pat on the head. Nathan looked like he wanted to bite Jody's hand.

"Come on over here, Nathan, you can sit with me."

"I want to sit with Aunt Randi, too." Julie said.

Steve cleared his throat.

"You can sit over here, too, Jules."

I winked, ignoring Steve's glare, and patted the seat next to me. The table went silent as we moved the kids and rearranged the plates around the table.

"Are you finished, Randi?" Steve asked.

"Just a minute."

Steve sighed and waited impatiently for us to get settled. While Julie squeezed in between her mother and me, I tucked Nathan on my other side. When the kids were busy with their breakfast again, I smiled and told Steve he could continue.

He gave me an *it's about time* look and went on with his elaborate battle scenario. I ignored him and finished eating while Nathan prattled in my ear about his new kitten.

We finally made it through the meal and went back to the house to turn ourselves into commandos. That's not much of a stretch for my brothers; they are commandos. I suspect it's not much of a stretch for Lex either. My boys, growing up with this stuff, take to it naturally. Me, I feel a little silly dressed like a SWAT cop.

We converged at The War Zone an hour later. My heart made a little lurch as a piece of forgotten police tape fluttered in the breeze. That was the only sign left that an investigation had taken place in the area. Lisa's face flashed across my mind as Steve outlined the teams and went over the mission one more time. I shook off thoughts of the dead girl and tuned in as Steve droned on.

"For God's sake, let's just break some paint," I muttered under my breath.

AJ heard me and snickered. Steve glanced over and I rearranged my face to show the interest he deserved. AJ watched the transformation and broke into a fit of coughing to cover his laughter.

Basically, it amounted to this: Devin, Steve, Chad and Lex were the bad guys. Travis, AJ, Jody and I were the good guys. I tried not to gag when I found out Jody was on my team.

The playing field for this game was an old farmhouse, a barn, and a bunch of wrecked mobile homes—a real redneck haven. We loaded our weapons and gave the bad guys twenty minutes to get set before we started our attack. We huddled together for AJ to give us our battle orders. AJ kneeled and drew a map in the dirt with his finger. Travis stood next to him. I leaned forward so I could see, and Jody pressed close behind me to watch over my shoulder. I stiffened as his body touched mine and heard him chuckle.

"Jody, you'll scout forward and signal when it's safe to move," AJ said. "Travis, you'll..."

I didn't hear the rest. Jody's hand had come to rest on my hip. I took a quick step back and landed firmly on his instep. He yelped. I stifled a grin.

"God, Jody. I'm sorry. I'm such a klutz."

AJ glanced up from where he and Travis were drawing in the dirt.

"Sorry. I stepped on Jody's foot."

AJ shook his head and finished telling Travis what to do. Jody gave me the evil eye as we scattered to take our places.

Travis and I were together on the backside of one of the mobile homes waiting for everyone to get into position.

"That Jody guy was at the baseball party the other night, wasn't he?" Travis asked.

"Yeah, he was."

"I don't like him, there's something fake about him."

"I don't like him either."

I wanted to get into it with Travis and find out what kind of vibes he was getting. Teenagers have an almost infallible bullshit detector, but Jody was in place so it was almost time to start the game.

A whistle sounded signaling our guys were all in position. Jody was forty feet or so in front of me, hidden behind a big oak tree. I couldn't see AJ. I suspected he had climbed onto the roof of one of the buildings ahead of us. He wasn't that far away. If I'd known that, I might not have done what I did, but my little devil got the best of me. As Travis and I waited for Jody to signal us, I took aim.

"Watch this," I whispered to Travis.

Jody motioned us forward and stepped from behind his tree. I pulled the trigger and a paintball spat from the barrel of my gun and hit Jody right in the back of the head.

"God dammit! Son of a Bitch." Jody yelled, and threw his paintball gun to the ground.

It was a one in a million shot. One I couldn't duplicate if I'd tried. I'd wanted to pop one on the tree or the ground around him, just to get him to hit the dirt. Instead, I'd taken him out of the game.

Whoops.

Travis was crouched behind the mobile home in a fit of giggles. I ducked down next to him and hoped Jody hadn't seen who fired.

"Nice shot, Mom," Travis whispered and snickered again.

That got me laughing and we huddled on the ground trying to stay quiet. Our laughter ended abruptly when a hand snatched the back of my shirt and jerked me to my feet. I gulped. Shit, captured already. I turned to see who the hand belonged to. It was AJ, and he wasn't very happy with me. He'd seen the whole thing from the top of the building we were hiding behind. So much for him being somewhere out in front.

"What the hell was that all about?" he snapped.

"It was an accident," I sputtered.

Travis exploded into another fit of almost silent laughter and I joined him. AJ dragged us underneath the mobile home and told us to be quiet. Travis and I shook as the giggles bubbled up and tried to escape. Sometimes the harder you try not to laugh the worse it gets, but AJ wasn't laughing. He glared Travis into silence and I finally gathered myself together.

"Now, do you mind telling me what that was all about?"

I almost said it was an accident, but I was afraid if I said that again, Travis and I would both break down.

"I didn't mean to hit him; I just wanted him to dive."

"He's on our team, Randi."

"That guy's a dick," Travis said.

I snorted. Travis turned away so he didn't start laughing again.

"Look, I didn't mean to hit him, AJ. But I'm not sorry he's out of the game. I can't stand that guy."

"What do you have against Jody?"

"I thought we were playing paintball, not twenty questions."

"Randi?"

"He's stalking me, okay?"

AJ stepped back like he'd been slapped. His hand dropped the hold he had on my shirt, and he stared at me in disbelief.

"Stalking you?"

"Stalking, harassing, whatever you want to call it. He's bugging me, I asked him to stop and he's still doing it."

"Randi, cops don't stalk."

"Right, I forgot. Cops are perfect."

"I didn't say that, Randi."

"Look, just forget it; let's just get back to the game so I can go home."

Paintballs were popping against the house and the trailers up ahead.

"Uh, guys," Travis said. "You might want to wrap this up."

"We'll continue this discussion later," AJ said.

"Why don't we just go home and continue it now?"

AJ's eyes crinkled at the corners as he smiled.

"Tempting, but we're already here."

Oh well, it was worth a shot. I scooped up my gun from where I'd dropped it when AJ grabbed my shirt.

"Trav, you and I will go around and try to get them out in the open," AJ said. "Randi, since you like to sit in the shadows and shoot, you can be our sniper."

"Watch out you don't get in my line of fire, AJ."

"You wouldn't shoot me, darlin'," he said with a wink.

"Don't count on it," I mumbled as he slipped off into the shadows.

I crawled out from under the mansion on wheels and climbed the oak tree Jody had used for cover. Jody stared up from the weeds at the edge of the field and flipped me off. Hmm, not in your wildest dreams, scumbag.

I pointed my gun at him and his eyes got wide behind his mask. I snickered and started scanning for targets. In the distance, I could see Steve working his way around one of the mobile homes. I took aim and waited for him to get into shooting range. He came around the corner and I splattered him with red paint.

"Good, that evens things up."

Devin leaned from a window of the farmhouse and I shot him on the top of his head. He jerked off his hat, frowned at it, and threw it down. Two down, two to go. I hadn't seen Lex. I thought he might be the most dangerous one. I climbed down from the tree and snuck around the nearest mobile home. I was looking over my shoulder and ran right into AJ. He caught me before I fell and held me close.

"I don't think we have time for this right now, darlin'."

I rolled my eyes. "I hit Steve and Devin. You have any idea where Chad and Lex are?"

"Chad is out, Travis hit him. Lex is tough. He's invisible."

We met up with Travis and regrouped. While we were planning our next move, a paintball splattered above my head.

"Shit." I ducked and slithered under the porch. Travis hit the deck and crawled under one of the trailers. AJ scooted in next to me.

"This is cozy," he said.

"Would be better if no one was shooting at us."

"You and Travis cover me. I know where he is and I think I know where he's going."

I joined Travis under his trailer, gave him the game plan, and we slithered out to get into position. AJ bounced from cover to cover. Travis and I tried to stay close enough to give him covering fire, but mostly he was on his own. As I ran toward an old burned-out car, paint balls pelted the area around me. I dove behind the wreck and checked myself for paint. Still clean. I peered through the broken side window of the car and took a direct hit to the facemask. Gogged, dammit. I sagged to the ground, the car at my back and tried to catch my breath. I'm really not in good enough shape to do this.

I heard someone give a whoop and recognized AJ. Great, we won. Now we could go home. I stood and headed toward the sound of AJ's yell. I stepped past the big oak, fumbling the barrel plug into my gun. Jody grabbed me by the shirt collar and jerked me against the tree. My gun smacked against the trunk. The hopper popped open and deposited paintballs into a pile at my feet.

"Shooting me wasn't very nice, Twinkie."

"Better than you deserve."

"You can't win against me."

"I know why you left your last job."

"Doesn't matter, no one here is going to believe you. They all think I'm a peach of a guy."

"That's fine. I'll take care of you myself if I have to."

"Bitch."

"I can be, now let me go. I won't have to take care of you if AJ catches you man-handling me." Maybe.

"I thought you two were just friends," Jody snarled.

"Commandos make nice friends."

"Fuck you!" Jody said slamming me against the tree. My head smacked into the bark, the mask perched on top of my head slid over my face and I dropped my gun.

I shoved the mask back up on my head as I watched Jody stalk off, then leaned down to gather my gun and barrel plug from the base of the tree. Jeez, that had hurt. I rubbed the back of my head and ambled along slowly. I wasn't in any hurry to catch Jody; he scared the hell out of me.

I finally met up with the rest of the group. AJ draped an arm over my shoulders. Jody sent ten-thousand watt death rays in my direction. Lex caught his look and sidled over behind Jody. He whispered something in his ear. Jody's body stiffened and his expression narrowed. He shot me a seriously diminished death glare and shifted his gaze elsewhere. Travis and Devin showed up, paint-covered as usual and begged to play another round.

"We could play in the forest this time. Please, Mom. Please?" Devin whined.

Did I want to play in the forest? Did I want to play another game with Jody? He might retaliate for his semi accidental shooting in the last game.

"Come on, Mom, it'll be fun." Travis said.

I checked the time. If we played a quick game, I could squeeze in another round before work. As soon as I looked at my watch, the boys knew they had won. They whooped and started rounding up more players. AJ was in. Chad said he'd play. Steve had to get home for his weekend honeydo duties, so he took off. Lex was having trouble with his gun and decided to sit out the game and try to get it fixed. As I filled my hopper with paintballs and topped off one of my ammo canisters, Devin asked Jody if he wanted to stay for a woods game.

"The woods, no. I...Um. I need to go. I have... something else I need to do," he stuttered.

He glanced at Lex, then stared at me without his normal arrogance. He grabbed his gear from the ground at his feet and shifted from foot to foot before starting toward the parking lot.

"I'll see you guys later, I guess. I've got to go."

"What was that all about?" I asked Lex.

He shrugged.

"Maybe he doesn't like trees."

I laughed as he went on tearing down his gun. I watched Jody almost run toward the parking lot as I twisted the top back on my ammo pod. I couldn't say I was sorry to see him go, but his exit was kind of out of character.

AJ, Chad, and the boys were huddled together sorting out teams when I joined them. Chad and AJ decided to take on the boys and me. I felt terribly outclassed, two fifteen-year-olds and me playing war games against an ex Navy SEAL and a retired Army Ranger. Hmmm. I wonder who's going to win this round?

We decided to play a capture-the-flag game. We, the good guys, owned the real estate and Chad and AJ, the bad guys, were trying to take it away. Steve wasn't here so everybody was relaxed. AJ fell out of a tree and we could hear him swearing and laughing all the way across the field. Chad tripped over Devin, dropped his gun and took a shot in the butt from Travis. I was laughing so hard I didn't hear AJ sneak up behind me. He took a handful of the back of my shirt and dropped me over his knee onto the leaves.

"You lose," he said, standing over me.

I kicked my leg out and swept his feet from under him. He landed with a thud on the ground beside me. He lifted my mask and kissed me till I was dizzy.

I smiled, "I think I won actually."

"Maybe we'll call it a draw."

He kissed me again and helped me up from the ground. I swayed and swallowed.

"Maybe."

He grinned and we started walking toward the others. I scuffed behind him through the scrub enjoying the view. We joined Chad and the boys and trooped to the parking lot. Devin and Travis were ducking behind trees, taking pot shots at each other. Chad and AJ raced forward and joined the fight. I trudged through the underbrush watching the running gunfight going on in front of me. As I stumbled down an embankment, my foot caught on something. I experienced a moment of deja vu as I yelled, "Shit," and my gun flew from my hands. I picked myself up from the ground and tried to figure out what I had tripped over. It could have been nothing; I've been known to fall over my own feet. Not this time, though. Something shone white through the underbrush. I moved the leaves aside and uncovered a hand wearing shiny red nail polish.

"No."

Not again. I closed my eyes, paused for a minute, then took another look. The hand was still there and appeared to be attached to a body. Flies swarmed up as I let the foliage snap back into place. I waved them away from my face and stepped out of the heavy brush. The smell hit me as the flies buzzed back through the leaves to their meal. I pulled my sweat-soaked tee shirt over my nose to try and filter the stench.

"AJ!" I yelled. I stepped away, and sank to the ground.

"AJ, Chad! Get down here!"

I put my head between my knees and swallowed hard as bile rose in my throat. Chad slipped and slithered down the embankment toward me. I lifted my head from my knees and saw Devin as Chad started to follow him down.

"Get the boys away from here."

"What?"

"Chad, get the boys out of here. Take them home and come back."

Chad turned to look at where I pointed and scrambled up the bank to intercept the twins.

"Come on guys, let's head on to the truck," I heard Chad say as he reached the top.

"Is Mom coming?" Devin asked.

"She'll be home later. I'm going to have to go in to work so I'm going to take you guys to the farm."

They moved away and the rest of their conversation was lost as AJ picked his way down the bank.

"Oh, Christ, Randi. Not again," he said.

He pulled me to my feet and guided me to the top of the ditch. When we stopped at the top, he pulled me against him.

"You okay?"

"No, dammit. I'm tired of tripping over dead bodies."

My stomach felt queasy and I gagged once, but managed not to throw up. AJ handed me a bottle of water and gave my shoulder a squeeze. I rinsed my mouth and spit before I took a drink.

"AJ, I need to use your phone."

I called Morgan and asked him if he would cover my shift at the bar. When I punched off the call, AJ called the station and reported the body. We sat down to await the arrival of the crime scene team. Chad pulled into the parking lot just ahead of the CSI guys. He led them to where we were sitting.

"I need to go to work now, you going to be alright?" AJ asked as he stood.

"I'm okay."

A couple of officers showed up to assist; one of them was George Williams. He sketched a wave my way and went to talk to AJ. CSI showed up next and roped off the scene. I walked to the parking lot and sat on the hood of the Mustang to wait. I could have gone on home, AJ would have gotten a ride, but actually getting into the car and driving back into town seemed like it required too much energy. I closed my eyes and leaned back against the windshield. The sun was warm on my face and the car was warm against my back, but I was cold inside, and scared.

A car drove up and I heard Steve ask if I was okay as he started out to the crime scene. I waved to him without opening my eyes and he went on without stopping. I heard someone crunch across the gravel toward me and looked up to see Lex walking my way. He leaned against the hood and crossed his arms.

"You want me to take your shift tonight, Ran?"

"I already called Morgan, but thanks."

"You okay?"

I nodded and stared toward the edge of the paintball range where I could see the guys walking around. The coroner drove up and parked near the site.

"What'd you say to Jody?" I asked.

"Just reminded him he had to work with AJ and he might want to chill as long as he was around."

I wasn't sure that's what he'd said, but whatever it was, it had cooled Jody off, so I wasn't going to press the issue.

AJ came out of the woods and Lex walked over to meet him. They talked for a minute looking my way once as I slid off the hood of the car, but they were too far away for me to make out what they said. I heard AJ laugh as Lex turned to go.

"Catch you later, Ski." Lex said as he walked toward his truck.

I cocked my head at the nickname. I'd never heard anyone but Steve use it. I wondered briefly where Lex had picked it up. But I didn't care enough at the moment to ask AJ about it.

"I figured you went on home," AJ said as he stopped by my side.

"Too lazy to drive."

"I'm pretty much done until forensics gets finished. Let's get out of here."

I climbed in and collapsed against the seatback as AJ started the car. I couldn't believe I'd actually stumbled on another body; it was like that movie, Groundhog Day, only people were dying. Two bodies in two weeks. Mom was never going to let me hear the end of this. Somehow, I knew she would find a way to make it all my fault.

Chapter 13

Wilson gave us his usual enthusiastic greeting when we stepped inside. AJ went through the kitchen to let him out. I tossed my purse on the table and stared through the back door. AJ slid his arms around my waist and I leaned back against his chest.

"You okay, darlin'?"

"Uh-huh."

He kissed the top of my head and turned me around to face him.

"Look me in the eye and say that."

"I'm fine." I said, as tears trickled down my cheeks. He pulled me close.

"You have to stop this guy, AJ," I mumbled against his chest.

"We're working on it, babe. We're working on it."

We stood that way for a long time. His arms wrapped around me, my cheek pressed against his shoulder.

"Why don't you tell me what's going on with Jody?" AJ asked softly.

I pulled away and wiped my face. If this was an attempt to get my mind off the murders, it wasn't working. I still thought Jody was the killer. I'd noticed how quickly he'd taken off when we decided to play a round in the woods. I'd bet money he knew what we might find out there. Could I prove it? No. Did I believe it? More than ever.

I had to tell AJ something, but if I told him the reasons I thought Jody was the killer, he'd blow me off because there wasn't any evidence. On the other hand, if I told him what Jody had been doing to me, he was gonna run off half-cocked and start something with the guy. That would cause a mess in the department and Steve would hold me personally responsible. I'd just need to tone my story down so AJ could understand my feelings without starting a civil war in the Alden PD. Besides that, if Jody started having problems at work because of something I told AJ, it might make him cause more trouble for me. Jody was a loose cannon and I didn't want to do anything to set him off.

"Randi?" AJ said when my pause went on too long.

"Do we really have to get into this now?" I asked.

"You got something else to do? Come on, talk to me."

I sighed. "Jody seems to have a fixation on me. I told you he asked me out the other night when he was over here. I told him no, but he doesn't seem to want to take no for an answer. He's been calling me and stopping by and I can't seem to get through to him that I'm not interested."

Okay, technically what I said was the truth. I just didn't give him all the details.

"Well, babe. I can't fault his taste, but it sounds like his methods need a little work. But don't you think popping him in the head with a paintball was a little extreme?"

Personally, I thought he'd gotten off easy, but I was trying to diffuse this situation, so I agreed that it was, while carefully crossing my fingers behind my back.

AJ kissed me and brushed my cheek. "Do I need to worry about the competition, babe?"

"I don't think so."

He pulled me close and I relaxed against him. AJ didn't have any competition. Somehow, we were right back where we'd been before he left and I wasn't fighting it anymore. It felt right. It always had. That's what had made his leaving so awful.

"I'm here to stay this time," he whispered, reading my thoughts.

I lifted my head and he brushed my lips with a soft kiss.

"Go take a shower, babe. You look done in."

I took his advice and headed for the bathroom. As I closed the door, I heard the click, click, click of Wilson's toenails as he trotted across the kitchen floor. I turned on the water and started the shower only to realize I didn't have a shower curtain. I'd taken the old one down because Jody had ripped it when he jerked it open. I hadn't gotten to the store to replace it yet. I stoppered the tub and turned off the shower to let it fill. I guess I could have gone upstairs and used the boys' shower, but that required, well, going upstairs. It was just more trouble than it was worth.

I poured in some lavender bath salts and sank into the steaming water. "Ahh." Maybe a bath was better than a shower anyway. I could feel my muscles relax, but my brain wouldn't be still. It just kept darting between Jody and the two murdered girls I'd had the misfortune to see. Maybe it would have been better if I'd taken Kira's suggestion and lit some candles. Or maybe I should consider having her come over and show me how to cleanse my crystals.

"You're not going to fall asleep in there, are you?"

I snapped awake.

"Not now."

I lifted my hands from the water and stared at the pruned flesh of my fingertips. Apparently I'd slept for quite a while. Maybe I didn't need those crystals after all.

AJ came in and held up a towel. He wrapped it around me when I stepped from the tub and tucked the end between my breasts.

"I liked you better without the towel."

"Please tell me you aren't hitting on me right now," I said.

"Hey, can't blame a guy for trying."

I laughed. "Get out of here and let me get dressed."

AJ was sitting at the kitchen table when I came out. I dropped down across from him.

"Aren't you going to race tonight?" I asked.

"Nah, I'll stay here with you."

"I don't need a babysitter, AJ."

"I know that, just thought you might want company."

"Liar. You thought I might be scared."

I went to the refrigerator and poured a soda. AJ twisted around in his chair.

"You want one?" I asked.

He shook his head.

"You sure you're okay here by yourself, darlin'?"

"AJ, I'm not going to trip over a dead body in my own home and I'm not going anywhere else. Go grab Devin from Mom and Dad's and get out of here."

"Are you sure?"

"I'm sure. Go already. You're going to be late."

I laughed as he jumped up from the table and trotted down the hall. He came back, dropped a kiss on my cheek and ran out to his truck. I called Devin and told him to be ready when AJ arrived. Wilson and I snuggled on the couch. I was watching the Cardinals pre-game when Travis and Chad came through the front door.

"Hi, Mom. Alan's coming over. We're gonna watch the game upstairs. We got any chips left?" Travis said.

"Hi. Okay. Yes, in the pantry."

Travis thundered up the stairs with his chips. Chad sank onto the other end of the couch. I put my feet in his lap and settled in to watch the game. Before the first pitch, someone knocked on the door. I got up and padded across the room. It was Alan. The only one of the boys' friends that didn't just walk in and announce himself.

"Hey, Mrs. B."

"Hi, Alan. Trav's in his bedroom."

He headed upstairs. I went back to my spot on the couch. Chad had shoved the coffee table out of the way and was on the floor with a pillow.

"Birds win tonight, we have to play the Dodgers," Chad said.

"Piece of cake. The Dodgers suck this year."

"Uh-huh."

I laughed softly to myself. The Dodgers definitely did not suck. We just say that. It's our whistling in the dark defense.

"You stay at the crime scene today?" I asked.

"I was there for a while. Jody got there right after Steve showed up. Steve was going nuts because Jody wouldn't go in the woods."

"He wouldn't go in the woods?"

"Yeah, I guess this morning at breakfast he mentioned something about being afraid of snakes. After the game today, one of the boys, he wasn't sure which one, told him the woods were teeming with copperheads."

"And he believed it?"

"Apparently. I'm guessing that's why he wouldn't stay and play this afternoon. Steve had a hell of a time convincing him he'd been had. Of course, the guys weren't helping, every time he'd start to relax a little, one of them would grab his pant leg and hiss."

I laughed; there was no question in my mind which twin was responsible. This little escapade had Travis written all over it. I'd have to remember to thank him later. I settled in to watch the game, more relaxed than I'd been in days and doubly glad that I hadn't told AJ my suspicions about Jody. I would have felt like a real idiot after AJ heard the snake story.

We watched in silence as the Cards went down in order. When it went to commercial, I asked Chad if they knew the name of the latest victim.

"Her name was Amy Welsh. She hung out at the Jungle. Pinch hit behind the bar if somebody didn't show."

"She a working girl?"

"I don't think so, just wild. Smoked a little weed, hung with a pretty rough bunch. I don't think she was as tough as she pretended to be. I busted her once, a while back. She was pretty broken up about it. I thought she'd gotten her act together."

Chad left to grab a couple of beers from the fridge and came back. I twisted the top off mine while he settled himself back on the floor with his pillow.

"You seem to know Liz pretty well," I said.

"I'm a vice-cop, Ran. I know all the working girls pretty well. We have a professional relationship."

"Didn't seem too professional at Mabel's. Come to think of it, didn't look all that professional at the Roger the other night either."

"She's a nice girl, just had a pretty rough life. She helps me out some with work. Keeps tabs on what's going on. In exchange, I leave her alone."

"Mom's gonna flip when you bring Elisabeth Appleton home for dinner."

"It's a good thing I'm not bringing her home then, isn't it?"

I made a face at the back of his head.

"I saw that."

"Did not."

Chad stared at the TV not looking at me. I picked at the corner of the label on my bottle, the St. Louis batter hit into a double play to end the inning. They cut away to a commercial. Chad focused on the screen, still ignoring me.

"Your face goes all soft when you talk about her," I said.

"You're imagining things, Randi."

I smiled and quit picking at him. We watched the Cards blow a three-run lead in the seventh. I was having a hard time concentrating on the game. I kept seeing that white hand with those blood red fingernails.

"Do you ever get used to it, Chad?" I asked.

"Get used to what?"

"The brutality."

"You learn to live with it. People do some pretty bad shit to each other."

"How do you sleep at night? How do you get rid of the images?" I asked.

"You just learn to turn it off after a while."

"I guess I haven't figured out how to do that yet."

Chad turned toward me. "I hope to God you never do, Ranna."

Wilson hopped up with me, rooted in behind my legs, and lay down with his feet sticking up in the air. The game came on, but I didn't really pay attention. Chad shifted position on the floor and fluffed up his pillow.

"You ever lose friends on missions? You never talk much about it."

"I can't talk about a lot of it. It's still classified. And yeah, I lost a couple. It's not usually something I want to discuss. Better to leave it buried."

Better or easier, I wondered.

"Why'd you go into the SEALs?"

"We gonna talk about this again?"

"Come on, Chad. The three of you were gone forever, doing something that I've never experienced. I can't even imagine most of it. But you all came back here, to Alden. You traveled all over the world, and then the three of you came home and slid into the police department like you'd never left this place. Maybe I'm just trying to understand what it was you all went to find and why you came back." Why AJ came back.

"I came home because I didn't see anything any better in my travels. Steve came back because he promised Sara Beth he would. AJ came back for you."

"He did not," I said. But inside I suspected it was true. AJ had as much as told me. And it still felt right, AJ and me. I shook the thoughts out of my head. Chad had sidetracked me, but I still wanted to know about the SEALs.

"You didn't answer my question, Chadly."

Chad sighed. "It just seemed like the ultimate test. I guess I wanted to see if I could do it."

"Were you good at it?"

"Yeah, I was good at it. You sure ask a lot of questions."

I took the hint and shut up for the rest of the game. When it was over, Chad stood and tossed the pillow back on the couch. "You going to be alright if I go home? I'm dog tired."

"I'll be fine."

I followed him to the door. He stepped outside and tripped over Bill on the porch.

"God damn cat!"

I laughed and locked up behind him. I turned around as Alan walked across the room. I jumped in surprise.

"Jesus, I forgot you were here."

"Sorry, Mrs. B. I'll try to make more noise next time."

I laughed and let him out. I flopped onto the couch to watch the news. The second body at Timber Bridge was the lead story. I flipped to The Weather Channel. An hour later, when I woke, they were giving the weather in Europe. I decided I could live without that knowledge and went to check on Travis. He was lying across the bed sound asleep with his guitar on the pillow beside him. I stood his guitar in the stand next to his desk and went down to bed. My .32 was under my pillow and I was asleep in minutes. My dreams weren't exactly nightmares, but I was glad to wake up. I crawled out of bed and heard voices so I stumbled into the kitchen to see who was there. AJ and the boys were cooking breakfast. I grabbed a Pepsi and sat down at the kitchen table to oversee.

"Good morning, beautiful," AJ said as he stopped to kiss me. "How do you like your eggs?"

"Cooked would be good."

Devin was at the stove in charge of egg preparation. He turned around and stuck out his tongue at me. Travis was making toast and AJ was cooking bacon in the microwave. The kitchen was a disaster.

"How do you make a mess this big cooking eggs, toast, and bacon?" I asked.

"You just hush. You are watching genius at work," AJ said.

"I hope you geniuses know how to do dishes. I am not cleaning this kitchen."

All three of them stuck out their tongues at me. AJ put a plate full of bacon on the table. Travis added toast, butter, and jelly. Devin started passing around eggs. The plate he plopped in front of me had one raw egg slithering around in the middle. Teenage humor. I tackled him and tickled until he surrendered and gave me cooked eggs. After breakfast, the boys trooped upstairs to play video games while AJ and I did the dishes. I knew I was going to get stuck cleaning the kitchen.

We worked in companionable silence.

"You know, if you could just find out who Lisa left the bar with, you might break this case wide open."

"I wish we had a clue. We don't have any leads at all. We've talked to everybody that we think was at the Jolly Roger that night. Too bad the Roger doesn't have security cameras."

"Morgan checked into it a while back."

AJ sighed, "Too bad he didn't get them installed. We could use a break. I hate cases like this."

"You going racing tonight?" I asked, changing the subject.

"Yep, and you're coming with us."

"Okay."

"No argument?" he seemed surprised.

"Nope."

"Cool, then you won't mind if I take Devin with me to get the car ready to go?"

"Nope. What time are you picking us up?"

"We'll be here around three."

"That works."

We almost had the dishes done when AJ rat-tailed me with the dishtowel. I poured a glass of water over his head and we started wrestling. I slipped in the soapy water and pulled AJ down on top of me. He darted a hand underneath my shirt.

"If the boys weren't home, I'd make the most of this opportunity," he said.

"Yeah, promises, promises."

He kissed my nose and lifted me to my feet.

"Hey, Devin!" AJ yelled up the stairs. "Get your butt down here. We got work to do."

Dev thundered down the stairs. After they left, Travis and I ran to town to get a new shower curtain and I installed it while the laundry ran in the background. After the dryer stopped, Travis and I went to Mabel's for lunch. We got home with just enough time to change clothes before Devin and AJ arrived. We dumped ice in the cooler, crowded into the truck, and we were off.

I hadn't been to the races with AJ since he came home from the Army. When I was younger, I went all the time. AJ and I had been a team then; we didn't even have to talk as we worked. I didn't think it would be like that now, too many years since we'd been at the track together.

We pulled into the pit area and unloaded the car. The air was already heavy with the smell of burnt fuel and grilled cheeseburgers. Engines rumbled and rapped as guys made last minute adjustments. The track, a quarter mile, high-banked dirt oval, was still muddy. Push-trucks made endless circles, packing the mud down into a relatively smooth racing surface. The turns were bordered by metal Armco barriers that were still mottled with clods of dirt from last week's race. The aluminum grandstands, new since my last trip, glittered in the setting sun; a welcome change from the old wood plank bleachers that would leave you with uncomfortable splinters if you scooted across their surface. They filled with a steady stream of fans carrying coolers and stadium blankets.

Kids yelped and squealed, scampered in and out from under the bleachers and along the fencing that ran beside the front straightaway. Older children sold official race programs for a quarter each. People bought them to use as fans. Nobody needed a program to know who the drivers were; some of these race fans had been coming to this track long enough to have cheered on the fathers and grandfathers of the current crop of racers. They sat in little groups in the stands, same place every weekend. It was like an extended family. If someone didn't show up for a race, everyone worried until they found out the reason why they'd missed. They cheered and ate bad cheeseburgers, watched each other's children grow, and marry, and bring children of their own to the track. I hadn't realized how much I'd missed it until I got that first whiff of burnt fuel.

I slid down from the truck to help get things ready. Rear end gears needed to be changed and fresh grease added; the oil checked, fuel topped off; tires swapped; a hundred and one little tasks to complete before the rubber met the racetrack. We fell into the old routine without thought. When AJ went into the trailer to change into his Nomex uniform, I sat down on a tire and drank a soda. Devin had disappeared to scope out the competition. It never hurts to have someone sneaky enough to find out what everybody else is doing. I leaned back and closed my eyes. I turned and opened them as AJ stepped from the trailer in his uniform. God he looked good. He winked and tossed me his helmet and a package of tear-offs.

"You remember how to put those on?"

"I remember. How many do you need?"

"Four or five ought to do it."

I put the thin plastic lens covers on AJ's helmet visor, so he could tear them away when they became covered with mud, then I perched the helmet on the thin aluminum hood of his car. Devin wandered back eating a cheeseburger. The sight of him underscored the years that had passed since I was a regular at the races. A lot of water under the bridge since the last time I'd been on this side of the fence.

Travis was over in the grandstands with his stopwatch. He was sitting in a clutch of fans that knew the stats on every car and every driver that had ever raced at our little speedway. They'd also known the twins since they were born and treated them like their own kids. As much as Devin likes working on the racecar, I think sometimes he misses those nights sitting in the grandstand with his second family. To tell the truth, I'd missed them too, and wondered why I'd worked so hard to stay away from something I used to enjoy so much.

I waved at Travis when he looked up. He stopped talking long enough to wave, then went back to his conversation. The pit steward came by and told us to line up for hot laps. Devin and I pushed the car out of the pit area, melding my past with my present.

The car was fast in hot laps and we won our eight-lap heat race. That meant we started fourth in the feature. AJ buckled in for the big race of the night, a thirty-lap main event. It would be worth twelve hundred bucks to the winner, just barely enough to cover the night's expenses. For everyone else, the night was gonna cost money, even if they didn't tear up any equipment. This was down and dirty, grass-roots dirt track racing; and you didn't do it for the money, you did it for love. I'd heard girls at the bar bitching about being football widows, but that was nothing compared to being in love with a racecar driver. At least football only consumed a few hours a week. A racecar took the top spot three hundred and sixty-five days a year. If they weren't driving it, they were working on it; and in the off-season, they were building a new one for the next year. It was an addiction worse than drugs.

AJ finished with the belts and Devin tightened them up for him. I handed over his helmet and received a wink before he snapped down the visor. I was a nervous wreck. Devin and AJ appeared relaxed. I wondered if they really were or if that was just for me. I climbed to the roof of the trailer as they pushed the car off for the start. My shaking hands were stuck deep in the pockets of my jeans and I wished I had a cigarette. Devin, perfectly calm, climbed up beside me to watch. The green flag flew and my heart rate soared. Twenty-two cars thundered into turn one. I watched through squinted eyes, afraid to look right at them in case they didn't all make it. I started breathing again when the cars came out of turn two in one piece, and tried to sort AJ from the pack. He passed the third place car and moved up to work on second. A bobble a couple of laps later by the second place car and AJ darted by. My hands weren't shaking any more. "Come on, AJ," I muttered as he closed in on the leader. Two laps from the end, he made his move.

"Come on, AJ," I yelled.

A lapped car slid across in front of him, and blocked the track. My heart stopped as AJ rode over a wheel, cartwheeled down the back straight and disappeared over the wall. Devin, no longer calm and relaxed, was off the trailer before the car stopped rolling. I climbed down slower. My knees weren't working very well. My trembling legs took me slowly across the pit area as I waited for AJ to appear. Devin reached the track as AJ climbed the embankment and stepped over the guardrail. I huffed a huge sigh of relief and tried to act like that hadn't scared the hell out of me. AJ talked to Devin for a minute. When he turned away, Dev scrambled over the fence and disappeared down the embankment to help get the car back onto the track. AJ waved off the EMT and headed across the track. I met him at the pit gate. He handed me his helmet, draped an arm over my shoulder, and we walked to the trailer.

"You okay?" I asked.

"Uh huh."

I grinned to myself. Unless there was a bone sticking through somewhere, he would say he was fine.

AJ sat on a tire. I stowed his helmet in the truck and started putting away tools. When the wrecker brought the car in, we were ready to load. When everything was locked up and put away, AJ went back to lean on the trailer and talk to the fans. Travis arrived while I was digging in the cooler for a Coors Light.

"Wow, I bet AJ was pulling at least four G's when he went over the fence."

I handed him a soda. "You might keep that observation to yourself I doubt if AJ's gonna want to hear it tonight."

"Oh. Right, Mom."

"Hey," I caught Travis before he got away. "I heard there's a snake infestation out at Timber Bridge."

His face went red, but he laughed and skipped off before I could say anything else. Devin was assing around with the guys in the next pit, so I closed the lid on the cooler and took a beer to AJ. He thanked me and hooked an arm around my waist so I couldn't leave. It felt like we'd been doing this without a break for the past twenty years. The only thing different was having the boys around instead of my brothers.

The crowd thinned. Travis corralled Devin, and they crawled in the rear seat of the truck. I slid behind the wheel, and AJ eased down beside me.

"You sure you can still back one of these things up?" he asked.

"Just go until you hear glass break," I said.

AJ grinned and laid his head against the seat. He liked to act tough, but if he didn't feel bad, he would never let me drive. I pointed the truck toward home while the boys slept in the back, and AJ nodded off up front. I tuned in an oldies station and drove into the night. AJ woke when we stopped in front of the house.

"You could probably leave your rig here for the night, AJ."

"Nah, I'd have to get up early and unload before work. I'd better take it on home tonight before I get really sore. It's going to be hard enough to get out of bed tomorrow as it is."

I roused the boys. They stumbled into the house, still half asleep, and went straight to bed. AJ leaned against the truck and pulled me into his arms.

"Kind of seemed like old times tonight. Will you come with me next weekend?"

"I wouldn't miss it."

He tipped my face toward his and kissed me.

"I gotta go, darlin'. It's late."

I stepped away and watched him wince his way behind the wheel. I waved as he drove down the street. I didn't want to go to bed. I was tired of dreaming about dead women. Wilson stood patiently at the slider in the kitchen, so I let him out, ate a bagel, let him in and took a shower. I sat huddled against the headboard of my bed trying to think of something to do besides sleep. I picked up a book, and my eyes drooped as I tried to read so I switched off the lamp and scooted under the covers. Wilson curled beside me and laid his head on my chest. I patted him absently, my mind wandering, my eyes no longer heavy enough for sleep. Images of the two dead women I'd found started running through my mind. I gave up on sleep and stared at the ceiling.

"Who did you leave with, Lisa?" I whispered in the dark. Suddenly I sat up. Wilson leapt to the floor and barked.

"The video cameras at the bar, Wilson. Morgan didn't buy them, but they were set up for a while. Shit, why didn't I think of that when AJ mentioned it earlier?"

The security company was supposed to send Morgan a DVD sample with the recordings they made the days the cameras were there. I tried to remember if Morgan had mentioned when they had installed the cameras or just when they removed them. I couldn't remember, but I was still excited by the idea.

"Wilson, we might be able to see who Lisa left the bar with."

Wilson studied me from beside the bed, pondered my words, and decided food didn't figure into the conversation, so he'd opt for more sleep. He snorted and trotted from the room. The recliner squeaked in the dark as he circled on the seat.

I checked the clock. It was after three. Morgan would already be home. Probably already asleep. I'd have to go over and talk to him first thing in the morning. That decided, I lay down and closed my eyes. My last thought of the night was about Jody and snakes. I dropped off with a smile. Considering I didn't like Jody or snakes, all in all it was a pretty good end to the day.

Chapter 14

called Morgan and got him out of bed the next morning. He wasn't happy. I don't know why he got into the bar business, he doesn't function well on short nights. He agreed to meet me at the Jolly Roger after I dropped the boys off at school. The coffee pot was going and he was sitting at the bar looking grouchy when I walked in.

"You want coffee?" he asked.

I rolled my eyes. We were married five years and he couldn't remember that I don't drink coffee? Or maybe he does, and he just doesn't care. I shook my head.

"No, thanks." I squirted soda over ice and sat down at a table. "Join me," I said nodding at the chair across from me.

Morgan turned the chair around and straddled it.

"Does this have something to do with the boys? What'd they do now?"

"What?"

"You rousted me out at the crack of dawn by telling me it was really important you talk to me right away. That usually means there's a problem with the kids. So what's the big emergency?"

"The boys are fine."

"Then get on with it, I've had about two hours sleep."

"When did the security company set up the test cameras in the bar?"

"You got me out of bed to find out about the security camera test?"

"Morgan, trust me. This is really important."

He strangled his coffee cup on the table in front of me. He probably wished his hands were around my neck. "I don't remember. It was a couple of weeks ago. Is that all?"

"Were they set up Friday before last?"

"Shit, Randi. I don't have a clue. What is so damned important about a security system I didn't buy?"

"Were they running the night Lisa got murdered?"

Morgan dropped the stranglehold on his cup and stared at me wide-eyed. Coffee splashed onto the tabletop.

"I don't know. They might have been, now that you mention it. I got a letter from the security company yesterday. It should be on my desk."

I followed Morgan into the office and sat on the edge of his desk. He rooted through the mess until he found a DVD mailer from Kauffman Security. He slid the DVD out and popped it into his computer. The computer clicked and whirred until the software opened. Morgan hit play and a dark picture of the bar became clear. There was a time/date stamp in the upper right hand corner. The recording started the day before Lisa's murder.

We fast-forwarded through the next day, and stopped at eleven the following night. Morgan slowly moved through the images until Lisa came into the frame with a group of girls.

"What are we looking for, Ran?"

"We need to see who Lisa left the bar with."

Morgan nodded and hunched forward in his chair. I leaned over his shoulder and squinted at the dark video image. Just before the time stamp reached midnight, Lisa appeared in the frame. She ordered a beer and waved goodbye to someone off camera. The guy in the cowboy hat wasn't in the picture. I wondered if he was the man Lisa had left with, then remembered that she'd supposedly been meeting a cop. I willed the recording to move faster, but didn't ask Morgan to fast forward. I was afraid we'd miss something.

At twelve fifteen, a man walked up to Lisa. They spoke, but he was facing away from the camera. I leaned forward waiting for him to turn around. At twelve thirty, Lisa turned from the bar, slipped her arm through her companion's, and pulled him toward the door. He turned with her and stared directly at the camera. The man with Lisa Woods was Jody McIntire.

I slapped the desk beside the monitor. "I knew it. I knew that guy was trouble."

Morgan stopped and backed the image up so we could see it again. "You think this is the guy, Ran?"

"I'm sure of it. I felt it the first time we met. Set the video back to where Lisa first comes into view, I'll get in touch with Chad."

I called the police station, but Chad wasn't in. I asked for Steve and drummed my fingers on the desktop until he answered.

"Detective Jennings."

"Steve, this is Randi."

"Hi, kid, what's up?"

"I need you to meet me at the Jolly Roger."

"Randi, I'm really up to my ass in alligators right now."

"Steve, I know who Lisa Woods left the bar with."

Silence came over the phone. "How do you know that?"

"Steve, please just meet me at the Roger."

"I'm on my way."

I punched off and paced the office. It felt like an hour before Steve and AJ walked in. It was probably closer to fifteen minutes. Morgan started the program and stepped out of the way. Steve and AJ leaned over the desk chair and watched silently as the video played out. I watched their faces as Jody turned toward the camera.

"Oh, shit," said Steve.

AJ slammed Morgan against the wall of the office and got in his face. "Why the hell didn't you tell us about this video before? Sonovabitch. I should take you in for obstructing justice."

Morgan shoved AJ out of his face. A move that was so entirely out of character that I almost laughed.

"You just wait a minute Weleski. I'm not taking any crap from you over this. First, I just got the disc in the mail yesterday. If Randi hadn't asked me about it, I wouldn't have even bothered to open the envelope. I'd have just tossed it into the trash. I'm not gonna save enough on insurance to pay for the damn cameras so as far as I was concerned it was junk mail. Second—"

Steve held up his hands in a stop sign and stepped between them before they came to blows. AJ spun away and caught me smiling.

"I don't need any shit from you either."

"AJ," Steve snapped.

AJ went silent. Steve turned to Morgan. "I know you wouldn't withhold evidence on purpose, just relax."

Morgan rolled his shoulders and took a deep breath. Steve pulled AJ aside for a quick conference, then AJ opened his cell phone and stepped out of the office.

"We need to take this disc with us, Morgan."

"Yeah, fine, whatever you need."

Steve dropped the DVD into an evidence bag, labeled it, wrote out a receipt for Morgan and turned toward the door.

"Thanks for calling, Randi. I'll talk to you later."

He slipped out and I heard the outer door close behind him. AJ stepped back into the office and pinned me with his cop stare.

"I don't need to tell you guys not to mention this to anyone," he said.

He spoke to both of us, but he was watching me. I don't know who he thought I was going to run out and tell. AJ left to find Jody. I thanked Morgan and took off. I felt like skipping to my car. Finally, I wouldn't have to worry about Jody anymore. I drove home and sat on the porch with Bill. It was the first time I'd felt safe in days.

Mrs. Litton started out her front door, so I scrambled up and ran inside, leaving Bill staring after me. I straightened up the house, played fetch in the backyard with Wilson, and tried to figure out how Bill was getting on the roof; he must be the bionic cat. There aren't any trees close enough for him to jump from. I didn't solve the mystery of the rooftop cat. I was fixing a sandwich when Steve stopped by later. I made one for him and asked what he'd found out from Jody.

"He says he left the bar with Lisa around twelve thirty. They drove around for a little while and Lisa wanted to get high. They got in a big fight over the drugs and Jody says he dropped her off at the Jungle around one. After he left her, he supposedly drove around for a while, then decided to go see his cousin in St. Louis."

"Are you buying this?" I asked in disbelief.

"I didn't want to, but it all checks out. Lisa was at the Jungle around one a.m. Saturday morning. The bartender remembered seeing her. Jody's got credit card receipts for gas and stuff showing he was in route to or in St. Louis in the early hours of Saturday morning. We talked to his cousin and he verified it. Jody got there about four a.m. He didn't have a chance to set up an alibi, Randi. He was in our custody the whole time we were verifying his story. I've got a couple of officers checking the receipts but I'm pretty sure it's all legit."

"Shit."

"We've got him for withholding information in a murder investigation, and we've got a lot more to work with now. We're going to interview everyone we can find that was at the Jungle that night. Maybe we'll find someone that wasn't too drunk to remember something."

"Is Jody in jail?"

"Out on bail."

I sighed. "I was sure that disc was the answer."

"Not this time, Ran. Just more questions, I'm afraid."

Steve finished eating and stood to go. I picked at my sandwich and fed chips to Wilson. My appetite had disappeared. Steve stopped halfway down the hall.

"Be careful, Randi, he's still out there."

I watched him walk out the front door and wondered if he was talking about Jody or the murderer. I cleaned up the kitchen, then dressed for work. I stepped into the bar just before four o'clock. Morgan glanced at his watch in surprise.

"Trying to ruin a perfect record?" he asked.

I grinned and slipped behind the bar. "Just get out of here."

He left to pick up the boys from football practice. I pulled a stool behind the bar and watched TV until business picked up around six. From six to ten, we had about ten customers. At ten it was like someone threw a switch, they all just left. I was about to close up when a bunch of bowlers showed up. I poured beer into the already well-lubricated bowlers until closing time, then shooed them out and started to sweep. AJ called at two to tell me he was going to be late and for me to wait at the bar for him. I agreed and went back to sweeping the floor.

A few minutes later, I heard a scuffing noise behind me. Thinking it was AJ, I smiled and started to turn around when someone grabbed my arm and twisted it up between my shoulder blades. The broom clattered to the floor. I grunted in pain and tried to pull away. He twisted it higher until the pain made me stop struggling. He slipped my gun out of the holster at my back and tossed it onto a table.

"Let me go, dammit."

"Shut up," he hissed.

I didn't recognize the voice. It felt like he was pulling my arm out of the socket. I tried to move and release the pressure on my shoulder. As I sidestepped, he slammed me nose first into the wall. I bit my tongue, tasted blood, and gagged. He swung me around to face him and my head smacked hard against the wall. Lights exploded in my head. I blinked my eyes clear and saw Jody standing in front of me. My stomach clenched in fear. Before I could move, he smacked me across the cheek with his gun.

"Bitch!"

Blood from my mouth and cheek was running down and soaking the front of my shirt. With my fingers, I probed the bloody mess. Jody pulled my hands away, stretched them over my head, and anchored them against the wall with one muscled fist. I struggled to get free, but his grasp was like a vice. He leaned in close, pinning me against the wall with his body.

"Be still."

His eyes were cold and dark with menace. I stopped moving and tried to take a deep breath.

"What are you doing here, Jody?"

"I came by to see you. You caused me a hell of a lot of trouble today, bitch. Now you're going to pay for it."

He pressed his body closer, and brushed his gun hand across my breasts. The look on his face changed, and a small smile curved his lips.

"I'm going to enjoy this, Twinkie."

I swallowed and tried to back through the wall. The wall held. Shit.

"I'm going to make you wish you had kept your pretty little nose out of my business."

Tears ran down my face, and my breath shuddered in my chest. I was hurt, and scared, and getting more pissed off by the second. This asshole was not going to rape me. I stared Jody in the eye and made sure he focused on me. Then I glanced over his shoulder in what I thought looked like surprise, as if I had seen someone come in the door behind him. Jody relaxed for just an instant and I head-butted him. Lights exploded in my head and I fought to stay upright. Jody's eyes widened and before he could recover, I kneed him in the groin. He made a noise like a deflating balloon. The gun dropped from his fingers, and he folded to the floor groaning. I grabbed my .32 from the table, put my knee in his back and shoved the barrel against his temple. Tears and blood mingled as they ran and dripped onto his back.

"You rotten piece of shit. If you ever come close to me again, I...will...kill...you."

"You couldn't do it," he mumbled. "You're afraid to pull the trigger."

I tapped his temple with the barrel. "Don't tempt me."

I straightened up and stepped away, keeping my weapon trained on Jody's head. I backed across the floor and kicked his Glock across the room into the darkness.

He rolled over and sat up.

"You're in way over your head, girlie," he said.

"I'm the one holding the gun."

"Too bad you're afraid to use it."

He lunged toward me as he spat out the words. I fired into the floor in front of him and he stopped.

AJ would be here any minute. I had to keep Jody there until he showed up, but I wasn't confident I could do it without actually shooting him.

"Get back against the wall, Jody."

"NOW!" I shouted when he didn't move.

He scooted across the floor until his back was against the wall. I walked over to stand in front of him.

"Put your hands on your head."

"You are making the mistake of a lifetime here, Twinkie. You'll be looking over your shoulder for me for the rest of your life."

"I heard you had a little snake problem the other day."

"Oh, I've got something for that little brat of yours too."

My finger twitched on the trigger as he threatened Travis. I just managed to keep from shooting him then and there.

"You leave my children out of this."

My head was starting to pound. My legs felt weak and my arms were starting to shake from the strain of holding the gun out in front of me. I needed AJ to get there soon. I was almost at the end of my rope.

The latch on the front door clicked and I jumped and turned away for an instant. Jody lunged from the floor and hit me with a football tackle that threw us both to the floor. I screamed and my gun skittered away.

"I'm not finished with you, bitch," Jody hissed, as he scrambled to his feet and ran toward the back door.

I felt frantically around the floor for my gun, but the back door slammed behind Jody before my fingers closed around it.

The front door scraped open and I rolled to my stomach and aimed at the intruder. Lex stopped and raised his hands.

"Easy, angel. It's just me."

I dropped the gun and put my head down till my forehead rested on the floor. Lex ran over and helped me up.

"Jesus, Randi. Who did this to you?"

I swallowed and didn't say anything. Lex guided me to a table and into a chair before ducking behind the bar to fill a plastic bag with ice. He wrapped a bar towel around it and brought it to me. I didn't know what part of my head to put it on so I just pressed it against my cheek and closed my eyes.

"What are you doing here, Lex?" I mumbled. Where were you ten minutes ago?

"I drove by and your car was still here, it was late, I wanted to make sure you were okay. Who did this, Randi?"

I removed the ice pack and looked across the table at Lex.

"Jody."

Lex narrowed his eyes. "Jody," he said. "Jody McIntire? The cop we played paintball with?"

I nodded my head. Pain shot through my eyeballs. I gritted my teeth and groaned.

"Come on, hon. I'm taking you home. Then we're going to call AJ."

"AJ's supposed to meet me here. Let's just wait."

"Come on, I'll call him and he can meet us at the house."

Lex pulled me gently to my feet. I got dizzy when I stood. I swallowed the bile that rose in my throat, and leaned against the table. Lex slipped his arm around me and guided me out to his truck.

"What did you do to the guy, anyway? Head-butt him?"

"Yeah, then I kneed him in the nuts. I couldn't think of anything else."

"I think you probably got your point across." Lex laughed softly. "Somebody better teach you how to do a head-butt without cracking your skull before you try it again."

"I hope I don't ever have to do it again."

I sank onto the seat of Lex's car and he closed the door. He crawled behind the wheel and took off.

"I'm gonna stop by the hospital, let them have a look at your head."

"Just take me home, Lex. Please. I'll be fine."

"I don't like it, Randi. You need to get checked out."

I felt like I was going to crumble into a million pieces. If I had to sit in the emergency room for hours until someone had time to look at me, I was going to shatter.

"Please, I just want to go home."

Lex must have heard something of the panic in my voice. He didn't press the issue, just pointed his truck toward my neighborhood and drove. I leaned my head back against the seat in relief. My insides were starting to shake as the adrenaline high wore off. As it left my system, little aches and pains battled with each other to claim my attention. I shifted in the seat so I could look at Lex.

"You're really a pretty nice guy, aren't you?"

He smiled. "Don't let that get out."

"So what was with all the groping?"

He grinned. "I like to work alone. Thought if I made a pest of myself you'd quit."

I wondered why he was lying about something so innocuous. Didn't matter. My head hurt too much to worry about it. I put the icepack on my face and drifted in and out for the rest of the ride. Lex helped me out of the car, and I stumbled to the bathroom to make repairs. I peeled off the bloodstained shirt and slipped into my robe. I washed the blood off my face. It didn't make a lot of improvement. My lip was puffed up twice-normal size and the skin around my eyes was already turning purple. I had a gash across my left cheek and a goose egg on my forehead. I gave it up as hopeless and went into the living room and sagged onto the couch. Lex brought a fresh ice pack and I pressed it against my forehead.

"I called AJ. He's on his way. Want to tell me what happened?"

I gave him a run down of Jody's attack. His face went hard while I talked.

"I told him I would kill him if he ever came close to me again."

Lex grinned and brushed his fingers gently across my bruised cheek.

"It won't come to that, angel."

"I hope not, it was an empty threat."

I tried a trembly smile. Lex laughed softly. "You need to tell all this to AJ when he gets here."

I wasn't sure I could go through it all again. It was all I could do to keep my eyes open. "It's over. Jody's had his fun. I just want to go to sleep and forget about it."

"Doesn't work that way, Randi. You had the advantage this time because he thought you would be too scared to fight back. Now that he knows you're not, he'll make it a lot harder on you. You won't get off next time with a couple of black eyes and headache."

AJ walked in looking completely exhausted. It was almost three a.m. and he'd been at work since eight that morning. He strode into the living room, saw my face, and the exhaustion disappeared.

"Who did this, Randi?" he asked very quietly.

I sat up on the couch. He knelt in front of me, and gently brushed my cheek. "Randi, who did this?"

"Jody."

"I think this qualifies as more than a little harassment."

"I, he..." I took a shaky breath and continued. "He threatened Travis."

"Where are the boys now?" AJ asked.

"They're at Morgan's. They stay there most nights when I work."

Lex stood and headed for the phone. "I've got it, Ski. I'll have Chad go over there."

"Baby, I'm so sorry. You've been hinting to me about Jody for a while."

"I didn't want for it to end up being a big deal at the department."

"Shh." AJ brushed my hair away from my face and kissed me lightly on the lips. "You're way more important than work. I need to get my priorities in line."

Lex came back from the kitchen and we both looked up.

"The boys are fine, I talked to Morgan. Chad's on his way over there now."

"Thanks, Lex."

"I'll meet you downtown, Ski," Lex said as he walked out the door.

"Will you be okay if I leave you for a little bit?" AJ asked.

"I'll be fine."

"I'll be back in a little while."

I shuddered at the look in his eyes. The man behind those eyes was a dangerous stranger. The door closed softly as AJ left. I lay on the couch and put the ice pack on my face. Wilson curled up next to me and licked the outside of the pack. I dropped it to the floor when it was more water than ice, and drifted in and out of sleep. As the sky was starting to lighten, I heard the door open and close softly. I hoped it was AJ, but it wouldn't matter. I was all out of fight. Wilson wiggled in greeting and hopped down. I felt someone tuck the blanket in around me. The next time I was conscious it was daytime and AJ, was sitting in the chair next to the couch.

"Did you arrest him?"

"He's being processed. You're going to have to come down to the station so we can file an assault charge. We've got to get you to a doctor to get checked out and get photos of the damage."

"Does that have to happen now?"

"It does if we want to have any chance at all of getting the charge to stick. We know he did it, but we still don't have a witness or any evidence."

"So you're telling me he's going to get off?"

"Maybe, but he'll be suspended pending an internal investigation. Apparently they've had other complaints."

I guess that was good news. He wouldn't be able to hide behind his badge now, but I was more concerned with myself. I had to get dressed, go to the station and deal with the emergency room at the hospital. To top it off, Jody probably wasn't going to stay in jail. I wasn't sure which thing was more disturbing. At the moment, it was probably the thought that I was going to have to get off the couch.

It was full daylight by the time that ordeal was finished. I refused the opportunity to spend a day in the hospital and begged AJ to take me home. I probably arrived there about the same time Jody managed to make bail. I walked into the house, zeroed in on the couch and closed my eyes to rest just for a minute. When I was conscious again, it was dark and Chad was sitting in my recliner.

"Hey, Ranna."

"Hi, Chadly."

"How ya doing?"

"I feel like hell."

"You've looked better."

"Thanks, you're all heart."

"I just stopped by to see if you were awake yet."

"Not really."

"Okay."

I lay quietly and thought about going back to sleep, expecting to hear Chad go out the front door. I opened my eyes and found him staring down at me.

"You were right about Jody, Ranna. I'm sorry I didn't do more to keep this from happening."

I flapped a hand at him. "Not your fault."

He moved forward and kneeled next to the couch. "God dammit, it is my fault. My job is to keep stuff like this from happening."

"Stop it, Chad."

"No. You're going to hear me out."

I struggled to a sitting position so I could see him without breaking my neck.

"Okay, I'm listening."

He sat on the coffee table so we were knee to knee, then he took my hands.

"I've ignored your fears. I've made fun of you. I've blown off your instincts and suggestions, not just the last few weeks, but pretty much since I got home. I've been the big returning hero. The rough tough Navy SEAL. Too arrogant to pay attention even when my gut told me you were telling the truth. And I almost got you killed."

"Chad..."

He put a finger to my lips to hush me.

"I'm sorry, Ranna..."

His eyes filled with tears and he cleared his throat so he could continue.

"I promise you will never again be hurt because I'm being an asshole."

His tears finally fell as we leaned together in a hug.

"God, Ranna. I don't know what I would have done if that jerk had killed you."

"Oh, I imagine a rough tough Navy SEAL like yourself would have come up with something."

"Oh, you can count that, Ran."

I smiled as we drew apart.

"Forgive me?" he asked.

"Don't be an ass, of course I do."

"God, Randi."

"Enough. It's over, don't mention it again."

"But..."

"No more, I mean it."

"Okay."

He walked across the room and dropped into the recliner. I sat on the couch trying to breathe without moving.

"You feel like eating something?" Chad asked.

My stomach lurched at the thought and I shook my head. I didn't need to eat, my stomach wasn't ready for that, but I did need to pee. Couldn't decide if it was worth the trip. I sat without moving for a while, then decided it was. I started to stand, and Chad jumped up from the recliner.

"What, what do you need?"

I fell back on the couch snickering.

"Relax, I just need to pee."

Chad busted out laughing. I was trying to quit giggling. I really needed to pee and the giggles weren't helping.

"Stop laughing at me and help me up."

Chad gave me a hand and I swayed on my feet letting him hold me steady while I tried to control the giggles.

"You okay, can I let go now?"

I nodded. I was afraid to talk or I'd start laughing again.

I wasn't laughing as I navigated my way back to the living room. My whole body was throbbing. The trip down the hall and back had taken all my strength.

Chad tucked me in on the couch and told me to go to sleep. He didn't have to tell me twice.

Chapter 15

I spent most of the next week on the couch interrupted only by brief trips to the bathroom and the fridge. Morgan worked my shifts at the bar and Steve took the boys home to stay with him and Sara Beth. I called to make sure Sara Beth was okay with the extra kids. She assured me they were fine, so I took the week off from motherhood.

The skin around my eyes changed from black to green, to yellow, then faded. The goose egg on my forehead disappeared and the cut on my cheek started to heal. I endured jokes from my sons, teasing from my brothers and pampering from AJ. I slept in snatches, startled awake by nightmares, and by Saturday, I was climbing the walls. The boys came home and I sent them to the races with AJ and Chad.

Wilson and I camped on the couch and prepared to watch the Cardinals destroy the Dodgers. Just before the game started, Lex knocked on the door. I invited him to watch the game with us, told him to help himself to a beer, and sank back to my spot on the couch. Tired and grouchy from inactivity I might be, but much vertical movement was still beyond me.

Lex grabbed a Bud Light and parked in the squeaking recliner.

"How's the head?" he asked.

"Better."

"Shiners are almost gone."

"Still feel like hell though."

Lex kicked the footrest up on the recliner and settled in to watch the game. I decided I'd been vertical long enough and went from a sitting to reclining position. The dizziness washed over me. I pinched the bridge of my nose between my thumb and forefinger, and waited for it to pass.

"That should go away in a few more days," Lex said.

"That's what everybody tells me."

"It's true."

The Birds started the game with a four run first inning. We were off to a good start.

"Were you a Ranger, Lex?" I asked.

"Special Forces."

"With AJ and Steve?"

"And a few others."

"If I keep asking questions am I going to learn anything else about you?"

"Not necessarily."

"Okay, different subject. Why'd you move down here?"

"I had enough of St. Louis. Got tired of all the city bullshit. When we were stationed overseas, I listened to your brother and AJ talk about this place. Decided I might move down here when I got out."

His answer sounded practiced, I wasn't sure I believed him, but I let it slide.

"How long have you been out of the service?" I asked.

"Almost three years."

I watched the Dodgers tee off on the Redbird pitcher. It was going to be a long ballgame. When they went to commercial, I started talking again.

"AJ wouldn't tell me what went on with Jody. All he told me was that Jody's free on bail again, but that I don't need to worry about it. What did you guys do to him?"

"What makes you think we did anything?"

"Come on, Lex."

"We convinced him it was in his best interest to keep a low profile for a while, especially where you and your boys are concerned."

My heart clenched. I'd seen first hand how violent Jody could be. The thought of one of my boys having to face him terrified me.

"He can't get to the boys can he?"

"Relax, Ran. I don't think you are going to have any more problems with Jody, but we're keeping a close eye on Devin and Travis. We're not going to let anything happen to them, I promise."

His words did little to calm my fears. I knew the boys were fine right now; they were with Chad and AJ. But what about when they went back to school Monday? What about football practice, or away games? Jody wouldn't try to get at them here, I was sure of that. He'd wait until they were away from home. He could get at them on a school bus or after some school activity during the chaos of kids grabbing backpacks, or getting in their cars. We just couldn't be with them twenty-four hours a day.

"Maybe I should keep the kids home from school for a while."

"Randi, we're not going to let him get to your boys."

I prayed he was right. Until Jody was locked up or dead, I wasn't going to be able to relax. I almost wished I'd shot him when I had the chance. That was a disturbing thought and it gave me chills, because I knew I meant it. I'd never wished anyone dead before. It was a side of me that I wasn't ready to acknowledge. I tried to turn my attention to the ballgame, but the Redbirds weren't helping. The Dodgers tied the game in the fourth.

"Did AJ ask you to stay with me while he was gone?" I asked Lex when the game went to commercial.

"No."

"Would you tell me if he did?"

"Probably not."

I sighed and went back to watching the game. The Birds scored two runs. Things were improving. I dozed off, and when I woke, the game was in the top of the ninth.

The score was tied, and the Redbirds had one last chance to pull it out of the hat. They hit a two-run homer to take the lead, and held the Dodgers scoreless for the bottom half of the inning.

"I don't need a babysitter, Lex."

"I know."

"You don't have to stick around if you don't want to."

"I know."

"Okay."

Lex sat quietly watching TV. It didn't appear that he was planning to go anywhere. I fell asleep again. I slept without nightmares for the first time since the attack. I don't know if that was because Lex was there or if I was just exhausted. Either way it was refreshing to sleep without dreams. When I woke, Lex was gone and AJ was in the recliner.

"Have a nice nap?" he asked.

"I guess. I wasn't a very good host. When did Lex leave?"

"Few minutes ago."

"You just get home?" I asked.

"Uh-huh."

"Do any good?"

"We won."

"I bet the boys are happy. Where are they?"

"They went home with Chad."

I sighed. I wanted them home where I could see them. I wanted to hear their music thumping the ceiling above my head, and find their dirty socks scattered all over the floor. Maybe I had more than a concussion. Perhaps I was brain damaged.

I scooted to sit up on the couch, and AJ dropped down next to me. I leaned into him and he slipped his arm around me.

"I've done nothing but sleep and I'm still tired."

"Concussion will do that to ya, darlin'."

"I'm tired of it."

"You'll start feeling better in another day or two," he assured me.

I sighed and laid my head on his shoulder.

"Getting any closer to finding the murderer?"

"We have a few leads."

"You found out anything about the cowboy?"

"Nobody's seen him in town for a few days. Could be he was just passing through."

"If he's the killer, you'll never be able to solve this thing."

"Right now, we don't have any reason to think he did it. Just like to talk to him. Be nice to eliminate him from the picture completely."

"So what kind of leads do you have?"

"Nothin' really to share, darlin'."

"That's no fair. I've told you everything I know."

AJ laughed. "That's the way it's supposed to work. We ask the questions, you give us the answers."

"That sucks. I found the bodies. I should get some details."

"If I get any good details, I promise I'll share, okay?"

I nodded and closed my eyes. My head was starting to pound. Maybe a little less than it had the day before. I hoped that was a sign of improvement. AJ shifted and held me close. I breathed in the scent of sweat, Nomex, and methanol. Not an entirely unpleasant combination. I wished I felt better.

"You smell like the racetrack."

"I know, babe. I need a shower."

AJ rested his head against the couch cushion and sighed. He was tired. I could feel it in his muscles, hear it in his voice when he spoke. I hoped he'd spend the night.

"I've got to get out of this house tomorrow. Think I'll go to the shooting range and see Harold."

"You feel up to it?"

"I don't know if I'm gonna be able to shoot. Be nice to stare at four different walls for a while. I'm going stir crazy."

"Want some company?"

"Nah, I'll wait and go after you guys leave for the races."

"Lex could go with you."

"AJ, I don't need a babysitter."

"I know."

"I'm wiped. Let's call it a night."

He pulled me to my feet. I noticed the dizziness was less and didn't last as long. Recovery was starting to seem like a distinct possibility. I followed him to the bedroom and slid under the covers while AJ took his shower. I woke when he eased in beside me. Now he smelled like soap and that wasn't unpleasant either. He held me against his chest and a little tingle settled in the pit of my stomach. Unfortunately before the tingle could turn into something more, I was asleep. Head injuries are not conducive to night games.

We had just gotten up when Chad brought the boys over at eleven. They left with AJ to work on the racecar. Chad parked at the kitchen table. I was definitely feeling better. I'd been vertical for more than ten minutes and my head wasn't pounding. I poured iced tea for both of us and joined him.

"What have you heard on the murder case, Chad?"

"I'm pretty much out of the loop. I have something else going and they don't really need my help right now."

"You think they have anything?"

"Nothing big."

"Do you think this guy just started, or is this a continuation?"

"I don't know, Ranna. Serial killers are fairly rare. We've checked with other departments. I think they found a couple of similar murders, but they all have some pretty significant differences. We don't have any reason at this point to think it's the same guy."

He went to the refrigerator to refill his tea glass, and asked if I wanted more. I shook my head and he sat back down.

"I'm going to be out of touch for a while. I have an undercover assignment starting tonight. It'll probably last for a week or so. It's a real hush hush deal, so don't mention it to anybody."

"Okay."

"We've been working on this case for a while. I hope we can wrap it up this time."

I asked him a little about his case, but he didn't want to share any details. Said he just wanted me to know he was going to be out of touch, so I changed the subject.

"I'm going to Sure Shot, want to come with me?" I asked.

"I could do that."

I gathered my guns and followed Chad down the hallway. He opened the door and Bill flew off the porch.

"What's with the cat?" Chad asked.

"I think he's getting tired of being stepped on."

We took Chad's truck and left it in the Sure Shot parking lot. A police car and two sheriff's cars were sitting next to the front of The War Zone. They had the entrance roped off with yellow crime scene tape.

"What's going on out here?" I asked as we crunched across the parking lot.

"I think they got an anonymous tip about another body. It's probably bullshit. Most of those are, but they don't have many leads, so they can't afford to ignore it. I don't think Harold's in a huge hurry to open the range back up anyway. He's pretty freaked out about the whole thing."

We stepped inside and Harold greeted us from behind the counter. Mouse was sitting at a table in the corner, backpack on the floor beside him, chair tipped against the wall. His bruised and battered face had healed. Just a pale yellow shadow showed around his eyes.

I glanced at him and quickly turned away toward the counter. Chad stopped to talk with him for a minute before he went on through to the range. When I turned back toward Mouse, he was staring out the window. Probably Chad told him to ignore me.

I visited with Harold for a few minutes. He said he'd talked to the cops three times about the girls that had been murdered and what—if anything—he'd seen around the place the nights they died.

"I didn't see or hear a thing, Randi. I'm afraid to open the range until they catch the monster that's killed those girls. I've put new locks on the gates, so if anybody's gonna get in there now, they'll have to climb the fence. I didn't used to even pull the gates shut. I didn't really care if the kids wanted to hike there at night. Now I've gotta keep the place locked tight. It's a shame somebody's messed things up for everybody else."

I agreed that it was. We chatted a little more and I bought ammo before I turned to go. Chad was already shooting when I started into the range. On my way to the door, I stopped and said hello to Mouse. He started at the sound of my voice and stared at me, his eyes wide with fear. I smiled.

"Ma'am," he said.

"You doin' okay?" I asked.

"Yes, ma'am. Thank you."

He acted like he wished I would just leave him alone, so I pushed on into the range. I didn't care what Chad said. Mouse hadn't killed anybody. I was sure of it.

I had my .32 and my 9mm with me. I shot half a box of bullets through the .32. My aim was off, and my headache was starting up. I wondered if it was from wearing the earmuffs, or just from standing up and trying to sight down the range. I switched to the nine, and popped a few rounds, but my heart wasn't really in it and my headache was getting worse. I broke the guns down and cleaned them while Chad finished shooting. When we left, Mouse was gone and Harold was waiting for us.

"Chad, they have any new leads on the killer?" he asked.

"I'm not really on the case anymore, Harold," Chad answered. "I was just helping. I'm sure something will break soon, though."

"It's a terrible thing. You make sure you keep that gun with you, girl," he said to me.

"I will, Harold."

My head was really throbbing and I just wanted to go lie down. I'd really overdone my first trip out of the house.

I started through the door, hoping Chad would follow, when Harold called me back.

"I was wondering, Randi," he said. "Would you mind helping me with a class on Tuesday night? Got a bunch of first timers coming in. This whole murder thing has 'em spooked."

"I'll try."

It would depend on how I felt; and what kind of arrangements I could make for the boys. I was not going to leave them home alone to help teach a class.

"Let me know; I could really use the help."

"If you don't hear from me, I'll be here, Harold."

We finally made our exit and went out to the truck. I felt awful. As soon as I walked inside the house, I swallowed two aspirin and slumped onto the couch. Chad turned on the game and we watched the Cards beat up on the Dodgers again. Well, Chad watched and I slept, but I was thinking about the game. Chad left at ten to change into undercover cop. I hate it when he's working UC. I keep hoping he'll get a promotion or something and won't have to do it anymore. AJ and the twins arrived home an hour or so later. The boys said goodnight and went straight to bed. AJ joined me on the couch.

"Have a good night?" I asked.

"Not bad."

"What's that mean?"

"Means we won again," he said with a smile.

"How come you only win if I'm not there?"

"Just lucky, I guess."

AJ kneaded my neck and kissed me behind the ear. I felt it in the pit of my stomach. I was pretty sure if AJ spent the night, I'd be able to stay awake.

"You need to get to bed, darlin'."

"Hmm."

"Wish I could stay."

I sighed. So did I.

"You don't have to leave yet do you?"

"Not yet."

He stretched out on the couch. I laid my head on his chest, and fell asleep with his heartbeat gently thrumming in my ear. A couple of hours later, AJ kissed me on top of the head.

"Wake up, darlin'. I really do need to get home."

"Why don't you stay here tonight?"

"I need to get the car unloaded and you go into a coma whenever you get horizontal."

I laughed and sat up. AJ stood and I followed him to the truck.

"Have you guys discovered anything about the killer at all?"

"He's right-handed."

"That's it?"

"He's pretty strong. It takes a lot of strength to strangle someone."

"So, basically you've eliminated all left-handed men and all guys a hundred and fifty pounds or less."

"You got it."

"Well, that only leaves about a hundred million suspects."

AJ winked. "Yeah. Like I said, we're narrowing it down."

I kissed him through the open window. The taillights disappeared around the corner as Bill peered over the roof at me. I told him goodnight and went inside. Wilson went for his nightly run. When he came in, I told him it was bedtime. I fell asleep wondering if AJ and I would ever end up awake and in bed together.

Chapter 16

made it through work on Monday without anyone trying to knock my head off. Liz stopped in for a visit and asked about my colorful eye. I shared my adventure with Jody. I'm sure she already knew the basics. It made the front page of the paper. Mom was so proud.

I asked Liz if she'd ever had any dealings with Jody.

"I had a run in with him right after he went to work down here," she said.

"Did he hit you?"

"No, just lots of threats. He gets off on scaring women. Lots of guys are like that. Most of 'em can't get it up."

I laughed.

"Girl, I'm telling you the truth."

It was late when Liz left and I decided to lock up. I threw the dead bolts on the front door and glanced uneasily around. Understandably, I was a little uncomfortable there all by myself. It was my own fault. Morgan, Lex, and AJ had offered to come in and close with me. I told them I would be fine and to quit babying me. Truth was, I'd wanted someone with the boys more than with me. Now that I was alone, I wasn't sure I'd made the right decision.

I cranked up the dimmer to brighten the room and circled it with my eyes as I dumped the trashcans into a big plastic bag. Behind me, the ice settled in the cooler with a crunch. My heart rate spiked. I laughed at myself. The sound fell flat in the big empty room.

"For God's sake, Randi, get a grip," I muttered.

I dragged the black trash bag down the hall to the back door. I slipped the lock and hefted the bag through behind me. The door snicked closed and I paused outside and glanced around the parking lot. I was standing in a sickly pool of yellow leaking from the bug lamp on the back stoop. Puddles of light from the streetlamps scalloped the edges of the gravel lot. The rest was in darkness. Nothing moved in my field of vision. The only sounds I heard were the chirring of tree frogs. Certain I was alone, I swung the heavy bag over my shoulder and marched toward the trash bin.

I flipped the lid open and it crashed with a satisfying clang. I thought I heard a small scuffling noise and stood still, but it didn't come again. The last time I was out here, the cowboy had snuck up on me. I jerked around at the thought and peered out across the parking lot. I was still alone. The tree frogs were still singing their chorus. I was being stupid. I started to swing the bag into the dumpster and the scuffling noise came again. I stopped, the bag clattered against my leg. There was the noise again, this time followed by a dull thump and a groan. I dropped the bag and eased my gun from the holster. I was straining over the sound of my crashing heart to hear the noise. There was a soft moan coming from the darkness beyond the dumpster. Gun drawn, I slowly stepped around it and out of the light. Something moved in the shadow of the building.

"Who's there?"

My voice was high and shaky, barely above a whisper. I repeated myself. There was no answer. I stepped closer and squinted into the shadows at a human-shaped form. I heard the moan again and sank to my knees next to the man on the ground. He moved and his face came in view. Black streaks mottled his cheeks in the yellow glow of the bug light. His eyes were almost swollen shut, blood trickled from his nose and dripped on the ground. I recognized him by the threadbare cammies. It was Mouse and he was in bad shape.

"Oh, God, Mouse."

His swollen eyes opened a fraction and he reached toward me.

"Hang on, Mouse. I've gotta get some help."

I snapped my cell phone off my belt and dialed 911. I gave my name, the location and stated the problem, then dropped the phone and ran into the bar. I scooped some ice into a baggie, grabbed a bar towel and ran back outside. Mouse lay motionless.

"Mouse stay with me, you hear?"

He moaned and rolled onto his back.

"Come on, Mouse. You need to sit up."

I grabbed him under the arms and tried to balance him against the wall. He groaned in pain. I stopped. I didn't try to move him again. He lay there, his hand wrapped protectively around his ribs. Blood ran from his nose and soaked the collar of his shirt and the rocks below. His hair was matted and bloody. Rocks were stuck in the mess from his crawl across the parking lot. His trail through the gravel was obvious in the moonlight, now that I was looking for it.

I ran to the car and grabbed a blanket and coat from the trunk. I covered Mouse with the blanket and wadded the coat into a pillow behind his head. His lids fluttered and a small moan escaped from his lips. I knelt in the gravel next to him.

"Mouse? Mouse talk to me."

I brushed my fingers across his brow. He was damp and cold to the touch. I laid my hand on his shoulder and his eyes shot open as he jerked away.

"It's just me, Mouse. You're okay."

"My friend," he mumbled.

"I'm your friend, Mouse."

He shook his head and gritted his teeth in pain.

"Shhh. Help's on the way."

He tried to take a deep breath and groaned. I willed the ambulance to hurry.

"What happened, Mouse? Who did this?"

"Thought he was...friend."

"Who, Mouse? Who was your friend? Did Jody do this?"

He coughed and blood trickled between his lips. I wiped it away with the damp bar towel.

"Not Jody," he whispered.

A siren sounded in the distance. Oh, hurry up...Mouse shifted his body and groaned. He coughed and blood spattered from his mouth, frothy and thick. His breathing sounded damp. His lips moved and I leaned closer to hear.

"...didn't kill those girls..."

"What?"

He tried to take a breath. His face was almost translucent in the yellow bug light. I wiped his forehead with the edge of the blanket. Blood dripped in a steady stream from the corner of his mouth.

"I didn't...kill...those...girls."

The words were strong, and when he finished, he rolled onto his side, coughing and gagging. The sirens were getting closer. I squeezed his shoulder as he tried to catch his breath.

"Hang on, Mouse. The ambulance is almost here."

His lips moved and I strained to hear him.

"...know who killed them."

"Who, Mouse? Who was it?"

His lips started to move again but the blood rushed into his mouth. He coughed, and choked. Headlights threw our shadows against the wall as an ambulance and a police car slid to a stop a few feet away. The EMTs pushed me aside and went to work. I slumped against the dumpster, and watched them try to save his life. Steve slipped his arm around my waist.

"Jesus, who would do something like that to Mouse?" he asked.

"I asked him if it was Jody."

"I don't think Jody did this, Ran."

"He said it wasn't. Steve, he said he knows who killed those girls."

"What did he say?"

I told him what little I'd heard. "He started coughing and couldn't finish."

"Goddammit."

"He might know, Steve. He walks all over. People are so used to seeing him, he's almost invisible."

Steve stepped forward and spoke to the EMT. He shook his head as they loaded Mouse on a stretcher. Steve's shoulders slumped as he stepped away. They pushed the stretcher into the rear of the ambulance, and slammed the door. Gravel spewed from the tires as they raced out of the lot. Steve walked the lot looking down to study the marks in the gravel where Mouse had dragged himself. He sent an officer to search the perimeter near the trees, and directed the CSI crew to take photos of where I'd found Mouse and the marks in the gravel. He came back and motioned me inside. He sat at the bar while I locked up and told him again everything that Mouse had said. I sagged onto the stool next to him when I finished.

"Is he going to live?" I asked.

"They didn't sound too hopeful."

"Poor Mouse."

"We're back to square one. We didn't have much evidence to begin with, and all of it was circumstantial. But we could put Mouse in the picture so that all of the pieces fit. Now we don't have a damn thing. Shit!"

"I'm sorry, Steve."

"Not your fault."

It was late. I yawned and rubbed my forehead. My shirt was blood-spattered and my head hurt. I finished closing and Steve nudged me out toward my car. He trailed me home and stopped in the street in front of the house. I leaned in his open window.

"You going to the hospital?" I asked.

"Uh-huh."

"You need me to do anything?"

"Not now."

"Let me know…"

He nodded and drove away. Bill stood up from his spot on the porch, stretched, and blinked at me while I unlocked the door. I told him goodnight, blocked the dog before he could run out and get beat up again, and pushed the door closed behind me. The house was quiet. No one had left a television on, or a stereo playing. I was getting an early taste of my empty nest while the boys were staying at Morgan's, and I didn't like it. I wanted my babies home, dirty laundry, loud music and all.

I peeled off my bloody shirt and tossed it into the trash. After a shower, I climbed into bed and wondered what information Mouse had that had almost gotten him killed.

The phone woke me in the morning. It was Steve calling from the hospital. Mouse was still alive, in critical condition. They still weren't sure if he would make it. He said he'd let me know if he heard anything else. I tried to go back to sleep, but it was no use. I called Dad and told him what had happened to Mouse. If he had family around here, I figured Dad would know them. He didn't know of any family, but he said he'd go to the hospital so Mouse wouldn't be alone.

I thought about going to the hospital, but they weren't going to let Dad and me both go in. I wasn't going to do him any good sitting in the waiting room. I puttered around the house, edgy and unfocused. I couldn't settle on anything. I did some laundry, then went out into the yard to play with Wilson. I felt like I should be doing something, but I couldn't think what. I went back into the house. Wilson settled in for a nap. I decided to go get lunch.

I went to Mabel's and stayed to talk to Granny Bert. She left with Fred when she finished her shift. I moved to Mabel's table and bummed a cigarette from her. She chattered on for an hour or so. I left once to call the hospital and check on Mouse. There was no change. I told Mabel goodbye and drove to the high school. Football practice was still going on. I sat in the bleachers and watched. Lex was working and Steve and AJ were both out of touch for the moment, but an Alden police car idled in the lot overlooking the practice field. It should have made me feel better, but it just scared me. I wanted Jody McIntire locked up.

After practice, I took the boys to Mom's. On the way over, they told me what had happened to Mouse. I didn't tell them I had found him. I noticed the story had started to grow with the retelling. I wondered how my name had stayed out of it so far. After I delivered the kids, I drove to The War Zone to help Harold with his class. I was early, so I bought some shells and went in to shoot before class started. After my last outing, I felt I needed the brush up. Harold was in his office sorting through handouts for tonight's lesson.

AJ and Steve came in to qualify with their new backup weapons. That's the excuse they used anyway. I think it was just a chance to get away from the case for a while.

After spending the better part of a year teasing me about my little .32, Steve and AJ had both decided they liked it and bought one for themselves. I just managed to keep from saying I told you so. It wasn't easy.

When they finished, Steve stopped at the counter to talk to Harold. AJ held the outside door for me. As I turned to walk through, I saw Harold and Steve both look over at me. When I caught Steve's eye, he quickly looked away. He came out the door behind us, but before I could ask what he was talking to Harold about he peeled off toward his car.

"I'm meeting Sara and the kids at the farm, I'll keep an eye on the twins, Ran."

With a wave, he slipped behind the wheel and drove out of the gravel lot. I leaned a hip against the front fender of AJ's truck and watched the women as they arrived for class. AJ tossed his gun cleaning kit onto the front seat, then closed the door and draped his arm over my shoulder.

"You haven't forgotten about Dad's birthday party have you? It's Thursday at six."

"I had actually. The way this case is going, I'll probably be stuck somewhere else."

"Chad's already said he wouldn't be there. Mom's gonna flip if Steve's not there."

"I'd say the chances are pretty slim."

"Great, that leaves me, Sara Beth, and the kids. You do know it's always my fault if Steve and Chad manage to get out of some family gathering."

AJ laughed and dropped a kiss on the top of my head.

"You can handle it, darlin'."

As we talked, the parking lot was slowly filling up. AJ glanced around at the women heading in to Sure Shot, and looked at me with a serious frown on his face.

"Darlin', I'm not sure this is a good idea."

"What's not?"

"Teaching all these women to shoot."

"And why's that?"

"Now, every time a cop takes a domestic call he's got to worry about some woman with PMS waving around a gun."

I laughed for the first time all day and some of the tension that had me pacing the floors trickled away.

"You are a pig. A big, fat, male chauvinist pig."

"Just thinkin' about the safety of our officers, babe."

"I gotta go."

I shrugged out from under his arm and started to walk into the building. AJ hooked the collar of my shirt, spun me close and kissed me until my knees went weak. He let me go, winked, ducked into his truck and drove away. I stood in the parking lot in a stupor for a couple of minutes before I turned to go inside. Harold was waiting for me when I came in. I asked if he'd heard about Mouse.

"This town is going to hell in a hand basket, Randi."

I couldn't disagree with that. I stashed my purse behind the counter, so I wouldn't have to mess with it during class, and slipped back around to the front.

"You dating that detective?" Harold asked.

"Sort of, I think."

"He's a good man. You ready to get started?"

"Sure, let's do it."

I grabbed the box of ammo Harold had laid out on the counter for me and followed him into the range. The women were sitting in chairs against the wall. Harold stepped in front of them and started his spiel about how it was every woman's responsibility to protect herself and a gun was just one more tool for the job, blah, blah, blah. I'd heard it before so I tuned out. Harold passed around earmuffs to all the ladies, and showed them what kind of damage his weapon could do to a paper target. Then it was my turn. Since I was trying to be somewhat accurate, I used my nine. I put four shots into the torso of the target and laid my weapon down on the shooting table.

The women teamed up and we went over their weapons with them, showed them how to load and unload, and had them practice for a while. I glanced around at the group. It was an eclectic bunch, housewives, clerks, a lawyer, and a checker from the grocery store. Liz and Ann Marie were there. They handled their guns like old friends. I guess they were just there for a brush up. Both of them were in Harold's group.

I went down the line showing the women how to sight their guns and letting them squeeze off some shots. I gave them a few pointers and moved on to the next. None of them had much confidence and that translated into poor shooting skills. Only practice would make them comfortable with a handgun. I doubted many of them would put in the time to get that way. I glanced down the the range and saw Harold giving Ann Marie some extra attention. He was standing behind her, with his hands covering hers on the grip of the gun. I assume he was giving her tips on her shooting stance. Looked like a cheap feel to me. Liz saw me watching and raised her eyebrows. I smirked and went back to the ladies under my care. When they were finished, I suggested they spend an hour or two a week at the range putting some ammo through their guns. I hoped none of them would ever actually have to use them.

When most of the women were gone, I signaled Harold that I was leaving. He waved and gave his attention to the young woman he was helping. Liz and Ann Marie followed me outside.

"Hey, Randi?"

"Yeah."

"Could you give us a ride to town? My car's in the shop. Miss Bertie gave us a ride over on her way home from work."

"Sure. Hop in. You guys should have called me, I'd have given you a ride."

"It was no big deal. We'd pretty much decided to stay home tonight, but then your granny offered to give us a ride, so we came on out."

I left them at Liz's house. It was twice as big as mine, and probably twice as nice. As I drove home, I pondered whether or not I'd made the wrong career choice. Probably not. I don't think I could handle their job. I deal with drunks every day, but at least they have their clothes on most of the time.

Chapter 17

I went into the house and checked my answering machine for messages. No one wanted to talk to me enough to leave a message. I let Wilson out, made a sandwich and slumped at the table while I ate. I was thinking about the murders. Didn't look to me like they were any closer to catching the killer than they had been when this all began. I didn't think this guy had just started killing. I knew the police had searched for related murders, but I couldn't settle down. I needed to be doing something that at least felt productive. I decided to call on a friend and see what I could find. I let Wilson in and drove to the newspaper office. When I stepped through the door, the sports editor's eyes went wide and he scooted off to his cubbyhole. I laughed and roamed around until I found the guy I was searching for: Tom Wallace, the managing editor.

"Hey, Tom. What's up?"

"Hi, Randi. Here to beg for your old job back?" He asked grinning.

"Fat chance."

"I got it. You've finally come to your senses and came down here to profess your undying love?"

"Nope, that's not it either. I could use your help, though."

"You're breaking my heart, lusting after my brain instead of my body."

"God, you're such a squirrel. You have time to help me before you put the paper to bed?"

"Anything for you, love. Have a seat."

I ignored the chair and perched on the end of his desk.

"If I wanted to find information on unsolved murders in Missouri, where would I start searching?"

"We can tap into Lexis/Nexis. We just feed it some key words and it hits on news stories that fit the parameters. If they made the papers, it might give us a place to start."

"Cool, can I use it?"

"It's a subscription service. And, it's not cheap if you're doing a lot of research."

"How much is not cheap?"

"I don't know, say dinner, a movie, and then a night at my place."

"Oh, ha ha."

"Hey, it was worth a shot."

"Would it be worth it to you to make some inquiries? It might lead to a big story."

Tom grinned at me. "You're just trying to get out of having to pay."

"Well, yeah, your price is a little out of my league."

"Kiddo, I'm telling you, it would be the bargain of a lifetime."

"I'm serious Tom, would you check something out for me?"

Tom glanced at his watch, "I could give it an hour or so, but it is gonna cost you. Let's call it a debt to be named later. Now, what are you looking for?"

"You've been doing stories on the murders, right?"

I didn't have to explain which murders. The Timber Bridge killings were the first murders in Alden in eons. Tom scooted forward in his chair and started acting like a journalist instead of a lecher. I definitely had his attention.

"Could you use the details from those stories to set your parameters and see if you get any matches in Missouri?"

"Sure. Why?"

"Just a hunch."

"You think he killed before he came to Alden?"

"Maybe."

"Is that an official hunch?"

"Nope, it's just my hunch."

"You wouldn't happen to have any official details about the case that the police haven't released, would you?"

"Probably, but I can't tell you."

"I'll buy you dinner."

"I already ate. Besides my brothers would kill me. Not worth it."

"We could make other arrangements," he said with a wink.

I laughed. "I don't think AJ would appreciate that."

"You're dating AJ Weleski again?"

"I guess so."

"Shit," he sighed. "I'll do it, but unless I get a story out of it, you're gonna owe me."

"I'll stand you at the bar some night. Free beer for you and a guest."

"Sam Adams beer and cheeseburgers."

"Fine, Sam Adams and cheeseburgers, geez."

"You've got a deal."

"Thanks, Tom. You want me to hang around or what?"

"It's gonna take a while, how 'bout I call you? It might be tomorrow."

"Okay. You have my cell number?"

He didn't, so I gave it to him and left the newsroom. I met the sports editor in the doorway as I was leaving. He almost tripped over his feet getting out of my way. Ahhh, sometimes life is sweet.

Wilson greeted me when I arrived home. But instead of his usual exuberant greeting, he just hunkered down with his ears lowered and his tail tucked between his legs. I rubbed his head and walked down the hall to the bathroom. Before I went in, he growled and let out one sharp bark.

"What's the matter with you buddy?"

He licked my hand when I reached down to pet him and I shook my head and went into the bathroom. When I flipped on the light, my breath whooshed out like I'd been hit in the gut. On the mirror, written with my lipstick, was a note from Jody. *I'm still watching you, Twinkie.*

"Son of a bitch."

I grabbed the Windex from under the counter and scrubbed the greasy mess off the glass. Wilson watched warily from the doorway as I muttered under my breath. I was furious, and scared, but at that moment, my anger was stronger than my fear.

In the living room later, I sat rigid on the couch, staring at the television. As my anger faded, fear crept in to take its place. A knock at the door jerked me out of my head and into the present. I glanced at the clock; it was after eleven-thirty. Who the hell was at my door this time of night? I palmed my gun and peered out the window. Chad was standing on my front porch with Bill wrapping himself around his legs. I sagged with relief, only then realizing I had expected to see Jody. I opened the door with relief. Chad stumbled over the cat, pushed past me, and shoved the door closed behind him.

"That cat is a pain in the ass."

I wrinkled my nose and stepped away.

"Jesus, you smell like pot."

"No shit."

His eyes were red and squinty. "Are you stoned?" I asked.

"Just a little bit."

I couldn't help it, I laughed. A little bit stoned is kind of like a little bit pregnant. He weaved his way into my living room and flopped onto the couch.

"Aren't you supposed to stay straight?"

"Contact high, occupational hazard sometimes."

"I hope you don't get popped for a drug test any time soon."

"Oh, Jesus, me too."

He let his head fall to the back of the couch and his eyes drooped closed.

"Why don't you get out of those clothes and go take a shower. I'll throw your stuff in to wash."

"No, don't wash 'em. That'd be too hard to explain. I will take you up on the shower, though."

While Chad was in the bathroom, I pondered telling him about Jody's latest visit. He came out of the shower, slumped into one of my kitchen chairs and laid his head on his arms. I decided he wasn't in any condition to help me right now. Tomorrow, I'd call a locksmith.

I poured him a glass of tea and sat back down at the table.

"You hear about Mouse?" I asked.

"Uh huh. How's he doing?"

"Still alive, as far as I know. Aren't you supposed to be undercover?"

"I am. I just needed to get away for a while."

"You look terrible."

"I blend in with the crowd, that's all that matters."

He sat up, picked up the tea glass, and drank it off in one gulp.

"God, Ran. I can't wait to get finished with this job. I've got a bad feeling about this one."

"Don't go back. You don't have to stay if you think you're in danger."

"Too much riding on me to back out now."

I bit back my comments. Nothing I could say was going to change his mind. I changed the subject instead.

"How'd you get away?"

"Told 'em I needed to see a man about a dog," he said grinning.

"Where's your car?"

"What?"

"Your car, Chad. Where is it?"

"Oh," he said laughing. "The car. I left it at Liz Appleton's place. Figured if they saw it there they wouldn't suspect anything. We kind of have an arrangement with Liz 'bout that kind of stuff."

"We have an arrangement, or you have an arrangement?"

Chad actually blushed. I had a hard time not laughing at him. He leaned forward on his elbows and his eyes closed. I tapped him on the arm.

"When do you need to be out of here, Chadly? Do you have time for a nap?"

He sat up and took a long look at his watch before he came up with the time.

"Midnight, one o'clock, somewhere around there," he finally answered.

"Go crash in my bedroom. I'll wake you."

"Thanks, Ran. I could use some sleep."

I watched TV, then fixed Chad a sandwich and woke him. He'd slept in his clothes and, if possible, looked more disreputable than he had when he arrived.

"How much longer are you going to be under?"

"Couple days."

"Why can't you make the bust now?"

"These guys are just little fish. We're waiting for the big one to swim in. He's supposed to be down Thursday or Friday. They call him The Duke."

"Like the Duke of Earl?"

"I don't know. They've just been talking about some guy called The Duke."

"Maybe he looks like John Wayne."

"Yeah, Ran, I bet that's it."

"You wearing a wire?" I asked.

"Nope, I'm on my own. This is a Federal sting. Completely off the books as far as the department goes. My super doesn't even know where I am. Far as he knows, I took of couple of days vacation."

"What's going on, Chad?"

"Look, I already told you more than I should have. I just didn't want you to worry or break my cover."

"They think a cop's involved," I said.

"You didn't hear that from me."

He glanced at the clock and finished his sandwich.

"I gotta go. Thanks, Ranna."

"Come by again if you want."

"Be hard to get away twice. Thanks, though."

"Be careful."

"I always am," he said with a wink. "Hey, I mean it. Don't bust my cover. Not to Mom, Steve, nobody. It could get me killed."

"Not a word. I promise."

"Thanks, Ran. Love you."

Chad stepped around Bill, slid down the stair rail, and strolled down the street. I checked the time when I went inside. It was one fifteen. I rubbed my eyes and decided it was time for Wilson and me to call it a day.

The phone rang at six a.m. I snatched up the receiver and mumbled hello.

"Randi."

"AJ?"

"Yeah, get up. We're on our way over."

Uh oh, this can't be good. The phone clicked and I scrambled out of bed and stumbled into my clothes. In the bathroom, I splashed water on my face. It didn't help; I was still half asleep. I guzzled a soda to get a caffeine infusion, let Wilson out, and unlocked the front door. I was on my way to the kitchen when AJ and Steve came in. They followed me and sat down at the table. Steve sniffed the air.

"You been smoking pot?"

Oh, shit.

"No."

"What about the boys?"

"They're at Mom's. Are you accusing my kids of using drugs? Seriously, Steve. Have you lost your mind?"

He sniffed the air again like a hound dog.

"Somebody around here has been smoking pot."

"Is that what was so urgent you had to get me up a six a.m.? You had a hot tip somebody was at my house burning some weed?"

AJ stifled a laugh. Steve didn't. It was too early in the morning for his sense of humor.

"Have you seen Chad?" Steve asked.

My stomach dropped. My heart rate doubled. It's hard to lie to a cop, especially if you're related. And I'm a rotten liar.

"He told me he was taking a couple of days vacation. I figured he was going to the lake. Why?"

To my surprise, the lie came off without a hitch. I tried to make sure my face didn't give me away.

"There's been another murder."

"What's that have to do with Chad?"

Steve sat and didn't say anything.

"AJ, what does that have to do with Chad?"

"The girl that was murdered was Ann Marie Austin."

"Ann Marie? Oh my God. I just saw her last night. I gave her and Liz a ride home. That's awful, but I still don't understand what that has to do with Chad."

"We think she was murdered around midnight." Steve said. "Becca got up in the night and went to her mom's room. When she didn't find her, she went downstairs. She found Liz unconscious in the living room and called 911 about one thirty. When the EMTs arrived, Ann Marie's car was there, but no one could find her. They took Liz off in the ambulance. They found Ann's body in the woods behind the house."

I blew out a breath in frustration.

"You're still not explaining what this all has to do with Chad, Steve."

"According to one of the neighbors, Chad's vehicle was parked at Liz's place from eleven thirty until some time after one. He wrote down the license plate number, we verified it. So we've placed Chad at the house during the time Ann Marie died. We need to talk to him."

"You're telling me you think Chad killed Ann Marie?"

"We have his fingerprints in the house and his car parked in the drive at the time of the murder."

"Well of course his fingerprints are in the house. He's dating Liz."

Oops, Chad was going to kill me.

"Who told you Chad and Liz were dating?"

"Um, well, nobody. I've just seen them together... talking." Man that sounded lame.

Steve stared at me like a stranger. I swallowed and looked guilty as hell and I hadn't done anything. Yet.

"Liz said the only contact she'd ever had with Chad was purely professional. She denied any kind of relationship between them."

"She's lying," I said.

"Or you are."

"Jesus, Steve. Why would I lie to you?"

"You tell me."

"Tell you what? What is it you want from me?"

"I want you to tell me what time Chad was here last night."

"He wasn't here. I haven't seen him for...I don't know a couple of days anyway."

My heart was pounding. What if he already knew Chad had been here last night? Maybe he'd spoken to Mrs. Litton. I wasn't going to hell for lying, I was going to jail.

"Think real hard, when did you see Chad last?"

"We went shooting the other day; I don't remember if I've seen him since then or not."

"Where is he?"

"How the hell should I know? He said he was taking a couple of days off; I assumed he went to the lake."

"Randi, we're talking murder here and Chad is a suspect. I hope you're not lying to me," Steve said.

I hoped he didn't find out I was. I decided to go on the defensive.

"Do you really think Chad did it?"

"It doesn't matter what I think. It's what I can prove. Right now, Chad is in deep shit. The sooner we talk to him the better."

I turned away from Steve and AJ and stared through the window. Shit, I wondered if I should say anything. If I kept quiet, Chad could end up in prison. If I said something, he could end up dead. Don't tell anybody, he'd said. It could get me killed. His words flashed through my mind. Was he just setting me up as his alibi?

"No way," I said out loud.

Steve and AJ stared at me as I turned around.

"Come on, Randi, spill. What's going on?" Steve asked.

I knew Chad didn't kill Ann Marie. I decided to stand my ground.

"There's nothing to spill, Steve. I haven't seen Chad."

"Randi, if you lie for him that makes you an accessory to murder."

"Dammit, Steve, I know that. I said I haven't seen Chad and I haven't."

Steve glared at me from across the room. He knew I was lying, but he couldn't figure out why. I glared back. AJ cleared his throat and we broke eye contact. Wilson whined to come in. I walked away from them to open the door.

"Is Liz okay?" I asked.

"They'll probably keep her in the hospital for a day or two," AJ answered.

"Where's Becca?"

Steve's shoulders relaxed a little and he stared down at the tabletop.

"I took her home and Sara Beth put her to bed," he said. "I didn't want to get family services involved."

I stared at Steve. The same guy that was trying to convince me his own brother had just committed a murder, couldn't bear to see the daughter of a virtual stranger sucked into social services. He glanced up and caught my stare.

"Don't look at me like that, Randi. Chad makes his own decisions. I'm just following the evidence. He has no alibi for any of the murders that we can pinpoint a date on."

"He also doesn't have a motive."

"No, we just don't know what the motive is."

"Exactly how long have you been looking at Chad as a suspect, Steve?"

"Randi, I'm a cop. All I have is the evidence and right now the evidence points to Chad as a suspect or at the very least a material witness."

"Gee, yesterday you thought the evidence pointed to Mouse and that worked out real well."

"Can it Randi, and tell me where he is, or you'll end up behind bars with him."

"Listen to yourself, Steve. You're talking about family here."

"That has nothing to do with it and you know it."

"Look, Steve, you said whoever killed Ann Marie hit Liz. I know Chad would never hurt her, regardless of what she told you about their relationship."

Steve stood up from the table and sighed.

"You don't know that, Randi. You don't know what he's capable of."

I got the impression Steve and I weren't talking about the same man. The Chad I knew couldn't murder a woman in cold blood. But Steve knew Chad the SEAL, and he was right, I didn't know what that man was capable of. I shook those thoughts away. Steve was poisoning my mind against my twin brother.

"You don't really believe that Chad committed these murders. I know you don't, Stevie. You can't."

He turned to leave the kitchen.

"You let me know if Chad gets in touch with you."

"I will, Steve." I was lying through my teeth.

He turned and leveled a cop stare at me. He knew I was lying.

"Understand this, Randi, if you protect him, you will go to jail."

I snapped off a salute.

"Yes, sir, Colonel, sir!"

AJ grinned and turned his head so Steve wouldn't see. Steve narrowed his eyes, leaned toward me and placed his hands flat on the kitchen table.

"Joke if you want to, Randi. But, if I find you've been lying to me, I will bust you. There's nothing funny about what's going on here. This is a murder investigation."

He turned and stalked down the hall and out the front door.

"God damn cat!" he muttered as he tripped down the steps.

I sent Bill a silent thank you.

Chapter 18

You need to cut Steve some slack, Randi. This case has him pretty stressed," AJ said.

"He needs to quit treating me like some flunky. He's my brother, not my commanding officer."

"He's the lead detective on a murder investigation. If you've been holding back information from him, he has a right to be pissed."

"I should have known you'd take his side."

"It's not about sides, Randi."

"Right. I suppose you think Chad killed Ann Marie, too."

I got up, pulled a Pepsi out of the fridge, and took a long drink.

"What I think is that Chad was over here last night. What I don't understand is why you are lying about it."

I choked and sat the can on the table.

"He wasn't here." I coughed. "I already told you that."

"Hmm. You sure you want to stick with that story? This isn't a game, Randi. Chad's in a world of hurt right now."

"Dammit, AJ, I know that. I'm telling you the truth. I can't believe you and Steve are pulling this good cop bad cop shit on me."

"Fine, Chad wasn't here last night, you were just hanging around the house with nothing to do and decided to get stoned. So where's your stash? Let's burn one. I have some time before I have to get back to work."

"Ha, Ha, funny guy."

I decided at this point, I'd be better off just keeping my mouth shut. I wasn't gaining any brownie points for Chad or myself. AJ went to the refrigerator and poured himself a glass of iced tea. I turned and gazed out the window into the backyard.

"Was Ann Marie's murder the same as the others, AJ?"

"Except this time he's left us a witness."

"Liz saw the killer?"

"She didn't get a good look. Just her bad luck she was even there. She wasn't supposed to be. She had an appointment scheduled, but she wasn't feeling well so she cancelled and went to bed early. She went down to answer the door because she thought Ann Marie was out. She opened it and got knocked in the head. That's all she remembers. We're hoping she comes up with more details as her memory comes back."

"You think it's the same guy, then?"

"Yes we do."

"Then why isn't Liz dead?"

"I don't know, Randi, maybe he got interrupted. Maybe he liked the way she smelled. Maybe, he liked Liz and he just had it in for Ann Marie. When we get him locked up, I'll ask him for you and let you know."

"And you're telling me you believe Chad killed those women?"

"Randi, we're just following the evidence. This is the first hard lead we've gotten on this case. We can place Chad not just at the scene of the crime, but at the scene during the time the murder was committed. We need to talk to him, and suddenly he's dropped off the radar. It doesn't matter what I believe, I'm just following the trail."

"And Chad's your only suspect? Come on, what about the cowboy from the bar?"

AJ massaged his temples.

"We're still interested in your cowboy, Ran. But we can't place him at the scene of any of the murders. And right now, he's in the wind. Nobody's seen him for days."

"Maybe Mouse will wake up today and you can talk to him. He said he knows who the killer is."

"Mouse is in bad shape, Randi. If he wakes up again, I'm not sure he's going to be able to tell us anything."

As AJ walked down the hall to the bathroom, I thought over what Mouse had mumbled to me before he lost consciousness. He said his attacker was a friend. Wonder if he considered Chad a friend. I crumpled my aluminum soda can and tossed it into the trash. Dammit, they were starting to make me seriously wonder if Chad had something to do with the murders.

AJ walked in and sat across from me.

"What ties all these women together, AJ? There has to be a pattern."

"If there is, we haven't picked up on it yet."

AJ rubbed his bloodshot eyes and sighed.

"I better get downtown."

"You'd better get some sleep."

"Too much to do, I'll sleep later. Could you give me a ride to the house? I need to get my truck. I came in to town with Steve this morning."

"Let me get my keys."

On the drive to AJ's house, I finally remembered the lipstick note.

"And you didn't tell me this sooner, because?"

"I just didn't think about it. There's been a lot going on in case you haven't noticed."

"He was in your house, Randi. That's a big deal. What the hell were you thinking?"

I went from friend to wicked bitch of the west in about two seconds.

"What was I thinking? I was mad as hell. I was thinking if I could have gotten any of you to listen to me when this all started, he wouldn't still be writing notes on my mirror and ruining my lipstick."

I took a deep breath so I could go on and AJ squeezed my arm.

"You're right, darlin'. I'm sorry. I didn't mean it to come out like that. I just wish we could have checked for prints, or at least gotten photos," AJ said.

"I'm sorry. It pissed me off so bad, I just wanted it gone."

"Don't worry about it. I'm glad you told me. I'll have a patrol officer run through your neighborhood more often. That may dissuade him from dropping in unannounced. If you get any other messages, call me immediately. Wouldn't be a bad idea to change the locks on your doors, too."

"That's already on my list of things to do today."

AJ gave me a goodbye kiss when I dropped him off in his driveway. I drove back toward town and stopped at Mabel's to get breakfast before I went home. Larry Foreman was sitting at the front table with Mabel. He owned a lock shop in town and I asked him when he could come by and install new locks on my front and back doors. He said he could do it today, so I told him I'd meet him at the house in about an hour. I sat at the counter and picked up a newspaper. They were calling the killer the Timber Bridge Strangler, even though they found Ann Marie in a wooded area south of her house. I read the article. As usual, they had done an outstanding job of saying a lot about nothing. The Major Crime Task Force had been activated and they weren't releasing much information. Probably because at this point, there wasn't a lot to release. The story about Mouse was three inches long and buried on an inside page. According to the paper, the police didn't have any suspects. I knew that wasn't true. If they thought Chad killed Ann Marie, they'd have to think he was the one that beat up Mouse.

I finished breakfast and the paper and met Larry at the house. He showed me a couple of different locks. I told him I didn't care what it looked like; I wanted the best he had. He said he'd leave the keys with Mrs. Litton when he was finished. I ran over to tell her of the arrangement.

"That would be just fine, Randi. I'm always glad to help out a neighbor."

"I really appreciate it. I need to run some errands and I won't be here when he finishes up."

I turned to go and she stopped me in my tracks.

"I have something here for you. That little Baldwin boy from down the street said you weren't home so it got left over there. I don't know why UPS didn't just leave it with me. We've been neighbors for so long we're practically family. Anyway he came over, the little Baldwin boy, not the UPS man, you see, and you still weren't home and he had to go to soccer practice, so I told him to just leave it with me, that I'd be more than happy to see that you got it. So he left it here, and I'm so glad you stopped over today so I could give it to you, because I'm so forgetful, I might not have remembered otherwise."

While I stood there trying to sort out that flood of information, Mrs. Litton toddled back into the house to locate the mysterious package. I was pretty sure she wouldn't have forgotten about the package, she would probably have steamed it open and peeked inside before she delivered it, if I hadn't shown up to get it.

She came back with a shoebox-sized package addressed to Travis. I glanced at the return address, but the ink was smeared and I couldn't read it. I thanked Mrs. Litton and walked to the car. I gave the package a tentative shake. Something slid inside with a soft thump. My hands started shaking and I wondered if this was more of Jody's handiwork. I stopped next to the car and examined the label again. Through the smeared ink, I could just make out the name CompuTech. My breath whooshed out in relief. I'd have felt like an idiot if I'd run down to the police station with a mysterious box of computer parts. I snickered under my breath at the fun AJ and Steve would have had with that one.

The box was a little beat up. I hoped whatever computer parts Travis had ordered hadn't been damaged in transit. I tossed the box on the rear seat for Travis to get later and started the car. I waved at Larry and drove to

Steve's house to see if Sara Beth needed any help. When I arrived, Julie and Becca were watching TV.

"She doing okay, Sara?" I asked.

"She's fine. Isn't she a beautiful little girl?"

I glanced into the living room. Becca and Julie were huddled together in front of the television. The shiny black head next to the sparkling blonde one made them look like a positive and a negative.

"You need me to do anything for you?" I asked.

"No, we're fine."

Becca followed Julie into the kitchen to get a snack. She sat down at the table directly across the room from me. Liz's daughter had clouds of dark curly hair and dazzling, green eyes framed by lashes I would kill for.

"Hi, Aunt Randi," Julie said.

"Hi, kiddo."

Julie sat down at the table, stared across at Becca, and then over at me. I scooped Nathan off the floor as he toddled through the kitchen and tickled him until he screamed with laughter.

"Becca," Julie said. "You look just like my Aunt Randi."

I stopped tickling and turned Nathan loose. He resumed his interrupted trip to the table for his snack. Sara Beth looked back and forth, between Becca and me.

"I think it's just the hair," she said. "They've both got lots of curly, dark hair, but your Aunt Randi doesn't have green eyes."

"Becca's prettier than your old Aunt Randi, Jules," I said.

I did some quick mental math to see if Becca could actually be my long lost niece, but I couldn't see how that would work. Unless Chad hooked up with Liz sometime before she moved to Alden, Becca and I weren't related.

The girls finished their peanut butter and jelly sandwiches and skipped off back to the family room. I stood and planted a kiss on top of Nathan's head. He ducked and said ick, but I don't think he really hated it.

"Bethy, if you're sure you don't need anything, I'd better get going. I have to run home and let the dog out, then run to town to get supplies for the boys' class homecoming float."

"Napkins, paint, and chicken wire," she said laughing.

"Yep, that's it. I'd better get going. I have my cell phone with me. If you need anything just call."

"Thanks, Randi."

Sara Beth followed me to the car.

"You think Becca could be Chad's daughter?" she asked.

"Nah, I don't think the timing fits. I can't get it to add up anyway."

Beth laughed. "Probably a good thing; your mom would have a coronary."

If Mom got an inkling that Steve thought Chad was a murderer, a coronary would be the least of it. I waved goodbye and went back to the house. Larry had finished, so I got the new keys from Mrs. Litton and checked to make sure Wilson hadn't escaped while the locks were being installed. He was safe and sound and begging to go outside. I let him out for a run and found a note from Chad on the kitchen table. He must have slipped in while Larry was there. The note asked me to go to the hospital and tell Liz he'd see her as soon as he could.

I read it twice and hoped Mrs. Litton hadn't seen Chad's latest entry. Then I soaked it in the sink and ran it through the garbage disposal. I felt like a secret agent or something.

I ignored the little squiggle of unease that lodged in my stomach. I should have called Steve and shown him the note, but right now, I thought it was in Chad's best interests to stay missing.

While I waited for Wilson to come back in, I thought about Chad and Liz and Becca. Becca might not be Chad's daughter, but she might end up as his stepdaughter one of these days. Assuming Chad didn't end up in prison. I couldn't wait to see Mom's face when Chad showed up with Liz at some family dinner. It would be worth paying admission.

Wilson barked to come in and I topped off his food and water dishes before I left. As I crossed the drive to the car, Bill shot out from underneath and dove between my legs.

"Jesus, Bill. You're going to give me a heart attack."

He didn't appear terribly concerned about my health. He just sat on the porch steps and blinked at me. I drove to the hospital, asked for Liz's room number, and wandered around lost until I finally found her. She had fallen asleep sitting up with the television on. I waited in the chair next to the bed. She woke slowly and smiled when she realized she had a visitor.

"Hi," she said.

"How are you feeling?"

"I have an awful headache."

"I know how that is. Chad asked me to stop by. He said he'd see you as soon as he could. The cops think he killed Anne Marie, Liz. Because his car was at your place last night."

She shook her head and stared down at her hands. When her eyes met mine, they were bright with unshed tears.

"Your brother is a very nice man. I don't think he could have killed Ann Marie."

I tried to ignore the fact that she didn't say definitively, "Chad didn't kill Ann Marie." It was just semantics. I hoped.

"If he gets in touch with you, tell him Steve needs to talk to him."

She nodded and looked back down at her lap.

"He loves you," I said.

"He'll get over that."

"Why would he want to? Liz, what's that supposed to mean?"

"He can't get hooked up with me. He's a cop."

"That doesn't have anything to do with it."

"Oh, Randi. That has everything to do with it. It just wouldn't work. What would his family think?"

"I'm his family, I think you're great."

She raised her head and smiled.

"What about Steve?"

"Steve took Becca home so she could play with Julie. I don't think he has a problem with you and Chad either."

Right now, his problem was with Chad alone. I pushed that thought aside. Steve was wrong. He had to be.

"And your parents?"

"My Dad will love you. Mom is another story, but she doesn't really like me either, so I wouldn't worry about it too much," I said smiling.

"You make it sound easy."

"It is easy."

"You just don't understand, Randi. He's a cop, I'm a prostitute. It would never work."

"Don't let other people decide your happiness, Liz. If you guys love each other, that's all that's important."

Liz blinked away her tears and I gave her a hug.

"I have to go. Here's my cell phone number. If you need anything call me."

"Thank you, Randi."

"That's what family's for."

A lone tear tracked down her cheek. I gave her hand a squeeze before I stood to go. I started through the door then stopped and turned back.

"Do you guys keep an appointment book?" I asked.

"What?"

"When someone calls for an...um...appointment. Do you write it down somewhere?"

"Oh," Liz laughed. "Nope. Strictly off the record."

"I was just wondering."

"Why?"

"I thought maybe whoever killed Ann Marie might have called ahead."

"He might have. I didn't take the call so there's no way to know now." Liz blinked and took a deep shuddering breath. "I hope they catch the bastard that did this."

"They will."

I left Liz and went looking for Mouse. I finally found Lex in the intensive care waiting room.

"Hey, Lex. I didn't know you knew Mouse."

"We talk some."

"You been in to see him?"

"He's still unconscious. I don't think they have much hope."

I stayed with Lex until the nurse came to let him in Mouse's room again. He offered to let me go instead, but I waved him away and left the hospital. I needed to get to the farm and drop off the float supplies. While I was there, I wandered out to the garage to check on my truck. I found Dad under the hood of Devin's black Mustang.

"Hey, Dad."

He jumped and hit his head on the hood. Guilty conscience.

"Hi, hon," he said rubbing his head.

"How's my truck?"

He grinned and looked a little sheepish. I walked over and peered under the hood. I couldn't tell that anything had been done since the last time I was there.

"Ready in about a week, you said."

He smiled again. "Well, Devin really wanted to work on the car, so we took a break from your truck."

"Took a break. Have you worked on it at all?"

"A little."

"Uh-huh."

"Well, I didn't think it was critical since you had something to drive."

"Jeez, Dad. You have any idea what AJ will do if something happens to his car? I want my truck back."

"We'll start working on it again this weekend, I promise. Why don't you run in for a minute and say hi to your mom?"

I couldn't come up with a way to get out of it, so I followed Dad inside and we sat down at the kitchen table.

"Hi, Mom."

"Hello, Miranda. You're not getting enough sleep, dear."

That was the understatement of the year.

"It's just awful about these murders, isn't it? I don't know why Steve hasn't solved this thing yet."

I wondered what she'd think if I told her Steve was trying to arrest Chad for the murders.

"He's not Superman, Mom. He's human like the rest of us."

Mom sniffed. Before she could start telling me how incredible my big brother Steve was, my cell phone rang. Thank God, saved by the bell. I answered and walked into the dining room.

"Hey, Randi. This is Tom down at the paper."

"What's up?"

"I don't know if it's what you were searching for, but I found some stuff here you might be interested in. There's something else I need to talk to you about, if you can run by tonight."

"I'm on my way. Be there in twenty minutes."

I walked back into the kitchen and picked up my keys.

"I have to run. See you guys later."

"Don't forget your Dad's birthday, dinner. We eat at six."

"Okay, Mom, see you. Happy birthday, Dad."

Chapter 19

I parked in front of the newspaper office in something less than thirty minutes. I would have made it sooner, but old man Roth's cows were out and I had to come into town the long way. I ran in through the rear entrance and tripped over a stack of newspapers. I landed on my knees in front of a surprised newspaper editor. Tom cocked his head and smirked.

"I know you worship me, but please, not in public."

I laughed. I couldn't help it. I'd kill to be able to think on my feet like that. He offered me a hand up.

"I assume you're here to see what treasures I've found for you," he said when I was vertical again.

I said I was and he motioned for me to follow him to the conference room.

He closed the door behind us and scooped up a folder full of printouts.

"I haven't shown these to anyone else. Check them out. See what you think."

Tom had found twenty-six articles covering similar cases, most within a hundred miles of Alden.

I fanned the pages, reading a sentence here, a word there, glancing at the pictures.

"What do you think, Tom?"

"There were some big differences. Some of the victims were gagged. Some were beaten or seriously disfigured. There were enough similarities to make you wonder, but I wouldn't think the cops are looking very closely at these. Just not enough to tie them together."

I was disappointed and my face must have shown it.

"Hey, it was a good idea. Probably one of the first things the cops checked out. Unless this guy bounces from town to town and changes his pattern every time, I don't think you have anything to go on. That would be pretty atypical serial killer behavior."

"Thanks anyway, Tom. I appreciate you checking into it for me."

"Hey, you know how newspapermen are. We'll do almost anything for a pretty girl or a free Sam Adams."

I skimmed through one of the articles and shuffled it back in the stack. I was so sure I was right. Dammit. I tossed the printouts down on the table and thanked Tom again.

"I made those copies for you. You can take them."

I didn't see much point; I was obviously chasing the wild goose. But since Tom had gone to the trouble to make the copies, I felt bad not taking them. I stuffed them into my shoulder bag.

One of the reporters stuck his head in to ask Tom a question and I waggled my fingers at him in goodbye as I squeezed past.

"Hey, Randi, wait a sec."

I stopped and waited for Tom to finish and he escorted me to my car. I figured he was going to ask me out again. Despite what Chad believes, I have actually had a few dates in the last twenty years. We stopped next to the Mustang and he ran his hand along the fender in a fond caress. I waited for him to speak. He fondled the car.

"Uh, Tom. Did you want something?"

"Oh, yeah."

He glanced up from the Mustang, met my gaze and dropped it back to the car.

"Okay, you want me to guess what it is?"

He smiled and shook his head.

"I um. I heard." He paused and blew out his breath. "Look, I heard something about your brother, and I wondered if you could confirm it for me."

My heart sank. If news of the department's suspicions of Chad made it into the newspaper, my mother would die. I wondered how I should handle this. Play dumb? Beg for mercy?

"Which brother?" I asked.

"Um, Chad. The rumor was about Chad."

"Well, spit it out, Tom. What'd you hear?"

"Look, Randi. I hate this. It's the worst thing about being a small town newsman. You know everybody. Don't take this personally, okay? It's just my job."

"Tom, I have no idea what you're talking about." I'd decided on the play dumb defense.

"Well, um."

"Just spit it out already."

"We have information that your brother is the main suspect in the Timber Bridge murders." He held up his hand before I could interrupt. "We were also told that he is missing. That no one knows where he is. My police reporter also heard that an arrest warrant has been issued, but I haven't confirmed that."

"That's why you gave me those files. That's why you think my theory is all wet. You are going to stand there and look me in the eye and tell me you think my twin brother is a murderer."

My voice rose in anger. I had started off trying to play dumb, act affronted, but by the time I'd finished, I wasn't faking it. Tom knew my brother. He'd known him since before he went into the service.

"Dammit, Randi, keep your voice down."

"You know he couldn't do something like that. You know Chad."

"He's an ex Navy SEAL, a trained killer. Frankly, I don't find it that hard to believe."

I took a step back and glared at Tom. He flinched as if I'd struck him.

"Where is he, Randi? Let me talk to him. If he didn't do it, he shouldn't have any problem telling me that."

"He went to the lake. Took a couple of days vacation."

"Well, then give me his cell number. I'll give him a call. Look, I'll handle this myself."

"He, uh. He didn't take his phone. Said he wanted to get completely away for a few days."

Man that sounded weak. I wasn't doing Chad any favors. Tom knew I was lying.

"You can't protect a killer, Randi. He has to be stopped. You hide him or lie for him and you'll go to jail, too."

"I'm not hiding anyone. I can't believe you're going to print crap like this. Who is telling you these lies about my brother?"

"I can't tell you that, Randi. I have the information from more than one source. I'm going to press with this."

"You bastard. You're going to kill my mother."

Tom's reporter poked his head through the door.

"We have confirmation on the warrant, Tee."

I felt the blood drain from my face. Tom stepped forward and tried to take my hand. I slapped him away.

"Don't touch me. I can't believe you are doing this, Tom. I thought we were friends."

"This isn't about friendship, Randi. It's about news. I can't not follow up on this story."

I waved off his explanation and slid behind the wheel. He tapped on my window and I lowered it an inch so I could hear him.

"If Chad is innocent, get me in touch with him."

I rolled up the glass without answering and started the car. Tom stepped aside and watched me drive away.

My eyes were stinging with unshed tears. I could alibi Chad for part of the time in question, but he still had time to commit the murder after he left my house or even before he showed up. I pulled into my driveway and stared at the house. Bill was sharpening his claws on the shake shingles above the door.

I grabbed my cell phone and dialed Chad's number. It rang twice, then a recording came on. "I'm sorry, the number you have dialed is not in service." I punched end before the message finished and dialed again, making sure I dialed the number correctly. I got the same message. Why would Chad's cell number be disconnected? What the hell was going on?

I went inside and sat down at the kitchen table. The information Tom copied was in front of me, but I wasn't reading. I was thinking of Chad, my brother, my closest friend in the entire world. The one person I could always count on to be there for me. I couldn't believe he was a murderer. Still, it was time to tell Steve and AJ what I knew. I just hoped it didn't get him killed. I dialed the Alden police department and waited for AJ to answer the phone.

"Detective Weleski."

"AJ, it's Randi. I need to talk to you. Can you come over here?"

"It's gonna be a while."

"It's about Chad."

AJ was silent on the other end. I heard the muffled sound of conversation in the background before he spoke again.

"I'll be there as soon as I can. May be half hour or so. I'm in the middle of something here and I can't leave it. Don't go anywhere."

"I won't."

I cradled the phone and stared at the file folder. My hands were shaking. What had I just done? I was turning on my own flesh and blood. But what if he was a killer? I glanced at the clock. Two minutes had passed. At this rate, I would be a complete basket case by the time AJ arrived.

I opened the file and started reading the articles Tom had found, more for something to do than anything else. I was almost convinced that the man we were searching for was Chad.

I sorted the articles into stacks. In the last six years, twelve women had been brutally murdered and the police had never solved the crimes. I read the articles. They all died late at night. They were all discovered in wooded areas. They were all raped. Those were the only similarities. Cause of death was varied. Some were strangled, some were stabbed, one was shot. One died from blunt force trauma. The only other similarity was that all of them had lived in towns the size of Alden or smaller. Despite myself, I was interested in the cases.

I dug out a map and made marks at each town where the murders had taken place. They were roughly in a circle with Alden on the Western edge. The furthest east was near Owensville. The closest was Mexico. I sat staring at the map then reread the articles. There was nothing in the newspaper files that lead me to believe that the cases were related, but I felt in my gut that they were. That meant Chad couldn't be the killer. He was overseas when the first murders occurred.

Someone knocked at the front door. I jumped and glanced at the clock. It had been over an hour since I'd called AJ. Shit, AJ. What was I going to tell him? I certainly wasn't going to blow Chad's case by telling them he was here the night of the murder. Not now. Not after I'd seen the articles. Not when there was a chance it could get him killed.

Wilson was barking ferociously at the front door. I nudged him out of the way and opened it, still trying to decide what I was going to tell AJ. As soon as Wilson saw who it was, he flopped over to get his belly rubbed.

"Hey there, Wil, old buddy," AJ said as he kneeled down to rub his tummy.

Wilson moaned with pleasure.

"Hey there to you, too, beautiful."

"Hi."

He straightened and followed me into the kitchen.

"You look exhausted," I said.

He dropped a kiss on my head.

"It's been a bitch of a week. So, what'd you need to tell me?"

"I talked to Tom Wallace this afternoon. He said you've issued a warrant for Chad's arrest."

AJ looked surprised.

"I don't know how he got that information."

"But it's true, isn't it?"

"Yeah, it's true."

I sat down at the table. The map I'd marked up earlier was blurry through my unshed tears. AJ put his hands on my shoulders and gave them a gentle squeeze.

"Tell me you really think he did this, AJ. Tell me the man you've known since childhood is a killer."

"I don't think he did it. But I can't prove he didn't."

I twisted away from his hands. He sat in the chair next to mine.

"Randi, if you know anything about where his is, you have to let me know."

"I don't know where he is." That, at least, was the truth.

"We just need to talk to him, Ran."

"If all you needed was talk, you wouldn't have issued a warrant."

I was idly tracing the circle of death on my map.

"It's going to be in the newspaper tomorrow. This is going to kill Mom."

"We can probably get the newspapers to hold off for a day or so, at least from giving the name. If they scare him underground, we'll never find him."

I looked up from the map into AJ's eyes.

"Tell me where he is, Ran."

"I don't know. All I know is that his cell phone has been disconnected."

"Shit."

"This is wrong, AJ. Chad couldn't kill those women."

"The sooner we find him, the sooner we can prove that."

He took my hand in his. "Tell me where he is, Randi."

I shook my head no. He let go of my hand and noticed the map on the table for the first time.

"What's that?"

"Just some stuff I got from Tom down at the paper. He pulled some old articles for me about murders and I plotted them out on the map."

"Let me see."

I handed him the stack of articles. He skimmed through them and studied the map.

"We've been through all these cases. None of them matches our killer, Ran."

"What if he changed his MO every time he changed towns?"

Tom had mentioned that earlier. I hadn't checked the articles to see if the murders in each town were the same. I wasn't going to get a chance either. AJ folded the map into a sloppy fan and stuffed it into the folder along with the articles.

"I've talked to the departments on some of these, but I think I'll go over it again," he said.

"If the same person did all of those, it couldn't be Chad."

"Don't get your hopes up, Randi. I'll check into it, but I think it's a long shot. I'll try and stop by after work."

"I'm closing at the bar tonight. I'm going in late after Dad's birthday party."

"Tell him I said happy birthday."

AJ brushed my lips with a kiss and started for the door.

"You know this is going to take some time to check out. We still need to talk to Chad."

"Just keep it out of the papers if you can."

"I'll try, babe. No promises."

On that up note, AJ took off with my map, and all my notes. I glanced at my watch and realized it was time to pick up the boys from practice. I grabbed my keys and ran out the door. I had to get the kids home, herd them into the shower, and get them dressed and back out the door in time to get to the farm for Dad's party. God save me if we arrived late, even if it wasn't my fault I'd never hear the end of it.

At the high school, the boys scooted into the back seat. Travis picked up the package that I'd tossed there earlier and shook it. It made the same soft shuffling noise, but no rattle of broken parts.

"What's this, Mom?"

"I don't know. I think it says CompuTech on the label."

"I don't have anything ordered right now."

He started peeling the tape from the ends of the package.

"Travis, don't mess with that right now. We are barely going to get to Dad's party on time as it is."

He ignored me and ripped the paper from the outside of the box. I turned off of Main Street as he lifted the lid.

"Holy shit," Travis yelped and flung the box into the front seat. "Snake! Copperhead! In the box."

I slammed on the brakes at the word snake, threw open the door before he finished the word copperhead and leapt from the car sliding and stumbling, barely keeping my feet. Travis and Devin tumbled out after me, rolled and came up standing behind me. The snake peered out the open car door. He did not look happy; he'd been in that box a long time. Of course, snakes don't ever really look happy, so I might have been reading more into his expression than was actually there. With a flick of his tongue the possibly angry snake disappeared from sight. The boys and I stood in the street gazing into the car while traffic slowed to pass and people gawked at us. Devin sidled closer for a look. The snake poked his head out from under the seat. He leapt back, and he and Travis broke into nervous giggles. The snake flicked his tongue at us a couple of times, looked around, then dropped out of the car and slithered into the ditch as we watched.

"Who mails a snake?" Travis demanded.

Jody McIntire.

Devin leaned into the car and reached for the box.

"Don't touch it. There might be fingerprints."

Devin pulled his hand back and leaned closer for a look.

"There's a note, Mom."

"Just leave it. I'll get a grocery sack to put it in and I'll take it to AJ later. Right now we need to get home."

I drove the rest of the way across town, glancing at the floor periodically just to make sure there hadn't been two snakes in that box. I pulled into the driveway and hopped out of the car.

"You guys run and get done in the shower or we're going to be late for Granddad's party."

Devin loped up to the house. Travis hung back with me.

"That dickwad from the paintball game sent that, didn't he?"

"That would be my guess. Are you okay?"

"Yeah. That jerk. I'd like to send him a rattlesnake."

"Your Uncle Steve will take care of it, I promise. Now, run in and take your shower. We'll leave as soon as you guys are ready."

After Travis went inside, I walked down the street to the Baldwin's house. Kevin, the package delivery boy, had just gotten home from soccer and was out front dribbling the ball back and forth across the yard.

"Hey, Kevin."

"Hey, Mrs. B. What's up?"

"We got that package you dropped off at Mrs. Litton's house."

"Good, sorry I couldn't bring it to you, but I had soccer."

"That's okay, hon. Did somebody drop it off here?"

"It was just on the porch when I got home. I saw Travis's name and figured UPS must have left it or something. Don't know why they didn't just leave it on your porch."

"I don't either. Thanks for getting it to us."

I walked back to the house. The boys were coming out the door as I got there. I ran in, grabbed a paper sack from under the kitchen sink, and went out to collect the package and the wrapping. The note in the bottom of the box said, "I've got a snake for you, Brat." I dropped it into the sack and put it in the trunk of the car. We headed out to the farm and I called AJ on the way to tell him what had happened. He promised to drop by and get the package from the trunk of the car while I was at work. Neither one of us thought we'd find any useful evidence.

It was five minutes before six when we pulled into the drive at the farm. Sara Beth arrived with her two kids and Becca before we were out of the car. Even though we weren't late, Mom was in a snit when we walked in.

"Steve just called to say he wasn't going to be able to make it. Something to do with that case he's on."

"They got a new lead this afternoon," I said. "They've probably called in everyone on the major case squad to work it."

Mom ignored my interruption and continued.

"God knows where your brother Chad is. I can't believe he'd go off on vacation when he knew Dad's birthday was coming up."

God, if she only knew.

"I have this huge mountain of food," she went on. "And nobody but us to eat it all."

"Sorry, Mom. We'll do our best to get through it."

"You need to start watching what you eat young lady. You're not some teenager anymore. Everything you eat goes straight to the hips at your age."

Well, yeah, but I didn't really need to hear that, especially not today. This would be a great day for some nice comfortable calories. In the other room, Devin and Travis were telling Dad about the snake. I hoped they wouldn't bring it up at dinner. It would just be something else for Mom to bitch at me about and she was doing fine without any help. With only a small pause to stir one of the pots on the stove, she hit me with her next broadside.

"And what's this I hear about you smoking again? I thought you gave up that filthy habit. I don't know what's gotten into you lately."

She glared at me while I tried to think of something to say. I had no comeback. I had people sending my kids poisonous snakes in the mail. Cigarettes seemed pretty harmless after that. In fact, I wished I had one right then.

The back door slammed and Mom cringed as Granny Bert swung through the archway into the kitchen. She swooped into the dining room to pounce on Dad. I heard her wish him happy birthday as Fred Baxter shuffled through the door and stood there glancing around. Oh my God, Granny Bert brought Fred Baxter to dinner. Mom was going to spontaneously combust. At least it took the heat off me for a while.

"I brought company," Granny Bert said. "I didn't think you'd mind, Alice, you always cook way too much."

Mom's eye narrowed, her back stiffened, and she turned to the stove. I stared at the tabletop and smiled.

"Well, hello Fred," said Dad, standing up to shake hands.

"What?" yelled Fred.

Sara Beth and I laughed. Mom looked pained. Dad snickered and Granny just grinned.

"I said, hello," Dad yelled.

"Sure I like Jell-O," Fred answered.

I snorted with laughter and got a glare from Mom. I tried to turn it into a cough. Sara sat next to me silently shaking. I caught Dad's eye and lost it again. I left the room before Mom could hit me with a serving spoon. When I could breathe again, I went back to the kitchen and sat down.

"Do you have an extra child tonight?" Dad asked Sara Beth.

"I'm babysitting for a friend."

I bit my lip. Mom would have kittens if she knew whose little girl that was. Mom poked an elbow in my ribs as she walked by. A preemptive poke, just to make sure I was on my best behavior.

"Try to behave like a lady for once," she hissed.

I swallowed a laugh and tried to sit ladylike at the table. We bulldozed our way through dinner. Fred did an admirable job of making up for Chad and Steve's absence.

"Did you put in a garden this year, Fred?" Mom asked.

"I don't think the chicken is hard at all, ma'am," Fred answered.

I choked on a carrot. While I coughed and tried to get a drink, Sara excused herself to the other room. I quit trying to eat and just tried to act like a lady for the rest of the meal. Devin and Travis were in stitches. They had tears streaming down their faces. Mom was shooting daggers at all of us.

After Fred and Granny Bert left, Mom said, "Well, I have never been so mortified in all my life."

"But Gran," Devin said. "When you asked if he'd like some pie, he thought you were talking about his tie."

We all burst out laughing again and Mom finally cracked a smile.

"I swear, Mel. Your mother is going to be the death of me yet."

Devin and Travis headed out to the shed where their classmates were working on the homecoming float. I took off for the Jolly Roger, leaving Sara Beth to deal with Mom. Lex was behind the bar when I walked in.

"How'd the birthday dinner go?" he asked.

I scooted behind the bar and laughed as I described Dad's birthday dinner. A visit from Fred had been just what I'd needed. I was almost in tears again just telling the story. I hadn't thought about Chad, snakes, or murder for hours.

The bar got busy and we started tag teaming. Lex flipped a whiskey bottle at me. The noise level in the bar changed while it was in mid-air. Oh shit, a fight. I took my eye off the bottle and it crashed to the floor as Lex went over the bar. He was in the middle of the fight before it even got started. He jerked the two idiots apart and propelled them outside. They seemed quite eager to leave. Lex has that effect on drunks. He slid behind the bar and slowly the noise level rose to normal. I was still on the floor cleaning up whiskey and glass. I dumped it into the trash and looked over at Lex.

"You move like a snake. All coiled up nice and quiet and then, boom," I said.

Lex smiled and flipped a glass at me. I missed it and it splintered against the tile. The bar went silent for a minute then the noise started again. I sighed, and swept broken glass a second time. While I swept up my mess, I told Lex about the snake Travis had gotten in the mail. He was livid and agreed that Jody was probably the culprit.

Eleven o'clock came and went and Lex was still behind the bar. The crowd started to thin.

"I thought you left at eleven every day except Friday."

"Not anymore."

"Why?"

"Don't need to leave early anymore," he answered.

"Why were you leaving early before?"

"You ask a lot of questions."

"Yeah, but you don't answer most of them so it doesn't count."

Lex laughed and wiped the bar down, then chucked the towel at my head. I caught it and dropped it in the sink.

"So, why'd you used to leave early?"

"Had to pick someone up from work."

"This someone a woman?"

"Uh-huh."

"She doesn't work the night shift anymore?"

"Jeez, you just don't quit, do you?"

"Guess it runs in the family. That's probably why my brothers are cops."

At least one of them was. I wondered if Chad was still a good guy. Distracted, I almost missed Lex's answer.

"She doesn't work in Alden anymore, she split," he said.

It took a minute for that to compute.

"Is that a good thing or a bad thing?" I asked.

"Jury's still out on that," he said as he gave me a long, dark-eyed look. My breath caught in my throat. I'd seen that look before, but not from Lex.

"Oh."

Gulp. I quit asking questions.

The bar cleared out by one, so I swept the upstairs and started on the main room. I stopped sweeping and leaned against the bar. Lex grabbed my ponytail and pulled my head back until he could look in my eyes.

"Why don't you go on home? You're wiped out."

I turned around and smiled.

"I'm not going to give you a chance to change your mind, so I hope you meant that."

"I did. Get out of here."

I grabbed my purse from the office and scooted for the back door. As I passed the last table before the hallway, a hand reached out and grabbed me. I squealed in surprise. It was Harold. I hadn't even seen him come in.

"Hey, Harold. You startled me."

"Sorry, Randi. Wanted to say hi before you got outta here. Who's that guy behind the bar?"

"Boy, you haven't been in here for a while have you?" I smiled. "That's Arlen Lexington. Everybody calls him Lex."

"You guys look pretty chummy. Thought you were dating that cop."

"Lex and I just work together."

"You finished for the night?" he asked.

"Yep, I'm heading for the house."

"See you at the range tomorrow? I'm doing another class."

"I can't. I have to supervise the freshman class float. Sorry."

"No problem. Maybe next week."

I waved and continued out to my car. When I pulled into my drive, Bill was sitting on top of AJ's truck. I parked behind it and stepped out. Bill hopped down to greet me and led me up the walk. I reached down to rub his head and scratch his ears. A car drove slowly down the street as I stood up to unlock the door. It looked like

Harold's old truck. I waved and slipped into my dark house. AJ was sound asleep on the couch. I closed and locked the door and tiptoed across the room. He didn't wake, so I covered him with a blanket and kissed him on the forehead. Wilson lay with his head on AJ's shoulder and never even opened an eye when I covered them. Once again, I went to bed alone. Too bad, I could have used a distraction. Everything I'd managed to forget about during the party and later at work, came back to haunt me as soon as I closed my eyes. Where was Chad? Should I tell AJ and Steve what I knew? Where was Jody? The snake was the first we'd heard from him in days. Waiting for his next appearance was almost as bad as meeting up with him. Poor Mouse. I hadn't given him a thought. And what about the cowboy? How did he fit in? Was he even still around? Needless to say, it was a while before I slept.

Chapter 20

"Wake up, Beautiful," AJ whispered in my ear.

I opened my eyes and smiled. He was sitting on the bed, still damp from the shower, wearing nothing but his boxers. I had to remind myself to breathe. He leaned over and kissed me. Good thing I was lying down. If I'd been standing, my knees would have buckled.

I ran my hands through the hair on his chest, his gaze darkened and a smile twitched the corner of his mouth. He lifted away the cover and slipped his hand under my shirt. He lifted it and trailed kisses across my breasts and down my stomach. My brain stopped functioning. He ran his hand lightly up the inside of my thigh, bent down to kiss me, and his pager went off.

He let out a deep sigh. "I do not fucking believe this."

He fumbled his pager off the nightstand to check the number.

"You don't have to answer it," I said hopefully.

He grinned. "Yeah, I do. It's Steve."

He kissed me again.

"Do you think I'd get prison time if I offed him?" I asked. "You know, if the jury had all the details."

AJ laughed. "I don't know. Be a tough call."

He zipped into his jeans and sat down while he called my brother.

I ran my fingers lightly down his back while he talked. He grinned. I brushed them over his ribs and his breath caught. I dropped to the waistband of his Levi's and felt his stomach muscles quiver. He grabbed my hand, so he could finish his conversation. He pounced as soon as he punched off the call, pinning me to the bed and capturing my lips.

"That was not nice."

"Wasn't supposed to be."

I pulled him down for another kiss. But I let him go when I felt him lean away.

"Babe, I really gotta go," he said.

I gave up. I just couldn't compete with my brother Steve. That was a hell of a note.

AJ finished dressing.

"Go to sleep, Randi. It's early yet."

Yeah, right. Like that was going to happen. He must have read the disappointment on my face. He sat down on the bed.

"I'll make you a promise," he said, brushing the hair away from my face. "When this is all over, we're going to go away for a while. No kids, no phones, no pagers, just you and me."

That was a fantasy I could live with. He kissed me breathless and stood to leave.

"Hey, did Steve know you were staying here last night?" I asked.

"Probably."

"Think he did that on purpose?"

AJ laughed. "No, Steve's not really the morning sex kind of guy. He probably can't even imagine morning sex."

I sighed. "All I can do is imagine it."

"I'm sorry, darlin'. I really need to go."

I closed my eyes and heard the front door shut softly behind him. If this went on much longer, I was going to start hitting people, and Steve was going to be first on the list. I lay in bed for a while and tried to go back to sleep. Finally, I gave up and took a shower. When I walked into the kitchen, Wilson trotted in with a big doggy smile on his face.

"Don't start with me, you traitor," I said.

He cocked his head sideways and tried to figure out what he'd done wrong. I shared breakfast with him so he didn't think I was really mad. Then it was off to town. I made the rounds, bought groceries, paid the electric bill, returned a library book, and finished off with a stop at Mabel's for lunch. I shot the breeze with Granny Bert for an hour or so and tried to take a nap after I got home. Wilson was ready, but I couldn't sleep. I grabbed his leash and we drove to the park. We were strolling a hiking path through the woods when someone stepped onto the trail in front of us.

"Jesus!" I jumped and put a hand to my heart. "You scared the hell out of me."

We were in the shadows. I couldn't make out the features of the man in front of me until he took a step forward. My knees went weak. It was Jody. I tightened my hold on Wilson's leash and took a step back. Jody snatched my arm and jerked me against his chest. Wilson growled low in his throat and went tense beside me.

"Shut up the fucking dog or I'll kill him," he hissed.

"Shhh, Wilson, it's okay," I whispered.

He sat down and stopped growling, but he didn't relax. I could feel the tension humming through the leash to my arm.

"What do you want, Jody?"

"We have some unfinished business, you and I. I just wanted to make sure you hadn't forgotten me."

"Forgotten you? You sent my son a poisonous snake yesterday."

"You can't keep them safe from me."

I struggled to free myself from his grip. Wilson growled and lunged to the end of his leash. Jody kicked him aside and twisted my arm until I went still. Wilson yelped with pain and surprise and hunkered down at my feet.

"Don't hurt him."

"He's safe for today, and so are you. This is just a little reminder that I'm still around."

Abruptly, he released my arm, and disappeared into the trees. My knees buckled and I slumped down next to

Wilson. He crawled trembling into my lap and licked my face while I checked to make sure he wasn't hurt. We stayed that way for an hour. I couldn't trust my legs to take me to the car even though I was afraid to stay where I was. I'd heard the term 'paralyzed with fear,' and now I knew what it meant. I finally coaxed my legs to stand and we made our way out of the park.

I sat behind the wheel and glanced at my reflection in the rearview mirror. Tears and mascara streaked my pasty white face. I found a Kleenex and tried to repair the damage. A car drove slowly by and stopped behind me. I stared in the rear view mirror. Jody smiled and waved. I shuddered and fumbled to lock the doors. Jody drove away. I tried to stab the key into the ignition. It took three tries before I got the car started. I drove slowly home watching my mirrors. If he was following me, he was invisible. I shivered. I couldn't see him, but I could feel him—a malevolent presence lurking just beyond my line of sight.

I made it home and huddled on the couch with Wilson. I checked him over again to make sure he wasn't hurt, then hugged him until he wriggled away. My hands were still shaking. I did not want to leave the house, but I had to pick the boys up from school. I forced myself to move off the couch, wash my face, put on makeup, and change into warm clothes. It was my turn to supervise the boys' homecoming float. I didn't think surrounding myself with teenagers was going to do much to keep Jody at bay.

I went into town and picked up the last of the float supplies and enough pizza to feed a small army. The boys walked out of school just as I parked. They scrambled into the car and I drove to the farm. I kept an eye on the rearview mirror all the way, but Jody was a no show. Somehow, I didn't find that comforting.

I found a spot on the hay bales where I had a good view of the float and the float builders and settled in. If this float was going to be in a parade tomorrow, we were going to be here all night. I fumbled my phone out of my purse and called AJ.

"Weleski," he answered.

"AJ."

"Randi?"

"Yeah, you going to be late tonight?"

"I should be done here in an hour or so, why?"

"Can you keep me company while I supervise the homecoming float?"

"Sure," he said laughing. "You okay?"

I didn't want to tell AJ about Jody on the phone. I lied and told him everything was fine. I punched off my cell and dropped it into my pocket. The boys were showing signs of an impending spray paint fight. I clambered down off my perch and stopped it before it started. One of the kids handed me a piece of pizza. I scooped a Pepsi from the cooler and climbed up to my perch on the hay bales. After I finished my pizza, I called Lex at the bar.

"I need to talk to you about something," I said when he answered.

"Right now?"

"Tomorrow will be okay."

"Want me to come to your place?" he asked.

"If you could."

"Hang on."

I heard him talking to someone in the background, then he came on.

"I'll be there at eight."

"Thanks, Lex."

I stuck my phone in my jacket pocket and huddled in my blanket. I was going to talk to Lex about Jody. I didn't want to analyze why I'd called Lex instead of waiting to talk to AJ. There'd been a subtle shift in my relationship with Lex since the night Jody had attacked me. I knew without a doubt that he would help me, no questions asked. Maybe it was because we didn't have any past history to slog through. I just knew he would listen, and I was too tired and too scared to argue.

I waved as AJ strolled into the shed. He crawled onto the hay bales and pulled me close. He still looked exhausted even after last night's sleep. He was too tired to deal with Jody right now. That's what I told myself, anyway.

"You heard anything about Mouse?" I asked.

"He's still alive. Still unconscious. We'll get this guy with or without Mouse's help."

His answer gave me a little hope. He hadn't said they'd find Chad with or without Mouse's help. I was afraid to ask if they were still searching for him.

"What the hell is that thing supposed to be anyway?" he asked looking down at the float.

"I think it's going to be a skunk."

"It's gonna be a long night."

I laughed. Around us, teenage boys and girls flirted, joked, and sometimes actually worked. AJ slid down on the hay bales and went to sleep with his head cradled on his arms. Shortly before midnight, I shook him awake.

"Hey, check it out," I said.

On the trailer in front of us was an enormous skunk, complete with moving tail. AJ stretched and rubbed his eyes.

"When I got here I didn't think there was any way in hell they would get that thing done," he said. "It looks pretty good."

And it did. It was sitting on its hind legs peering around, and when the tail lifted up a puff from a fire extinguisher was supposed to shoot out the back. If it worked, it was going to be great. Travis crawled up next to us and threw himself down on the bales.

"What's up?" I asked.

"Uncle Chad's supposed to drive the float in the parade."

"Uh oh, better implement plan B."

"AJ?" he said.

"Sorry, bud. I have to go out of town tomorrow on a case and your Uncle Steve is going with me."

"Great. What are we going to do now, Mom? We don't have a driver."

"What about your dad or granddad?"

"Granddad's the grand marshal."

"Oh, yeah. I forgot about that. Guess you'd better call your dad."

I dug my phone out of my jacket pocket and handed it to him. He dialed and AJ's pager went off.

"Did Travis call you?" I asked.

AJ laughed. "No. It's Steve."

He called Steve, talked for a minute, dropped his cell phone in his pocket, and stood to go.

"Steve wants to leave tonight instead of in the morning."

"I'm going to kill him. You can tell him I said that."

"I'll let you tell him. He said to tell you Mouse has been upgraded to serious condition."

"Have you been able to talk to him yet?"

"No. He's out of danger, but still hasn't really regained consciousness."

"I wish you guys could talk to him before you go."

"Me too, darlin'. I better get a move on."

He took off walking, but stopped when I called out.

"Hey, wait. When will you guys be home?"

"Saturday maybe," he said over his shoulder. "Or Sunday. Depends. I'll call you."

"Dad said he'd do it, but you have to cover for him at the bar," Travis said, handing me my phone.

"I can do that."

"Thanks, Mom."

Well, one crisis averted. What next? Lucky for me there weren't many more. I had to crawl up inside the skunk and install the fire extinguisher under the tail. None of the guys were small enough and none of the girls would do it. Other than that, it was a piece of cake. No parts fell off. We didn't run out of paint, pizza, or soda. The float rolled from the shed in all its glory at four thirty a.m. And on the test run, the tail raised, the fire extinguisher squirted, and everyone still standing cheered. Skunk 'Em was ready to roll.

The kids that were left headed home to shower and change. I squeezed the kids that didn't have cars into the Mustang and dropped them off. Then I drove the boys to

Morgan's before I finally made it home. I was a walking zombie. At six a.m., feet dragging, I approached my front door. The keys were in my hand, but I was afraid to unlock it. Twice before, Jody had entered my locked home. I was terrified he was inside waiting for me. I went and got back into the Mustang, ran to the quick shop, bought a soda, and drove back to the house. I still couldn't bring myself to unlock the door. Instead, I sat on the porch, shivering as the sun came up. Bill curled on my lap and tried to keep me warm. At eight on the dot, Lex parked in front of me.

"You look frozen. How long have you been sitting out here?"

"I don't know, couple of hours."

"Randi, why didn't you call? I could have come over sooner."

"I didn't want to wake you. You had to work last night."

"I would have come over."

"It's no big deal," I said.

"You gonna tell me why you've been sitting on your front porch for the last two hours?"

"It's a long story. If you'll unlock my door and check out my house, I'll fix breakfast and tell you about it."

"Okay. And what am I checking your house for?"

"Jody."

Lex went still.

"He was here again?"

"Not here."

"So this isn't about the snake."

"No, I ran into him again yesterday."

I handed Lex my keys, and as he unlocked the door, I told him about meeting Jody in the park. Teeth chattering, I followed him into the house. Wilson came yawning to greet me and padded down the hallway to the kitchen. I let him out and waited for him by the sliding door. Lex made a quick search of the house and walked into the kitchen.

"This was on your bed," he said handing me the note.

'I'm watching you' was all it said. I turned away as tears rolled down my cheeks. Lex held me in his arms while I cried.

"Shhh," he whispered. "I won't let him bother you any more."

He tightened his arms around me and kissed my hair. I stiffened and pushed away from his embrace. I wiped my face with a dishtowel and tried to get myself under control. Lex smiled a half smile and sat down at the table. I dropped into the chair across from him.

"That boy's not too smart," he said.

"He's very smart, that's why he scares me so much. He's been in this house twice, no, three times now. Then, yesterday he grabbed me at the park. Lex, I never see him. He's like a ghost."

I stood up from the table and pulled my cast iron skillet from the cabinet. It clattered against the stovetop when I banged it down. I opened the refrigerator searching for the bacon. Lex put his hands on my shoulders and turned me around, pushing the fridge closed behind me.

"Forget about breakfast, Randi. Go take a shower and get in bed. I'll call AJ, and see what he can find out."

"He and Steve are out of town for the weekend."

"Fine, then I'll get in touch with Chad."

"Nobody knows where he is and his cell phone's been turned off."

"Then I'll see if I can find him. Now, go to bed. Try to get some sleep."

I was too terrified to sleep and too exhausted to stay awake. Sleep finally won. At one o'clock, the phone woke me.

"Hi, Randi."

"Morgan?" I mumbled.

"Just thought I'd give you a wake up call. The boys said you were awake all night."

"So were they."

Morgan laughed. "Yeah, you've got a couple of years on them. Makes a difference."

That, and I haven't had a decent night's sleep in a week. I sighed and crawled out of bed. I told him I'd be there in about half an hour and hung up the phone.

I washed my face and pulled on some clothes, let the dog out, and loaded my guns. My .32 I slid into my ankle holster, the nine went on my belt. Wilson came back in. I told him goodbye, grabbed my jacket and left for the bar. It had taken me twenty minutes. The sky was clouding over. The weather matched my mood. I waved Morgan and the boys out, poured a soda, and sat down on a barstool to wait through the dead time 'til the parade was over. I couldn't sit still. Every little noise made me jump.

I stepped outside when the parade went by. The boys waved from the football team float. Morgan waved when he drove past pulling the freshman class float, and several of the kids I'd spent the night with waved and hollered. I went inside after they passed and got ready for the rush. Lex slipped in the back door and slid behind the bar. I jumped when he touched my shoulder.

"Just me, thought you might need some help."

"Thanks. Did you find Jody?"

"Huh-uh. Our boy's gone to ground somewhere."

I shivered. Lex ruffled my hair.

"Relax. I told you I won't let him bother you anymore."

"You said that last time."

"Yeah, kind of underestimated his tenacity."

"Tenacity?" I said with eyebrows raised. "Have you been reading books?"

Lex grinned. "Cute."

The crowd poured through the doors and we didn't get a chance to talk again until after seven.

"You going to the game?" Lex asked.

"Not tonight. I told Morgan I'd work."

I turned on the TV to watch the Cardinals game. The series was tied. The Redbirds needed a win tonight or they'd be done for the year. The baseball game got over the same time as the football game and with the same result. The good guys lost both of them. The bar filled up and got loud, just another normal Friday night. Lex made a phone call around eleven, looked pleased with himself, and went back to work. I didn't get a chance to talk to him and then I forgot about it. Every time the door opened, I glanced up expecting the cowboy. He never showed. After I locked the door behind the last drunk, Lex went to the back door and let someone in. I turned around as Chad strolled into the room.

"Hi, Ranna."

"Don't you hi, Ranna me! Where the hell have you been?"

Then I burst into tears. Chad pulled me into his arms.

"Don't cry, Ranna. I really put you in a bind, didn't I? I'm sorry."

"Steve thinks you killed Ann Marie. You have to get out of here."

He pulled away and wiped my tears away with his thumbs.

"Relax. I talked to Steve. Everything's cool."

"Don't you ever do that to me again."

He smiled. "I won't. I promise. I didn't enjoy it too much myself."

I cleaned up behind the bar while Chad and Lex had a pow wow. They shook hands and Chad strode out the back door.

"Where's he going?"

"Hunting."

"For Jody?" I asked.

Lex nodded. I tried to swallow a yawn.

"Let's go. I'll take you home. Chad can bring your car later."

I was too tired to argue. I followed Lex across the parking lot and sank into the car. I fell asleep on the short ride to the house. He woke me when we arrived and I trailed him inside. No love notes from Jody this time. I offered to lock up after he left, but he said he'd stay for a while. I handed him the remote and dragged my tired bones into the bedroom. Still dressed, I flopped across the bed and fell asleep.

Chapter 21

When I woke, my gun was digging into my back. I snapped off the holster and set it on the bedside table. I felt grimy and smelled like cigarette smoke from the bar the night before. I needed a shower. I peeled off my sleep rumpled clothes and walked down the hall to the bathroom. I stopped with my hand on the doorknob. I heard voices coming from the kitchen that suddenly went silent. Voices meant people. Shit, I wasn't wearing any clothes. I looked into the kitchen and froze. Chad and Lex were sitting at the table. Chad had his back to me, but Lex had a clear view over Chad's right shoulder. He raised his eyebrows and his lips curled into a slow smile. Then he winked. Lovely!

I slammed the bathroom door as they said good morning. I was blushing all the way to my toes. I could hear their laughter as I stepped into the shower. After I was clean, I stood wrapped in my robe and willed Lex to leave. Of course he didn't. He wouldn't. I took a deep breath and walked into the kitchen. I didn't meet Lex's gaze. He tipped his chair, reached into the fridge for a soda and slid it across the table. I thanked him without looking up.

"Good morning," he said.

"That depends on your point of view," I answered.

"Mine was pretty good," he said.

"Oh, ha, ha."

My face flamed.

"Ah, lighten up, Ranna," Chad said.

I stuck my tongue out at him. I'm never at my best in the morning. And I'd had enough stress because of Chad over the last week to last me a lifetime.

"Not to change the subject, but what are we going to do about Jody?" I asked.

"You are going to do nothing. And while you're doing it, one of us is going to be with you."

"And I guess the kids are going to have to stay with Morgan?"

"Or Mom and Dad."

"I want them here. They belong here."

"Right now, you shouldn't even be here. But I know better than to try and talk you into moving in with me or back to the farm until this is all over. So, you get to stay home, and Lex and I get to stay here."

"I hate this. What if I want to go shopping or something?" Lex and Chad both looked alarmed at the thought.

"You aren't really going shopping, are you?" Lex asked.

"Probably not, but I could."

"Why are you being so difficult?"

"Because I just woke up and strolled naked through my house in front of Lex. That's why."

"I promise I won't tell anyone," Lex said, trying to stifle a laugh. "It can just be our little secret."

"I'm going to get dressed," I said as I stalked into my bedroom.

I hurried into my clothes, checked my guns and strapped them on. I gathered the dirty laundry scattered on my bedroom floor and stuck it in to wash. When I walked into the kitchen, Lex was gone.

"Sorry, Ranna. It never occurred to me you might walk down the hall naked," Chad said laughing.

I grinned and sat down at the table. "It was kind of funny, wasn't it? Did you track down Jody last night?"

"Didn't see a sign of him anywhere. So far, all I've determined is where he's not."

"What should I do? Do I have to stay here and hide out in the house, or what?"

"Just do whatever you would normally do and one of us will go with you."

The phone rang while I decided what was on the schedule for the day. It was AJ.

"Hi, beautiful."

"Hi, AJ. Where are you?"

"On the road, between stops."

"Guess that means you're not going to tell me."

"Steve would rather I didn't share right now."

I grabbed the orange juice from the fridge and poured a glass.

"Can you tell me what you're doing?"

"Just making a circuit of the towns on your map. Right now we've got nothing. We're just trying to find a link."

"Any luck so far?" I asked.

"Not yet."

"I thought of something yesterday. All the girls that have been killed have either been party girls or hookers."

"Yeah, we noticed that. Us being professional investigators and all."

"Hey, don't be smart. I thought of it, and I wanted to share it with you."

"Appreciate it. Glad you've turned over a new leaf of cooperation."

"It's probably not permanent."

AJ's laugh drifted over the phone.

"I wish you were here."

"I wish I was too, darlin'. This case is going to break soon. I can feel it. We're going to find something. We have all the pieces to the puzzle. We just need to figure out how they fit together."

"I hope you're better at puzzles than I am."

"I need to go, babe. I just wanted to tell you good morning. I love you."

My heart stuttered. He'd just thrown out the L word like he did it all the time. I hung up the phone and tried to stifle my smile.

Chad gave me a funny look.

"I thought you said you weren't dating AJ."

"So I lied, sue me. Speaking of relationships, how long have you and Liz been a couple?"

"We're not."

"Liar."

"I go over and talk to her some. She won't go out with me."

"She likes you."

"I know that. She's freaked out about what everybody would say if we started dating."

"What do you think about it, Chadly?"

"I don't give a damn what anybody else thinks."

"Did you tell her that?" I asked.

"She's not buying it."

"She still working?"

"She just does escort stuff. That's all she's done for a long time. So, what's the plan for the day?" he asked, changing the subject.

"I don't know. I'm so strung out I can't even think."

"Why don't we go see how the truck's coming along?"

"I already know the answer to that. It isn't. Morgan has the boys this weekend. Besides, I'm not in the mood to fence with Mom today."

"We could go to the gym."

"No!"

Chad snickered. "Randi, you can't let this guy get inside your head."

"He's already there. He's blindsided me too many times. He's been in my house. He beat the shit out of me. My God, he sent a poisonous snake to my son."

"I know, Randi. I know. Now try to put him out of your mind. It's not going to happen again."

I stood and paced around the room. I stopped and pressed my forehead against the glass of the sliding door.

"You can't guarantee that, Chad."

"Yeah, I can," he said.

"Don't make promises you can't keep."

"He won't get close to you again, Randi."

I stepped out of the kitchen and went to change the laundry around. Chad followed and leaned against the wall.

"I wish I was as confident as you, Chadly."

I started the dryer, got the washer going, and dropped the lid.

"You working tonight?" Chad asked.

"Yes."

"So you only have to kill time until you go in to work."

"I hate being babysat."

"I'm hungry, you want to go get something to eat?"

"Not really; I'll cook something if you want."

"We could order a pizza."

"I had pizza yesterday. I don't want it again. I'll cook."

I fixed smothered chicken breasts with rice and gravy. Chad thought he'd died and gone to heaven.

"I forget you can cook," he said when he'd finished eating.

"You guys were gone a long time. I learned all kinds of stuff while you were off protecting the free world."

Chad laughed and got up to clear the table. We washed the dishes and settled down in front of the TV—normal Saturday, four hundred channels and nothing on but college football.

"You make your big bust?"

"Nuh uh. The Duke never showed."

"That sucks."

"Yeah, we'll get him next time."

"Did you find out if you have a leak in the department?"

His face hardened into a scowl and he shook his head. I took that as a no and didn't pursue it.

I flipped through the channels again. Now we had infomercials and college football. I tossed the remote on the table. The cover popped off and the batteries skittered across the coffee table. Chad snapped the pieces of the remote together and laid it on the end table away from me.

"This is boring. I need to get groceries."

"Okay, let's go."

Chad stood and scooped his keys from the table.

If he was that excited about grocery shopping, he must've been as bored as I was. We walked out the front door and Mrs. Litton caught me as I crossed the porch. Chad kept going down the walk, but I was stuck.

"I need to talk to you, Randi."

I swallowed a groan and pasted on a smile.

"Sure. What about?"

"Well, dear. I know it's none of my business and you can do anything you want, but it's really..." she paused. "Well, really dear, having two different young men stay the night in the same week. People are going to talk."

"What?"

"Well, there was that police officer and then that scruffy bartender. I personally don't think he's much of a catch. Anyway, you should be more discreet. Really, Randi, what will your poor mother think?"

I was speechless. I just stared at Mrs. Litton while Bill made figure eights around my ankles. I opened my mouth to say something, but I didn't have any words. I snapped my mouth closed and shook my head. Chad tooted the horn and I turned and walked to the truck leaving Mrs. Litton staring after me in surprise.

"What was that?" Chad asked.

"Mrs. Litton told me I should be more discreet with my lovers."

Chad started the truck and backed out of the drive. Mrs. Litton gave us a tentative wave as we went past.

"Lovers? You have more than one? I thought there was only AJ."

"There's not even AJ."

Chad glanced at me in surprise.

"He spends the night and you guys don't sleep together?"

"I don't want to talk about it."

"No wonder he's such a grouch," he said.

"Just drop it okay."

"Sorry."

But he didn't. He was laughing at me.

We turned off Main and circled around to the Happy Harry's entrance. Chad drove up and down the aisles looking for a place to park.

"Wonder how soon before Mom calls and gives me a lecture?" I asked.

"Oh, she'll know within the hour. You can bet on that."

"God, if I'm going to have to put up with all the crap, you'd think I could at least have sex first."

Chad laughed silently beside me. I tried to glare at him, but I started laughing too. An old lady backed out of a parking spot. Chad dove in before a soccer mom could maneuver her SUV into it. She glared at us as we sauntered across the lot.

Killing time more than shopping, we wandered the aisles of the grocery store. I picked up a bag of shredded cheese when we stopped by the dairy case.

"I'll make tacos before I go to work if you want."

"Sounds good to me," Chad said.

"Go get some taco shells and whatever you want to have with them."

Chad took off to find the taco shells and I moved on down the case. I picked up a dozen eggs and opened them to make sure none were broken. As I did, a hand grasped my shoulder. I squealed and dropped the eggs. Egg goo dripped off my shoes as lips pressed against my ear.

"Your bodyguards can't follow you all the time, Twinkie," he whispered, "but I can."

I held the grocery cart handle with shaking hands and willed my legs to keep standing. I turned in time to see Jody disappear around the corner. Chad came from the other direction and tossed the taco shells in the cart.

"What's wrong?"

When I didn't answer right away, he grabbed my arm to get my attention.

"Randi, what's wrong?"

"He was here."

"That son of a bitch. Come on. Let's go."

He pulled me by the arm and marched me from the store leaving the cart next to the dairy case and a dozen eggs splattered on the floor. I sank onto the seat of the truck and pressed my hands together to keep them from shaking.

"This is ridiculous, Chad. I can't even go to the grocery store. You guys have to find him. I can't stand this," I ended in a sob.

Chad pulled me into his arms.

"I'm sorry, Ranna. We're trying to find him."

"Dammit, that's not good enough."

"I know, Ran. I know."

I pulled away and sniffed. Chad dug through the console for Kleenex or a napkin. He handed me one that had seen better days and I dried my eyes. Chad drove us home and called Lex. When Lex arrived at the house, Chad told him what had happened and then left.

"Where's he going?" I asked.

"Didn't say," Lex answered.

"I'm going to lie down. Help yourself to whatever you can find."

I went to my room and flopped down on the bed. Wilson nosed his way in and joined me. He crawled up beside me and put his head on my shoulder. I buried my face in his fur and cried. He licked my face until I smiled, then he curled up for a nap. I fell asleep, but Jody kept intruding in my dreams. After jolting awake for the fourth time, I gave up. When I walked into the kitchen, Chad was there with groceries.

"I don't know where anything goes," he said, helplessly looking around.

"You wouldn't even if you lived here," I said smiling. "It's a genetic thing."

He tossed a head of lettuce my direction. I caught it before it hit the floor and put it in the fridge.

"Is Lex gone?" I asked.

"He left when I got back."

"Did you find what you were looking for?"

"No. I was hoping there was a security camera at the store, but they only have those around the registers. Apparently he didn't use the front door."

I finished stowing the groceries and pulled out the stuff for tacos.

"You don't have to cook if you don't want to, Ranna."

"Keeps me busy. I can't stand to be cooped up here doing nothing."

"I'm sorry, Ranna. It's probably best if you hang here for the most part. I thought it would be enough for us to be with you, but he seems to be able to get around that."

"Chop a tomato and some lettuce," I said, handing him a knife.

I stirred the seasoning in the taco meat and turned it down to simmer. Chad was mutilating the tomato so I sat down at the table and took the knife away from him.

Chad stirred the taco meat and put the shells in the oven. I finished the tomato and the lettuce and grabbed the cheese from the refrigerator. We put the meat and shells in the middle and crunched tacos while Wilson waited on the floor between our chairs hoping for a taco spill. After we washed up, I changed into work clothes and Chad drove me to the Roger. Lex was already behind the bar when I walked in.

"Randi, long time no see," Lex said with a grin.

"You're going to make jokes like that for weeks, aren't you?"

"I don't know, I might. It isn't every day a guy gets to see his co-worker parading around in the nude."

"I wasn't parading. I was walking down the hall of my own home."

"Yeah, nude," Chad put in, laughing.

"You stay out of this, Chad."

"Boy, Lex. It is a primo opportunity. Man probably only gets an opportunity like this once in a lifetime."

"Yeah, I think I'm going to have to make the most of it."

"I'll start wearing my boots to work again."

Lex lifted his hands in surrender. "Okay, I'll be good. You want a beer, Chad?"

"Yeah, set me up."

Chad stayed at the bar as the regular Saturday night crew started trickling in. I kept glancing at the back door and jumping at loud noises. During a lull, Lex stepped behind me and put his hands on my waist. I jumped.

"Relax, Randi," he whispered in my ear. "He's not going to come in while Chad and I are both here."

I took a deep breath and tried to do as he said. He was probably right, but knowing that didn't help much. I kept getting Kira's drinks wrong. She was ready to shoot me by closing time. She counted out her tips, handed Lex a twenty and shot me a dirty look before she left.

"I think I'm off her Christmas card list," I said.

"She'll get over it. She doesn't hold a grudge. She'll probably go and buy you a new aromatherapy candle or a crystal or something. Why don't you guys go on home? I'll close up."

He didn't have to say it twice. I grabbed my purse from the safe and followed Chad to his truck.

"How many beers did you have tonight?" I asked.

"Just one, I was drinking soda the rest of the time."

"Just wondered if I needed to drive."

"I'm okay."

Bill blinked down at us from the roof as we parked. I stopped halfway up the walk and watched him.

"He's kind of like Yertle the Turtle up there," I said.

"Yertle the what?" asked Chad.

"Dr. Seuss. You know. Yertle…never mind," I muttered.

Chad shook his head and unlocked the front door. Wilson didn't hear us drive in. He came padding into the room looking shamefaced and depressed.

"It's okay, buddy." I said.

His ears perked up a little, but he still had his tail tucked between his legs.

"Come on, Wilson, want to go outside?" At that, he started bouncing and charged to the door.

I let him out and Chad flopped down on the couch and turned on the TV. I changed into sweats and sat in the recliner. Chad let Wilson in. He hopped up with Chad and turned circles until he had his spot softened up. Minutes later, he was snoring. I gathered a blanket around me and scrunched down in the recliner.

"Why don't you go to bed?" Chad asked.

"I'd rather stay here. He's been in my bedroom."

"Want me to sleep in there. You could have the sofa."

"This is fine."

"Your call, Ran."

He scooted down until his head was pillowed on the armrest. Soon his heavy even breathing joined Wilson's little snorts. I flipped to the weather channel. Surely, that would put me out. Wilson woke and burrowed under my blanket. I cuddled him in my lap and he went back to sleep. I drifted off while they were giving the weather in Afghanistan.

Chapter 22

woke with a stiff neck. It happens every time I fall asleep in the recliner. I kicked the footrest down and rolled to my feet in one motion. I could see Chad in the backyard playing with Wilson as I walked into the kitchen. I poured a bowl of cereal and sat down to eat. Chad and Wilson came bouncing through the door.

"Morning, Ranna."

"Hey, Chad. You hungry? I fixed breakfast."

I pointed to the cereal box.

"I already ate."

He poured a cup of coffee and sat down across from me.

"I wish I knew how Bill gets on your roof," he said.

"Is he up there again?"

"Yeah. Saw him just now."

"Maybe he's a magic cat."

"Yeah, Randi, I'm sure that's it."

"You have a better theory?"

"I don't have any theory. I haven't actually given it a lot of thought."

"So he could be magic."

Chad made a face at me. I grinned and went to rinse my cereal bowl.

"What's the plan for the day?" Chad asked.

"I don't know."

"What do you usually do on Sunday?"

"Read, watch TV. I don't know. Just hang out with the kids."

"Okay, this week you can hang out with me instead."

Chad kicked back in the recliner to watch the Chiefs game. I settled onto the couch with a Dana Stabenow mystery, but I couldn't concentrate. After reading the same page five times, I put the book down. I obviously wasn't in the mood to read. I paced around the house for a while, then went out with Wilson. He barked at some squirrels and watered all the fence posts.

"Wilson, I'm going stir crazy."

He cocked his head and gave me his worried dog face. I rubbed his ears and we went inside. In the kitchen, I stood and stared at the cabinets waiting for inspiration. Wilson slurped a drink from his water dish and trotted to the living room for a nap. A drink sounded like a good idea, so I poured a glass of iced tea. Chad came in and grabbed a Bud Light.

"What are you doing?" he asked.

"I'm going crazy. I hate being stuck in the house."

"You said you usually hang around at home on Sunday anyway."

"Yeah, but I could leave if I wanted to. I feel like I'm in prison here."

"You need to chill out, Randi."

"You chill out," I snapped.

"Okay, Okay. Don't go all PMS on me. I'm going into the living room now. You let me know when it's safe to come back."

I stuck out my tongue at his retreating form. Wilson came in for a snack and watched me as I stared unseeing out the window. He started whining, so I sat down at the table. Wilson doesn't like it if you just stand around staring at things. I grabbed a cookbook off the shelf and it fell open to the chocolate chip cookie recipe. Hmm. That wasn't a half-bad idea.

I turned on the oven and started mixing cookie dough. Chad, still afraid to get too close, stayed in the living room until the smell of cookies wafted down the hall. He peeked around the corner into the kitchen.

"Is it safe to come in?"

"Yeah."

I pulled the first batch of cookies from the oven and Chad poured us each a glass of milk. We ate all of that batch and most of the second one.

"You want, I could move in here permanently," Chad said.

"I don't make cookies very often, and half the time we live on macaroni and cheese and Ramen noodles."

"Well, that's a disappointment. I guess I'll keep my place."

"Chad, how long am I going to be trapped like this?"

"I don't know, Ran. Not long, a few days at the most. He'll make a mistake soon."

"You hope he makes a mistake soon."

"Okay, we hope he makes a mistake soon."

I finished baking the cookies and cleaned up my mess in the kitchen. It didn't take long, and I was again at loose ends, staring across the back yard seeing nothing. Chad was talking about something he wanted to do to his truck, but I wasn't really listening. My thoughts were on Ann Marie. Specifically, how she and Liz acted at Harold's gun use and safety class. Other than me, they were the only women there that seemed comfortable with handguns.

"Earth to Randi, where are you?"

I shook my head. "Sorry. What did you say?"

"Nothing. Wasn't important. What were you thinking about?"

"Was there a gun found with Ann Marie's body or at the house with Liz?"

"I don't think so."

"So they knew whoever it was that came to the house, and they didn't have any reason to be frightened."

"Why do you say that?"

"What Ann Marie did for a living was a fairly high risk profession. I think she usually carried a gun. I saw her at the range. She was familiar with handguns. Probably went to the range and shot fairly regularly. She wasn't a newby like some of those women at class."

"So?"

"She and Liz were really spooked by the murders. They'd been through something similar back when they lived in Kansas City and weren't taking any chances. We talked about it when I gave them a ride home after Harold's class. She had to have known whoever came into her home. If it had been a stranger, she would have been armed."

"She was in her own home, Randi. I doubt if she answered the door with her gun."

"I have since this all started. I think she would have too."

"You psychic now?"

"Don't be a smart ass. I think whoever it was called ahead and made an appointment like a regular john, expecting to find Ann Marie home alone. When Liz opened the door, she surprised him, and he knocked her out. Then he dragged Ann Marie from the house."

"You have it all worked out, don't you?"

"Yeah, all except who did it."

"That's always the tough part," he agreed.

I dropped into the chair across from Chad and fiddled with the salt and pepper shakers in the middle of the table.

"How much longer are you going to work undercover around here?" I asked, changing the subject.

"I'm pretty much done locally. I'll still be available for the Feds or to other departments if they need someone. It's getting pretty dicey for me around here, though."

"I'm surprised you've gotten away with it as long as you have."

"I don't look much like I did in high school."

That was an understatement. He left as a clean-cut scrawny high school kid and came back as the incredible hulk.

"You glad to be out of it?" I asked.

"I guess. It's a rush sometimes, but I get sick of hanging with sleaze bags all the time. It's easy to get sucked into that mindset. The longer you do it, the harder it is to remember you're one of the good guys. I think I'm ready to get out."

"Uh oh, better watch it. Next thing you know, you'll get a haircut, start wearing suits and move to homicide. Or maybe you'll run off to join the FBI."

"Not a chance. Besides, I'm too old to join the feebies. They take themselves too damn seriously. I don't know how Steve and AJ can stand it. The Feds have been all over this murder case."

"Lot of good it's done. They have this huge major case squad with state troopers and sheriff's deputies, Feds and everything else, and the killer is still running around free."

"Yeah, but think how far behind we'd be if we didn't have all those detectives working this thing. They bring a lot of resources to the table. I can guarantee Steve and AJ wouldn't be following hunches in God knows where. They'd be stuck here sorting through the murder book or jacking around with paperwork."

"I guess that's true."

"Come on, Ran. I'm sick of this place. Let me take you to lunch."

"I thought I wasn't supposed to go out."

"I think you'll be safe at a restaurant."

"Where we going?"

"I don't know. You want Chinese or Mexican?"

"Mexican. That should be good on top of chocolate chip cookies."

Chad made a face. "I guess."

We drove to La Casa and ordered lunch.

"Why so quiet?" Chad asked over his burrito.

"I think we're missing something important on these murders. Some kind of connection."

"We?" Chad asked.

I flipped a tortilla chip at him and he ducked.

"I still say you should become a cop, Randi."

"Why?"

"You have good instincts."

"Yeah, just one problem. I don't want to be a cop."

"Whatever, you're wasting your talent," he said.

"No, I'm not. I'm sharing it with you."

"Oh, thank you."

We stretched lunch until dinnertime, then decided to go visit Lex at the bar. It was almost empty when we arrived, just a few hard-core drinkers nursing beers and staring at the silent TV.

"Hey guys, want a beer?" Lex asked.

"I don't think so. I'd like to go to the range and shoot. Can we do that, Chad?"

"That should be okay," Chad said.

We stayed until the bar started to get crowded around seven. As we walked outside, Chad's pager went off. He glanced at it and gave me a *just a minute* sign. I went in and parked on a barstool while he made his phone call.

Chad came back inside looking tense.

"Ran. I have to go. We've got a...situation in town. Why don't you hang here? You'll be safe with Lex."

"Don't I get any say in this?"

"Randi, I've got to go. Now. I don't have time for a debate.

His tone and the look on his face stopped my whining. I didn't know what was going on, but it was serious.

"Be careful, Chad," I said, as he walked back out the door.

He didn't even respond. Just pushed through the door and sprinted to his truck. I heard gravel spray and the chirp of tires on pavement a minute before his siren wailed to life.

I absolutely did not want to be at the Roger. It was dark, and this evening, it felt dreary even as the crowd picked up and the jukebox started blaring. I hunched at the bar, tension knotted the muscles in my back and shoulders until I thought I'd scream. I needed to be doing something. Before I completely melted down, rescue arrived from an unlikely source. Fred Baxter walked through the door. He stopped at the bar to pick up a to-go order from the kitchen. I practically attacked the poor man.

"Fred, I'm so glad to see you. Chad had to leave and left me stranded here. Could you please give me a ride to my house?"

"What?" he said, cupping a hand to his ear.

"Randi, I don't think that's a good idea," Lex said.

"I'm going to get in my car and drive straight to Sure Shot. I'll be safe there with Harold."

"I wish you would wait until someone can go with you."

"Lex, I have to get out of here. I've been killing time all day because I'm afraid to go out. I won't live like this. Jody can't get past Harold. Please, Fred," I said turning to him. "Can you give me a ride?"

"I didn't order any pie."

"A ride," I shouted. "Can you give me a ride home?"

"Oh, sure."

"Please, Randi," Lex said. "Stay here, or let me call Morgan to cover the bar, and I'll go with you.

I shook my head. "Don't be silly. I'll be fine. Harold won't let anything happen to me."

Lex was not happy. He was probably on the phone to Chad the instant I walked out the door, but I couldn't stay there another second. I was ready to start climbing the walls.

Fred chattered nonstop as he drove to my house. I gave up trying to give him directions and just pointed when it was time to turn. It was easier that way. He dropped me off and gave me a cheery wave as he drove away. I ran inside, strapped my .32 into my ankle holster, grabbed my 9mm and my cleaning kit, and trotted back out to the car. Wilson shadowed my every footstep as I ran down the hall and back to the front door. I told him to guard the house and trotted out to the Mustang, a little nervous, but happy to be doing anything besides sitting and waiting for something to happen.

Harold was behind the counter as usual when I rushed through the door.

"Hey, Harold. What's going on?"

"Nothing much, Randi. What can I do for ya?"

"Give me a box of nines. I think I'll go gut a few targets."

"Sounds like a good way to pass the time. Where's Chad?"

"He's at work and AJ's out of town, so it's just me tonight."

"Where's that other guy, the one that works at the bar?"

"Lex?"

"Yeah, that's the one."

"He's working tonight."

"Well, sounds like the men folk just left you to your own devices."

"Yep, so I decided to come and visit with you. Anything good going on around here?"

"Guess it depends on your point of view. The Zone's still shut down. So I'm not workin' nearly as hard as I have been, but ain't making near as much money either."

"Surely you can open the range back up, can't you?"

"I don't know if I'm going to. Folks in small towns have long memories. Don't know that they'll want to play out there where they found those poor girls."

I didn't know what to say. He might be right. I didn't think anyone would blame him for owning the property where the bodies were found. But, they might not want to come out and play there either.

"Say," Harold said, before I could summon up anything positive to say. "There was a fellow out here the other day asking about you."

"Really?"

"Yeah, nice looking boy, around your age I guess. Said he'd seen you around and wanted to meet you."

"Wow, I have a secret admirer. I don't know whether to be flattered or creeped out."

I opened a Gun World magazine that was on the counter and idly paged through it while we talked.

"He seemed nice enough," Harold said. "I told him I'd introduce you if he ever showed up when you were here."

"Ah, thanks, I guess."

"I told him he was wasting his time mooning after you. You already had too many men sniffing around."

His last sentence snapped out like something my Mom would have said about my clothes. I looked up from my magazine in surprise, but Harold was bent down looking for something under the counter.

"Well, um...I guess I'll go on in and shoot a few rounds. Talk to you later."

He grunted something unintelligible from behind the counter as I pushed my way into the range. It was empty so I picked a spot in the middle and set a target. I was halfway through the box of shells when another shooter came in. I reloaded and set my next target. The range lights flickered off before I fired a shot. My heart thudded into overdrive. I could hear footsteps coming toward me, then they stopped. I checked the clip in my gun to make sure it was seated and called out.

"Who's there? Harold? Is that you?"

The footsteps started again. I peered through the darkness, trying to see who was coming. The emergency lights glowed at the exits, but left the rest of the cavernous room in either deep shadow or total darkness. Whoever was walking had stopped just on the other side of my shooting cubicle. I swallowed, took a slow step forward and glanced around the wall. Jody was standing on the other side. I let out an aborted scream and stumbled away from his grinning face.

"What's the matter, Twinkie? Aren't you glad to see me?"

"Jody, how did you know I was here?"

"Just followed you, sweetheart. It was easy once I got rid of your bodyguard."

Oh, God. "What have you done to Chad?"

"Relax, I didn't hurt him, just made sure he'd be busy for a while."

"What do you want from me?"

"That's easy. Payback. You cost me my job. I'm going to take it out of your hide. But first, we're going to have a little fun. Or at least I am."

"Harold won't let you do this."

"I can handle the old man. He thinks I'm an awful nice guy."

"My brothers know where I am."

I took a step back and felt the shooting table behind me digging into my back. I was as far as I was going to go, that way.

"Steve ain't even in town, and that asswipe boyfriend of yours is gone with him. You're not the only one I've been watching. As for Chad, I created a little diversion that should keep him busy for a while. Looks like it's just you and me at last."

He moved toward me and for the first time I saw the shadow of something in his hand.

He's got a gun! Shoot! My brain screamed.

Before I could put thought into motion, he peeled the gun out of my fingers and tossed it onto the range. I tried to scramble over the counter as it skittered across the floor. Jody made a lunge toward me and I saw something glitter in his hand. Not a gun, a knife.

"Harold!" I screamed.

The door to the gun shop smacked the wall as Harold rushed through. Jody turned toward the sound. I flipped myself backwards over the counter and rolled away. Jody scrambled after me.

"What the fuck's going on here?" Harold yelled, charging toward us.

Jody stopped and turned around. "Stay out of this old man. This is between me and the bitch."

I crabbed across the floor toward my nine. Jody started after me while Harold climbed into the range. I rolled over, scooped up my gun and turned as Jody came rushing at me. He kicked my hand and the nine flew across the range. My hand exploded with pain and my arm went numb.

"God damn it! Leave her alone!" Harold shouted.

I cradled my hand against my stomach and scooted away from the two men.

"I warned you to stay out of this old man."

Jody turned toward Harold and a gunshot cracked. Jody jerked and stumbled. He dropped the knife and grabbed his stomach as he sank to the floor. I sat trying to catch my breath. Harold walked toward Jody and kicked the knife away.

"Is he dead?" I croaked.

"No."

"You'd better call an ambulance."

"I'll do that in a little bit. Are you all right? Did he hurt you?

"No, just scared me. Thank you, Harold. I thought he was going to kill me."

"I'm glad he didn't. It would have been a shame to waste your death like that."

"Wh...what?"

"I thought he was a nice fellow." Harold muttered to himself, as he stared at Jody. "Too nice for a fallen woman."

"What do you mean, Harold?"

He looked over at me in surprise, as if he'd forgotten I was there.

"Now you stay right where you are, Randi. Let me get you some water and an ice pack for that hand."

"Really, I'm fine." I said as I started to get to my feet."

"Don't move," he snapped. "You might injure that hand worse," he added as an afterthought.

"Okay."

I shook my head as he disappeared up front to the cooler. Maybe he was reacting to the adrenaline rush from the attack by Jody. I felt jittery, like my muscles were trying to jump out of my skin. I held my injured hand against my chest and rocked back and forth. Harold strode across the range, handed me a water bottle, and tossed a chemical ice pack at my feet. I tried to open the bottle, but my fingers refused to cooperate. Harold jerked it from me, snapped the seal, and handed it back. I took a drink and tried to look away from Jody. Blood was starting to pool on the floor around him. He moved and a weak groan escaped.

"We should probably call the cops and get an ambulance on the way, Harold," I said.

He was staring toward Jody's inert form and didn't answer. I wondered if he was in shock.

"Harold?"

He didn't respond, so I stood and started to turn away. He whirled toward me, grabbed the water bottle and flung it to the floor.

"What are you doing?" I asked.

He grabbed my arms and jerked me against his chest.

"Harold, what's going on?"

"I thought you were different. Pure and chaste. A good woman, like my mother."

"What are you talking about? Harold you're hurting me."

"A Jezebel," he shouted.

Spittle sprayed my face as I jerked against his hold.

"A floozy, a tramp, a slut," he screamed. "Fornicating with that cop, whoring with that bartender. I watched your house; I saw them slipping in and out at all hours, sometimes both on the same day. One leaving as the other came in. Shameful."

When he spoke again, his voice was soft. He sounded like a father scolding a well loved, but wayward child.

"You've been such a disappointment to me."

My mind raced to make sense of Harold's rant. Jezebel, whore, men around at all hours, I couldn't believe it. I was getting lectured on adult behavior in a darkened shooting range by a knife wielding man I'd thought of as a friend, while Jody McIntire quietly bled out on the floor.

"Harold, I'm sorry I've disappointed you." This was surreal. I was apologizing for having sex with two men I'd never slept with. If I hadn't been so scared, I might have laughed. "We can talk this out if you just let me go."

"I'm going to let you go, very soon."

"Um, now would be good."

I strained against him, trying to break free. He tightened his grip and my eyes teared with pain.

"Harold, please."

"Mother told me about women like you. You've broken the laws of God. Used your body to taunt and abuse those poor men. But I can bring you to the light."

Oh my God. I was trapped in a redneck version of Psycho.

"Harold, you've got it wrong. It's not like that," I stammered.

"Don't lie to me. I've seen them at your house, with my own eyes. Do not lie!" He hissed.

Harold's gaze was fixed on me, but I don't think he was seeing me any more; he was looking at something deep inside. His eyes were just dark empty pools.

"You have to be cleansed," he whispered. "They all had to be cleansed. They profaned themselves. I'm doing God's work."

I gasped as understanding dawned.

"It was you," I whispered. "You killed those girls."

"It had to be done. They were dirty. They had to be cleansed."

Jody moved his leg. The toe of his boot made a squeak noise as he dragged it on the floor. Harold turned toward him and I jerked my right arm free. He tightened his grip on my left and eased his knife from the scabbard on his belt. The knife blade flashed in front of my face as he drug the tip gently across my cheek and down my neck. I didn't twitch. I didn't even breathe.

He flicked the knife at my shirt and one by one, the buttons dropped and bounced on the floor. I flinched and tried to jerk away from the blade. Harold's grip slipped on my arm. I pulled free and stumbled across the range away from him. I fell, and swore as my injured hand smacked the floor. In a panic, I pushed to my feet, Harold's steps loud behind me. I turned to see where he was and a gunshot cracked. A stabbing pain shot through my left shoulder. My arm went slack as my knees buckled. Tears flooded my eyes. I thumped to my butt and pushed myself away with my feet. Harold kept walking deliberately toward me.

"Don't fight me, Randi," he said softly. "Let me cleanse you. In purity, you can meet God."

"I'm not ready to meet God," I sobbed. I stopped scooting backward and fumbled with my ankle holster. Harold tossed his gun aside and came toward me with the knife.

"Don't struggle. Soon you'll be free."

His voice was soft and low. His eyes were still empty.

"Don't come any closer, Harold."

He didn't change his pace.

"Stop or I'll shoot."

"You can't fight it," he whispered, as I finally jerked my .32 free of the holster.

Harold's eyes widened as I pointed the barrel toward him. He face went ugly with fury and he lunged forward. I fired, and his steps halted for just a second, then he started toward me again. I fired twice more and he stopped. His hand went to his chest and came away bloody; he staggered once and the knife clattered to the floor. He stared down in surprise at the blood on his fingers. When he raised his head, his expression was hurt. Like he'd tried to do me a favor and I'd refused.

"I just needed to cleanse you," he whispered.

He sank to his knees still staring at me. "You needed to be cleansed."

I dropped my gun and scooted until my back hit the wall. My blood soaked shirt was wet and cold where it stuck to my skin. I pressed my hand against my shoulder and gasped in pain. I closed my eyes. A shiver racked my body. I was so cold, so tired.

Chapter 23

andi, sweetheart, talk to me."

AJ's voice sounded very far away. I opened my eyes to find him kneeling in front of me.

"Oh, God, darlin'. I thought you were dead."

"How did you get here?"

He brushed the hair away from my face and kissed my cheek.

"Shhh. We'll talk later. Let's get you to the hospital."

"AJ, Harold killed those girls. He was going to kill me."

Tears trickled down my cheeks. AJ brushed them away.

"Hush. I know."

I moved and gasped as pain stabbed my shoulder. I stopped and concentrated on catching my breath. When I looked up at AJ, there were tears in his eyes.

"You're going to be okay," he said.

I tried to smile. AJ nodded to the EMTs. I gritted my teeth as they placed me on a stretcher and jolted it into the back of the ambulance.

AJ touched my cheek and kissed my forehead before the doors slammed closed. "I'll be there as soon as I can, darlin'. I love you."

I smiled and closed my eyes.

When I woke, AJ was asleep in the chair beside my bed. I moved and a gasp of pain slipped out. His eyes snapped open. He came to stand by the bed and brushed my hair away from my forehead before he leaned down and kissed me. When I woke again, the doctor was walking into my room. He was the first in a long line of visitors. Most bearing flowers and candy and cheerful get well soon faces. None of them willing to tell me how AJ had shown up at Sure Shot.

The next day, freshly showered, and with my arm in a sling, they sent me home. My bandaged shoulder hurt like hell. I reclined on the couch, stoked on painkillers. AJ, Chad, and Steve were there to finally fill me in on what I'd missed.

"For two days, we drove all over hell's half acre and found absolutely nothing," Steve said.

"I knew we were missing a piece of the puzzle. It was niggling at the back of my mind, but I couldn't get a handle on it," AJ added. "Something clicked the day I looked at the map you had marked all the murder sites on. It wasn't anything specific, just a gut feeling. I convinced Steve it couldn't hurt to check them closer. He hadn't been crazy about the idea from the start. By that afternoon, he just figured we'd wasted the better part of two days and was antsy to get home and get to work.

"We stopped for coffee on the drive back. I started flipping through the yellow pages of a phone book from Owensville when an ad for a paintball range called The Free Fire Zone caught my eye. I grabbed the phone book from one of the other towns and checked. There was a paintball range there called The Battle Zone. That's when I got it. I grabbed my cell phone and started to make a call."

"I couldn't figure out what he was so fired up about," Steve said.

"I stopped dialing and told him all the towns on the map had paintball ranges. We'd played at most of them last summer when we were in the Splat League. He still wasn't buying it, just stared at me like I was nuts. I finally convinced him it couldn't hurt to check. Hell we'd already wasted a day and a half. We started calling the police stations in each town, and asked if they had paintball ranges. They thought we were crazy, but they gave us the names and phone numbers. We called the ranges and talked to the owners and I was beginning to think we were off on a tangent."

"We took a few minutes to regroup, then started home," Steve said, taking over the story. "I started wondering if the people that had owned the ranges were the original owners, so we stopped at the police station in Jefferson City and borrowed a phone. We called all of the ranges and spoke to the owners a second time. We asked each of them if they were the original owners. They all said they'd purchased the property from someone as a going concern. When we asked for purchase dates, they all fit in with the dates of the murders. Every one of them was bought within a few weeks after the last murder. It fit in each town. When we asked who the original owner was, it was the same every time: Harold Baker."

AJ took over the story. "I called Chad to give him a quick rundown of what we'd found. Before I could start, he told me all hell was breaking loose in town. They'd had a bomb threat hand-delivered to the police station by a kid. Another dropped into the collection plate during evening mass at the Catholic Church. At the same time, a department-wide email came in telling them a sniper was about to start shooting people in the vicinity of the courthouse. They had tactical teams in town from Jefferson City and Columbia. The bomb squad was on its way, and every officer and sheriff's deputy had mobilized to evacuate people and maintain order. He was about to hang up on me when I asked about you. He told me you were at the Jolly Roger with Lex and hung up. Something was hinky about the crap going down in Alden, but there wasn't anything I could do about it. We were still twenty-five miles away. I told Steve we needed to get our butts to town, and gave him a brief synopsis of the chaos. Then I called the Roger to check on you. When Lex told me you weren't there, something clicked. There were only two scenarios other than natural disaster that would mobilize the entire police and sheriff's department. One was multiple bomb threats; the other was a sniper or sniper threat in town. I couldn't believe that both things were happening in Alden on a Sunday evening. It had to be a diversion and the only person that could know the effect those two things would have was someone in the department, or someone that used to be in the department."

"Jody," said Steve. "It had to be. It was a sure way for him to get Chad away from you. All he had to do was put his plan in motion and follow you until he got you in a vulnerable position."

"But how'd he know I would leave the bar?" I asked.

"Just dumb luck. He'd gone to a lot of trouble for nothing until you left the bar. As long as you were with Lex, he wouldn't have even considered getting close to you," answered Steve.

AJ took up the story again.

"I tried to get in touch with you on your cell phone, but just kept getting your voicemail. By the time I called Chad again, they'd begun to suspect they were dealing with a hoax. I told him my suspicions about Jody being responsible and he instantly agreed."

"I was relieved, because I knew you were safe with Lex," Chad said.

"That's when I told him you had left with Fred. Chad went quiet on the phone for a minute then shouted, Sure Shot, she's at the shooting range with Harold.

"My heart stopped. As Steve and I ran for the car, I tried to fill Chad in on what we'd discovered about the murders."

Steve took over the story.

"We jumped in the car, hit the lights and siren and flew home at ninety. AJ was driving like a maniac. I thought we were going to die."

"While I was playing Indy 500," AJ said, "Steve was talking to the dispatcher, trying to get a force mobilized and trying to get through on your cell phone. There was no one available to go to Sure Shot; everyone was tied up in town. And you still weren't answering your cell phone."

"It was in my purse, in the car."

AJ shook his head at me and continued.

"Chad broke away from the mess in town and slid into the parking lot of Sure Shot just ahead of us. We ran inside, but didn't see Harold. Chad and I charged into the shooting range and Steve ran around the building to the back entrance where he found Jody's car parked next to Harold's truck. He called the department and finally got them to send out some officers."

"The lights were off when we pushed into the range," Chad said, "we crawled over the shooting bench to search the area, I almost fell over Jody. I checked to see if he had a pulse. He was still alive, so I called an ambulance and continued searching the range. AJ was across the room when I heard him shout. I went running toward his voice, tripped over Harold, and fell flat on my face. I was starting to feel like you, Ranna, couldn't take a step without tripping over a body."

I laughed and waited for the rest.

"AJ was kneeling in front of someone. I knew it had to be you."

"I felt for a pulse and almost cried when I found it." AJ said. "The ambulance arrived out front and Chad left to direct them around to the rear. They came in and that's when you woke up."

"I couldn't believe it when he started going weird on me," I said. "He must have really been disturbed. It was just a total meltdown. He was crazy."

I shuddered and AJ slipped his arm around me.

"I can't believe he killed sixteen women," I said quietly.

"We're not sure it wasn't more than that," said Steve.

"We cleared our cases and handed the rest over to the Feds. Let them worry about the others."

"When he was screaming at me, he said the women he killed were polluted and had to be cleansed," I said. "The Harold I knew just disappeared in front of my eyes."

"Almost all the women he killed were either pros like Ann Marie or part timers like Lisa. Call girls or just good-time girls that liked to hang out with different guys," said Steve.

"What I don't understand," said Chad, "is why he went after Randi."

"I know the answer to that," I said. "He was watching my house. I don't know why."

"Um, I asked him to run by whenever he had a chance," Steve said, looking down at the floor. "I was worried about you. We were all putting in so many hours. I'm sorry, Ran. If I hadn't done that, you might have stayed under his radar."

"He must have taken your directions to heart. I saw him drive by once, and he came to the Roger one night. When he went completely nutso on me, he said I was unclean because I was sleeping with Lex and AJ."

AJ and I looked at each other and laughed.

"If we hadn't been trying to keep Jody from killing you, Harold would have left you alone," Steve said.

"Yeah, something like that."

"He was one disturbed individual. We got some information on him this morning. Talked to some of his teachers, a couple of guys he was in the service with. I guess his mom was a nut case. Some of the stuff she supposedly did to him when he was just a kid makes Joan Crawford seem like Mother of the Year.

We all went quiet, thinking about the Harold that we'd known and the one he'd kept hidden. I shuddered and broke the silence.

"How's Jody?"

"He's going to live, unfortunately," Chad said. "He's going to be in the hospital for a long time."

"He'll be a resident of the state longer," AJ added.

"Well, they both got what they had coming to them," Steve said as he stood to go. "You need anything, Randi, give us call."

"Thanks, Stevie."

He ruffled my hair and walked out the door. The painkillers were starting to wear off and I was gritting my teeth in pain. Chad went in the kitchen and came back with two pills and a glass of water. I shook my head.

"I hate that stuff, Chad. I'm not taking it."

"Yes, you are."

"I'm not, they make me sleep."

"They're supposed to make you sleep. Your body needs sleep to heal."

I swallowed the pills under protest. Chad perched on the arm of the couch.

"I think we found your cowboy."

I jerked upright and hissed with pain when I moved my shoulder. Jesus, the cowboy, I'd forgotten all about him.

"Where'd he turn up?" I asked.

"One of Sheriff Logan's guys stopped him out on Route E. Doing seventy in a fifty five."

"He got busted for speeding?"

"They were already on the lookout for the truck. Just turned out it was for my case and not Steve's. Seems he had a tool box full of product he didn't get delivered."

"He was The Duke?"

"Yeah."

"Guess that's why he was so nervous when he found out Steve was a cop."

"Yeah, he wasn't in any hurry to make his acquaintance."

Chad got up off the arm of the couch and leaned down to kiss my cheek.

"I'm gonna get out of here, Ran." Chad said. "I'm glad you're home."

So was I. The boys were upstairs, and I could hear their music thumping the ceiling over my head. Wilson was curled up on my lap and no one was trying to kill me. I scooted down till I was lying on the couch and waited for the pills to kick in. I must have fallen asleep. When I woke, AJ and the boys were playing a video game and eating pizza. I sat up and AJ turned away from the game.

"Hey, darlin'. You feeling any better?"

"Hmm." I thought about it for a minute. "Not really."

"Want some pizza?"

"Yeah, pizza would make it better, I think."

I ate a piece of pizza. The boys each grabbed another slice and headed upstairs to their rooms. That first slice of pizza tasted pretty good, so I had another one. I pondered a third, but decided I'd rather sleep.

"I'm going to bed," I said as I stood.

"Mind if I join you?" AJ ask with a smile.

"Long as all you want is sleep."

AJ sighed. "I'm getting used to that."

He switched off the television and followed me to the bedroom. AJ undressed and slipped between the sheets. I joined him, and he took me gently in his arms, trying not to move my shoulder and hand. Wilson rooted under the covers and curled at my feet. If I hadn't been in so much pain, it might have been perfect.

"I love you, Randi. I thought you were dead when I found you," AJ whispered. "You were so pale and there was so much blood. I don't ever want to go through that again."

"I could do without a repeat, myself."

AJ's lips were warm against my neck. I shivered and wished I felt better. The painkillers I'd taken before we lay down were starting to kick in. I was awake but I was getting fuzzy. AJ's words sounded far away.

"You need to get healed up. I have a week's vacation coming. Make sure you get plenty of rest, too. I don't think we'll be doing a lot of sleeping."

My lips curled into a smile and then I slept.

KD EASLEY
Author of MURDER at TIMBER BRIDGE
Jolly Roger
(ATTEMPTED)
MURDER at the
JOLLY ROGER
A Randi Black Mystery
SNEAK PEEK!

Chapter 1

It was five after four and I was late. Again. After the argument I'd had with Morgan last night it might be just the excuse he needed to fire me. My boots skidded on the yellowed linoleum as I burst through the door. Then three things happened at once. First, the door I'd just slapped open crashed against the wall. Next, my boots hit the edge of the hardwood floor and came to a sudden stop without notifying the rest of my body, which continued into the room landing with a thud and a slap as knees and hands saved me from a full face-plant. Do I know how to make an entrance or what?

I glanced around the bar to see if anyone witnessed my grand entrance. If nothing else, Morgan should have been laughing his ass off. The only noise I heard was a soft snick that could have been the backdoor closing. It was quiet, creepy quiet. I rose to my feet and brushed futilely at the dirt now embedded in the knees of my jeans.

"Morgan," I called.

I stared down the length of the bar and the breath whooshed out of my lungs. Morgan lay half leaning against the paneling between the open end of the bar, and the hallway that led to the bathrooms. A bloody streak marked the wall above him like an exclamation point.

"Oh shit! Oh God! Morgan, please don't be dead."

Adrenaline surged through my system. I fumbled my gun from the holster at my back, glad for the first time that Morgan insisted I wear it to work. I couldn't tell if he was breathing. I ran forward on shaking legs and scanned the room, listening to the silence, trying to determine if we were alone. The pounding of my heart was so loud, the only thing I heard was blood thundering in my ears. I knelt at Morgan's side, and felt his neck for a pulse. It was faint, but it was there. His breathing was quick and shallow. His tanned complexion was pale and shiny with sweat. His sandy hair, always perfect, was matted with blood. Stuff like this wasn't supposed to happen in small Missouri towns like Alden. I laid my gun on the floor, worked my iPhone out of my pocket and dialed 911.

Morgan Black, the man on the floor, was my boss, my ex-husband, and the father of my teenage sons. There was a time when I daydreamed of killing him, hell; the thought crossed my mind last night. The reality was I didn't want him dead. I definitely didn't want to be the one to find the body.

The 911 dispatcher answered, and my voice came out as a croak. I cleared my throat and tried again. Even then my voice was an octave high.

"This is Randi Black. There's been a shooting, I need an ambulance at the Jolly Roger." I paused and tried not to give in to panic, but the pool of blood around Morgan was growing. "Please hurry."

The dispatcher assured me help was on the way. He was advising me to stay on the line until they arrived as I tossed the phone to the floor. With shaking fingers I brushed the hair off Morgan's forehead. His skin was cold and clammy. I didn't think that was a good sign.

I ripped open his shirt and tried to figure out where the blood was coming from so I could put pressure on the wound. From the blood on the wall and the pool on the floor, I didn't think pressing on his chest was going to help much, but I was afraid to move him.

I found a bullet hole, wadded up his shirttail and pressed. Morgan groaned.

"Morgan, hang on. Don't die on me now."

His green eyes fluttered open. Dull and pain-filled, conscious thought seeped into them slowly as he woke. He blinked once, swallowed, and squinted at me.

"Randi," he whispered.

He lifted his hand a few inches toward me, too weak to raise it all the way.

"Stay still, you're going to be okay. The ambulance is on the way."

"I'm sorry, Randi," he paused and licked his lips. "I still love you, I always have," he whispered. "Tell the boys I love them."

"You tell them yourself," I choked out.

His voice grew weaker. I leaned in close to hear as his breath whistled in his chest. He coughed and blood trickled from the corner of his mouth. I wiped it away with my sleeve and scooted closer to hear what he was trying to say. Blood soaked into the knees of my jeans and squeezed through my fingers as it saturated the flannel wadded up in my hand. I heard a noise from behind me and grabbed my gun from the floor before Morgan could continue. The front door opened with a crash. I leapt to my feet and jerked my gun toward the intruder. A police officer charged in.

I lowered my gun, and sighed with relief.

"Thank God you're here."

"Put the weapon down and step away from the victim," the officer screamed.

His voice cracked and his gun barrel wobbled in a sloppy circle as he pointed it in my general direction. He sounded like Barney Fife and he acted like he wanted an excuse to shoot me.

"Wha—What?" I stammered.

The situation was almost comical except that the gun wavering at me was real and the cop behind it was seriously juiced on an adrenaline buzz.

"I said drop it!" he yelled again.

A younger officer came in and stood slightly to the rear of Barney. I stared down at Morgan. He was still, eyes closed, face slack.

"Put down the weapon and step away." Barney enunciated very clearly like he was speaking to a slow child.

The officer's words took a moment to process, but the message finally got through. He motioned with his head for me to move aside. I took a long step to the right and raised my arms, the gun forgotten in my right hand. Two semi-automatics immediately pointed my way. That didn't take long to get through. I swallowed, let my gun dangle from my finger and reached down to lay it on the floor. The two officers tracked my every move.

"Kick it toward me and put your hands on top of your head."

"But, I..."

"Shut up and do it."

"Okay. Okay."

I laced my fingers over my head and risked another glance at Morgan. His color had gone from pasty white to gray, but the whistling wound in his chest told me he was still breathing.

I kicked the gun toward Barney and took a step back.

He tracked my movements with the 9mm, his muscles quivering with excitement. I hoped he didn't shoot me by accident. He was hefty, with a nice doughnut ring hanging over his utility belt, and he was breathing like he'd just run a hundred-yard dash. The second officer took a step toward my gun on the floor. He was a rookie named Benson. I recognized him as he stepped from the shadows behind Barney. I'd met him at the Alden Police Department's annual charity barbeque. He glanced up and stopped in surprise when he recognized me.

"Um, Nixon. That's Randi Black. She's..."

Nixon interrupted the kid before he could finish.

"Get that weapon bagged and tagged, you need a damn invitation, or what?"

"But, sir. She's, um, her brothers are..."

"Kid, I ain't gonna tell you again. Get that gun bagged and tagged."

Benson gave me a wide-eyed look as he knelt to pick up my PF-9. He slipped his ink pen through the trigger guard of my gun and dropped it into an evidence bag.

"Take that out and put it in the car, then call dispatch and have them send the detectives," Nixon said.

"Yes, sir. Sir, I think you..."

"Kid, you ain't been on the force long enough to think. Now get out there and wait for the detectives."

"Yes, sir."

Nixon continued to stare at me. I stood unmoving, my hands still clasped on my head. When the ambulance crew came in rolling a stretcher, I dropped my hands and moved toward Morgan.

"I'm glad you're here," I said. "He's lost a..."

I didn't finish my sentence. Nixon grabbed me from behind and shoved me face first into wall.

"Reach toward the ceiling, palms on the wall and spread 'em."

It was becoming increasingly evident that I might be in some trouble. That notion gained some momentum as my cheek smacked the paneling. How was it that the only cop on the force that didn't know me by sight, had to find me kneeling over Morgan Black with a gun in my hand.

"What'd you shoot him for?" Nixon asked. "Huh? Lovers quarrel?"

I turned my head to speak. "I didn't."

Guess that was a rhetorical question, because my face thunked against the wall before I could answer.

"Don't move unless I tell you to."

I swallowed and tried not to breathe too deeply.

"You got any more weapons?"

I wasn't sure I was allowed to speak so I stayed silent.

"I said do you have any more weapons?"

His nine-millimeter poked into my kidneys punctuating every word.

"No," I mumbled against the wall.

Out of the corner of my eye I could see the EMTs working on Morgan. At least that meant he was still alive. My friend in blue stuck his gun into its holster and started to frisk me. He started at my hands, ran down my arms and copped a two-handed feel of my breasts. I stiffened.

"I don't keep weapons in my bra," I snapped.

"I thought I told you to be quiet."

He kicked my legs further apart for emphasis and ran both hands up my left leg. When he reached the top, he paused, then grabbed a handful. That was too much, and instinct took over. I pushed away from the wall and planted my cowboy boot on his right instep.

"Ow, Jesus! I think you broke my foot. Bitch!"

He backhanded me. My head snapped against the wall and a light show went off inside my brain. Upon reconsideration, stomping his foot was probably not my best move.

"Think that was cute?" he snarled.

I was trying to remember my name so I didn't answer. Nixon jerked my right arm behind me, slapped the cuff down tight on my wrist, then grabbed my left arm and repeated the procedure.

He clamped his hand around my bicep and jerked me toward him. "You should never have messed with me."

He kicked my feet out from under me for emphasis, and I whomped onto the floor. I landed on my chest, my cheek smacked the polished wood, and stars sparkled behind my eyelids.

"Don't move."

I was almost comatose so I thought that was unnecessary advice. I stayed still until my brain began functioning again, then raised my head. I half expected a boot to the side of my skull. When it didn't come, I watched the EMTs load Morgan onto a stretcher and trundle him off to the waiting ambulance. After they disappeared from my line of sight, I lowered my head to the floor. My mouth had the metallic, coppery taste of blood. The floor smelled of stale beer, dust, and lemon floor polish. The combination was nauseating. I scrunched my eyes closed and willed my stomach into submission. I didn't want to lie on the floor in a puddle of vomit. I drifted for a while somewhere just below consciousness until

Nixon brought me around with a sharp kick to the kidneys.

"Oof."

My stomach flopped. I clamped my teeth and swallowed.

"Get up," he ordered.

That simple order is surprisingly difficult when your arms are cuffed behind your back. After some initial grunting and squirming, I rolled onto my side, curled my knees, eased onto them and teetered unsteadily to my feet as he read my Miranda rights off a little card.

"Do you understand your rights?" he asked.

I nodded. He propelled me toward the door with a vice-like grip on my upper arm. I was going to have finger shaped bruises there tomorrow. I resisted the urge to kick him in the shin and concentrated on staying upright. He pushed me outside and heat settled around us like a blanket. I blinked in the bright sunshine. Before my eyes adjusted to the change, he pushed me forward. I tripped on the curb and went down hard on one knee. I struggled to my feet and stared down at my leg. The knee of my jeans had a ragged tear, and I could feel blood trickling into my sock.

"You just ruined a brand new pair of jeans."

"Don't worry about it, doll. Pretty soon you'll have a brand new orange jumpsuit."

A shadow fell across us as someone stepped out of a car angled in next to the front entrance.

"Officer Nixon," the newcomer said in greeting.

"Detective," Nixon answered.

"There a problem here?"

"I was just going to put the perp in my car, get her out of the way of the crime scene team."

"Why don't you go inside and make sure the scene stays secure until they get here. I'll watch your...perp," he said.

"Sure, thanks...detective."

Nixon said detective like it had a foul taste. He sent one last glare my way, then spun around and hobbled into the bar.

The detective that led me away from Officer Nixon was my twin brother, Chad Jennings. When Nixon was gone, I slumped over and tried to ease the pain from the kidney kick. Chad spun me around and pushed me against his car. I shrugged off his grip and hunched forward to take the pressure off my cuffed hands.

"What the hell's going on here, Randi? Benson was so rattled he wasn't making any sense at all.

"I can't talk to you. I've already been Mirandized."

"I'm your brother; you can talk to me."

"You're also a cop."

Chad sighed, leaned into the police cruiser and pulled the radio mic through the window of the car.

"Dispatch, this is fifteen ninety-three, I'm gonna be out of touch for a while."

A mumbled reply followed and Chad tossed the mic onto the car seat.

"Okay, I'm off the clock. Talk."

It was a command.

"I came into the bar and found Morgan lying on the floor bleeding. I called 911 and Barney fucking Fife came in, grabbed my gun, fondled my breasts and slapped me in cuffs."

Chad's eyes narrowed. He stared toward the battle-scarred front door of the Roger that Officer Nixon had disappeared through, then back at me. He paused to gather his thoughts before he spoke again.

"Um...you didn't shoot Morgan, though. Right?"

"No, dammit! I didn't shoot Morgan. If I was going to shoot Morgan, I would have done it years ago," I yelled.

Several officers stopped and stared in our direction.

"It's okay," Chad said waving them off, and they continued into the bar. "I was just checking. You guys had a hell of an argument last night."

"I didn't shoot Morgan."

"What happened to your face?"

I gave Chad another withering glare. "I walked into a door. What do you think happened to it?"

"I don't know, Ran. That's why I'm asking."

"I was backhanded by one of Alden's finest."

Officer Nixon came outside limping toward us and muttering to himself, "Goddamn crime scene guys, think they're the goddamn rulers of the earth."

"Him?" Chad asked.

I nodded.

Chad went rigid. He glared at Nixon as he hobbled toward us down the sidewalk.

"What happened to your foot, Nixon?" Chad asked.

"That bitch stomped on it. I think it's broken."

I smiled. The muscles tightened in Chad's face. His eyes went dark and dangerous and he rolled onto the balls of his feet. Chad's an ex Navy SEAL and he was very close to going into warrior mode.

"Save it, Chad," I hissed out of the corner of my mouth.

He relaxed and took a deep breath, but the look on his face didn't change.

"The...perp have those bruises when you showed up, Nixon?"

"Oh, yes, sir. Probably why she popped the vic."

I groaned to myself. This guy was unbelievable. I'd like to shoot him. I gritted my teeth, counted to ten, and still wanted to shoot the fat little weasel. Unfortunately he had my gun and I was in cuffs. Lucky day for him I guess.

"See that she doesn't arrive at the station with any more bruises than she has now, officer," Chad said quietly.

"Sure thing, detective."

Nixon nudged me forward and shoveled me into the rear seat of his black and white. He wedged in behind the wheel and we motored toward the police station.

"Fucking detectives. Think they can order us uniforms around. I hate that long-haired, muscle-bound prick."

Chad works vice and is on perpetual loan to whatever regional police force needs another undercover officer. He has long hair, usually tied into a ponytail, a neatly trimmed beard, and a diamond stud in one ear. He doesn't look like a cop, he looks dangerous, and he is.

"That long-haired, muscle-bound prick is my brother, my twin brother actually." I said softly from behind him.

All the color drained out of Nixon's face. I thought he was going to pass out and run us into a bridge abutment. When he caught my eye in the rearview mirror, I stifled the urge to wink. I almost felt sorry for him. Adulthood had brought changes that kept Chad and I from looking much alike. Our coloring is the same and we both have long dark hair, but I doubt that Chad's neat ponytail and my tangled curls were much of a clue. Maybe I should make a habit of introducing myself around the station to any new officers that hire in.

Nixon parked in the rear lot of the police station and helped me gently from the car. He guided me through the station with his hand lightly at the small of my back, a huge improvement over being dragged around by the arm.

Detective AJ Weleski looked out from the window of an interview room as we passed. He leapt to his feet in surprise as we strode by. His interviewee, thinking he was under attack, hurled himself to the floor and cowered under the table. I stopped moving and laughed. Nixon nudged me forward. I could feel AJ's eyes boring into my back as we continued down the hallway.

Nixon led me into an interview room and offered me a seat. He might have bowed on his way out, but I wasn't really watching. My adrenaline level was falling and my new collection of bruises was starting to hurt. I hunched forward in the chair, my cuffed hands behind me, and glanced around the room.

A two-way mirror covered the wall in front of me. My right eye was beginning to swell, and dried blood made a line down my cheek. That was an unpleasant sight so I turned away and checked out the rest of the room. It was about eight feet by eight feet. A gray metal table ran down the center. An ashtray sat in the middle and I longed for a cigarette. I'd mostly quit smoking, but I thought I'd earned one today.

Four scarred wooden chairs flanked the table, and all of it stood on stained linoleum that might once have been white. A security camera peered down from the corner, focused on the table. I twisted in my seat to ease the strain on my shoulders and closed my eyes against the pounding in my head. When the door latch clicked, I jumped. AJ let himself into the room and stood across the table from me. AJ and I have been dating off and on since he moved home to Alden almost a year ago. Right now was an on period. He reached over and brushed the hair away from my face. I winced as his fingers brushed my bruised cheek.

"Randi, what the hell's going on?" he asked.

"Officer Nixon arrested me for shooting Morgan."

AJ paused for a second before he spoke again. "You didn't shoot Morgan, right?"

"No, dammit, I didn't shoot him. What is wrong with you people?"

"Just making sure. You were pretty pissed off last night."

"I didn't shoot Morgan." I sighed.

"Hang tough. We'll get this straightened out, darlin'."

"While you're straightening, mind taking these cuffs off, my shoulder is killing me."

A few months ago I was shot in the shoulder. After months of physical therapy, it was finally starting to function again.

"Jesus, hang on." AJ fumbled on his belt for his handcuff key and freed my arms.

I rubbed my wrists, then rubbed my shoulder, and eased back in the chair.

"I guess you haven't heard how Morgan is doing."

"Sorry, darlin'. I hadn't even heard about the shooting. Been tied up with a suspect all afternoon."

His tone of voice said that not only hadn't he heard, but he didn't really care. The antagonism between Morgan and AJ started before puberty and hadn't lessened over the intervening years.

I stared longingly at the ashtray. "You got a cigarette?"

"No. I can get you one if you want."

"Don't bother."

We were both quiet, deep in our own thoughts. I finally broke the silence.

"I guess our weekend getaway will have to be postponed."

"Yeah, I guess so. Thanks to Morgan."

"I don't think he got shot just to ruin our vacation."

AJ and I were high school sweethearts, but the Army snagged him first. I still haven't completely forgiven him for that and I still wasn't sure getting together with him was a good idea. Things had been a little rocky the last few weeks. AJ finally convinced me the two of us needed to get away for a few days—no kids, no pagers, and no cell phones. We were supposed to leave tomorrow. My bags were packed, the dog was at Chad's, the kids were spending the week with Mom and Dad, and I was in an interrogation room at the local police station.

AJ sighed. "You want to tell me what's going on?"

"Nope, I'm waiting for my attorney."

"What?"

"I've been Mirandized and you are a cop. I'm not saying one word about what happened to you or anyone else until Allen gets here."

"Jesus H. Christ, Randi!"

I folded my arms on the table and lay my head down on top of them. AJ stomped across the linoleum and slammed the door as he left.

(ATTEMPTED) MURDER at the JOLLY ROGER

COMING 2011 FROM NUKEWORKS PUBLISHING.

Photo by Justin Easley

KD Easley lives and writes in Fulton, MO. She is the mother of two grown sons, one a nuclear technician and the other a United States Sailor, that have and continue to provide her with more material than she will ever be able to use. She also shares her home with two feline writing partners, Luna and Merlin who make sure she doesn't develop carpel tunnel syndrome by dragging her away from the keyboard for ear scratches and snacks when they've decided she's been working long enough. KD has been writing for over ten years and has published both short mysteries and novel length fiction.

Her first mystery, Where the Dreams End, featuring repo man, Brocs Harley and her short mystery collection, Nine Kinds of Trouble, are out and available now.

Visit KD online at
www.kdwrites.com
or drop by her blog at
http://kdblog.kdwrites.com.

www.ingramcontent.com/pod-product-compliance
Lightning Source LLC
Chambersburg PA
CBHW032046050726
47590CB00001B/155